A Novel by Emory Jones

The Valley Where They
DANCED

For more information, contact
Emory Jones LLC
480 High Ridge Road, Cleveland, GA 30528
Call 706-348-7372 or visit www.yonahtreasures.com

Cover design by Luciano Georgescu based on his wood sculpture *The Nacoochee Valley Indian Mound*.

Legal review by William M. House

ISBN 978-0-9887325-6-8

The Valley Where They
DANCED

DEDICATION

This novel is dedicated to the late John Kollock,
whose historical paintings conjured up so many of
the descriptions in this book, and to the late Dr.
Tom Lumsden, a true son of the Valley.

So now faith, hope, and love abide, these three,
but the greatest of these is love.

I Corinthians 13:13

PREFACE

My name is Kelvin Boggs. My family has ties to the Sautee Valley and its secrets — old ones maybe, and mostly hidden, but honest ties nonetheless. Charles Boggs was my grandfather. His older brother, Alton — my great-uncle — is buried on our family's homeplace just down the road. When Granddaddy was 19, he left the Valley. He wound up near Asheville, North Carolina. I still live in the farmhouse he built.

The elderly woman I'm here to see on this January day in 1979, Hannah Conley, knows more about my connections to this valley than I do. Being a reporter, I'm naturally curious, and stubborn, too, I guess. I met Hannah a few years ago. We've visited several times since. However, despite my cajoling — begging really — she's never told me much about my family, or hers either, for that matter.

But there's a big difference between this visit and the others I've made to her North Georgia hill-country home — this time she sent for me. This day was also the first time she didn't meet me at the door. Instead, wrapped in quilts as faded as her face, she beckoned from her rocking chair.

Everything else was the same, though. As they always did, even in summer, embers smoldered in her fireplace. The old shawl that hugged her shoulders still smelled of cornbread. Her dog-eared Bible lay open to the same passage; her frail finger tap, tap, tapping that verse.

As is the nature of deep-rooted Appalachian women, she wasted no time with pleasantries. She only nodded for me to sit and leaned forward to stoke the fire.

Then, finally, on this cold, winter afternoon, she told me the story I'd waited so many years to hear.

This is how

Hannah Conley began...

"Let me say this first, Mr. Writer Man: Heaven 'n earth mingle more'n folks know. I've studied on that a lot.

"Love is a powerful thing. You only need to read what it says here in First Corinthians 13:13 to know that.

"Was a time nobody 'round here'd talk about it a'tall. Now days, this 'un or that'un will say their daddy told 'em so-and-so, when nothing like it ever did happen. But they'll swear by it.

"No matter. It all come about just the way I'm fixin' to say it did. Only, promise you won't write nothin' about it 'til I lay a corpse. You won't have to wait long — I'll be 98 come spring.

"All right then, I reckon you got a right to know. Here's exactly what happened all them years ago, right here in this valley..."

❧

CHAPTER ONE

Tom

June 12, 1919

S omehow, Tom Garrison knew this letter was going to change his life. As soon as he took it out of the mailbox, the newly licensed doctor felt that profound sense of knowing he'd come to call the feeling. He remembered the first time he had this sensation — it was 18 years ago — the day he turned 6.

That Sunday afternoon, several cousins and Barbara Baker, the pretty girl who lived down the road, were climbing in the Garrison family's backyard cherry tree, when Barbara fell. The other children scattered like yard hens when they saw her fractured arm — but not Tom.

"Don't cry," he told the wailing Barbara. "I'll take care of you." But, when Tom ran back from the barn with planks and twine, the adults had taken over. Her daddy was already galloping his horse toward Macon to fetch Dr. Neal.

During the uproar, a conviction that he would become a doctor settled in and built a home in Tom's heart — it became something he simply knew. Once Dr. Neal finished setting Barbara's arm, the grown-ups sorted out the various family broods and headed home. When his mother, Wirtha Garrison, saw Tom standing alone in the yard watching them go, she walked over to her youngest child and knelt in front of him.

"What's the matter, son?"

"Mama, I want to tell you something." The boy's face assumed a look of absolute confidence.

"Of course, honey. You can always tell me something."

"When I grow up, I'm going to be a doctor."

His mother hugged him and kissed his cheek. "Of course you are, darling, if that's what you want."

And just like that, Tom's future vocation was settled. He graduated from high school at the top of his class, and had recently earned the coveted degree from the Medical College of Georgia in Augusta.

The letter he'd just read was from a doctor in Clarkesville, Georgia, named David Dyer. Tom had never been there, but he knew Clarkesville was a small Habersham County town in the northeastern part of the state, near the mountains. Two words in this letter were new to him. He thought they must be Indian expressions whittled by whites to better fit European tongues.

"Nacoochee."

"Sautee."

Native names like those—Oconee and Ocmulgee, for example—had long been assigned to towns and streams around Clinton, Georgia, where he grew up. His mother still lived in this small community, just outside Macon.

Wirtha Garrison, the refined woman who birthed Tom and his two older brothers, was the great-niece of men who, between them, had been governors of both Georgia and Texas. A South Georgia town and county already bore her maiden name of Colquitt when she married up-and-coming Macon attorney, Dennis Garrison, twenty-eight years ago.

As a child, Tom sensed that in some way he was different, somehow, from other boys his age. He possessed a sort of sixth sense, and it made the normally capable and clever youngster a bit reserved—sometimes even shy, at least during his early years.

When it came to this *feeling* that sometimes enveloped him, Tom's mother suggested he keep it just between the two of them. He'd done that—except for telling Big Mama Nell, of course. Employed by the Garrison family as a cook and housekeeper, Nell was a descendant of slaves, who were, at this place and in this time, called "colored." Naturally, Tom would tell *her*. With no children of her own, Big Mama was like a second mother to him and his two brothers.

"It's a gift from the other side, honey chile," she said, when he first told her about it. "It means God Hisself sees you as 'specially special."

Six feet tall and strong, with a personality as big as her build, Nell stood in sharp contrast to Wirtha. When Tom's older brother, Christopher, was a toddler, he called the two women his *big* mama and his *little* mama. They let the tradition stand, and before long, everybody knew her as Big Mama Nell or, to the Garrison boys, just Big Mama.

Uncle Isaac and Big Mama lived in a cabin behind the larger house where Tom grew up. Isaac had a shop next door where he mended harnesses and such. He also cobbled shoes. Isaac could fit anyone after studying their feet for a moment. He never took measurements, and no matter how odd-shaped the foot, the shoes always fit.

Growing up, Tom spent many pleasant hours in Isaac's shop. He read while Isaac worked. Even as a boy, Tom was always reading. Once, Isaac asked Tom the name of a particular book he was browsing.

"It's called *Lord Jim*," said Tom, without looking up. "Joseph Conrad wrote it."

"What's it 'bout?" Isaac paused from his work and peered at Tom as he asked.

"About a British sailor who abandoned his ship. It's good. You can read it when I'm finished," Tom offered.

Isaac went back to working his awl through a piece of leather. "Naw, you can jes' tell me 'bout it sometime."

That was when Tom first realized Isaac couldn't read. Until then, he assumed everybody could. "I'll just read it out loud," said Tom. "That way you can keep working." After that, he read to Isaac every day until they finished the book.

Now, nearly two decades later, with the required medical education behind him, Tom was eager to start his calling. Between The Great War and the recent worldwide influenza pandemic, much of the country faced a shortage of medical men. But for some reason, the communities in middle Georgia, where his mother lived, had a surplus. None of the letters he'd mailed to various officials in nearby towns asking about opportunities had been answered — at least not favorably.

He'd had his medical skills tested last October when that dreaded flu crept into the Army's Camp Hancock outside Augusta. With hundreds of soldiers mustering in and out every week, the post was a prime target.

The medical college held one institute-wide lecture on respiratory infections and promptly suspended classes. Tom and the other fourth-year students put on white masks and joined the fight against one of the deadliest contagions the world had ever known.

Two months later, when the ordeal was over, the head of the school called Tom into his office. "I have an assistant teaching position available," he said. "It's yours if you want it. You can do advanced studies while you work. This is quite an opportunity."

It was, but Tom turned him down. He wanted to *practice* medicine, not teach it.

He'd been back in Clinton for two months now. The rest and escape from the rigors of studying had been a welcomed diversion at first. But the afternoon chess games with his childhood friends — the few who still had time to play — were beginning to feel indulgent. Tom was ready for a change. He needed to get to work.

That's why this letter he'd just read had his full attention. His eyes followed the lines on the paper as he read it for the second time. Dr. Dyer wrote that a group of community-minded citizens would even subsidize his accommodations, for the first year at least.

"I've looked after the people over in these two valleys for thirty years," Dr. Dyer wrote. "I'm getting too old for it." He explained that the Sautee and Nacoochee Valleys were twelve miles from Clarkesville, and he was often sent for late at night. Wild dashes over dirt roads were taking their toll.

Tom wondered how this doctor from Clarkesville had ever heard of him — let alone would want to offer up a goodly portion of his practice. He decided to talk to his mother about it.

The young doctor folded the crisp stationery back into its envelope, put it in his shirt pocket and ran both hands through his hair — thick and brown to its roots. He closed the mailbox and walked up the sandy lane to the rambling, two-story house his grandfather, former Confederate Colonel, Pope Garrison, built in 1852. Even with the forced neglect that followed that awful war, visitors could still catch glimpses of the home's former grandeur.

The old house might not be majestic anymore, but no Garrison man had ever let her roof leak.

The past two years had been hard on Tom's mother. She'd not only lost her oldest son in the war, but her husband died soon after that, leaving her aching and alone.

His mother's ordeal began when the United States entered the war in Europe on April 6, 1917. Her two oldest boys raced to Macon the very next morning to sign up. Ray joined the infantry, but the more thrill-seeking Christopher, or "Crick" as everyone called him, wanted to try his hand with those new-fangled flying machines. Their daddy had to pull some strings, but he qualified, and the Army obliged. They sent him to France as an aviator in the fledgling U.S. Army Air Service.

Tom didn't know much about airplanes, but in a picture Crick sent home last fall, he stood, cocky and proud in his leather jacket and high boots, beside the French-made Nieuport 28 biplane he flew. In the picture with him was the new friend he wrote home about with near reverence, Quentin Roosevelt, the son of the former President.

Dennis Garrison, clearly proud of his son, showed the picture to everyone he knew, always pointing out that Crick was the first Garrison man in history to either fly an airplane or to have his picture taken with a Republican.

Tom would never forget the day Christopher died. He was playing chess with one of the other students, instead of studying for tomorrow's exam on liver diseases, when *the feeling* came to him. He suddenly *knew* his oldest brother was dead.

A German flier shot Crick's airplane down on June 24, 1918, the day before he would have been 27. The communique said Lt. Garrison's body was retrieved and buried with a Christian cross in a French town whose name no one in Tom's family could pronounce. Tom's father died three weeks later.

His other brother, Ray, survived the war, physically at least, and brought home a brown and black pup he called Jack. Black-headed and shorter than Tom, Ray didn't talk much about the war, but he did tell Big Mama that he found Jack in the foul mud of a German trench, somewhere in France.

There was a strong bond between Ray and that dog. Before Jack, any animal that put a paw inside the Garrison home was quickly chased out by Big Mama's broom. "Der'll be no fleas or ticks in dis house," she'd yell. "Now git on out from here!"

But the day Ray brought the young German shepherd home, Big Mama looked at Wirtha and said, "I'll make dat pup a little pallet so he kin sleep by your bed, Mister Ray."

Because he was in medical school with two brothers at the front, the Army didn't call Tom up. He felt guilty about that. He told himself, if the war had lasted longer, he'd have gone in, too.

When he reached the house, Tom walked down the hall and knocked at the open door of the sitting room, where his mother was reading her Bible. Behind her rocking chair, sunlight poured through the multi-paned windows to light her pages.

"Mother, do you feel like a walk?"

Wirtha closed her Bible and gave him one of her rare smiles. "All right, son. A walk would be nice. Only let's not go far. I'm a bit tired today."

They strolled down the front porch steps and past the two magnolias at the garden's entrance. At the dewpond's mossy ledge, goldfish darted from the shadows Tom and his mother cast over the water. She sat on the little rock seat, but her son stood as he told her about the letter, not knowing if she'd be pleased or disappointed.

When he finished, he sat beside her. She leaned against his arm. "Son, when you get to be my age, you'll find the world is a right small place. You've had so much going on with school and all, I'm not surprised you don't remember that my cousin, Emma, and her husband own a farm in this valley named Nacoochee. They think a lot of you, Tom. I'm sure they're the ones who told this Dr. Dyer you'd make them a fine doctor."

Now, after absorbing his mother's words, the letter from Clarkesville made more sense. Emma Hardman was his mother's first cousin. Her husband, an older, well-regarded physician named Lamartine, was also a cousin on her father's side. Most folks knew him less formally as, Dr. Lam.

The former Emma Griffin and Tom's mother grew up in Valdosta near the Florida line. They were as close as sisters, and even though she was a cousin, all three Garrison boys called her Aunt Emma. The woman brimmed with old-style Southernisms.

At 25, she married Dr. Lam who, at 51, was twice her age. Tom was a child when they wed, but he remembered the small ceremony in the parlor of Aunt Emma's parent's house in Valdosta.

"Dr. Lam bought that place in Nacoochee Valley to get away from his business dealings," Wirtha continued. "It's supposed to be where they go to relax," she said with a smile. "But according to Emma, he's turned that into a money-making operation, too. He has a herd of Jersey cows, and they've even got an old gristmill of some sort up and running. I don't believe that man is much for relaxing — poor Emma!"

Wirtha sighed. "Your father and I planned to go see it one day, but we never did. I wish we had. Emma's letters make it sound so beautiful." She took her son's hands in hers. "I guess if my fine-looking boy is the new doctor up there, I might get to see that place yet." Wirtha, as she always did when deep in thought, rolled her lower lip between her teeth. "But... it's a long way off, and without your father...well, it won't be the same, will it?"

Tom hated seeing his mother still in so much pain over the loss of her husband and son. So, mostly to change the subject, he asked her, "Mother, since Dr. Lam is a doctor himself, why would he want another physician up there?"

The question amused her even further. "Goodness gracious, son. With all that man has going on, he doesn't have time to doctor anybody." She laughed. "He's tried to get elected governor of Georgia twice, and Emma says he'll run again before long. I expect he'll win next time."

Wirtha dropped her hands to her lap and studied a minute before she continued. "A year or two back, Emma sent us a picture of an old Indian mound in the field by their house. It has the cutest little gazebo on top. I'll have Big Mama find it for you tomorrow."

When his mother stood, Tom did, too. She had to look up at him. At six feet, he was the tallest of her three boys, and the only one with brown hair, like hers once was. "Son, you're an exceptional man. Your daddy taught you to always do right, so you'll be fine wherever you go. But I know you've already decided about this, and you have my blessing if that's what you want. Naturally, I'll miss you, but I have Big Mama and Isaac to look after me — and of course, your brother, Ray..."

Tom frowned when she brought up his brother. As boys who were closer in temperament, Ray and Crick always spent more time with each other than with him. They roved the local countryside while Tom kept to his books and read. His brothers had always wanted to include him, but they never had much luck teaching him to hunt or fish. He could never get them interested in chess, either—a game he found fascinating. But his older brothers did make sure he could hold his own when it came to fighting and such. The few times Tom had been called a sissy, the boy who'd made the mistake of calling him that soon regretted it.

Tom ran his hand over his face. "Ray's not easy to talk to anymore, Mother. I don't know if it's losing Crick and Dad, or whatever happened to him in the war, but sometimes I think he's the unhappiest man I've ever seen."

This time it was his mother who changed the subject. "There's good train service between Macon and Atlanta, son. Emma says a lumber company has put in a railroad between Gainesville and that new settlement—Helen, I believe it's called—above this Nacoochee Valley. But she says you'll want to take the train that goes by Clarkesville the first time you go up. That way, you can spend some time with Dr. Dyer."

Tom looked at his mother with a mixture of awe and understanding. Clearly, she knew more about this letter than she was letting on. "Mother, did you and Aunt Emma cook up this whole North Georgia thing together? Because it sure sounds to me like you did."

Wirtha ignored the question as she continued. "You can come home anytime you want, Tom. My goodness, the way things are going, you might even get one of those new automobiles and make your rounds that way. Wouldn't that be something?"

Tom patted his mother's hand and smiled at her. He certainly didn't have any extra money himself, and he knew his mother and father had spent most of theirs sending him to medical school. "A buggy will do me fine, Mother. Besides, I'm not sure automobiles are all that reliable, at least not yet."

A water spider sprinted across the dewpond, surface-tension keeping the insect afloat. Tom watched it for a moment. Not really surprised at her perception, he asked anyway, "Mother, how did you know I'd already decided to go?"

His mother smiled at him. "Well, for one thing, I'm your mother. And for another, you have a certain look about you when you get your special feeling, remember? It's the same one you had when you first told me you were going to be a doctor—the day Barbara broke her arm."

"And you see it now?"

"Oh, yes. I surely do." His mother beamed.

And so, standing on the spot where he experienced *the feeling*, for the first time, the next part of Tom's life was sealed the same way as the first—with a hug and a kiss on his cheek from his mother.

CHAPTER TWO

Lenore

July 7, 1919

L enore Conley loosened the strings of her calico bonnet and
pulled it back to cool her face. Her blue eyes regarded the tree-
covered hillside that an early settler — likely one of her own blood —
had named Grimes Nose. She wiped her hands on her apron, then
straightened her back and stared.

Strictly speaking, Grimes Nose wasn't *really* a mountain.
Neither was Lynch on the other side of her family's Sautee Valley
farm. Instead, both knolls were members of a close-knit league of
hills that linger where the Southern Appalachians surrender their
majesty to the flatlands. But to Lenore, these hills were not only
mountains; they were *her* mountains.

As she stretched, Lenore thought, apparently out loud, "It's just
plain hot today!"

From the next row of cornfield beans, whose vines coiled
around head-high stalks of sweetcorn, her mother answered.
"Lord-a-mercy, girl. Surely not! July in Georgia, and it's turned off
hot? You reckon we ought to get word to the newspaper?"

Lenore peeked through the stalks at the older woman. "Oh,
Mama, I didn't mean to say that out loud. Now you'll think I'm
slothful."

"Not likely I would," replied Hannah Conley, not pausing in
her work. "But the Good Lord might. Of course, even I wouldn't
mind if He sent us a breeze."

The two women went back to their work and settled into the comfortable silence that typically existed between them in the garden. Their right hands deftly plucked beans from their vines and, quick as a wink, dropped them into the pocket they made by holding the ends of their aprons together.

Once their makeshift pouches were full, the women emptied them into one of the bushel-sized containers scattered everywhere. This meant more walking, but it kept them from pulling an increasingly heavier basket by its wire handle as they picked their way down the rows.

Nothing had ever been said about it, but Lenore knew this method of harvesting the garden was an accommodation to her. Lenore's left leg was shorter than her right. That made dragging anything cumbersome.

Years earlier, the doctor told her parents the femur in that leg had stopped growing as it should. He believed it was caused by a peculiar illness that struck Lenore just before she turned four. On that summer afternoon, she woke up from her nap crying, with a terrible headache and fever. Her daddy rode to Clarkesville to fetch Dr. Dyer. While the doctor didn't know what caused the illness, he did know that none of his medicines were calming it.

"I've never seen anything like this," he told Lanier and Hannah on the third night. "This child may not live 'til morning. You need to prepare yourselves."

But just before sunrise, as the heartbroken couple, along with Lenore's grandparents, James and Aldie Chambers, prayed by the girl's side, her fever broke. A few minutes later, Lenore, not fully awake, opened her eyes a bit and asked, "Isn't Lana pretty, Mama?" Not knowing what to say, Hannah just nodded.

"She's nice, too," said Lenore. "She looks at me the way you do. And Lana made the hot go 'way."

While she was growing up, her parents never let their only child think of herself as "sickly." They gave her the same chores any farm girl would have, even if they did allow her a little extra time to do them.

Although she was, Lenore didn't think of herself as pretty — especially when she looked at her leg. But boys did. She loved to read, and by the 7th grade, there weren't many books in the library at the Nacoochee Institute she hadn't checked out at least once.

Because of her natural charm, most people who knew Lenore didn't notice her limp. If they did, they soon forgot about it and focused on her face. It was one that made boys dream and girls — at least until they got to know her — jealous.

Once, a new teacher asked Lenore if she had infantile paralysis. "What's that?" Lenore asked innocently.

"Oh, never mind," said the teacher, embarrassed. Later, Lenore looked up the term in the library. At least now she had a name for this thing that caused her to limp.

Every year, Lenore's daddy hired a cobbler in Gainesville to make her two pairs of special shoes — one for work, one for church. The left shoe always had a thick cork sole. They were practical, but not pretty. Still, the only time she thought about that was on Sundays or during the fall dances, which she seldom attended anyway. Boys would ask her to dance when she went, but Lenore always refused them — she'd never danced, even once.

She knew it was vain, but Lenore longed for a fashionable pair of shoes. She pictured her dream footwear as smart, low-heeled pumps with glass beading on the toes. But shoes like that were beyond the Gainesville man's skills, so she never said anything.

Here in the garden, as they reached the end of the last row, Lenore's mother said, "Well, it worked."

"What worked, Mama?"

"Praying for a breeze. Can't you feel it?"

Lenore held out her arms. She did feel it, but it was still mighty warm. The brochures those resort hotels mailed out to entice vacationers to the mountains didn't mention hot days like this — or working in gardens. Still, Lenore reminded herself, while those visitors might get to rest and relax for a while, they couldn't call these old mountains home the way she did.

She didn't have to leave them at all if she didn't want to, and she seldom did. Of course, a short visit to Tallulah Falls might be nice. Her parents enjoyed visiting that gorge as much as she did, and were usually up for any excuse to go.

To get there, they took their surrey to Clarkesville and then embarked on a thrilling, twelve-mile, high-trestle train ride to the little resort town and its deep canyon. She made a mental note to suggest that trip to her daddy at supper.

Both her parents had an attachment to the town of Tallulah Falls. They'd visited there separately as children, and in 1901, together as newlyweds. They spent their honeymoon at the town's Cliff House Hotel, and Lenore was born nine months later.

She came into this world of 10,000 things, as her grandmother, Aldie, called it, one hour before the first sunrise of 1902 spread its light across the Valley. That's what folks here called it—the Valley—as if no other valley held any significance, excepting, of course, the converging Nacoochee right below.

The waters that formed these two vales sprang from underground sources high in the mountains. Large streams like Sautee and Chickamauga, along with smaller ones with names like Vandiver Branch and Bean Creek, had spent eons molding this stretch of land.

Sautee Valley ran north and south. Below it, Nacoochee Valley lay east to west alongside the Chattahoochee River like a contented lover. The river became bolder after Sautee Creek gathered her sister streams and herded them into it, two miles below Lenore's home. Reinforced yet again from the opposite side by Dukes Creek just upriver, the bolstered Chattahoochee roiled southward toward some pressing business on the Coastal Plain.

For the most part, folks here knew their neighbors—except for those rowdy newcomers in the sawmill town of Helen, three miles west. Most everyone else was descended from one or more of the first white families to put down roots here in 1822. Before them, countless bands of native people claimed these valleys, most recently the Cherokees.

"Honey, our baskets are nearly full," said Lenore's mother from the garden. "Sun'll be behind the mountain before long. It's time for you to milk the cows and for me to fix your daddy's supper."

"All right, Mama." Lenore answered. She thought it was funny how her mother called the evening meal "your daddy's supper." She did the same with breakfast and dinner, too, even though the three of them always ate together.

A few weeks from 40, Hannah Conley was still a handsome woman. Her blond hair had gray streaks now, but otherwise, she appeared to be an older, taller version of her daughter.

Each woman grabbed a wire handle on a basket filled with green beans and squash. They carried it down the row sideways, stopping to retrieve an occasional pod they'd missed or dropped earlier. Lenore's daddy, Lanier, would be back from the store soon; he'd bring the rest up then.

She and her mother put the basket on the porch between two rocking chairs, "I'll take in enough squash for us to have a mess for supper," said Hannah.

"Sounds good, Mama." Lenore took down the two milk pails hanging above the well. She cranked the handle on the windlass to bring up a dripping bucketful of water. After drinking from the aluminum dipper, she poured water into both pails and headed down the path to the barn.

"Remember now, don't let the calf get but half of May's milk," hollered Hannah. "I think you gave the little one more than her share yesterday."

"I know, Mama," Lenore said over her shoulder. "We get the right side. Her baby gets the left."

Her mother laughed. "Right or left, I don't care which. Just bring me half of what she's got."

Earlier, from the garden, Lenore had watched the two fawn-colored milk cows — mother and daughter themselves — spend the afternoon grazing their way toward the barn. Now they stood at the back entrance, heads lowered to peer between the two chestnut rails that blocked their entry.

Lenore lowered the barriers. "Welcome to the barn, June. Hello, Miss May," she said, curtsying to each animal as it entered.

After mooing at the stall that held her calf, May, the older cow, turned toward the feed trough on the opposite wall. Dappled by late afternoon sun slipping through gaps in the logs, the eager calf butted her head on the door, making it bang against its latch.

"Calm down, girl," Lenore gently chided the heifer she'd named Flower. The calf had been lying in a bed of blooming clover when Lenore first found her in the pasture a few weeks earlier.

"As soon as your mama gives me our part, you can have yours." Brown eyes stared through the cracks. Opening the feed-room door, Lenore dropped two scoopfuls of ground corn mixed with molasses in the feedbox. She looped the ropes, attached to a board above the trough, around each cow's horns. Tying them wasn't necessary, but both animals expected it.

While they munched their feed, Lenore pulled up a three-legged stool. She washed the cow's swollen udder and used another rag to dry it off. Once everything was clean, Lenore leaned her forehead into May's side and milked the two teats closest to her.

As she always did when she milked, Lenore quietly sang the old hymn *Amazing Grace*. Her daddy's parents died before Lenore was born, but her mama said this was their favorite song, so she sang it in tribute to them.

Although she was modest about it, Lenore was known for her singing—even as a girl, preachers asked her to sing at church. When she came to Grandma Ruth's favorite verse, she sang the words in her memory.

> *"When we've been there ten thousand years,*
> *bright shining as the sun.*
> *We've no less days to sing God's praise*
> *than when we've first begun."*

Another stanza, the one they usually skipped at church, she sang for her granddaddy, Bevel Conley. He'd left this world in good standing with both the Lord and the land 20 years ago. He was buried beside his wife beneath a leaning Confederate tombstone in the Methodist church cemetery.

> *"Yea, when this flesh and heart shall fail,*
> *And mortal life shall cease,*
> *I shall possess within the veil,*
> *A life of joy and peace."*

Somehow, the barn and its smells made Lenore think of the thing preachers called grace. Maybe it was the manger story, or perhaps because a barn seemed so serene, especially when it rained. Lenore thought rain on a barn roof, with the animals all safe inside, was as close to heaven as a person could get in this world.

Or maybe it was Lana. The barn was her favorite place, too. Lana hadn't appeared to Lenore for several years now, but she felt her presence often, especially here.

Once Lenore drained half of May's milk, she covered the pail and put it on a shelf. She slipped the rope off and guided the cow to the stall by her horn. When Lenore opened the door, the calf bounded out, raced past its mother, and started trying to nurse June, who wanted no part of it.

"That's not your mama," said Lenore, laughing. She grabbed Flower around her neck and pulled the heifer back towards the stable. When the calf saw her real mother, she raced inside and started nursing.

As Lenore milked the second cow, she leaned her head against the cow's warm side and felt the bump of the unborn calf against her forehead. Like May, June was bred to one of the high-grade Jersey bulls down at the Hardman farm. Her daddy was expecting this calf to be a fine one, as long as it turned out to be a heifer they could keep for a milk cow.

"Miss June, I think it's time we turned you dry before your baby comes," said Lenore, patting the cow's side. "It's daddy's call, but I'll talk to him about it tonight."

Lenore wondered if her father sang when he milked in the morning. She wasn't about to ask, though; milking was personal.

Below the barn, her black gelding, Custer, whinnied, reminding Lenore to put oats in his feedbox. "Don't worry, boy. I won't forget about you," she reassured him.

Her father had bought the gentle, four-year-old horse as Lenore's birthday present the year she turned 12. She took to riding immediately. Custer was another reason Lenore didn't think of her leg that much. On his back, she was as complete as anyone.

After she gave the black gelding his feed, Lenore poured a bit of fresh milk into a bowl for the two barn cats, Sly and Daisy. The pair scampered down the hayloft ladder at the first splash and brushed against her legs before lapping the frothy overflow of their expected treat.

As Lenore carried the milk pails to the house — one in each hand — she watched her father in the garden as he loaded the baskets into their wagon. The old but vital conveyance also held a salt block for the pasture and three boxes of those new Mason jars her mother wanted to try putting up beans in this year.

At 51, Lanier Conley had the bearing of a hill-country patriarch. With a head full of graying hair and his Cherokee grandmother's brown eyes, he was tall and still strong enough to outwork men half his age. His regular garb was overalls, brogans, and a crumpled fedora. But, Lenore thought, and her mother agreed, when he put on his Sunday go-to-meeting clothes, he was the handsomest man in the Valley.

Her daddy stopped Ole Burl by the porch just as she climbed the steps with the milk. "Whoa! Hold up there, mule." He leaned back as he pulled on the reins to stop the plodding creature. "Looks like I'm just in time for a cup of warm, sweet milk. Strain me some, Punkin, and set it aside 'til I get Ole Burl put up."

Lenore and her mother liked their milk cold, after it sat in the springhouse for a few hours and had the cream skimmed off. But Lanier Conley considered a glass of warm milk, as fresh from the cow as he could get it, to be the second best drink a man could have — third, if you counted spring water.

Lenore decided to put forth her suggestion about an outing. "I will, Daddy, if you'll take us to Tallulah Falls this Sunday."

Lanier feigned astonishment and teased, "Sugar Babe, come here and see what a young'un we've raised. A gal that won't pour her own daddy a glass of sweet milk without making him promise to take her on a trip first! I declare."

Hannah looked out the kitchen window at the reassuring appearance of her husband. They'd been married almost twenty years now, and she still liked looking at him. She loved him in spite of the one bad habit he'd developed not long after they married; Lanier liked whiskey.

He never came home intoxicated, but *any* drinking was too much for Hannah's temperance-based upbringing. It didn't happen often, so when he got back from a 'coon hunt or a trip to the store with liquor on his breath — as she could already tell he had today — she usually let it go.

They'd both wanted a big family, and with their first baby coming so soon after they married, they expected plenty more to follow. Since that didn't happen, they showered their love on this one daughter and looked forward to grandchildren.

"You two won't do," said Hannah through the open window. "Supper's ready, so hurry up and let's eat. We'll sort out any trips we need to be taking later."

Lanier sat the boxes of quart jars on the porch, climbed up on the wagon again and shouted "giddy-up," a bit louder than necessary. When he slapped the reins across the mule's back, Ole Burl pulled the wagon down the grassy centerline toward the barn. On the way, Lanier threw his head back and sang out his favorite song.

> *"Old Dan Tucker's a fine old man.*
> *Washed his face in a fryin' pan.*
> *Combed his hair with a wagon wheel.*
> *Died with a toothache in his heel!*

Get outa' the way of old Dan Tucker,
Lanier's come home to get his supper!"

Lenore thought her daddy must have found an excuse to have a drink with somebody at the store. As far as she knew, he didn't keep whiskey at home, but he never sang unless he'd had "the tiniest little nip," as he always called it.

Lenore poured the milk through one of the straining rags her mother kept washed and folded in the kitchen cupboard just for that. She sat his tall, clay mug, filled with milk, by her daddy's place at the head of the kitchen table.

She divided the rest of the milk between a five-gallon churn and a one-gallon pitcher. Her daddy would take the churn to the springhouse later. She put a cloth over the pitcher, sat it in the well bucket and lowered it to hang above the cool water at the bottom. That way, if anyone wanted a glass of milk after dark, they could get it from the porch instead of walking all the way down to the spring.

After they finished their supper of tomatoes, fried squash, okra, and the ever-present cornbread, Lenore and her mother rocked on the front porch, stringing beans. Hannah snapped her's into sections and dropped them in a pan. Lenore, however, used a darning needle to pull a thread through the center of the pods. She wrapped the string around each bean and tied a knot to keep them from touching each other. If they did, they'd mold.

Tomorrow she'd hang these "leather britches" on the wall behind the stove to dry and wrinkle. This winter, they'd simmer with a ham bone and onions to make her daddy's favorite winter dish, which was always served with crackling cornbread.

As dark settled in, mother and daughter spoke above the katydids—a million males answered in octave by an equal number of females in a singsong courtship only they understood. When she was little, Lenore believed these creatures, clinging to every tree and bush, chanted "Saw-Tee, Saw-Tee," as if even the insects knew her valley's name.

A whippoorwill called from down below the barn. From over near the Sautee Creek, a lonesome male answered.

The screen door's hinges squeaked as Lanier came outside and let it slam behind him. He stepped onto the porch holding his tobacco pouch and sat down with a grunt on the top step. He struck a match, lit his pipe, and tossed the dying flame into the grass. "We forgot to talk about it at supper," he said, "but I don't think we can go to the gorge Sunday."

Lenore felt a twinge of disappointment. Her daddy rarely denied any request from her or her mother. She didn't say anything, but her mother did.

"Why not, Lanier?" asked Hannah. "Don't you think your womenfolk deserve a day at the Falls?"

When she was a child, Lenore imagined she could hear those faraway waterfalls at night, like the faint hum of distant bees. Her daddy said it was the shoals on Chickamauga Creek and not the Tallulah River miles away, but Lenore liked to believe otherwise.

Anyway, the question didn't matter anymore — Tallulah's falls were quiet these days — at least compared to the way they roared before the Georgia Railway and Power Company built their dams.

Where mountain people saw majesty, engineers saw a fine place to put dams. The corporation bought the valley town of Burton, the second largest in Rabun County, and was now drowning it to make a reservoir they — mockingly, Lenore thought — had named, *Lake Burton.*

Everyone she knew hated those dams. Outsiders were destroying the jewel of the mountains to supply electricity for up-and-coming Atlanta — a place most had never visited. It was outrageous.

When she was 7, Lenore mailed a letter of support and a shiny new dime to Helen Dortch Longstreet, the plucky widow of Confederate General James Longstreet and the woman leading the charge to save those famous falls. She was Lenore's idol.

But her dime wasn't enough — Mrs. Longstreet's campaign failed, and construction started the year Lenore turned 8. The town still attracted tourists; only not as many. But Lenore still loved to visit the place.

On their trips over, her daddy would tell the story of Professor Leon. "When I was a boy," he'd say, "a tightrope walker named Professor Leon walked across that gorge on a cloth cable tied to trees. He did just fine 'til one of the support wires snapped."

At this point, her daddy always paused for effect. "Professor Leon crouched down," he'd say, "but after a minute, he stood up again. The man came toward us balancing his pole and mumbling something or other. Some of 'em said he was lecturing himself. But I'm here to tell you, that feller was praying! We went to praying, too. My mama always said we prayed him across, and I believe we did. It scared Mama so bad she took to bed for a week."

Lanier always added that he believed somebody tampered with a support cable to make the poor man fall. About everybody in town had bet against him, so Lenore supposed it could be true, but she hoped not.

Lanier's voice brought her mind back to the present. "There's big doin's at church Sunday," he said, "all-day singin' and dinner on the grounds to welcome that new doctor movin' here. We wouldn't want to miss that, would we?" He hoped the two women saw the matter the same way he did. "Besides, campmeetin' starts in three weeks. We got a lot to do to get ready for it."

Her daddy was right about that. To Lenore, it didn't seem possible that it was almost time for the annual, weeklong tradition of campmeeting, but it was. *Of course*, they wouldn't miss it—who would want to? This wasn't just an annual religious revival; campmeeting was the social event of the year!

Most people spent the week in one of these so-called "tents" around the open-air arbor where preachers held forth three or four times a day. The tents were mostly one-room structures with a door at each end and, for some, a window. Like most, the Conley tent had been in the same family since the 1830s.

Lanier puffed on his pipe. "It wouldn't be polite not to introduce ourselves to the new doctor Sunday. Anyhow, Lenore may want to see if he's good husband material."

Her daddy pretended to be gravely wounded by the bean she tossed at him. "Well, you've ruled out every other boy around here, including poor ol' Alton Boggs," he said. "By the way, I promised Alton you'd bring him a fried pie Sunday."

"Daddy, you're awful," Lenore protested. "And if this doctor thinks he can take Dr. Dyer's place, he's got another *think* coming. I hope we can still go see him in Clarkesville even if he won't come over here anymore."

When neither parent said anything, Lenore continued. "How 'bout if I marry Odell Stovall? He sits down at the store all day, complaining about how bad that leg he lost in France still hurts so much. I could marry *him*—between us, we'd have two good legs, at least."

Her father rubbed his chin and pretended to think about Odell's potential as a son-in-law. "Well, Punkin, I reckon Odell might be all right. But the truth is—he ain't got a pot to piss in. You ought to consider a man's prospects before you think on marrying him. Alton Boggs, on the other hand…"

"Oh, Daddy," said Lenore, interrupting. "Don't talk like that. Having an old maid daughter won't be too bad. I can cook for you after Mama leaves you for somebody better looking," she teased. "Anyhow, there's a shortage of men these days, and the ones left don't want to marry a gimpy girl like me."

Lenore's mother stopped snapping beans. She reached over and took her daughter's hand. "Don't say that, honey. You can have your pick of men." She gave her husband a look and added, "That is, if you think you can put up with one."

Lanier studied his pipe. In the yard, a purple martin swooped and swirled in the twilight, catching mosquitos in mid-flight. It soon flew back to the flock up near the string of gourds Lanier kept hanging by the barn to attract them.

Hannah took more beans from the basket between the two rocking chairs. "Alton Boggs is so slow, it wouldn't hurt him none to fall out of a tree," she said. "If you ask me, he's tetched. Alton has wanted to court Lenore since she blossomed, but she wants no part of it. He's nearly 10 years older than her, anyway."

Lanier studied his pipe some more and then looked kindly at his wife. "Ah, Sugar Babe, she knows I'm teasin', and Alton ain't no more tetched than the average feller moonin' over a girl. And don't forget, I'm 11 years older than *you*," he reminded her.

"That's different," said Hannah, snapping her beans a bit faster.

Lanier looked up at his daughter, "Your mama's right, honey. You *can* take your pick of men."

Lenore blushed at her daddy's praise. Secretly, she thought he might be right about Alton being her best bet for a husband. Lord knows he was interested. It seemed like he showed up every time she went to the store, and she couldn't *count* the times he'd offered to buy her a stick of licorice — as if she were a child!

Lately, Alton had started sitting on their bench at church, too. So far, she'd kept her parents between them. Because once a girl sat beside a man at church two Sundays in a row, folks considered them sweethearts.

Lenore took more beans out of the basket and looked at her daddy. "If you think I'm so pretty, why do you keep making out like you want me to marry Alton Boggs?" she asked him. "Don't you think I can do any better?"

Before giving him a chance to respond, she changed the subject. "By the way, Daddy, I think it's time we let June go dry. It won't be long 'til her calf comes."

Her daddy leaned against the post. "You may be right. I forget when she's due to drop." He scratched his head as if trying to tease out the date. "But I've got it marked on the calendar down at the barn. That'll be one less cow to milk during campmeetin', anyhow."

Not easily sidetracked, Lanier got right back to his pet subject. "You and your mama can say what you want about ol' Alton, but when his mama passes, he and his brother, Charles, up in Asheville, will get clear title to two hundred and forty acres of good bottomland. That ain't nothin' to sneeze at. A lot of it joins ours. You could do worse than Alton to help make Miss Hannah here a grandma."

Lenore sighed. "There *are* things more important than bottomland, you know."

"Like what?"

Lanier didn't duck fast enough to avoid the two beans that hit him at the same time.

Later, as he and Hannah lay in the handmade, walnut-wood bed her grandparents brought down from North Carolina a century earlier, they talked about their daughter's prospects. From a practical standpoint — and they were both practical people — when you considered the shortage of eligible men and Lenore's handicap, Alton Boggs might indeed be their best hope for grandchildren.

Still, Hannah had heard someone down at the store say this new doctor was single. So, with that in mind, she decided to help with Sunday's pies, and maybe even fry up a chicken.

CHAPTER THREE

The Arrival

July 8, 1919

om checked his pocket watch and gazed through the
passenger car window as the locomotive steamed to a halt at
Clarkesville Station. Somewhere, a few miles west, lay the valleys
of Nacoochee and Sautee.

To get to this part of Northeast Georgia, he'd changed trains in
Atlanta, and spent the night in a hamlet called Cornelia, before
catching the Tallulah Falls line up here. The train had been late
leaving Cornelia this morning. Instead of arriving in Clarkesville at
the scheduled time of 9:33, it was now noon.

Tom *finally* felt hungry again. He'd only eaten once since the
feast of ham, eggs, grits, and red-eye gravy Big Mama laid out for
him yesterday morning before he left for the Macon depot. Three
lumberjacks couldn't have finished that meal. "I don't know what
dey'll feed you up in dem mountains," she'd told him as she
pressed a bag of fried chicken into his hands. "But you ain't gonna
leave dis house hongry."

Big Mama waved the scarf she used to wipe her tears until the
buggy carrying him and his mother was out of sight. Isaac followed
in his wagon. It held Tom's trunk, which was too big for the
buggy — heavy with books more than clothes. Tom was taking the
tall, chestnut mare named Val with him to North Georgia, so Isaac
and his mule would have to come back for the buggy later.

Their father hadn't touched on Val in his will, but Tom's mother insisted the horse belonged to him now. "You're the one he'd want to have her, son," she said. When Tom asked his brother if that was all right with him, Ray only shrugged.

There was also the matter of the pocket watch — an E. Howard, made in 1850. Their Confederate grandfather had carried it through the entire war. He'd passed it on to his oldest son, Tom's father, and by rights the watch should belong to Tom's brother, Ray. But Ray had refused to take it. "Give it to Tom," he told his mother. "He's got more use for a watch than I do."

At the Macon depot, the colored man tending to the livestock didn't mind that Tom wanted to lead the horse onto the car himself. "Dat's one fine hoss, sir," he'd said, admiring Val.

Once his mare was safely inside, Tom tied Val's braided hemp halter to a rope that hung from the slatted wall. "Yes, she is," he said to the attendant. "I'd appreciate it if you take good care of her." He handed the man a nickel.

"Yes, sir, I surely will. Thank you, sir. I'll throw down some extra straw so she won't be as apt to slip. If she gets skittish, I'll blindfold her," the man offered. "But I don't think dat's gonna be necessary." Grabbing a curry comb, the attendant ran it across Val's back. "Ain't nothing like a good currying to calm a hoss down. I'll make sure dis filly gets a *fine* ride up to Atlanta."

Reassured that Val was in good hands, Tom kissed his mother goodbye and shook Isaac's hand. He looked around one last time for his brother, Ray, but didn't see him.

Tom and his mother had both hoped Ray would come with them to the depot. But when Tom peeked into his brother's room yesterday morning, the bed was made, and he and Jack were gone. Tom waited as long as he could, but he'd left home without telling his brother goodbye.

Now that he was here in Clarkesville, Tom's immediate concern was his horse. This trip was her first train ride. She'd stayed calm yesterday but seemed a bit more anxious when he loaded her in Cornelia this morning.

From his seat, Tom watched two men on the loading dock grind cigarettes under their shoes, then roll hand-dollies to the edge of the platform. A dozen or so people milled around the station. One of them — a silver-haired man with a moustache and an unbuttoned vest hanging over a wrinkled white shirt — held an umbrella in his hand.

Tom chuckled. The sky was clear, but in his last letter, Dr. Dyer wrote that if it *wasn't* raining, he'd bring an umbrella to the depot. If it *was*, the doctor would hold a newspaper over his head. Either way, he wrote, he'd be easy to spot.

A teenage boy stood beside the older man. When Tom raised his hand in their direction through the window, the elder gentleman touched his hat, acknowledging the gesture. As the other passengers collected their belongings, Tom looked around.

A little trolley with a roof, and enough open-air seats for ten or so people, sat on a set of tracks heading north. As if the trolley longed to be a real locomotive, both ends sported a miniature cowcatcher. The driver slouched in one of its seats reading a newspaper.

Once the other passengers were off, Tom stepped down from the car, walked to the man with the umbrella and put out his hand. "Dr. Livingstone, I presume?" he asked, smiling. "Please forgive me, but I've always wanted to say that."

The older man shook his head. "No. I'm sorry. I don't know anybody named Livingstone. I'm waiting for a Tom Garrison — thought you might be him."

Feeling sheepish, Tom said, "Oh. Well. Yes. I'm Tom Garrison. I was making a little joke there — sorry — nice to meet you, sir."

The doctor shook Tom's hand. "I'm Dr. David Dyer. Happy to make your acquaintance — finally. I've heard some mighty fine things about you from Dr. Hardman and his wife. I believe she's your aunt?"

"Well, kind of — I call her Aunt Emma, but she's actually my mother's first cousin." Tom started to explain further, but decided it was best not to — especially the part about Aunt Emma's husband also being a cousin on his father's side.

Dr. Dyer gestured toward the teenager. "This here is Frank — Frank Sosebee. Frank lives over in the Valley," he explained. "But he helps me out some. Frank wants to be a doctor."

The boy offered his hand. "Nice to meet you, sir. My name's Frank, but you can call me Dr. Stanley if you like." He winked.

Dr. Dyer rubbed his eyes. "Why on earth would he call you Stanley? That doesn't make any sense. Now make yourself useful and help with the bags. Put 'em on the white steamer. I declare, boy. Sometimes I don't know about you."

"The white steamer?" Tom asked, looking around, a little confused.

"That's what we call the freight buggy hitched to that mule over there," said Dr. Dyer. "They use that to haul the bags. We call it the white steamer because the mule is white. He pulls it, you see. The thing's not really steam-powered."

Tom laughed. He liked these people. "I'm sorry you had to wait on me. I don't know why the train was so late."

Dr. Dyer looked puzzled. "Wait on you? Why, we just got here. We knew you wouldn't be in before noon. Jordan Emerson, the engineer, stayed here in Clarkesville last night with his mama, Emily." He shook his head. "Poor woman's been ailing. Jordan didn't leave for Cornelia this morning 'til 8 o'clock. No, the way we figured it, you're a few minutes early."

Tom couldn't keep from laughing again. Then he looked down the track and turned serious. Two men had slid the livestock car door open and were trying to lead Val down a wooden ramp. The mare was nervous. Half-way out, she balked. The younger of the two attendants jerked on her halter rope.

Val tried to rear, but the move caused her to sit back on her haunches. While her front hooves flailed at the air, her back feet slid across the wood, splintering it. When she got all four feet on the ramp again, she squealed and bolted.

"Whoa, you stupid horse!" yelled the man holding the rope. He pulled back on it hard with both hands, which caused the mare to lose her footing and fall on her side at the bottom of the ramp. Instead of trying to calm the terrified animal, the young man whacked her across the back with the rope. When he raised the line for the third time, Tom's hand gripped his wrist.

"Watch out for my horse," Tom shouted at Frank as he pulled the man away from Val and shoved him to the ground. When Tom glared at the other fellow who'd been helping, he seemed to suddenly remember some pressing business behind the depot.

Val got to her feet, white-eyed and trembling. As Tom looked her over for injuries, someone shoved him chest-first against the car, nearly knocking the wind out of him. Tom caught his breath just in time to block a fist heading for his jaw. He countered with a right hook that dropped the man to one knee and a left cross that laid him on the ground.

Frank kept his grip on Val's halter, stroking her neck to calm her. "Wow," he said. "Where'd you learn to fight like that?"

"I had two brothers," said Tom, breathing hard.

Frank nodded as if that explained everything. "I bet you're the youngest," he said. "Like me."

"That's right," Tom said, grinning. He turned his attention back to the horse. Once he saw Val was all right, he put his hand out to the man on the ground. Pulling him up, he said, "Don't you *ever* mistreat an animal that way again—you understand me, mister?"

"Hell, it's just a horse," the man mumbled, rubbing his face. "I's jus' trying to get her up 'fore she hurt herself."

"You're the reason she went down in the first place," said Tom, as he rubbed the knuckles on his right hand. "Now get, before I lose my temper!"

The young man turned away, but Dr. Dyer yelled for him to wait, motioning with his umbrella. "Hold on there, Floyd," he said, walking toward him. "Let me look at you before you leave and make sure you're all right." The doctor felt the young man's jaw and probed his rib cage.

"He a friend of yours?" asked Tom.

"Well, his daddy is," Dr. Dyer replied. "Floyd and me aren't all that close, but I did deliver him, so I reckon you might say we're acquainted."

Dr. Dyer looked in the man's mouth and checked him over carefully. "You're fine," he told the subdued young fellow. "Put some ointment on that cut there. If anything gets to hurting ya, much come by my office. Meanwhile, try to learn something from this. Dr. Garrison's right about mistreating animals. There's no use in it."

Floyd Martin pointed at Tom. "He's a doctor?" The young man looked surprised. "Well, I'll be damned."

"That's another thing, Floyd," said Dr. Dyer. "I'm not a judge, and there ain't enough of me to make a jury, but I wish you wouldn't swear so much. Your daddy doesn't, 'less he's drunk. Now go on home, son. There's not much to unload today anyway."

Tom ran his hands over Val's legs. Except for a few scratches, the horse was sound. Frank took hold of her halter. "I'll take her around and tie her to the baggage cart."

"Come on," said Dr. Dyer to a suddenly tired Tom. "Let's you and me get on the trolley. As soon as those other two passengers get settled, it'll be leaving."

As if taking his cue from the doctor's words, the driver folded his newspaper, moved to the front of the trolley and started its two-cylinder gasoline engine. Instead of turning the vehicle around, he sat down in the seat facing town and drove from that end.

Once Dr. Dyer took his seat, he shouted at the driver, "Let's go, Fred. It's high-time we got started."

Shortly after the trolley pulled out, Tom saw the Blue Ridge Mountains for the first time. Their rugged ridges receded into the distance until the mountains blended with the sky. He couldn't look away. "They're beautiful," he whispered to himself. Speaking louder, he said to his companions, "Believe it or not, this is the first time I've ever seen mountains."

"Well," yelled Dr. Dyer above the engine noise. "I've never seen flatland, so I reckon we're even."

During the mile-long ride to town, Tom fell in love with Clarkesville. The trolley rolled up the tree-lined street past grand houses with flower-filled window boxes.

"This is Washington Street," yelled Dr. Dyer, "It's our main boulevard. I bet you didn't think we even had a boulevard, did you?"

Tom grinned and admitted that was true.

"You may not know it," Dr. Dyer continued, "but Clarkesville is a resort destination for wealthy folks—has been since about 1840."

Up ahead, a stately, red-brick courthouse with arched windows and a towering belfry marked the north end of town. Its huge clock showed twelve-fifteen.

"That's our courthouse," said Dr. Dyer. "Ain't it about the finest one you ever saw?" They stopped a few yards away from it in a small, circular park, whose centerpiece was a large gazebo with a roof pointing skyward like a witch's hat. Dr. Dyer motioned toward a two-story building on their left. A sign hanging from the second-floor porch read *Mountain View Hotel*.

"I took the liberty of booking you a room here," said Dr. Dyer. "I think you'll find it satisfactory." The trolley driver killed its engine, set the brake, and went back to his newspaper.

When the white mule pulled the baggage cart up behind the trolley, Frank jumped out to help the bellman. "Sam and me will take this up to your room," he said pulling hard on the trunk. "Good grief! What you got in this thing, Dr. Garrison?"

"It's just one of the cadavers from medical school," said Tom, grinning. "Be careful with him. I've become fond of old Pete. He's got my chess set in there with him, and he likes to take his time between moves, so try not to disturb him."

As Frank and the bellman wrestled with the trunk, Dr. Dyer slapped Tom on the back, "Let's get some dinner, son. Then we'll go by Brewer's pharmacy and get you stocked up on medicine and such. If you're not dog-tired, my wife and I would like to buy you supper. Tomorrow morning, we'll ride over to the Valley and get you settled."

Frank ran back and tossed Tom a room key. "You're all set, Dr. Garrison — Room 12 on the second floor. If you want me to, I'll take your mare over to the livery stable across the street."

"Sure," said Tom, untying Val and handing the rope to Frank. Dr. Dyer slapped the horse on her rump as Frank led her past him. "Tell Ed I said to make room for her. I don't think they've got rid of all those mules from Saturday's auction yet."

"I will," said Frank.

It was 5 o'clock before Tom saw the inside of room 12. But once he did, he found it accommodating. Outside his room, the side-porch had a view of the mountains, so he plopped in a rocking chair, put up his feet and stared at them. He'd seen pictures of these mountains, but pictures weren't the same.

An hour later, at 6 o'clock, someone rang a hand-held bell to announce the evening meal. Dr. Dyer and his wife strolled through the front door just as Tom got to the bottom of the stairs. The older doctor bowed graciously. "Howdy, son. I'd like you to meet my wife, Miss India." He gestured toward the attractive older woman.

"It's a pleasure to meet you, ma'am," Tom said, taking her hand. "What a beautiful name for a beautiful lady. Not many people are named for a country, but then, not many are worthy of such a tribute."

"Why, thank you," replied Mrs. Dyer.

Tom glanced around the lobby. "Will Frank be joining us?" He looked forward to the young man's company, but the doctor and his wife chuckled.

"We invited him," Dr. Dyer explained. "But Frank can barely break away from his books long enough to eat a cold sweet potato. We have an extra room he stays in when he's over this way. He's up there studying now. Like I said, he plans on being a doctor."

"Frank comes from good stock," said Mrs. Dyer. "He's got a head full of sense. But his family's been up against it lately."

She didn't elaborate. "Oh, India," said her husband. "You make him sound like an orphan. He's still got a daddy and two brothers who work. They've got all they want as long as they don't want much."

Eyeing Tom, he added, "If you don't watch out, Frank will ask more questions than you care to answer. But he can be a help to you, too, if you'll put up with his history talk."

His wife waggled her finger. "You take that back, David. Frank is a joy to be around, and you love answering his questions as much as he likes asking them. Anyway, he learned most of the history he knows from you."

Before her husband could answer, a waitress appeared, and ushered them into the dining room.

"Thank you, Marion, "said Mrs. Dyer to the girl. "How's Conrad?"

"Mean as ever," said the waitress. "I'll tell him you asked after him. Y'all enjoy your meal."

During their dinner of fried chicken, cornbread and more vegetables than Tom could count, he began to feel as if he'd known this couple for years.

"I understand you're single," said Mrs. Dyer mid-way through the meal. "Do you have a special girl back home?"

Tom blushed. There had been only one girl in his life, really, and that wasn't serious—at least from his standpoint. He'd always been friends with Barbara Baker, the girl whose arm he'd wanted to fix when he was six. But about two years ago, much to his surprise, Barbara told Tom she was in love with him. Then she kissed him.

When he didn't react, Barbara asked, "What's the matter, Tom? Don't you like me?"

"Of course I like you, Barbara," Tom stammered. "I've always liked you. I'm sorry. I...I, just don't love you. Not that way."

It was a year before Barbara spoke to him again. Then, on one of his trips home from school, she came to their front door and asked Tom's mother if he was home. When Tom came out, they sat together on the porch.

"Lester Allison asked me to marry him last night," she said.

"I'm not surprised. He's liked you since we were kids. He's a good man, Barbara. I wish the two of you the best."

She put her hand on his. "I wanted to tell you about it before I gave him my answer."

"Barbara, I..." Tom looked at the floor.

She hurried down the steps before he finished his thought.

Barbara and Lester married two months later.

"Well, ma'am," Tom said to Mrs. Dyer. "The truth is I've been so busy with school and all, I haven't had much time for girls. I won't say I haven't winked at one or two, but no, there's no one special — at least not yet."

Mrs. Dyer smiled and looked at her husband. "When you meet the right woman, you'll know. Isn't that right, David?"

Dr. Dyer glanced up from his plate. "Yes'm. Sure is. Tom, have you tried the ham? Taste of it and tell me how you like it."

Tom reached for the ham and asked Mrs. Dyer, "Do y'all have any children?"

"Yes, we have a daughter, Bonnie. She has two adorable boys, Seth and Ethan, but they live in Atlanta, so we don't see them as much as we'd like."

"She married a Yankee," said Dr. Dyer as if that explained something. "His name's Ted. He's from one of those states that start with an "I" — I forget which one."

"Illinois," said Mrs. Dyer, rolling her eyes. "Why can't you remember that?"

Later, over peach cobbler, Tom remarked that he planned to buy a buggy in the next few days. When he did, the doctor's wife glanced at her husband and nodded faintly.

Dr. Dyer took a sip of coffee and put his cup down. After wiping his mouth with his napkin, he said, "There's no need in that, son. I got a good buggy I don't plan to use much now that you're here. I've kept the axles greased, so it's got plenty of life left. You're welcome to it."

Tom didn't know what to say. This generous offer made so casually to a near stranger startled him. "Sir, I couldn't take your buggy," he protested. "I'm sure you'll still need it. I've put money back to buy one. I'd planned on doing it as soon as I got settled."

Dr. Dyer shook his head. "Save your money, son. I've figured out how to make do without a buggy. Besides, we live in walking distance of everything we need, church included," he assured Tom. "I'm keeping Rebel, my ol' gelding. You take that buggy and welcome — no use in lettin' it just sit."

The issue seemed settled. The three of them spent the rest of the evening talking about Clarkesville and the two valleys Tom would soon see. It was well after ten when they said goodnight.

Back on the hotel's side-porch, Tom sat in the rocking chair he'd used earlier. Two men on horseback trotted by on the street below. One laughed at something the other one said.

Tom lit the cigar Dr. Dyer had slipped him when his wife wasn't looking. He blew smoke in the directions of the mountains. The grandfather clock in the lobby had just struck midnight when he pulled off his boots and went to bed.

CHAPTER FOUR

First Day

July 9, 1919

W hen Tom got to the livery stable the next morning, Frank already had Val hitched to the buggy.

"Thanks," Tom said, impressed with the boy's resourcefulness. He was paying his stable bill when Dr. Dyer rode up on Rebel, patting the horse's brown neck before he dismounted. "Sorry I'm late boys," he said, "but it couldn't be helped. India made biscuits for breakfast, and you can't rush biscuits. Here, she sent y'all two apiece — even put a dab of butter on 'em. Eat 'em quick — early don't last long around here."

When Frank and Tom finished eating, they all headed west toward the place everyone here simply called "the Valley." Frank led the way, riding bareback on a molly mule named Trouble.

At Dr. Dyer's direction, Tom had left his trunk at the hotel. When he'd asked why, the doctor shrugged and said, "Oh, I hired a wagon to bring it over later today with a chair or two and a few things my wife wants you to have. It'll all be along directly."

It was a steamy morning, but a breeze kept it pleasant. A thunderstorm had rumbled through before daylight. It dropped enough rain to keep the dust down as the trio trotted along the dirt road with its red clay banks. The rolling land that wasn't in pasture or covered by trees grew corn, sorghum and, here and there, some cotton — though nothing like the big fields of it Tom was used to seeing further south.

Some things did remind him of home, though: every house had a garden—usually a big one—and they were never far from a barking dog or the smell of a barn.

Women straightened from their work to wave. Every traveler they met knew Dr. Dyer. "This is Dr. Garrison from Macon," he told a man named Guy Dorsey, who halted his peddler's wagon to chat. "He'll be staying in the Valley to take on some of my work over this way."

"So I hear," said the peddler. "Look-a-here Doc, I got some whetrocks in last week. You mentioned you was needin' one." Dorsey looked hopeful.

"I sure do," said Dr. Dyer, riding his horse up to the wagon. "They still a nickel apiece?"

"Yep." Dorsey reached inside the wagon and handed one of the sharpening stones to the doctor. He pocketed the coin Dr. Dyer handed him, then addressed Tom. "Folks say you're kin to the Hardmans."

Tom nodded.

"Nice folks for rich people. Look forward to knowin' you, Doc. Giddy up, mule." His wagon creaked out of sight behind them.

A half-mile down the road, a woman sweeping her dirt yard with a stick of tightly-bound broom sage, hollered that her youngest boy was feeling puny. She'd be obliged if Dr. Dyer could stop for a minute and take a look at him.

"Sure thing, Mildred," he said to her. "You boys ride on without me. I'll be along directly."

Tom and Frank continued along the road. Each mile brought the foothills closer; every curve a different view. One uniquely formed mountain west of their route seemed larger than the others—its rounded top almost always in sight.

"What's that hill yonder?" Tom asked, pointing toward it. "I've seen it off and on since we left Clarkesville."

"Oh, that's Yonah Mountain," said Frank, as if the mountain was an old friend he'd forgotten to introduce earlier. "Yonah is the granddaddy of all the hills around here. It means *bear* in the Cherokee language. If you ever get lost, just look for Yonah Mountain. She'll guide you home every time."

They rode along silently for a while. Then Frank walked his mule, Trouble, up alongside the buggy. "Can I ask you a question, Dr. Garrison?"

"Sure."

"Do you like healing people?"

Tom considered the question and took his time before he spoke. He sensed his answer was important to the boy. "Well, Frank," he said finally. "The truth is, I can't heal anybody. Doctors are instruments, and I know we play a role, but we can't heal."

Frank ran his hands across Trouble's closely-cropped mane. He looked straight ahead as Yonah Mountain came into view again. A good-news bee hovered above the mule's head.

"A doctor can set bones," said Tom, watching the bee zip away. "But we don't have anything to do with making them grow back together. All we can do is stand in awe when it happens."

Frank leaned forward to fiddle with the top of the mule's bridle. He pulled some of Trouble's mane out from under it. "That's what Dr. Dyer says. I want to be a doctor one day. I promised Mama I'd be one, so I will."

"I felt that way, too," said Tom. "When I was six, I knew medicine was my calling. I haven't practiced it much, though, other than during the flu scare."

When Frank seemed satisfied with how the mule's bridle fit, he straightened up. "That flu was bad. Mama—she died from it last fall—Daddy's sister, my Aunt Dora Lee, too." The boy's sadness was evident. "She lived down at Stone Mountain near Atlanta. I hear it was worse down there. People more bunched up, I reckon."

"Probably so," said Tom, remembering all the people he'd seen die from the flu in Augusta. "Frank, can I ask you a question now?"

"Sure."

"How did that mule of yours get her name, Trouble? There has to be a story behind that."

Frank reached forward to scratch the top of Trouble's head again. "Aw, Daddy named her that when we first got her. When she was young, she was bad to get out of the pasture and eat folk's corn and such. But you don't do that no more, do you, girl?" He patted the mule's neck, dark now with sweat.

They plodded along without speaking for a time. All of a sudden, Frank kicked Trouble into a trot and motioned for Tom to keep up. "Let's get on over to the Valley," he shouted back. "You're gonna love it!"

Before long, Dr. Dyer cantered up on Rebel and reined in his snorting horse. "Looks like I'm just in time," he said, pretending to hand Tom something. "I found one of your ears on the road a-ways back. Thank goodness I got here before Frank talked the other one off."

Tom laughed. "Actually, he's been filling me in on things — interesting stuff, too. How's that boy you looked in on back there?"

"Aw, he wasn't bad off — just a touch o' colic." Dr. Dyer laughed. "I gave him a dose of castor oil. His mama's the one with the real problem. She has the backdoor trots and didn't want you and Frank to know it."

Dr. Dyer shaded his eyes and looked down the road. "We're almost to the Valley. Let's stop at Allan Williams's store up the road a-ways and get you some supplies. After that, we'll ride on up to your place."

The sun was directly overhead when they pulled into the yard of the general store, which — Frank told him — also served as the community post office. Frank let their horses and mule drink from the watering trough before he pulled their dripping muzzles toward a hitching post by a giant oak whose shade, even at high noon, covered half the yard.

The store faced the main road; its west wall ran alongside another dirt road heading north. Metal signs on the outside pushed Dental Sweet Snuff, Lydia Pinkham's Tonic, Knox Knit Hosiery and an assortment of other products. The double front door stood open, giving flies free access.

Dr. Dyer pointed to a piece of flat ground to the north. "Yonder is the beginning of the Sautee Valley. Up the road a-ways is your house." Facing south, he said, "This valley between the road and the river is Nacoochee. Your kinfolk's place — you really ought to decide if Mrs. Hardman is your aunt or your cousin — is down at the west end of it. In fact, the feller who built it — his name was Nichols — called the house *West End*."

Frank followed both doctors up the steps to where two men sat playing checkers on the porch. The older one, a farmer by his dress, was winning, based on the number of checkers stacked at his end. The other man didn't seem to care much. He was more interested in spitting tobacco juice into a red, Hills Bros. coffee can and swatting flies.

The losing man's right leg had been amputated; his britches folded and pinned a few inches above where his knee should have been. Two handmade crutches leaned against the wall by the door.

"Pert nigh hot, ain't it, boys? Howdy, Sherry," said Dr. Dyer, surprising Tom with the change in his speech pattern. The old doctor slapped the farmer on his back and added, "Ain't seen you in a good long while."

"I'm here to tell ya," said Sherry, who jumped the crippled man's last checker and stood up. "I been working from can to can't since spring. Thought I'd give Odell a run for his money while they load up my wagon. Who's that you got with you?"

"This is Dr. Tom Garrison from down around Macon," said Dr. Dyer, gesturing toward Tom. "He's gonna be the new doctor over here. Tom, meet Sherry Collins and Odell Stovall. Odell here is one of our war heroes; donated his hind leg to the Kaiser—that missing leg still bothering you, son?"

Odell swatted a fly. "It hurts some." He spit tobacco juice into the can. "What's that you call it, Doc—phantom pain? Itches too. Wish now I'd a pickled the damn thing and brought it home with me. That way, I could scratch it once 'n awhile."

Sherry Collins shook Tom's hand. "Pleased to meet ya, Dr. Garrison. I heard you was coming. Think you can fill ol' Doc's shoes?"

"I don't plan to," said Tom. "From what I've seen, that would be impossible."

Odell ignored Tom's hand. "You in the war, Doc?" he asked.

Tom looked at the man's empty pants leg. "No," he answered. "My brothers were, though—both of them. The oldest was killed. The other one made it back."

Odell didn't seem impressed. "How come you didn't go?"

Tom didn't know what to say. Odell spat again, waiting for an answer.

"I was in medical school. Plus, the Army didn't like to take all the sons from the same family. There was just the three of us."

"Don't sound like much of an excuse to me. There wadn't but two boys in my family, but they took me and Grady both. The flu killed him, though—not the Germans. A fit man like you ought to of signed up."

Dr. Dyer spoke before Tom could answer. "Lots of men didn't go across the pond, Odell. You can't stay mad at everybody who didn't. How 'bout your buddy, Alton Boggs? He didn't go overseas, and you don't seem all that put out with him."

"He was drafted, ya know," said Odell. "Wadn't his fault the Army wouldn't have him."

Dr. Dyer shook his head and sighed. "Come on, Tom, let's quit gabbin'. I'll introduce you to a few folks. Frank, you're a good hand at checkers; see if you can beat Odell. We'll be back directly."

It was dark inside but their eyes soon adjusted. Packed shelves lined the front room. Advertisements and political slogans dangled everywhere. An ironic picture of Woodrow Wilson with his 1916 campaign slogan, "He Kept Us Out of War!" hung above a set of cast iron counter scales. Three pine coffins leaned against the back wall.

Tom didn't pay attention to any of it. "Odell's right, you know," he said to Dr. Dyer. "I *should* have gone. But everyone said it'd be best if I finished school first and went in as a doctor. By then, the war was over. I didn't mean to dodge anything."

Tom was clearly full of regret, and Dr. Dyer noticed. "Seems to me your family did their part and then some," he said. "Just count yourself lucky." He turned toward the postal counter and motioned for Tom to step up beside him. "Fannie, I want you to meet somebody."

A big woman, her hair pinned in a bun, peered across the counter by the door. "Well, hello, Dr. Dyer. This your new helper?" Without waiting for an answer, she stuck her hand out. "Nice to make your acquaintance. I'm Fannie Stover, the temporary postmaster here. I'm just filling in for Allan Williams while he's off fishing for a day or two. In the meantime, welcome to my post office." Fannie rattled on. "I understand you're kin to the Hardmans—good folks. They always come up around campmeetin' week. 'Course, they don't go."

Tom shook her hand. "Yes ma'am. I'm Tom Garrison. I believe you're right about Dr. Lam and Aunt Emma. I understand they're coming up the first week of August."

"Did you say Garrison?" asked the woman, looking behind her. "I knew you were coming, but I never heard your name before now. I got a package here for a Tom Garrison—now where'd I put it?" She looked underneath the counter. "Here it is. I wondered who'd show up for it."

"Are you sure it's for me?" Tom was surprised. "I've only left home yesterday. Nobody knows I'm here."

Fannie heaved the box onto the counter. "Well, it's addressed to Dr. Thomas Garrison—Sautee, Georgia. As far as I know, you're the only one we got."

Tom recognized his mother's handwriting on the package. "I wonder what this could be."

"I know a sure-fire way to find out," said Fannie, handing him a pocket knife. "I'm as curious as you are."

Tom cut the strings holding the box together, folded the blade, and handed the knife back. Now that he thought about it, he remembered seeing Uncle Isaac load a box like this on his wagon last week. Isaac had covered it with a cloth when he noticed Tom watching.

Inside, packed in newspapers, were three tin containers. The top one had an envelope with the words "For our much-loved doctor" written on it. There was something else, too. Wrapped in a hand-made quilt lay an engraved wooden sign with two metal hooks—clearly Isaac's handiwork. Carved into the wood were the words, *Dr. Thomas Garrison, M.D.*

Feeling a need to be busy, Tom stuffed the sign back in the box. He wiped his eyes on the back of his hand, grabbed one of the tins and pried the lid off. Inside was one of Big Mama's brown sugar pound cakes—Tom's favorite. The only thing he liked better was her oatmeal and molasses cookies, and the other two cans held dozens of those.

Their aroma flooded Tom with memories. "Big Mama sent me this," he said. "She wanted me to have something from home when I got here—a quilt, too. I guess she thought it'd be cold up here in the mountains. She wouldn't know any different, bless her heart."

Dr. Dyer cleared his throat. "All that's from your mama? How thoughtful."

"Well, yes and no," said Tom. "Nell is our housekeeper, but she's like my second mother. I call her Big Mama—we all do. My real mother doesn't bake cakes anymore."

"Let me see if I've got this straight," said Dr. Dyer, stroking his chin. "Your cousin is your aunt, and you call your housekeeper, Mama. Do you have a sister somewhere you think of as an uncle? You flatlanders beat a hen a rootin'."

"Don't try to figure it out," Tom said, laughing. "Here, have a cookie." The doctor took one, and Fannie grabbed three, saying she'd put two back for later. Dr. Dyer brushed crumbs from his moustache and ushered Tom across the creaky floor toward the back of the store.

Half an hour later, the two doctors started out the front door again. Tom had his arms full of things like salt, coffee, blackstrap molasses and a middling of meat. Dr. Dyer was picking up the box of things Tom's mother had sent when Fannie bellowed, "See ya Sunday, Dr. Garrison! You gonna bring that cake?"

"Bring it where?" Tom asked, looking at her over the boxes. "What happens Sunday?"

"Doggone it," said Dr. Dyer. "I clean forgot. I'm supposed to tell you there's gonna be an all-day singing and dinner on the grounds at the Methodist church Sunday. You're the guest of honor. It'll give you a chance to meet a few folks."

"But I'm Baptist."

"Don't matter—the Baptists will get around to welcomin' you soon enough. Especially after they figure out the Methodists beat 'em to it. Anyway, people from the other churches will come to eat and sing after the service. You'll meet all kinds of folks, ain't that right, Fannie?"

"Sure is. You'll get to hear me play the piano, too. I'm pretty good at it, if I do say so myself."

"All right then," said Tom. "I guess I'll see you Sunday."

Odell looked up when they walked back on the porch. Frank, who'd been half-heartedly setting up the checker board for yet another game, seemed relieved to see them. Not sure what to say, Tom, his arms too full to do it himself, nodded at Dr. Dyer to open one of the tin containers and offer them some of Big Mama's cookies. Frank took two, but Odell shook his head.

"I don't want nothin' from a dodger," he said, raising the coffee can to his mouth. Dr. Dyer took a cookie for himself and put the lid back on the container.

"Look," said Tom, looking at Odell. "I didn't dodge anything. I *planned* to join up, but the war ended before I could. I'm sorry about your leg *and* your brother, but there's nothing I can do about either one. I lost a brother, too, you know."

Odell swatted another fly. This time, he knocked the coffee can over in the process. Brown liquid dribbled through the cracks in the well-worn floorboards. He spat again. This time, the tobacco juice landed on the floor between Tom's boots.

Dr. Dyer put his hand on Odell's shoulder. "Son, there ain't no need carrying on like this. I know it's hard on you, but what's done is done. Get on with things."

Odell lowered his head and stared at the checkerboard. "I ain't got nothin' to get on with." He looked up at Frank. "Hand me my crutches, boy."

The one-legged man sat the nearly empty coffee can on the barrel holding the checker board, pulled himself up and hobbled down the steps at the other end of the porch. Tom and the rest watched as he propelled himself down the dirt road as fast as he could.

The two doctors walked down the opposite steps and arranged the boxes in the buggy. "Try not to have hard feelings toward Odell," said Dr. Dyer. He put his hand on Tom's back. "Before he got drafted, Odell was as good-natured a boy as you'd find anywhere. It's just taking a while to get used to being a war-cripple."

"I know," said Tom, unhitching Val and backing her toward the road. Before getting into the buggy, he asked, "Didn't the Army do anything for Odell? I mean, we've made big advances in artificial limbs since the 1800s."

"Oh, they gave him the standard-issue replacement leg," said the older doctor. "It's right heavy, though. Odell gets around better with just his crutches."

"Do you think you could get a plaster cast made of what's left of that leg?" Tom asked.

"Why?"

"I'm not sure. But one of my professors at Augusta went over to Queen Mary's Hospital in London last year to study replacement limbs. He may not be able to do anything, but it won't hurt to write him and ask. I know he'd need a cast — and money, of course."

"Well, it might take some doing," said Dr. Dyer, scratching his head, "but I guess I could. If it comes to it, I could always get him drunk."

Dr. Dyer untied Rebel. After mounting, he said, "About you doing your part in the war — I was a little over a year old when the War Between the States broke out." He looked toward the trees along the river. "It seems to me I can remember pulling off my daddy's gray hat the day he left home for it. But that's just because I heard so much about him when I was little. I was too young to remember anything like that. It's a fake memory, but it's the only one I have of him, so I treasure it."

Then, as if he'd forgotten something, Dr. Dyer turned around in the saddle. "Frank, before you hop on your mule, run back in and ask Fannie for an empty box. It don't have to be big, but don't get a little bitty one."

Frank sprinted inside and came back with a container. He handed it to Tom, who somehow found a place for it on the buggy seat.

Frank led the way as the Sautee Valley unfolded by the road. The land had lots of open spaces surrounded by woods and fed by streams, the main one being Sautee Creek.

About then, another mountain came into view. Its long tree-lined ridge lay on the far side of the land to their right. Tom called whoa to Val. He thought this rugged old hill was magnificent.

"That's Lynch Mountain," said Frank, stopping his mule. "It's named for Jeter Lynch. Not because anybody's ever been lynched up there, like some folks will tell you."

"Thanks for the information," said Tom. "Do all these mountains have names?"

"Most of 'em," said Frank, who began clicking them off one by one. "There's Yonah and Lynch, of course, then there's Pink, Hamby, Blood, Tray, Slaughter, Leadpole, Little Andy…"

Frank kept up his litany of mountain names as they passed fields of corn with waving tassels that reached toward the sun, as if praying for rain. A mile above the store, another mountain appeared on their left. Frank said this was Grimes Nose.

Below it stood a tin-roofed, two-story house with a covered porch on the front and along both sides. A garden filled the space between the road and front yard. On a grassy hill, across the lane that led to the house, two cows lay in the shade chewing their cud. Below them, under two strings of gourds hanging from wires, a horse and mule lazed head to tail, each swishing flies from the other's face.

On the porch, a man in overalls sat beside a woman in a white-collared work dress, shelling Crowder peas. A Bluetick hound ran toward the visitors, baying loudly, although his wagging tail betrayed the fierceness of his voice.

Dr. Dyer reined Rebel up and crossed his hands over the saddle horn. "Howdy, Lanier. Howdy, Miss Hannah. Nice looking garden. Not like last year's when everything dried up. Mind if I grab a tomato or two?"

"Take as many as you want," hollered the man from his porch. "They's a good many ripe, and a few good-sized ones. Tree leaves are showing their undersides, so it'll come up another cloud by evening." Finished with the weather report, he acknowledged Tom's presence. "He the new doctor we been hearing about?"

The woman on the porch cuffed her husband's arm. "Lanier, where's your manners?" Motioning toward the travelers, she said, "Y'all come up here and take dinner with us. Lenore's puttin' ever' thing on the table now. You ought not be traveling in the heat of the day anyhow."

Dr. Dyer dismounted and walked between two rows of tomatoes with vines tied to stakes that crossed at the top like tiny teepees. The hound accompanied him, enjoying having his ears scratched.

"Thanks kindly, but we got to keep moving," Dr. Dyer hollered toward the house. He gestured toward Tom. "This here is Tom Garrison. He is, in fact, the new doctor, up from Macon. Tom, this here is Lanier and Hannah Conley." The doctor examined tomato vines while he talked.

Tom waved. Before he put his hand down, the screen door opened, and the most beautiful girl he'd ever seen stepped onto the porch. She wore a peach-colored cotton dress under a white apron. The young woman walked with a limp as she moved behind her father. She put one hand on his shoulder and gestured toward them with the other. Then, or so it seemed to Tom, she looked right at him. Not at the buggy or at Frank or anything else — only him. For a moment, he couldn't breathe.

In the garden, Dr. Dyer pulled his shirt out of his britches and held up the ends to make a pouch. He used that to carry all the ripe tomatoes he could back to the buggy. As he dropped them into the box Frank had gotten from Fannie Stover, he whispered. "We'll have us a feast later — fresh tomatoes and cake — that's as good as it gets."

Dr. Dyer tucked his shirt back into his trousers, held his horse's bridle and continued his long-distance chat with Lanier, still mostly about the weather.

Frank noticed something didn't seem right with the new doctor, so he clucked Trouble up beside the buggy. Leaning down, he asked, "You all right, Dr. Garrison?"

When Tom didn't answer, Frank tugged on his sleeve. "Dr. Garrison, is something the matter? You look peak-ed."

Tom jumped, but his eyes stayed on the girl. "What? No, no. I'm sorry, Frank. I felt strange there for a minute. It's nothing." Then he whispered, "Who is she? Do you know her?"

The boy looked toward the house. "Sure. That's Lenore Conley. She was the smartest girl in her class down at the Nacoochee Institute. And Lord, can she sing! Lanier and Hannah are her mama and daddy. You aw' right, Doctor?"

"Yeah, I'm fine. It's just a feeling I get sometimes. Tell me more about her. She married?"

"Lenore? No, she ain't going with nobody, 'less you count Alton Boggs. Alton *wants* to court her, but he's not had much luck. Sometimes he makes out like she's his girl, but I doubt Lenore even knows it. If she does, she don't let on."

Frank looked at Lenore and openly declared, "I reckon she's about the prettiest girl I ever saw. You won't find a sweeter person, neither," he added. "She's always doing for old folks and them that needs help, and she won't never take a thing for it."

Frank swung himself down from Trouble's back and patted the mule's jaw. "Lenore sang *Amazing Grace* at my mama's funeral," he said. "She sounded like an angel. You can't tell it much from here, but she's got a game leg. Mama told me Lenore like to died the year I was born. Doc Dyer saved her. She limps some, but she don't let it hold her back none — works as hard as anybody."

On the porch, it looked to Tom like Hannah Conley whispered something to her daughter. The girl patted her mother's shoulder and started back inside. At the door, she turned and waved at Tom before she vanished.

"That corn across the road shore looks good," shouted Dr. Dyer.

"We got a fair to middlin' stand this spring," said Lanier. "Some of it down in the bottoms is running away with grass, though. Still, it might make thirty-bushel to the acre."

"I 'spec so, way it looks — be good it if does," Dr. Dyer replied as he waved goodbye.

A half-mile up the road from the Conley farm, they stopped in front of a covered bridge to let a wagon come through from the other direction. While they waited, Frank pointed toward the fast-moving stream below. "That's Chickamauga Creek. It's not the same one the battle of Chickamauga is named after, though. That one's up in Northwest Georgia."

Dr. Dyer laughed and motioned for Frank and Tom to go in ahead of him. The animals' metal shoes pounded the timbers as they walked through the cool, dark bridge. When they came out the other side, Dr. Dyer pointed to a house a half-mile ahead on the left side of the road. "Up there's your new home, Tom. I think you're gonna like it," he said somewhat proudly.

A few minutes later, they stopped in the yard of the small, whitewashed house this anonymous citizens' committee had rented for him. When Tom set the buggy brake, he looped the reins around the dashboard rail and tied the ends together in a bowtie knot.

"What on earth are you doin'?" asked Dr. Dyer, watching him. "I've never seen anyone tie their lines that way."

"It's just something my father taught me." Tom grinned at the man. "He said a horse appreciates it if their buggy looks fancier than the others. Tying the reins that way is just a habit now. I don't even think about it when I do it."

Dr. Dyer shook his head. "You flatlanders won't do."

Just then, a short, balding man scurried out the front door and down the porch steps. He dabbed his forehead with a handkerchief, but sweat still ran down his face.

Dr. Dyer dismounted and whispered, "That's Gus Miller, your new landlord. His ass weighs a ton."

"What?" Tom was taken aback.

"He's too big for his britches," muttered the doctor across his saddle.

"Howdy, Gus," said Dr. Dyer to the portly man. "This is Tom Garrison from Macon. You two get acquainted while I water the daisies. My old bladder ain't what it used to be."

"Welcome to the Valley, welcome, welcome!" said the pudgy man, as he pumped Tom's hand, ignoring Dr. Dyer and Frank. "I'm Gus Miller. Me and Pledger here were just putting the finishing touches on a few things for ya." His voice jangled on. "The house comes fully furnished, you know. They've even set you up with a tub of lard and enough flour to last 'til fall—had me lay in some hay down at the barn, too. This place'll only cost you a dollar a month, what with that citizens' committee putting in the other two, ta make up the difference."

Then, as if he'd suddenly had an idea, he added, "Say, since this is the ninth, why don't we say your rent's due on that day ever' month? If you give me your dollar now, you'll be paid up through the ninth of August."

Not sure what else to do, Tom took out his wallet and handed the man a dollar. When Miller wasn't looking, Dr. Dyer and Frank grinned at each other.

"Thank you, sir, thank you," said Miller. "I can see it's gonna be a pleasure doing business with you. Pledger! Get over here. Help Frank with these boxes. Hurry up now!"

A lean, colored man about 50, Tom guessed, walked through the door with a heavy box. Pledger's knees showed through the worn-out places in his overalls. He heaved the box onto a wagon parked by the porch and nodded at the newcomers.

Frank put the boxes from the buggy inside while Tom looked around his new home. The house was small, but it would do. A porch with a shed-like roof covered the door and two windows on either side of it. A galvanized tub hung from a peg on the end wall. Inside, a hallway led past two front rooms—empty except for a metal cot in one and two cane-back chairs in the other.

Miller saw Tom looking at the cot and the thin mattress lying across it. "My wife's gonna send over a nice counterpane to cover that little bed. She makes them herself, you know—she usually gets fifty-cents apiece for 'em."

When Tom went inside, Miller followed him. The room at the end of the hall had a rock fireplace on one wall and a woodstove on another. A single stick of firewood and a crumpled old newspaper lay on the floor beside a dry sink. The house looked to Tom as if it had been vacant for quite some time.

"That little side-room there will be a fine place for you to see patients," Mr. Miller continued. "You'll need an outside entryway, of course—won't do to have sick folks coming through your home." Miller was all wound up again. "I'm gonna have Pledger cut in a new door for you tomorrow—no charge. Just tell him where you want it. I'd put it there at the far end myself."

Tom thought the room *would* make a good doctor's office. In fact, the whole place was perfect, but for some reason, he didn't want to tell Miller that. Still, he had to admit, this mysterious citizens' committee that arranged his living quarters had chosen well.

A barn stood behind the house with enough pasture for Val, although the split-rail fence needed work. A springhouse sat above the barn — its branch running through the meadow. There was, he noticed through the kitchen window, even a shed for the buggy.

A creaking freight wagon pulling into the yard brought Tom and Gus Miller back to the porch. Its driver reined two chestnut Clydesdales to a stop.

"Howdy, Nolan," said Dr. Dyer. "I'd about give you out. Better late than never, I reckon."

"What are you talkin' about?" asked the driver. "I nearly beat you over here, dad-blame it. Don't be calling me late."

Pledger helped the man pull back the tarp covering the wagon's load. As it unfolded, Tom saw a cabinet, a bed, and quite a few other pieces of furniture along with his trunk.

"What's all this?" he asked Dr. Dyer. "You said you were gonna send over a couple of chairs. There's enough here to furnish a house."

Dr. Dyer chuckled. "Well, it looks like this house could stand some furnishin'. That's just a few things we've been meaning to get shed of. India wants you to have them. I tossed in my old medicine cabinet, too. I haven't used that one in years. And I threw in that old saddle — noticed you didn't have one."

Tom was flabbergasted at this generosity. He was also thrilled to see the bed. He'd not been looking forward to sleeping on that metal cot in the front room.

Frank and Tom helped Pledger and the delivery man take everything inside. They set up the new bed in the other front room. After that, they moved the medicine cabinet into the side-room that would soon be Tom's office and put everything else in a reasonably appropriate place.

When they went back outside, Dr. Dyer was on the porch steps, peeling tomatoes with his pocket knife. He piled the slices onto one of the plates that came on the freight wagon and sprinkled them copiously with salt and pepper. Gus Miller fairly drooled with anticipation.

"Gather 'round boys and let's eat," said Dr. Dyer. "Nothing better than fresh tomatoes right out of the garden — especially when it's not your garden. There ain't no women around, so feel free to use your fingers."

Frank picked up the bucket of cool water Dr. Dyer had brought up from the spring and poured it over everyone's hands. They wiped them dry on their britches' legs.

The hungry men stuffed the delicacies into their mouths and let the seed-laden juice dribble down their chins. Pledger stood a few feet away, watching. Miller scowled when Tom offered Pledger a slice, but he didn't say anything.

"Much obliged sir," said Pledger, looking at the plate. "But I ain't hongry just now — thank ya all da same."

"At least take this water," said Tom.

Pledger took the tin cup, but didn't drink from it. "What's your last name?" Tom asked him. "I don't think I heard it."

"It's Moss, sir — Pledger Moss. Thank you for askin'."

Gus Miller waggled his hand and said through a mouthful of tomato, "That'll be all, Pledger. You go on home now."

"Yassir," said Pledger, setting the cup of water down. He turned to Tom. "If you don't mind, show me where you wants dat door. I'll put it in tomorrow. You're gonna need a winder, too, for light."

Gus Miller glowered at Pledger. "A window wasn't never in the deal," he said. He looked at Tom and added, "But, if you think you need one, two dollars should cover it. I don't suppose the committee will pay for it, though." He glanced in Dr. Dyer's direction.

After Tom pointed to a different spot for the door than the one Miller suggested, Pledger walked down the lane toward the main road. He turned south when he reached it.

"How far does he have to go?" Tom asked.

"Not far," said Miller. "He lives out on Bean Creek with the rest of 'em. Pledger's a fair worker if you stay after him, but he's naturally lazy, like they all are."

"He didn't seem lazy to me," said Tom, staring at his new landlord. "In fact, he worked harder than any of us. And it looks to me like he'd been at it a while before we got here."

Miller reached for the last tomato slice. "That's because I kept him motivated," he said, wiping his mouth on the back of his hand. "If I hadn't, he'd be asleep by the springhouse — you mark my word."

Tom found it hard to hide his disdain for this man. Thankfully, once the last tomato was gone, Miller was ready to go, too. "If I don't see you before, I'll see you Sunday," he said as he drove his wagon out of the yard.

Once Miller was out of earshot, Dr. Dyer said, "Ol' Gus isn't too bad a feller. You do have to say this for him—his dinner bell is always in tune."

Frank watched the man drive away. "My daddy says he's sorta' quar," he volunteered. "And too stingy to give a man the time of day."

Dr. Dyer laughed. "Well, I don't want to say anything bad about Gus, but he does have a lot of the same characteristics you'll often find in an asshole."

The delivery man shook his head, turned the big draft horses around and climbed up on the wagon's seat. "I'm fixin' to head for Clarkesville, boys. Appreciate the 'maters." Looking at Tom he added, "Good luck to ya, Dr. Garrison."

As he drove off, Dr. Dyer shouted after him, "I'll catch up with you later, Nolan, and ride along a-ways—it'll give Rebel a rest."

When the big wagon rolled away, Dr. Dyer glanced over each of his shoulders once and leaned toward Tom. "I didn't want to say nothin' while there was a crowd here, but you plan on cutting that cake anytime soon?"

Tom grinned and went inside. He came back with a thick slice for each of them on his new saucers. The three sat on the porch steps and ate Big Mama's cake, their clinking forks the only sound.

When he finished, Dr. Dyer wiped a handkerchief across his mouth. "Mighty fine, boys. Mighty fine. Always eat cake with a fork, Frank—women or no women. You remember that." He slapped the boy on his knee. "If you don't learn nothin' else from me, son, you learn that."

The old doctor stood and stretched, leaving his saucer on the step. "I'm tuckered out. It's high time I hit the road. Y'all may not believe it, but this is the latest it's ever been around here."

He put out his hand toward Tom. "Son, I'm proud you're here. I've seen enough to know you're a good man, just like Lam said. Come see us when you can." The sincere welcome was written on his intelligent face. "You'll likely need a few more things from the pharmacy before long. Send word if you run into anything you can't handle."

He turned to Frank. "You help him stock up on yellow root and what-not. Some folks won't be happy with just a powder or two. And get up a few buckeyes for him to give anybody with arthritis."

"I will, sir," said Frank. "You can count on it." The affection between the two was evident.

"Show Dr. Garrison where Miss Lothridge lives," Dr. Dyer continued. "She's bad to get dropsy. And old man Hulsey is stove up with gout again. They need to be looked in on." He continued down the list. "Mrs. Kollock's baby is due next month, but they use a midwife—that Stiles woman I believe. Still, y'all keep an eye on her. I had to help with that last one."

After Dr. Dyer pulled himself into the saddle, Tom held on to the horses' bridle, not sure what to say. They'd only known each other for a few hours, but Tom felt a strong connection to this man.

"I can't thank you enough for everything you've done," he said. "The buggy, the furniture—it's all too much."

"Well," said Dr. Dyer. "My mama always said it don't take nothin' from one candle to light another."

"I'll come to Clarkesville when I can," said Tom.

"Well, if you don't bring Frank, you can stay at our place," said Dr. Dyer, winking. "Our latch string's always out for you." Once Dr. Dyer reached the main road, he nudged Rebel into a canter and waved his hat.

Before Frank left, he brought up another bucket of water from the spring and put it by the kitchen sink. "I reckon I'll head toward the house, then. I told Pa I'd be back before dark tonight. He'll worry if I'm not, and I've been gone since yesterday."

Tom and the teenager shook hands. "Thanks for all you've done, Frank. How much do I owe you?"

"Not anything," said Frank, as he climbed onto Trouble's back. "But I sure would appreciate it if you'd teach me to play chess sometime. You mentioned you had a board."

"Consider it done," said Tom. "But you need to get paid more than that for all your work."

Frank looked down at him from the mule's back. "Dr. Dyer pays me some to help out, so don't worry about it. He lets me read his books and pamphlets, too—says he's gonna see that I amount to somethin' one day."

"I expect you will. What other kind of books do you like?"

"Most anything, I reckon. I guess you've noticed I like history; geography, too," Frank mused. "I love the Valley, but books make me want to see more of the world."

Tom laughed. "Coming up here is seeing more of the world for me. But I know what you mean. Have you read *Huckleberry Finn*?"

"No. But I've heard about it. Mark Twain wrote it, didn't he?"

"That's right. Wait a minute. I'll loan you my copy." Tom went inside, retrieved the book from his trunk and handed it to the boy.

"Much obliged," said Frank. "That cadaver in your trunk must be pretty well-read." He grinned and put the book behind the bib of his overalls. "I'll take good care of this."

"I know you will. People who love books always take care of them. Dr. Dyer told me you have two brothers. How big is your family?" Tom was genuinely curious.

"I do have two older brothers—Reggie and Edwin. They work at the sawmill in Helen. I got a sister, too—Freda. She's the baby." There was that hint of sadness again. "It's just the five of us since Mama died. Her name was Teresa, but everybody called her Terry. My daddy is Will Sosebee."

Frank clucked to the mule and pulled on the right rein to turn her around. "Thanks again for the book."

"Wait a minute, Frank." Tom interrupted the boy's departure. "Can I ask you one more thing before you go?"

"Sure."

"What do you know about this 'committee' everybody keeps talking about?"

Frank tied the ends of the reins together and laid them across the mule's neck. "I'm not supposed to say, Dr. Garrison. But I'll give you a hint if you won't tell on me."

"I won't," Tom promised.

"Well, you had supper with the whole committee in Clarkesville last night. I reckon Miss India is the chairman."

"That's about what I thought."

Frank turned the mule toward his home at the foot of Lynch Mountain and trotted away. After he left, Tom led Val to the barn, unhitched the buggy and pushed it under the shed. He gave the mare a good rubdown before he led her to the stable and fetched a pail of water from the spring. After he put oats in the feed trough, and added more hay to the rack, he scratched the top of Val's head.

"Well, girl, this is our new home. What do you think of it?" The mare pressed her nose into his chest.

Back at the house, Tom lit a lantern, cut another piece of Big Mama's cake and went out to the porch to savor it. Remembering the envelope from the box he'd picked up at the store, he took it out of his pocket. The folded paper inside held no greeting; merely the words his mother had penned from something called A Physician's Prayer: *Give skill to my hand, clear vision to my mind, kindness and sympathy to my heart.*

The porch had a nice view of the Valley, and the evening air soon filled with the cadence of katydids. Thunder rumbled from the south. The flashes of lightning proceeding the sound offered brief glances of other, more distant mountains. Lightning bugs blinked in the yard.

Although this was his first night in the Valley, Tom already felt at home. And even if he had yet to touch her hand or feel her breath on his face, he knew that, earlier today, he'd seen the woman he would marry.

He could hardly wait to meet her.

CHAPTER FIVE

Hanging A Shingle

July 10, 1919

Harmonica music woke Tom from an extraordinarily real dream the next morning. In it, he was back inside Macon's Mt. Olive Baptist Church, sitting between his two brothers. Lenore Conley was in the choir, sharing a hymnal with his father.

Tom tried to hold on to his image of Lenore, but a faint sound of music lured him awake. When he looked through the open window, he saw Pledger Moss sitting by the old oak farthest from the house.

"Morning, Pledger," he yelled through the opening. "Didn't expect you so early. Didn't expect to wake up to music either."

Pledger put the harmonica back in the bib pocket of his overalls. "Nawsir. Didn't mean to wake ya, but it's gonna take most o' the day to get that winder and dor set in. Sorry if I made music too loud."

"I've slept too late already," said Tom, rubbing his eyes. "Music is a nice way to wake up."

"Yassir. I'll git started now if you don't mind." Pledger moved away from the tree and started toward the house.

By the time Tom visited the outhouse, washed his face and shaved at the dry sink, Pledger, his old brogans dark from the dew, had sawed through the wall of the side-room. His handsaw shined slick from the lard he'd rubbed on the blade to keep it from binding.

ATt#

By the time Tom made coffee, Pledger had the new door opening framed with two-by-fours.

"Where did this lumber come from?" Tom asked, knowing the boards weren't here earlier.

Pledger finished pounding in a nail before he answered. "I brung them over this mornin'. Made yore dor at my house last night. My boys gonna tote it over after dey get back from da mornin' milkin' at da Hardman barn."

Tom looked around the yard. "Don't you have a wagon to haul things on?"

"Yassir, I got a wagon—mule too. But ain't worth hitchin' Maude up to haul a few boards; got boys for dat. Best let the mule rest—don't have to feed her so much dat way." Pledger grinned and pointed in the direction of Williams' store. "You'll need to get one of dem store-bought winders, though, from down yonder."

Tom sat on the edge of the porch drinking coffee and watching Pledger work. "I've never been much of a hand at carpentry or I'd offer to help. The truth is, I'd just be in the way. But, I could take the buggy down and pick up that window for you."

Pledger nodded. "I figure Dr. Dyer paid fer it on his way home last evenin'."

Behind them, they heard giggling. Tom and Pledger turned their heads to see a boy about six and an even younger girl holding a cloth-covered basket. The thin boy's short pants were held up by a pair of black suspenders. The girl had on a simple cotton dress. Both children were barefoot.

"Well, hello there," said Tom. "Who are you two?"

The boy pushed dirt around with his big toe and studied the results carefully. The girl looked directly at Tom. "I'm Judy Gee. This is my brother, Aaron. He's bashful, but I'm not. Mama says I talk *too* much," she said, as if trying to prove it. "We're your neighbors. Mama told us to bring over this basket of food. She says a man by hisself will starve if some woman don't feed him, even if he *is* a doctor."

The girl pulled her brother's hand off the basket handle, walked over and put it on the porch step. She stopped to watch a June bug whir by, then, without saying another word, she and her brother raced down the lane, laughing.

"Be sure to thank your mama for me," Tom hollered after them. When he pulled back the cloth on the basket, he found a jar of honey and a dozen cat-head biscuits, still warm. Thick slices of salted ham were wrapped in another cloth. Until now, Tom hadn't thought about breakfast, but the smells from the basket made him hungry. He broke a biscuit in half, poured honey on it and offered it to Pledger.

"No thank ya, sir," said Pledger, shaking his head as he measured another two-by-four. "But what dat little gal said is right. My wife already fed me dis mornin'. Since you batchin', you bes' hold on to ever' biscuit you gets handed."

Tom laughed. "I may not have a wife yet, but you know what, Pledger? I feel like that's going to change before long."

"I 'spec you right. Word gets out you single, da mamas 'round here be linin' up der' daughters for you ta meet."

A half hour later, Tom let Val finish her oats before hitching her to the buggy. He waved bye to Pledger and headed down the road toward Williams store. Right before the Conley home came into view, he reined Val to a walk. The horse was feeling good and wanted to move, so she slung her head in protest. "Easy, girl," said Tom. "You can go faster in a minute."

The Conleys' black gelding neighed at Val, but Tom noticed the mule and wagon were gone. Inside the barn, a calf bawled.

Inside the Conley house, Tom thought he heard a woman laugh, but he couldn't be sure. After lingering as long as he dared, he clucked to Val, who trotted on down the road.

At the store, the old, homemade checkerboard was set up, but no one was on the porch. Inside, Fannie Stover was busy helping a middle-aged man sort through mail behind the counter. As soon as she saw Tom, she waved him over.

"Howdy, Doctor Garrison! You're out bright and early this mornin'. Come over here and meet your mail rider, Walter Lumsden. Walter, this is Tom Garrison."

Tom shook hands with Mr. Lumsden, but the mail carrier was too focused on his duties for small talk. "Nice to meet you," he said with a quick nod. "We'll talk more Sunday." He and Fannie went back to sorting mail.

A double-hinged window was leaning against the postal counter with his name on it. The ticket tied to it was marked *paid*, so he carried it to the buggy.

On the way home, Tom still didn't see anyone at the Conley farm. He considered pulling up to the house, but couldn't think of a plausible excuse. Still, before he drove out of sight, he did stop the buggy to get out, lift one of Val's forelegs and inspect the hoof. Even though he made as much noise as he possibly could, no one came to the door.

Foiled in his attempt to see Lenore again, he drove home. As he pulled up, Pledger's twin sons—he'd told Tom their names were Jody and Josh—were walking toward the house carrying his new door above their heads. They helped their father hold it in place while he fastened the hinges to the frame.

Tom put Val in the barn and waved to the boys as they left. He spent the rest of the day arranging furniture and setting up his office. After making a few repairs to the fence, he deemed it trustworthy enough to turn Val into the pasture.

When his landlord, Gus Miller, came by about six to inspect things, Pledger had the new door and window in place. Miller frowned while he inspected the work, but eventually nodded his approval and left.

Four more food baskets arrived over the course of the day—enough to last a week. One was from the Conley family but, to Tom's disappointment, Hannah delivered it, not Lenore. Like the other neighbors who dropped by, Hannah couldn't stay long—it was "puttin' up" time, and everyone was busy. But word was out that the new doctor wasn't much to cook.

Later, as Pledger gathered his tools, Tom remembered something. "Pledger, can you wait one more minute?"

He ran inside and came back with Isaac's sign. "Would you mind helping me hang this before you go?"

CHAPTER SIX

Dinner on the Grounds

July 13, 1919

T he rest of the week flew by for Tom. Getting settled took most of his time, and he hadn't found an excuse to leave the place since Wednesday. He had plenty of visitors, though—and even a few patients. A number of women brought children by with trifling ailments, but he suspected the object of most visits was to size up the new doctor. Still, he'd taken in two dollars, a banty rooster, three hens and a dozen eggs in payment.

At least the chickens might give him an excuse to ride by the Conley place again; he'd need materials to build a pen. A lot of folks let their chickens roam free, but Tom thought that wouldn't look good for a doctor, especially a new one. But, as he was getting ready to leave, Frank drove up in a wagon with lumber, two rolls of chicken wire and a few posts.

"I knew you'd be getting paid some in poultry," he said. "I figured you'd need this." Building a chicken pen and a covered roost took all of Saturday. Frank did most of the work, but he insisted on making the pen big enough to hold several dozen chickens.

Sunday morning broke right on schedule. Frank had promised yesterday that, although it'd be a little out of their way, he and his family would come by and give Tom a ride to the Methodist church in Nacoochee Valley for the service and festivities. Tom expected them any minute and was sitting on the porch when he heard an automobile coming up the road at a fast clip. A motorized vehicle was novel enough to make him stand for a better look.

He was further surprised when the black Tin Lizzy with the top down turned off the main road and came toward his house. He was absolutely astonished to see Dr. Dyer driving it—one hand on the steering wheel; the other clutching his hat. Miss India clung to her bonnet as the black automobile bounced toward him.

From somewhere under its hood, the car's horn sounded *AHOO-GA, AHOO-GA*. Dr. Dyer turned loose of his hat long enough to wave. The noise made the hens cackle in their pen and caused Val to flick her ears forward and stare from the pasture.

"Howdy, Tom," Dr. Dyer shouted. "I bet you're surprised to see us again this soon. Miss India insisted we come over for the doin's at the church. How ya like my new buggy?" He let go of the steering wheel to pull back a large handle by his left leg. The car rolled quite a few feet past the house before it stopped.

"Well, the horn works," said Tom, stepping off the porch.

"That's nothing," said Dr. Dyer, as he killed the engine. "You should have heard it down in the covered bridge—nearly made India jump plum out."

India Dyer adjusted the front of her dress. "I declare, David. You scared half the people in two counties on the way over. Not to mention almost spilling the food I brought."

The old doctor beamed. "We thought we'd give you a ride to church so you can show up in style. Make a grand entrance, so to speak." Stepping back, he spread both hands toward the vehicle. "I want you to meet Miss Percole."

"Who?"

"Miss Percole," said Dr. Dyer, indicating the car again. "We named her that because she just percolates right along. A car needs a name the same way a horse does, so that's what we've decided to call her."

"Don't say *we*," Mrs. Dyer corrected him as she jiggled the handle, trying to get the door open. "I didn't have any part in it. If I had, we'd a named it 'Trouble' like Frank's daddy did their mule."

Tom opened the car door for Mrs. Dyer. "Nice to see you again, ma'am. I'd love to ride to church with y'all, but I'm waiting on Frank and his family. I'd planned on going with them, you see. I didn't expect y'all."

Dr. Dyer shook his head. "No, no—we passed their wagon down the road a-ways. They're comin' on up here so Frank and

Freda can ride back down with us. It'll be their first automobile ride. They'll be here, but it's slow going without a car, you know."

As the doctor's wife busied herself rearranging her bowls in the food box, her husband guided Tom around the car, pointing out every feature. "I didn't mean to buy this thing," he said confidentially. "But a fellow offered me such a deal I couldn't pass it up. I bought her for two hundred dollars! He's gettin' a newer model with an electric starter. Don't see much use in that myself — just something else to break."

He was busy showing Tom the tool box mounted to the running-board when Frank's family pulled up in their wagon. Frank introduced Tom to his father, Will, his two older brothers, Reggie and Edwin, and his sister, Freda.

The girl was excited about riding in a car and showed it. She jumped from the wagon and into the car's back seat, rocking back and forth, running her hands over its surface. "Hurry, Frank," she urged, pushing the box of food to the side. "Come sit by me!"

Her obvious delight made everyone grin except Edwin and Reggie, who pretended to be indifferent. India thought they might be disappointed at not getting a ride themselves. "You boys can have a turn on the way back," she offered.

Edwin appeared hopeful, but Reggie shook his head. "Naw. Our boss over at the sawmill has a Cadillac. We've both rode in that. Boss says a T-Model's like a millionaire's baby — gets a new rattle ever' day." Edwin looked disappointed, but he didn't say anything.

"Let's light a shuck then," said Dr. Dyer, as he climbed into the driver's seat. "Tom, I'm fixin' to give you a lesson in how to start a car. Go to the front and take hold of that crank. I'll talk you through what to do."

Tom moved to the front of the car and put his hand on the iron handle below the radiator. Inside, Dr. Dyer pulled back on the brake and adjusted the throttle. "Now, move the crank to the 8 o'clock position. That's right. Push it in. Good. Now hold on — I gotta turn this here doohickey. Now, rotate it a half-turn clockwise and get out of the way quick."

Tom followed the instructions, and the little 20-horsepower engine jumped to life. Dr. Dyer adjusted the timing lever until the motor smoothed out. Tom climbed in the back seat between Frank and Freda and held Miss India's food box in his lap.

As they were about to pull away, Tom remembered something. "Wait!" he said. "I forgot the cake I meant to take."

Mrs. Dyer turned around in the front seat to look at Tom. "Nobody expects a single man to bring food. Anyway, I've brought enough for all of us. Let's go, David."

The car bounced down the road at what felt to Tom like a dangerous speed. But everyone else seemed to think the pace was perfect—if not a tad slow. Tom had his hands full keeping the box in his lap level.

As soon as the Methodist church came in view, Dr. Dyer pulled the throttle down, but didn't slow the car enough. The right rear tire hit a rock when he turned off the road, and the box full of food vaulted up to land sideways in Tom's lap. The butterbeans overturned, and Tom felt their warm juice spill across his legs.

By the time Dr. Dyer wrestled Miss Percole to a stop, Tom's britches were soaked—the seat, too. Frank and Freda avoided the mess by jumping out before the car stopped rolling.

"You've got to quit driving so fast!" said Mrs. Dyer, pulling her bonnet back in place. "You've made Tom spill my food."

Dr. Dyer got out and looked at the back seat. "How in tarnation did this happen?" He glanced around at the gathering crowd. "Jessie, you or Horace, one or the other, bring me a rag. And hurry! And bring a rock to scotch the back wheel while you're at it."

Several people ran up, and one handed Dr. Dyer a white tablecloth. Ignoring Tom, he rubbed the seat with it. "Stand up, son. Let me get it out from under you. Lord, I sure do hate you got my seat dirty."

Tom passed the empty dish to a stranger who put it beside the car. Quite a few beans clung to his trousers. A few dropped to the floor when he stood. Mrs. Dyer grabbed the tablecloth and handed it to Tom. "Clean up as best you can," she said. Frowning at her husband, she added, "So much for giving him a grand entrance, David."

"Aw, he don't look bad," Dr. Dyer said, rubbing his face. "That'll dry before long. They've got two preachers today, and each one will try to out-do the other. I wouldn't put it past 'em to preach 'til 1:30. Let's go—those back benches fill up fast."

Trying to make the best of things, Tom followed them up to the little wooden church with three tall windows on both sides. Freda stayed behind to describe the car ride to a group of excited girls.

Tom looked at the people they passed on the way. Frank noticed and whispered. "Lenore's not here yet. Don't worry, though, she's coming. She's gonna sing. So are me and my brothers — Pa, too."

Inside, they sat two pews from the rear. As Dr. Dyer predicted, the back benches were already taken. Frank slid in first and laid hymnals on the seat to hold a spot for his family.

Sitting on a stool with her back to the congregation, Fannie Stover thumbed through a stack of sheet music. Once she made her selection, she reverently placed her hands on the keyboard and began playing *Rock of Ages*. Mrs. Dyer opened a hymnal and discreetly motioned for Tom to cover the stain on his lap with it.

Tom had about given up on the Conley family when Lanier came through the door holding his hat in front of him with both hands. He nodded to Dr. Dyer, his wife and some others as he walked down the aisle to an open space on the second row. Close behind him were his own wife and daughter.

Lanier stepped aside to let Lenore go in first. As she scooted by him, Lanier looked toward the back of the church, and a tall man about thirty, wearing overalls, hurried down the aisle. He moved in front of Lanier to sit by Lenore. Hannah gave her husband a hard look but took a seat beside the man who was now between her and her daughter.

"That's Alton Boggs," Frank whispered to Tom, as the rest of the Sosebee clan filed in to his left. "I can't believe he's sittin' by Lenore! I think Lanier planned that."

Over the next two hours, both preachers pounded out lengthy sermons. Mothers bedded sleepy babies on quilts at their feet. Hand-held fans, like giant butterfly wings, moved the hot air around. They also kept horseflies at bay.

Tom didn't notice the fans or the flies — the preachers either. He only noticed the blond hairs that escaped the bun above Lenore's neck and shimmered like gold in the light.

At last, the visiting minister closed his Bible. He turned the service back to Preacher Yarbrough, who gave the benediction and dismissed the congregation for dinner.

Everyone moved outside, where men clustered to talk and smoke. The women scattered and reappeared with colorful tablecloths and white bed sheets to spread over a long row of wooden tables built under the trees. The other two churches in the area had let out early so their congregations could come here afterward, too. Several more buggies, wagons, and two other cars lined the road out front.

Once they had the tables covered, the women brought out pots, tin tubs, baskets, and even a couple of trunks filled with food. It was like every family tried to outdo the other.

Tom watched Lenore and her mother unload the delicacies they'd brought and join the other women. Lenore smiled often as she walked back and forth between the tables. Her thick, brown shoes kept her limp to a minimum. She stopped regularly to look at some play-pretty one of the children wanted to show her.

In minutes, plates of fried chicken, stews, roasts, puddings, fresh vegetables and cornbread were laid out until there were no empty spots left to fill. Two men heaved a galvanized washtub filled with lemonade up on the end of the last table and hung a half-dozen metal dippers around its side. Sliced lemons bobbed around a floating block of ice. Several women walked around the tables waving away flies with newspapers.

Frank and three other boys lugged two church pews outside and sat them face-to-face, forming another little table that was quickly covered in cloth and filled with dishes of banana pudding, meringue pies, apple cakes and cobblers.

"Ah, the dessert benches," Dr. Dyer said as he and Tom watched the feast materialize. "Always a popular spot—wait 'til you taste Virginia Hallford's pound cake! That's how India got me to come over here today."

The doctor grew nostalgic. "You know," he said, "this is nice and all, but I miss the old days when it really was dinner on the grounds. They'd spread everything out right on the ground— didn't mess with tables. You've never seen such bendin' and stoopin' and squattin' in all your life. That's how it ought to be— close to the earth. This here modern way just as well be called dinner on the tables."

Once everything was in place, the crowd hushed. Preacher Yarbrough asked Preacher Stack to return thanks. His enthusiastic blessing was punctuated by a crying baby and two dogs growling over a chicken leg someone had dropped while everything was being put together.

As soon as the preacher said "amen," Dr. Dyer banged a fork against a Mason jar. "Let me have your attention before we eat. I don't think there's gonna be a better time than now to introduce the new doctor." He pointed to Tom. "This fine-looking feller with the big stain on his britches is Tom Garrison. He's from Macon. That stain is my fault. My T-Model hit a rock and caused him to slosh Miss India's butterbeans in his lap. Most of you know he's settling in up at Gus Miller's renter house. And yes, girls, he is single."

Tom was surprised at the introduction but waved anyway. A few folks waved back. There was also a sprinkling of applause and a few giggles from the group. He'd nearly forgotten about the stain, but no one seemed to pay it any mind. They all went back to talking and lining up to fill their plates.

The two pastors moved to the front of the loosely formed ranks. Dr. Dyer pushed Tom ahead to get the two of them in line behind the preachers. "You're the guest of honor, son," he whispered. "Take advantage of it." He handed Tom a plate and urged him to fill it. Behind them, someone shouted good-naturedly, "What kind of way is that for preachers to act, going before everybody else?"

Preacher Yarbrough replied, "Well, the Bible says man can't live by bread alone. I'm following the scripture exactly so."

Everybody laughed, and the preacher piled on an extra helping of creamed corn. Behind them, Tom overheard bits of conversation and lots of teasing. "Gluttony's a sin, brother," said one man.

"That's right," answered another. "I aim to keep you from sinnin' by eating this piece of Sister Sarah's chicken—I saw you lusting after it."

Dr. Dyer pointed out various dishes for Tom to sample. "Be sure you try some of Bertie Mae's ham. And have a taste of Ruth Hunt's chow-chow. Nobody makes it like she does, but don't tell India I said so."

He also offered advice about dishes to shun. "Don't fool with that Lovell woman's mashed potatoes; she puts onions in 'em," he whispered. "There won't be enough salt in those," he said about Alice Hulsey's soup beans.

Once their plates were piled high, the two men sat them on the car hood, and stood on either side to eat. Miss India joined them and sat on the passenger seat with the door open, resting her plate on her lap.

Across the yard, the Conley women put their plates on the surrey's floor while Lanier plopped on the ground, leaned against a wheel and held his food in his lap. Alton Boggs squatted beside him.

"Are you going for seconds already?" India Dyer asked her husband when he started back toward the tables.

"Yes ma'am, I am. My granddaddy always said there's no feast so big that you can't eat a pickled peach and start over."

By the time most everybody else had gone back for seconds, conversations lulled. No one felt much like moving, so except for a few men wandering into the woods to answer the call of nature, no one did.

When Lenore and Jenny Gee covered the leftover food to keep the flies off, Tom watched every move Lenore made.

After Dr. Dyer finished his second helping of banana pudding, he stretched, and stood. "No rest for the weary," he said, patting his belly. "Come on Tom; let's get you introduced to a few folks before the singing starts."

Tom shook hands with more people than he could count or remember. He met a few more Stovalls—though Odell wasn't here—Bristols, Browns, Cantrells, and several people named Vandiver. He spoke briefly with Walter Lumsden, the mailman. Walter introduced him to his wife, Minnie, and their three-year-old daughter, Isabel. Fannie Stover mentioned how good Big Mama's cookies had tasted, but apparently didn't notice he'd forgotten to bring what was left of her pound cake. Gus Miller shook Tom's hand heartily and introduced his wife, Ruby.

It seemed to Tom he'd talked with everyone there except Lenore when Dr. Dyer finally guided him over to her family's surrey. "Tom, you remember Lanier, Miss Hannah, and Lenore, don't you? They gave us those nice tomatoes the other day," he reminded him—as if Tom needed reminding. "This here feller is Alton Boggs."

Tom shook hands with Lanier and Alton. Hannah offered hers, too, and he took it. Lenore smiled at him but was too busy balancing little Isabel Lumsden on her lap to do much else.

"Thank you for all that food you brought over this week," Tom stammered to Hannah. "I really appreciate it. It was good."

"Think nothing of it," she said. "I just brought the basket. Lenore did all the cooking."

"Well, then, thank you both," said Tom, eyeing Lenore. "You're not only pretty, but you can cook, too." As soon as the words left his mouth, his face glowed beet red. He knew that sounded foolish. The little girl in Lenore's lap giggled.

Alton Boggs pointed toward the stain on Tom's pants. "I reckon you can't hold your butterbeans, can ya, doc? You sure it wasn't *peas*? 'Cause it sure looks like a pee stain to me." Alton nudged Lanier with his elbow. Lanier didn't respond, but Lenore did.

"Hush, Alton. Don't be ill-mannered." Little Isabel jumped out of Lenore's lap and ran to her mama.

Alton stood up and sat his empty plate on the floor of the surrey. "I'm just joshin' the doc. He knows that." He put the last bit of fried apple pie in his mouth and stepped in front of Tom. His breath smelled bad. "Ain't that right, Doc?"

Before Tom could respond, Preacher Yarbrough clapped his hands and announced, "All right folks, it's time to kick things off. Fannie's gonna play the piano from inside the church." He pointed to two boys standing near him. "Max, you and Ralph open those windows and prop the door back so we can hear her music out here. Them that wants can go in and sit, but the church won't hold us all. We're going to start with a song from the Sosebee family."

Frank and his two brothers were already on the porch when their father walked up, adjusting the tuners on the headstock of his guitar. After strumming it a couple of times, he looked out over the crowd and belted out the first line.

"To Canaan's land I'm on my way!"

His three sons leaned their heads together to sing with him.

"Where the soul of man never dies!"

Most of the congregation accompanied them. The rest clapped or kept time with their feet. Inside the church, Fannie finally found the right sheet music and accompanied the guitar.

"My darkest night will turn to day!"

"Where the soul of man never dies!"
"Dear friend there'll be no sad farewells
There'll be no tear-dimmed eyes
Where all is joy peace and love."

"Where the soul of man never dies!"

The crowd demanded two more songs before letting the Sosebee men stop. When they did, Preacher Yarbrough bellowed, "How's that for a rousing start, folks? Praise the Lord! Now, Lenore Conley is going to sing. What a blessing! Come on up here, girl."

Lenore's dress sleeve brushed Tom's arm when she passed him. His eyes never left her as she made her way to the porch. Alton's eyes never left Tom.

At the porch, Lenore reached for a post and pulled herself up. Inside, Fannie began playing *In the Garden* on the piano. Apparently, she and everyone else knew what Lenore was about to sing. Lenore looked at the crowd, put her hands together in front of her and began singing in a voice that stirred Tom to his core.

At first, Lenore's words barely resonated beyond the porch. People leaned forward to listen. But no one joined in this time. While Lenore sang, no child cried, no dog barked. Her voice captivated Tom, just as it did everyone else.

> *"I come to the garden alone*
> *While the dew is still on the roses,*
> *And the voice I hear falling on my ear*
> *The Son of God discloses."*

At the chorus, Lenore threw her head back and sang out the words in the finest voice Tom had ever heard.

> *"And He walks with me, and He talks with me,*
> *And He tells me I am His own.*
> *And the joy we share as we tarry there,*
> *None other has ever known."*

Her effect on the crowd was incredible. Several women, and more than one man, dabbed their eyes. By the time Lenore finished the third stanza, Tom was head-over-heels in love.

The singing continued until late afternoon. More groups and individuals performed, and the congregation sang more hymns together. Musical instruments kept appearing out of nowhere, and folks played harps and fiddles until everyone was played out.

The crowd broke up gradually. Women packed empty dishes and folded tablecloths. Friends hugged, and children waved. First, one family, then another, went home. Tom watched the Conleys head up the road in their surrey.

Edwin and Reggie still refused a ride in the automobile, so when the Dyers were ready to go, Tom held the box of empty dishes on his lap, again sitting between Freda and Frank. Dr. Dyer drove slower on the way home, but still took curves a bit faster than Tom would have liked. That is, if he'd been paying attention.

Up the road a-ways, they overtook the Conley's surrey. Lanier pulled Custer over to let them pass and Tom turned in his seat to wave. He was pleased that Alton Boggs wasn't with them, but even more delighted that Lenore waved back.

India Dyer was gazing at him when he turned around, her eyes full of understanding. "I said you'd know, didn't I?"

Tom nodded. "I'm not sure she knows—but I do."

India Dyer held on to her bonnet with one hand and reached over with the other to touch her husband's shoulder.

CHAPTER SEVEN

Labor of Love

August 1, 1919

H annah Conley waved to Lenore as Ole Burl pulled the wagon onto the road in front of their house. "Bye, honey, we love you."

Lenore blew her parents a good-bye kiss from the porch. Campmeeting was only two days away, and Lanier and Hannah were spending today and tomorrow at the campground getting everything ready. Lenore usually went along on their annual pre-campmeeting pilgrimage, but this year, there was too much to do at home.

Their Bluetick 'coon hound, Cornbread, named for his favorite food, rode in the wagon with her parents. Lanier always insisted on taking the dog. "He'll sniff out snakes so we can get rid of 'em before the crowd comes," was his excuse. The notion of a snake in their tent made Hannah relent every year.

"Oh, all right," she always said. "But that dog is *not* coming with us next week." He never did either, much to Lanier's disappointment.

Early this morning, he'd loaded the wagon with sling blades, shovels, hoes, hammers, bed clothes and enough straw to cover their tent floor. He tossed in some additional straw for the arbor too; every family brought extra for the big, open-air building where they held the services.

Lenore's job this year was to stay home and get the house and garden ready to be more or less abandoned for the coming week. She had lots to do, but once the wagon rolled out of sight, she sat down in a rocker to think.

The thing with Alton that happened at the all-day singing three Sundays ago, still perplexed her. He'd come out of nowhere to sit by her before the service started. At one point, he even moved his hand to cover hers. She'd grabbed a hymnal and pretended to study a song to avoid the contact.

When her daddy insisted Alton eat with them at their surrey after the service, she was dismayed, but decided to make the best of it. She'd tried to use the little Lumsden girl as a distraction, but Isabel apparently didn't much like being around Alton either.

Alton missed church the following Sunday. But on the one after, he tried to sit by her again. This time, she excused herself and went to the back to organize the collection plates. It wasn't hard — there were only two. But instead of going back to her family's pew, she sat with her friend, Jenny Gee.

Lately, Lenore had been thinking a lot about that new doctor. But every time she brought his name up around her daddy, Lanier changed the subject back to Alton Boggs and his bottomland.

Lenore spent the day packing and cleaning. Tomorrow she'd pick everything in the garden that was ready. Pledger Moss and his wife would come over next week to gather anything that ripened while they were gone.

When the grandfather clock in the front room struck six, she walked to the barn to milk May. Lenore didn't see June, even after she banged on the bucket and yelled, "Su-Cow, Su-Cow."

Once she'd carried the milk to the house, strained it, and took the churn to the spring, Lenore walked across the pasture, calling June's name. She didn't see any sign of the cow until she got to the upper side, where June lay next to the fence rails, clearly in labor.

Lenore saw the calf's front legs protruding, but its nose wasn't resting on the forelegs the way she knew it should be. She knelt beside the cow and stroked her neck. "Oh, June, you poor thing. I should have checked on you before now. Don't worry, girl. I'll get you some help."

Before Lenore got up, she said a silent prayer, and then looked around her. "Lana, if you're here, show me what to do." She walked back to the barn as fast as she could and whistled for Custer. She bridled him but didn't bother with the saddle.

Lenore considered riding down to the Boggs farm and asking Alton to help. That's what her daddy would expect. Alton raised cattle and was well-versed in delivering calves. But that might just encourage him. Pledger Moss was another option. So was the new doctor. So, when Custer stopped on his own by their mailbox, she felt uncertain about which way to turn him.

"What do you think, boy?" She looked up the road toward Tom Garrison's place. "Would a doctor know anything about birthing a calf? Is that why I dreamed about him again last night?"

The horse pawed. When he turned his head toward the covered bridge, Lenore took a deep breath. "All right, boy. I'm taking this as a sign. Let's go."

Tom was reaching for an egg in the warm straw underneath a hen intent on pecking his hand when he heard the horse running up. A horse racing toward a doctor was never a good sign, so he clutched the egg, put it in his basket with the others and headed toward the house.

Lenore halted the black gelding in front of him.

"What is it?" he asked, grabbing Custer's bridle. "Is anything wrong with your parents?" Tom couldn't believe he was face-to-face with Lenore, alone.

Lenore shook her head. "No, they're not home today. I may have made a mistake coming for you, but one of our cows is in trouble. She's trying to have her calf. I thought you might help."

"A cow? I don't know too much about cows." He couldn't take his eyes off her.

Lenore suddenly felt foolish. "I don't know what I was thinking," she said, turning Custer. "You're a *doctor*. It's just that mama and daddy are over at Loudsville, and I wasn't sure what to do. I'll ride down to Alton's and get him."

Tom held on to the bridle. "No, wait. I'm pretty good with animals, so I can at least take a look. I suppose the basics are the same, and I did help out on some of the farms down home from time to time, when I could."

"I'd appreciate it. But we better hurry. She's been trying to have her calf for a while now."

"Let me get Val." Tom looked toward his office. "I don't suppose there's any need to take my doctor's bag. I don't have anything in it for livestock."

He bridled Val and, like Lenore, rode bareback beside her toward the Conley farm. Inside the covered bridge, Tom pulled Val up and waved for Lenore to stop, too. He didn't really have a reason to stop here, so he had to think fast.

"Tell me what's happening with this cow," he said. "Is she lying down or standing up?" He hoped that sounded important to Lenore.

"She's down. I should have checked on her before I did. I think the calf's neck is turned the wrong way. We had the same thing happen with another cow a few years back. Her name was Janie."

Now Lenore felt foolish. Why on earth would he care what that cow's name had been? She clucked to Custer who bolted out the bridge. Tom had no choice but to follow.

At the barn, Lenore turned Custer into his pen and motioned for Tom to tie Val in the hall of the barn. Val sniffed at May's calf through the stable door.

When Lenore lowered the rail at the end of the barn and started toward the woods, Tom hesitated. "Wait a second," he said, looking around. "Let's see if there's anything here we might need." He saw a plow-line hanging from a nail and grabbed it. Inside the feed-room, he found a burlap bag and dropped the rope inside it. "This should do it. Let's go."

Lenore walked ahead of him, and even with her limp, Tom had a hard time keeping up. May lifted her head to watch them pass, but soon went back to grazing.

"She's getting weak," Tom said when they got to June. Noticing the two protruding feet, he decided Lenore must be right about the calf's bent neck blocking what would otherwise be a normal birth. The bottom of the calf's feet pointed down, so it wasn't a breach. At least he knew that much.

"I think you're right about the head," he said, rolling up his sleeves. "I'll see if I can reposition it. Here, hold June's tail out of the way."

Lenore pulled back the cow's tail with one hand and stroked her neck with the other. "It's going to be all right, girl. Dr. Garrison is helping you. He'll save your baby." Lenore's touch seemed to calm the cow.

Tom took a deep breath. Then he positioned himself to reach inside the cow above the two protruding feet. June struggled to expel his invading arm.

As Tom pushed on the calf, June strained against his efforts, but she was weak. He finally felt the calf's face. Cupping his hand around it, he pulled it into the normal birth position. With that done, he reached for the rope. Making a double half-hitch around each leg, he waited for June's next contraction. When that happened, Tom pulled downward. After two more efforts, the calf's wet, brown shoulders came into view and, on the third try, its body gushed out.

Tom leaned back. The calf lay in the wet mess behind its mother. It didn't move, but Tom and Lenore both saw the new creature blink its eye.

"It's alive!" said Lenore. "You did it, Dr. Garrison! I knew Lana guided me to your house for a reason."

"Well, I don't know who Lana is," said Tom, "but I'd love to thank her for giving me the chance to do this. I'd seen it done, but I've never delivered a calf before." Tom soon remembered the task at hand and picked up the burlap bag. He wiped the calf off with it and cleared the fluid from its mouth and nostrils.

"Tickle its nose," Lenore said, handing Tom a pine needle. "That's what Daddy does. I think it helps them breathe."

Tom did, and the calf shook its head. They both laughed. "I remember when Val was born," he said. "I happened to be home that day and got to see it. Daddy poured water in her ear to make her head shake. I guess that gets everything going for them."

June thrashed about, but eventually made it to her feet and began licking the calf clean.

"Did you see if her new baby is a heifer?" Lenore asked. "Daddy will be pleased if it is."

"Let me check." Tom raised the calf's back leg to expose four pink teats protruding from wet, white hair. "It's a girl," he said. "Your daddy will be happy."

"That's good. You know, a doctor who doubles as veterinarian might be right popular around here."

"Not if you don't tell anybody about it," said Tom, as he rolled down his sleeves. "Most folks don't want their doctor doubling as a vet."

"Well, then, this may be something I can hold over your head, Dr. Garrison. Maybe I should have brought Daddy's new camera."

"Please, call me Tom. May I call you Lenore?"

She tilted her head. "That's my name. What else would you call me?"

Tom looked down at the first baby he'd delivered here in the Valley and felt pleased. Human or animal, the miracle of birth was the same. So was the satisfaction of being able to help.

"Look at the little white spot above her right knee," said Lenore. "I believe I'll call her Snowflake. Daddy lets me name the new calves."

"Snowflake is perfect," said Tom. "That's exactly what that white spot looks like." Tom patted the cow's hip. "I think these two will be fine. Let's give mama a chance to get to know her baby. She can take care of the calf better than we can now." He shifted his weight a bit and added, "I'll bring up some hay and a bucket of water later." He suddenly felt self-conscious about being so dirty in front of Lenore. "But I wouldn't mind washing up first."

"Let's go to the house then," she said. "I'll rinse out your shirt and find you one of Daddy's to wear. Then she smiled and chided gently, "I declare. I've never seen a man have so much trouble keeping his clothes clean."

At the house, Tom drew water from the well and poured it into a tub. Then he went behind the house to wash up with the homemade soap Lenore handed him out the door. When he came back, a blue cotton shirt lay folded beside the steps. His shirt was soaking in another bucket by the door.

As he put on Lanier's shirt, Tom heard Lenore moving about in the kitchen. "I'll take a some water up to the cow," he said through the door. "And some hay. Thanks for loaning me this shirt." He waited, but Lenore didn't answer. "Well, I guess I'll go see about that cow now."

Before he made it down the steps, she came to the door. "Are you hungry? We've got lots of vegetables to cook or put up before they ruin. Don't worry; I won't serve butterbeans—couldn't risk that, what with you wearing Daddy's shirt, and all."

Tom stood on the bottom step and looked back at her.

"I'd be pleased if you'd eat with me," she said, looking at him strangely. "Not that it matters, but you've got that shirt buttoned wrong."

Embarrassed, he rebuttoned the shirt. "I...well, I don't know. What would the neighbors think? I mean, about me eating with you...if they think anything, which they won't, I guess. They might, you know. Of course, I don't know your neighbors, so maybe not." He'd never felt so dumb.

"Well, I don't *think* the neighbors are watching," said Lenore from the kitchen. "Shame on them if they are. But, if it eases your mind, we can eat on the porch. It's cooler out there anyway."

"All right then. I'll take the hay and water up to the cow now." Tom studied a bit before adding, "Be back in a minute."

Lenore had the little porch table covered in a blue cloth when Tom came back. She'd put a vase of summer flowers in the middle. "How's June and her baby doing?" she asked, putting out the plates. "Everything all right?"

Tom brushed bits of hay off his clothes before he stepped back up on the porch. "They're both fine. The calf was nursing. Looks like June's already dropped her afterbirth."

He was horrified by the words as soon as they came out of his mouth. Why on earth did he mention afterbirth to a girl who was fixing him supper? What an idiot he must seem to her. Why couldn't he say anything intelligent around this girl? He was a doctor, for crying out loud! Red-faced, he sat down.

Lenore just nodded. "That's good. Do you think we should bring June and the calf down to the barn?"

Tom thought for a minute. "I don't know, but I imagine they're better off where they are. I'd think the woods would be cleaner than the barn, and they're both pretty worn out—but I can bring the calf down if you want me to. I'm sure June will follow."

"No. You're probably right. June's a good mama, and this *is* her third calf."

When Lenore started back inside to get the food, Tom jumped up to help, knocking over his chair in the process. To make matters worse, he tripped over the darn thing and fell sideways onto the floor.

"Are you all right? asked Lenore, wide-eyed. Here, let me help you up." She reached her hand toward Tom.

"No, no. I'm fine," he said, getting up on his own. He sat the chair upright. "I just...I mean, the chair tipped...Oh, Lord. I act like an idiot around you."

Lenore laughed. It was the most beautiful laugh he'd ever heard. "Why don't you try sitting down again, and let me bring the food out?" she asked.

Once she'd put everything on the table, Lenore filled two cups with water from the bucket Tom had drawn up earlier. When she sat down, she bowed her head for a moment, so Tom did, too—but just for a second. When Lenore looked up, Tom was staring at her.

She looked away and passed him the cornbread. By the time they finished eating, the sun was low, but there was enough light left for them to sit on the front porch a while.

They mostly rocked in silence. When the katydids started their nightly chant, Tom knew he'd stayed as long as he dared. "Well, I guess I better get Val and head on home. Thanks again for supper."

"Thank you for helping me with June's calf. I don't know what I'd have done if you hadn't come. How much do we owe you?"

"Supper is more than enough. Anyway, I'd lose my license if I charged money to care for livestock."

"Oh, I wasn't going to pay you with money," she teased. "I hear you like chickens."

Tom grinned. "Word spreads fast around here, doesn't it?"

Lenore stood when he did. "Well, goodnight then," she said. "Be careful going home. It's nearly dark."

"I will. I'll check on the calf in the morning if you want me to. I mean, I think she'll be fine, but still, you never know."

"That would be good. I'll hang your shirt on the line tonight. It should be dry by morning. You can pick that up, too."

Tom nodded in agreement. "I think that's a good plan. I'll see you tomorrow, Lenore."

He walked backward in the direction of the barn, but when he couldn't think of anything else to say, he turned around, waving at Lenore before he did. She waved back.

At the barn, he climbed on Val and headed up the road, the happiest he'd ever been in his life.

Behind the rows of corn in the Conley's garden, Alton Boggs trembled with rage. He'd come over earlier to check on Lenore, knowing Lanier and Hannah were at Loudsville.

Lenore wasn't home when he got there. He'd started to leave when he saw her racing home on Custer. That new doctor — the one who'd made such a fool out of himself by spilling beans in his lap — rode close beside her on his horse. Alton ducked behind the house before either of them saw him.

Later, he crept through the woods above where Lanier's cow was having her calf and watched everything from there. That man didn't know a damn thing about delivering calves. It was a wonder he hadn't paralyzed the cow.

Afterward, Alton listened while they talked on the porch like old friends.

Just wait till Lanier found out about his daughter consorting behind his back. There'd be hell to pay for that!

Alton had never been this mad before.

CHAPTER EIGHT

A Walk in the Woods

August 2, 1919

J une's bawling brought Lenore to the porch off the kitchen. The sun was barely up, but she saw the cow pacing the fence at the upper end of the pasture. Her swollen udder swung beneath her. As the cow walked, she kept her head turned toward the woods.

Lenore had started toward the pasture gate above the barn when she saw Tom riding up on Val. He was carrying Lanier's shirt. His own, freshly washed, hung on the clothesline.

"Good morning," Tom said, as he tied Val to a post near the house. "What's wrong with June? I've heard her carrying on for the last half-mile. Is something wrong with her calf?"

"I'm not sure," said Lenore, watching the cow look toward the woods. "But I'm afraid there may be. I was just about to go see. I didn't expect you so early, but I'm glad you're here."

Tom dismounted, tied Val, and laid Lanier's shirt on the porch. Then they walked through the gate and across the pasture toward the cow. June hurried along the upper fence back toward the spot her calf was born the evening before.

The hay Tom had brought up yesterday was trampled and the water bucket overturned, but the calf wasn't there. "Something's happened," said Lenore looking around her. "We should have moved them to the barn last night, Tom. That's my fault."

"No, it's not," said Tom. "I'm the one who said they'd be better off here. I'm sorry," he apologized. "Maybe the calf just wandered off. I'll head up that way and see what I can find."

Lenore shook her head. "No, her baby was too young to go far. Anyway, after it finished nursing, it would have been down for the night. Something got it. I'll get a bucket of sweet-feed and see if I can toll June to the barn with it before she hurts herself."

Tom lowered the top fence rail and stepped over the bottom ones, pausing to watch Lenore walk away. June saw the opening and started to jump across, but Tom blocked her with the rail and put it back in place. "You stay here, girl. I'll see if I can find your baby." The cow bawled after him but soon started walking along the fence again.

Tom went to the foot of Grimes Nose and back twice, but didn't see any sign of the calf. He eventually gave up, crossed the fence again and walked to the barn.

Inside, Lenore had June tied and was milking the cow's yellow colostrum into a pail. June wasn't eating and kept turning her head toward the trees, but she allowed Lenore's familiar hands to do their job.

"I didn't find the calf," said Tom.

"I know," said Lenore, continuing with her milking. "It's gone. If June hid it somewhere, the way cows do, she wouldn't be so upset. Poor little Snowflake."

Tom leaned against the wall and watched Lenore milk, amazed at her calm acceptance of the lost calf.

"It nursed once," she said, "but not this morning, so I'm going to give June some relief. I'll save this milk for Pledger. He likes to feed a cow's first milk to his hogs when he can get it."

Tom would have willingly stayed with Lenore all day, but before noon, she insisted he go home. "Someone up there may need you," she said. "I don't want to be the cause of somebody not finding their doctor when they need him."

He noticed his shirt hanging on the clothesline, but didn't say anything. Halfway home, he turned Val around. By pretending he'd forgotten it, he was able to spend ten more minutes with Lenore.

Her parents came home before dark, and when she told them about the calf, her daddy took his hound around the pasture. Cornbread struck a scent in the woods above the fence, but after a number of false starts, couldn't trace it any further.

Lanier searched again the next morning until it was time to leave for Loudsville. It was quite a few miles to the campground, and the first service started at 11 o'clock. He was reluctant to give up, but finally had to agree with Lenore that June's calf was gone. Some critter probably dragged it off, but still, he couldn't understand why Cornbread hadn't picked up the trail.

It baffled Lanier that Lenore got Dr. Garrison to help with the calf instead of Alton Boggs. Alton had more experience with cows than the new doctor, and he'd have been glad to come. He might have even brought the calf to the barn for the night. But what was done was done.

They'd keep June in the stable for a day or two. Pledger could let her back in the pasture next week. He'd be milking both cows and keeping an eye on things while they were at campmeeting.

CHAPTER NINE

Campmeetin'

August 3, 1919

W hen the Conleys left for campmeeting week, they rode in the surrey. Custer pulled it along briskly. Ole Burl was getting some well-deserved days off, but he brayed and paced by the fence until they were out of sight. He didn't like being left behind. "That ole mule sure is attached to Custer," said Hannah, looking back.

"Well, Sugar Babe, ever' mule has a horse for its mama," said Lanier, slapping the reins across Custer's back. "I reckon it's a natural thing." Cornbread followed them to the road, but sulked back to the house when Lanier pointed and yelled, "Stay!"

Campmeeting lasted from Sunday to Sunday—unless they decided to hold it over a day or two, which didn't happen as much as it used to. Folks brought what they needed for the week—plenty of food and chickens for eggs; some even brought their cows.

Guest clergymen drew the biggest crowds, and different ones preached during the week. Hannah sometimes let Lanier skip the morning services, and occasionally an afternoon one, but he knew better than to miss the evening's preaching. Those fire-and-brimstone sermons could last for hours. This was where most of the soul-saving happened, so that time was reserved for the preacher most aflame with righteousness, or at least the one who'd come the greatest distance.

In the early days, the folks attending the event used real tents for shelter, and the roof of the brush arbor was actually made from branches. But over the decades, both had grown more substantial. The temporary dwellings were still called tents, and the folks who used them were known as tenters. They all had natural gray exteriors. Lenore's daddy said that was because most folks were "too poor to paint and too proud to whitewash."

Tenters put straw on the dirt floors every year. Bed sheets, made from guano fertilizer sacks, were draped over ropes to serve as makeshift room-dividers. A few tents had stoves but most—like the Conleys'—had an outside fireplace at one end for cooking.

Folks customized their interiors to fit the needs of different families, but almost all had one thing in common: a shed-like roof over the end that faced the arbor. Preachers clustered there between services—men whittled, and women caught up with neighbors they seldom saw. From there, the feeble and infirm could hear the preaching and join the singing. That little front porch was the social center of every tent.

Campmeeting happened at lay-by time, when crops were "laid by" for the summer, and there wasn't much more to be done before fall. This was a necessary accommodation for an agrarian community, but the timing meant it always fell during the hottest days of summer.

For young folks—and even a few older ones—campmeeting was courting time. Over the years, Lenore heard many women say their husbands first made eyes at them during campmeeting. Courtships often began with a walk to the community spring, supposedly to fetch water. Some folks said you could tell how close a girl was to getting hitched by how much water her family's tent had in it.

Lenore remembered one irate daddy hurling a pail out the front door, and shouting at the boy running toward the arbor, "What the hell do you think we are—a family of fish?"

Folks still laughed about the incident, but by next campmeeting, that fellow and the man's daughter had married. Their union had already made the water-tossing man a grinning grandpa.

The first service of this year's campmeeting was about to start when the Conleys' surrey pulled up to the back of their tent just off the dirt road that circled the grounds. They barely had time to dust off their clothes before Oscar Howard blew the trumpet he sounded to announce the start of the service, just as he would for every other one this week.

On their way to the arbor, they shook hands with neighbors from near and far. The women were dressed in their best, and Lanier, like nearly all the males over age 10, sported a hat and white shirt. In spite of the heat, most men wore an unbuttoned dress jacket. Things would get less formal as the week wore on, but for this first service, everyone had on their finest—except Alton Boggs.

Alton came dressed in an ill-fitting coat over his everyday overalls. To make matters worse, Lenore noticed he'd taken to wearing a hat with the dried skin of a copperhead snake for a band. Alton and his widowed mother, Evelyn—with whom he lived—followed Lenore and her parents closely as they walked across the straw to find seats under the arbor.

Lenore felt certain Alton planned to sit by her again the way he'd done three Sundays ago in church. She was determined not to let that happen here. Still, Hannah was one of the widow Boggs' few friends. Her mother would not refuse to sit with her if that's what Evelyn wanted, and apparently, it was.

Right now, Lenore wished her mama and daddy had lost their battle twenty-five years ago, against having men and women sit on separately sides of the arbor. Her parents loved telling how, back in 1896, when they first "noticed" each other, a pastor named Cowen recommended the men sit on one side and the women on the other. That way, he felt, both groups would stay better focused on his sermons.

The idea was approved by the tent-holders, but lots of folks, including Lanier and Hannah, didn't like the decision. At the next service, several men ignored the rule. When Lanier sat by Hannah, one of the campground marshals asked him to move.

He refused. So did several other men and two women who'd sat down on the men's side. Some folks just got up and left, but not Lanier. When a marshal tried to move him by force, Lanier punched the man in the face, and a general ruckus broke out. It was quickly brought under control, but not before one of the Pope boys stabbed Riley Helton, another marshal. It wasn't fatal, but hard feelings lasted for years. That October, someone even set fire to some of the tents. They were eventually rebuilt, but that ended the separation of the sexes.

Out of the blue, Lenore thought of a way to avoid her predicament about sitting with Alton. "Mama, please excuse me a minute. I want to ask Preacher Yarbrough something." She moved down the aisle, lifting her dress a bit to keep it from dragging through the straw. Lenore motioned toward the minister who stepped down from the platform that held the podium.

After a quick conversation, Preacher Yarbrough summoned the other two pastors. They huddled for a time, then looked over the crowd and beckoned some of the people, including Frank Sosebee, his brothers and father, to come up to the stage.

When a dozen folks, all known for their singing, assembled, they held another discussion. Behind the podium, Preacher Yarbrough waved his hand and proclaimed, "Hallelujah, folks! We've got a special treat this year. Yes, we do. We're gonna have a choir!" His delight was evident. "They'll sit up here and sing backup all week and maybe even do a special number or two for us!"

People applauded as the new choir sat down on the benches behind the pulpit. Alton Boggs didn't look happy, but he took his place beside his mother, anyway.

Pastor Hoyt Ledford kicked things off with a prayer. Then he asked the choir to sing *There's Power in the Blood*. Once everybody found it in their song book, the entire congregation joined in.

Preacher Ledford opened his Bible and launched into the first sermon of campmeeting. He spoke slowly, at first, choosing his words carefully. But as The Spirit overtook him, he started talking faster. His sentences became shorter. Soon they rose and fell in rapid, poetic, rhythm with the pounding he gave his Bible. His words became harder to understand, and every sentence ended in an explosion of air that sounded like, "HA-AH!" as he strode back and forth across the platform.

The crowd responded enthusiastically. Now and then, someone hollered "Praise Jesus!" or "Hallelujah!" When they gave the altar call, eleven souls stepped forward, a record number for the first service, at least as far as anyone remembered.

Wednesday morning, as planned, Lanier took Custer from the makeshift corral folks put up every year for the horses and mules. He put the saddle he'd brought over last week on him and headed back to check on the farm. He felt sure Pledger had everything under control, but the mid-week trip home was a tradition for him and a few other men, too. Most would be back tonight in time for this evening's preaching.

Lenore and her mother went to the 11 o'clock morning service. Alton didn't show up, and Lenore hoped he'd gone home for the day, too. She'd foiled his plan to sit with her, but she'd caught him looking at her several times.

When the preaching was over, everyone went back to their tents to rest up for the ones yet to come. After dinner, her mother took an afternoon nap. She never did that at home, but it was a routine she followed faithfully at campmeeting. Other folks vanished into their tents, too. Even the three ministers disappeared, one by one, into the preacher's tent. It was the quietest time of the day. The only noise came from a horseshoe game up by the main road.

Lenore threw some shelled corn on the ground for the two chickens they'd brought over. These hens had about quit laying, but still, they might get one or two eggs from them this week. Either way, they would both be supper on Friday, the day the Conley family hosted the preachers.

Being careful not to wake her mother, Lenore decided to walk to the spring. As an excuse, she took the two pails they used for drinking water out behind the tent and emptied them — she always carried both pails with her for balance.

As soon as she started down the trail with its natural avenue of trees, the air felt cooler. At the spring, moss-covered boards created a little dam to hold the water in a foot-deep pool that shimmered in the sun. The cool bouquet of dampness here was one of Lenore's favorite smells — right up there with the comforting aroma of a barn.

When she stooped to fill her buckets, a spring lizard scurried off to hide in the ferns. A dragonfly — her daddy called them *snake doctors* — lit on a nearby branch. Lenore stared at its metallic-like finery. She imagined Indians gathering here, perhaps resting after a hunt. Lenore wondered how many lovers had met at this place — hundreds probably. This spring had always been one of her favorite places, and like the barn, was one where she often felt Lana's presence.

Lenore had only taken a few steps back up the path when a man stepped from behind a tree, startling her. The dragonfly winged to a nearby branch.

"Alton," she said, surprised. "My goodness! You almost made me spill my water. I thought you'd gone back home for the day."

"Naw, I left my cousin Sammy and his wife, Carol, in charge. They'll make sure ever' thing gets done how it should."

"That's good," said Lenore, attempting to walk past him.

"What's your hurry?" Alton asked, blocking her way. "Ain't nothing going on back there 'til 4 o'clock no how. Why don't we sit for a spell and talk?"

"I've got to get back, Alton. Mama is expecting me." She tried to move past him again and caught wind of his breath. It smelled like onions.

"Hold on," he said. "I got somethin' I need to ask, and you won't never give me a chance to do it. I aim to get it done right now." Alton reached into his overall's pocket, took out a piece of licorice and offered it to Lenore who shook her head no.

"Suite yourself," said Alton, biting off a piece of candy and putting the rest back in his pocket.

Lenore tried again to edge past him, but this time she stumbled on a root and fell, spilling both buckets of water on the ground and across her dress. The two empty pails rolled into the woods.

"Alton, look what you made me do. I've ruined my dress!"

He looked down at the muddy mess and the overturned buckets lying in the leaves. "Aw, you did that your own self. If you'd just sit and talked like I asked you to, there wouldn't a been no call for you to fall down."

Lenore picked herself up. Alton watched, but didn't offer to help. She was grateful because she couldn't stand the thought of him touching her. She'd never been drawn to this man, but she'd never been repulsed by him either, until now. Now she felt something else entirely — she was afraid of him.

"You're right, Alton — it *was* my fault. Now let me by so I can get back and change my dress."

Alton grabbed her wrist. "Hold on. I *told* you I had something to ask. Now you sit down there and let me ask it." He pointed to the big rock beside the path.

"All right. I'll sit. But please make it quick, Alton. I've got to get back."

When Lenore sat on the rock, Alton knelt on one knee in front of her. He took her hand and studied the back of it. "Lenore," he said, "I want to marry you. That's what I'm askin'. You ain't got to agree to it right now, but I want you to be studyin' on it."

She was shocked by his proposal. She didn't know what to say, so she just looked at Alton, who was still looking at her hand.

"They's reasons for us to marry," he continued without looking up. "I need a wife to help on the farm, and I don't mind you being crippled. That don't matter none to me. Even your daddy knows us marrying is a good idea. Just ask him."

Lenore wasn't sure what to say, but she knew she had to say something. "Alton, I'm flattered, but, well. I can't marry you. I just can't. I don't love you."

Alton looked like he'd been slapped. He slowly raised his head to look at her. "Ain't I good enough for you, Lenore? You think maybe you could do better—a cripple like you? Maybe you think you can marry that doctor. Is that what it is?"

"Alton, what on earth are you talking about?"

"I saw you feeding him last week while Lanier and Hannah were gone off. I ain't told on you yet, but I might. How you reckon your daddy will feel about that, huh?"

"Daddy and Mama already know about it. I fetched the new doctor to help deliver June's calf—she was having trouble. Were you spying on me?"

Flustered, Alton turned loose of Lenore's hand and stood. "Hell no! I wasn't spying on you! I's just passing by and saw y'all on the porch, that's all. But I don't believe you told them 'bout it. Lanier wouldn't stand for behavior like that from one of his womenfolk."

Lenore couldn't believe what she was hearing. "There wasn't anything indecent about it, Alton. He helped deliver the calf. I fed him supper for his trouble. If anything had been going on, we wouldn't have eaten on the porch. Anyway, this is none of your business."

Alton stiffened his back. He slowly became incensed. Lenore felt the change, and it scared her even more. When he drew his hand back to hit her, the rage she saw in his eyes made Lenore cringe. She pulled her hands away to protect her face.

When she did, Alton looked at her and dropped his own hands. "Come here to me," he said, stepping forward. "I wasn't really gonna slap you. I'm just tryin' to make you see things my way—the right way."

He pulled her off the rock and pinned her arms beneath his. Lenore struggled but couldn't break away from him. She moved her face from side to side trying to avoid his lips as he strained to plant them on hers. "Alton, stop this! Stop it right now! Please stop it! What's wrong with you?"

"Ain't nothin' wrong with me, girl. I just want to kiss you, honey. Come on now, quit carrying on so."

Lenore kicked Alton's shin with her good foot. When he didn't react, she kicked him again, harder. This time, he grabbed his leg

"Hell farr, girl. That hurt! Why are you being so willful?" Alton locked his arms around Lenore's waist and pulled her close. "I mean for us to marry, darlin'."

She shuddered.

Alton dropped his arms from her waist but quickly grabbed both Lenore's hands. She backed away as far as she could. "Let me go, Alton."

Alton noticed the buckets. As if he'd suddenly had an idea, he started toward them, pulling Lenore behind him by her wrist. He picked both buckets up and dragged her along to the spring. Holding on to her with his free hand, he filled the buckets with water and sat them in front of her like an offering. "Here," he said, finally turning her arm loose. "I'm sorry you spilled the first ones. But now we're right back where we was before you started carryin' on."

In spite of all that had just happened, Lenore felt sorry for him. "Alton," she said, stooping to lift a pail in each hand, "I won't tell anybody about this if you promise it won't happen again. Do you know what my daddy would do if I told him? Neither of us wants that."

Alton looked dazed. He turned away.

Lenore started back up the path. When she'd gone a few feet, he called after her. "Come back, Lenore, please."

She kept her composure, but something urged her on, so she walked faster.

"Lenore," Alton hollered louder.

She hurried even harder which exasperated her limp and caused water from the buckets to splash on her shoes.

"LENORE!"

Through the trees, she saw the backs of the closest tents and hurried toward them as fast as she could. Behind her, Alton, sounding mad again, shouted, "LENORE! I AIM TO MARRY YOU! YOU HEAR ME?"

CHAPTER TEN

The Hardmans

August 6, 1919

It was hot again, but the sky was clear when Tom headed the buggy toward the railroad depot below Helen. This would be the first time he'd been to the west end of the Nacoochee Valley. Before today, the farthest he'd come this way was the Methodist church he'd just passed. The road Val pulled him down was solid and ran parallel to the green fields of crops and pastures on his left.

A letter from his mother had arrived on Monday. She wrote that Dr. Lam and Aunt Emma would be on the train from Gainesville at 11:25 this morning. She'd asked that, if at all possible, Tom be there to meet them. He was honoring his mother's wish, although the Hardmans would hardly need a ride. From what he understood, the Nacoochee Station was right by the farm — their big house only a hundred yards away.

He hoped to get away in time to go to Loudsville tonight. Lenore and her mother had both invited him, and it would be rude not to go. Besides, seeing Lenore again was pretty much the only thing on his mind anymore.

He was plenty early, but Tom wanted time to look around some before the train came. Still, it was a pretty morning, so he let Val pull the buggy along at her own pace. Beyond the valley, on the other side of the Chattahoochee River, lay the long, tree-covered hill Frank had told him was known as Sal's Mountain.

"Most folks just call it Sal Mountain," Frank had said. "But on the old maps it's Sal's, with an apostrophe. A man named it after his wife, and her name was Sally. It's funny how names get changed over the years, ain't it?" Tom thought the boy's attention to historical detail was delightful.

Farther back stood Yonah Mountain—the one the Indians thought looked like a sleeping bear. Tom stared and squinted, but no matter how much he tried, he couldn't quite see what the Indians saw.

In the distance, sitting in a cornfield—big, even by middle Georgia standards—was the Indian Mound he'd seen in the picture Aunt Emma sent his mother. The little gazebo with its pointed oak-shingle roof looked exactly like it did in the photograph. Dozens of brown cows lay among the trees near the river. Tom was looking at the grass-covered mound when the most beautiful church he'd ever seen came into view on the other side of the road.

"Whoa, Val," said Tom, leaning forward for a better look. The wood-framed church sat tucked in the trees on a hill overlooking the Valley. The white structure had a green roof with matching shutters and accents. A bell tower reached skyward.

Beyond the church and farther down the road a-ways, he saw the pointed rooftop of a red cupola sticking up above the trees. From Dr. Dyer's description, he correctly guessed this to be the top of Dr. Lam and Aunt Emma's house.

"Come on, Val," he said. "Let's go see our kinfolks' place." The two-story residence looked even grander than he'd expected. Walnut trees formed a canopy over the road in front of the house. Matching buildings stood on either side of a fast-flowing stream that ran through the grounds. There was a separate kitchen a few yards from the main house and a smaller, reddish-colored building behind it.

As modest as they were, even those had whitewashed stone pillars and painted white trim. Across the stream sat a carriage house and a long dairy barn with two tall silos. Tom noticed poles with electrical wires leading from the residence. Electricity was rare, even in Macon, but his mother had mentioned that Dr. Lam had it generated from his grist mill up the road.

The road ahead curved past a cluster of buildings beside the railroad tracks. North of the depot, a covered bridge spanned the river that flowed down from Helen. Several people lolled around the buildings by the tracks, and Tom heard boys playing on the riverbank. Val stopped at the end of the brick building that, according to the signs, served as both a store and the Nacoochee Post Office.

He'd just finished tying the reins around the dashboard rail, in his usual bowtie knot, when he heard a familiar voice behind him. "What kind of fancy way is that to tie your reins?"

He looked around and saw Lanier Conley dismounting from Custer. "Just habit, I reckon," Tom said, walking to him.

"I never saw anybody tie 'em like that before," said Lanier, inspecting the knot. "You ain't already catching a train out of town, are you?"

"No, sir, I'm here to meet the Hardmans," Tom explained. "I thought you were at campmeeting. I'm hoping to get over there myself before it's over, maybe even tonight."

"Well, I'm just taking a little break from it all," said Lanier. "That young visitin' preacher's tongue is loose at both ends. I don't reckon he's done enough sinnin' yet to teach me much about it." Lanier grinned at Tom. "But I'll be back over there before dark," he said. "Hannah will light into me if I'm not."

Lanier tied Custer to the porch railing and stretched his arms. "I'm right beholden to you for delivering that calf Saturday. Sure do wish you'd a put it in the barn, though, and buttoned the door."

Tom scratched Custer's head. "Sir, I sure am sorry about what happened. Lenore and I talked about bringing them to the barn, but we decided they'd be better off where they were. I guess I made a mistake."

Lanier nodded to a man riding by on a horse and looked back at Tom. "You did, son. But what's done is done. That cow was bred to one of those Jersey bulls over there," he said, pointing to a pen near the Hardman's barn. "It woulda' made a fine milk cow one day."

Lanier stepped up on the covered porch of the brick building. "I got some business with the proprietor in here," he said. "I'll be back in a minute."

Tom strolled up to the covered bridge and looked down at the Chattahoochee. The boys were racing each other along the far bank now. From here, the river—somewhat polluted after its trip through Helen and past the big sawmill—curved into the bend that marked the west end of the Nacoochee Valley. After that, it made a graceful loop and flowed through the trees to the southeast.

Tom ambled back toward the buildings, keeping an eye out for Lanier. Three old men lounged on the depot's loading dock, smoking pipes and gazing south, although the train wasn't due for another twenty minutes.

When Lanier came back out, he had a small package wrapped in newspaper and tied with brown string. He was about to untie Custer when Tom stepped up. "Sir, I want to apologize again about that calf. I should have insisted on putting them both in the barn. I'm sorry."

Lanier left Custer tied and rubbed the back of his head. "Aw, it's all right, son. To tell the truth, I'd probably have done the same thing myself if I'd been there. I hear Lenore fed you supper."

Tom blushed. "Yes, sir, she did—on the porch. It was good, too. I mean the food. Really good. It was very good food."

Lanier frowned. "Normally, I'd take offense at a near stranger taking supper with my daughter without me or her ma there. But I reckon you was over on business—more or less anyhow. And you *did* bring my shirt back."

Tom blushed deeper. "Sir, I promise you it was all above suspicion—just supper on the porch. But about your daughter...she..."

"What about her?"

"Nothing...I mean, Lenore seems nice. That's all—and pretty."

Lanier seemed to relax a bit. Then he threw back his head and laughed. "Ay Gawd, she is pretty, ain't she? She took after her ma. I reckon I can't blame you none for asking after her. I'm more watchful than most, on account of her leg and all."

"Yes, sir. I understand. I've just met her, but I can tell she's an extraordinary girl." Tom was practically gushing. "I don't blame you for being protective."

Lanier seemed to soften a bit more. He looked around to see who was in the yard and motioned for Tom to follow him. "Walk with me, son."

Carrying the package, he led Tom to the end of the building. When they were out of sight of everybody in the yard, he flopped down on the ground and leaned against the brick wall that faced the Hardman's house. He looked up at Tom. "You a drinkin' man?" Without waiting for an answer, Lanier untied the string and revealed a pint jar of clear liquid, which he sat in the grass by his leg.

"Not really," said Tom, thinking this might not be the time to admit he'd never had a drink in his life.

"Good. Me neither. But, when old man Henderson in there gets up a new batch of snakebite prevention, a man sort of has an obligation to take a sip. We owe that to the womenfolk, don't you think?" Lanier patted the grass beside him. "Sit down, son. The train won't be here for another few minutes. You being a doctor, I'd think you'd have an interest in our mountain medicines."

Tom wasn't sure what to do, but he wanted to stay on this man's good side, so he plopped down next to him. Lanier slapped the jar hard against his left hand and held it up. "Look at the bead on that," he said. "And Henderson don't use no beadin' oil either. I reckon it's gonna take me a while to get used to these see-through glass jars, though."

Lanier unscrewed the ring, removed the lid, and poured the liquid down his throat. "Whew, that's smooth," he said, wiping his mouth on his sleeve. Lanier handed the jar to Tom. "Any ol' rattler gets close to me is gonna fall dead in mid-strike — copperheads, too. Go on son, vaccinate yourself."

Tom raised the jar to his nose and sniffed the contents. He frowned. Hoping to buy some time, Tom asked Lanier, "Don't you think it's a bit early for a drink?"

"Early?" asked Lanier indignantly. "Snakes don't know nothing 'bout early. Morning's the worst time for 'em! Just taste of it and see how you like it. Then give it back." Lanier watched him closely.

Just then, one of the bulls in the pen across the way bawled. When Tom still hesitated, Lanier leaned toward him. "One sip of this and you'll be bellowing like that big feller over there. Go on — you ain't too good to drink after me, are you?"

Tom felt he had no choice. Anyway, how bad could one sip be? Lanier said it was smooth. He decided to take one big gulp and get it over with. Tom pulled the jar to his lips, threw his head back and poured a goodly amount of whiskey into his mouth, swallowing fast. The result was not pretty.

He instinctively handed the jar back — hitting Lanier in the chest with it — leaned forward and gasped. He coughed so hard he lost his breath. When he could breathe again, it was with a sound he'd never made before.

Lanier calmly looked at him, took another swig from the jar and wiped his mouth again. "I reckon you're serious about not being a drinkin' man." With that fact firmly established, he offered the jar back. "Here, take another swallow, son. It'll clear you up."

Still coughing, Tom shook his head. "No, thanks. That's enough," he said, his voice hoarse. "If I get snake bit, I'll come find you."

"It'll be too late then," Lanier said, screwing the lid back on. "This medicine only *prevents* snakebites. It can't do nothin' much for you once you're bit."

"I'll keep that in mind," said Tom. He stood and extended his hand. Lanier took it to pull himself up. Tom felt a bit light-headed from the big gulp of whiskey that had made it past his tonsils, but Lanier seemed unaffected by the quarter-pint he'd swallowed.

The young doctor held the package of moonshine while Lanier climbed onto Custer's back. Once settled, he reached for the jar and said to Tom, "I forgot you're kin to the Hardmans — the doctor's wife is your aunt, isn't she?"

Tom started to correct him but decided to let it go. "That's right," he said.

Lenore's daddy stared down at him. "Being as how they're your kin and all, I hope you don't feel obliged to tell 'em about old man Henderson selling a little snakebite medicine in there. That'd put Henderson between a rock and a hard place."

"I won't say anything," said Tom. "But what does that have to do with the Hardmans?"

Lanier laughed. "Well, he owns this building. Hell, he owns everything around here." Lanier swept his arm in a wide circle. "Even Nora Mill, up the road there — the little church you passed back yonder, too. They use it for a chapel these days. I hear he's got three or four more big farms like this scattered around the state. You're kin to some high-cotton folks, son."

Lanier backed Custer up. "Good seeing you, Doc. Come to campmeetin' if you can. 'Course, you'll have to sing in the choir if you want to sit by Lenore. She's sittin' up there all week. Even ol' Alton ain't willing to go on the stage to sit by her." With that, he headed the horse up the road, threw his head back and sang the chorus of *Old Dan Tucker* as he rode away.

The elation Tom felt wasn't from the liquor that still burned his gullet. It came from knowing Alton Boggs wasn't sitting by Lenore at campmeeting. He was so delighted he tried clicking his heels together. After three attempts, he decided clicking one's heels is easier said than done.

Tom was checking his watch when he heard the train coming, right on time. He pivoted toward the station. Walking to the loading dock steps, he sauntered up them, but the heel of his boot caught on the top riser.

"You awright?" asked one of the old men.

"Never better," Tom replied. One of the men poked the other with his elbow.

Tom leaned against the front of the depot and watched the train pull into the station, its bell clanging. The locomotive and coal-tender pulled a passenger coach and one baggage car. The engineer waved at two boys standing by the building and rang the bell again just for them. The tender had the words *Gainesville & Northwestern* painted in large white letters on its side.

The conductor stepped off and placed a metal step below the spot where the two cars coupled. A man pushed the door of the baggage car open, and he and two others piled boxes and trunks on the platform. Inside the baggage car, a dog barked.

Three men with no luggage came off first. They walked to a waiting automobile with a *Morse Brothers Lumber Company* sign on the door. Once they were inside, its driver raced away.

Through the train windows, Tom saw the bulky form of Dr. Hardman rise and turn to his wife, Emma. She held their new baby daughter they'd also named Emma. Tom chuckled at the thought of explaining *that* to Dr. Dyer one day. She handed the baby to a colored woman who came from the rear of the car, took the child, and walked down the aisle behind Emma Hardman.

Dr. Hardman, who wore a suit in spite of the heat—although he carried his jacket—stepped off the train first and reached back to help his wife. At 63, he was still an impressive looking man. He had a moustache and a head full of gray hair just starting to recede.

Their other children exited in polite order; Lamartine Jr., 11, Josephine, 9, and Sue, 7. Another colored woman came down next with an arm-load of baby clothes. His mother had written that the Hardmans' cook, Delia, and her daughter, Alma, were coming with them from Commerce—Dr. Hardman's hometown—to help with the baby.

None of them noticed Tom standing on the dock, and he decided to keep his presence secret for a few more minutes. He might even jump off the dock and scare Lam, Jr.

The dog inside the baggage car barked again, and Tom wondered why someone didn't take it off. It had to be hot in there. He felt sweatier than usual himself.

He was about to make his presence known when Dr. Hardman extended his hand to another lady getting off the train. Tom had noticed the woman earlier through the window, holding a fan to her face, but hadn't given her much thought. Now she had his full attention. The woman was Wirtha Garrison.

"Mother!" Tom raced down the steps and tripped on the bottom one. He regained his footing and spread his arms. "Mother, what a surprise! I had no idea you were coming!"

She looked tired, but otherwise better than when Tom left her in Macon, three weeks ago. Sweeping her up, he hugged her. "I'm so happy to see you!"

"I'm glad to see you too, son." Then she pushed him away and looked at him. Tom shook hands with Dr. Hardman and Lamartine Jr., reintroduced himself to the two girls, and gushed over the baby.

"What a surprise!" Tom said again. "I am absolutely delighted!"

"Well, this isn't the end of it," said his mother. "Look behind you."

Tom turned around. Big Mama and Uncle Isaac stood on the loading dock with his brother, Ray, and Ray's dog, Jack. Tom raced up the stairs he'd just come down. At the top, Big Mama grabbed him in a bear hug that lifted him off the ground. Then she backed away, sniffed his face, and stared.

Tom shook hands with a grinning Isaac and moved toward Ray, who smiled, but took a step back when he saw Tom planned to hug him. Jack bristled, so Tom just shook his brother's hand. "What are you three doing in the baggage car? Coloreds can ride in the passenger car, can't they? I mean the Hardman's people did."

"Lawd-a-mercy, son," said Big Mama. "Dem ol' railroad folks wouldn't let dat dawg ride up front, and Mistah Ray wouldn't hear tell o' Jack being put 'n a box, so he 'lected to ride back here wif him ta keep that from happenin'. Me and Isaac jus rode back der ta keep dem company."

Tom danced a little jig. "I still can't believe this," he said, when he'd finished his dance. "I'm in shock."

"It was Emma's idea," said his mother, giving him an odd look. "She convinced me to come up and help with the baby, and I wanted to see your new place — we all did. Big Mama was the one who talked Ray into coming. We're going to stay a month at least, maybe longer. We'll see how things go."

Just then, a dark-green Cadillac car with a silver radiator and two brass headlights that looked like giant bug eyes, pulled up and parked at the end of the depot. Dr. Hardman shook hands with the driver, and introduced the man as Bob Minish, the farm's caretaker.

Minish opened the back door and Emma Hardman sat down inside. Alma handed her the baby and climbed in beside her. Dr. Hardman got in the front seat beside the driver and motioned out the window. "We've got room if anybody else wants to ride. That's the house right over there, though. It's not far."

"Thanks, but we'll walk," said Wirtha. "It'll do us good. We haven't done anything but sit since we left Macon." She took Tom by the arm and looked around. "It *is* beautiful here, son. Exactly the way Emma described it."

Josephine and Sue ran after Lamartine Jr., who won the race with the car as it rolled to the house. Tom had started walking in that direction with his mother when Ray called his name.

"Tom? Could I speak to you for a second? In private?"

"Sure thing." Tom let go of his mother's arm and turned back toward his brother. "Uncle Isaac, would you please escort Mother over to the house?"

Big Mama hung back with Ray. "I wants a word, too," she said to Tom.

"Go ahead, Big Mama," said Ray. "I'll give you first shot at him."

The big woman didn't waste any time. "Son, has you been drinkin'? 'Cause I smell liquor on yo' breath. You don't mean to tell me you ain't got no more gumption than that! You wadn' raised that way. Anyhow, it ain't even dinnertime yet!"

Before Tom could say anything in his defense, Ray joined in. "I think Mother smelled it, too. What's going on, little brother? And don't deny it, because I smelled enough booze in the Army to know it when I sniff it."

Big Mama put both hands on her hips and glared. "I oughta take a switch to you!"

"No, no, please! I can explain," said Tom. "It's not booze, it's snakebite medicine!"

Ray chuckled. "I've heard it called a lot of things, but that's a new one. You better hope Dr. Lam didn't notice it. He's the biggest teetotaler in the state. When he was in the legislature, he's the one who got prohibition passed in Georgia."

"I told you," said Tom. "I just swallowed a little by mistake. I wanted to make a good impression on Lenore's daddy. I delivered their calf, you see."

Ray sniffed Tom again. "Do they sell candy in there?"

"I don't know. I've never been inside. Why? Are you hungry?"

"Y'all stay here," said Ray. "Sit, Jack." He walked to the porch. Jack lay down by Big Mama but his eyes followed Ray as he went inside.

When Ray came back, he handed Tom two sticks of peppermint candy. "Suck on these, little brother. They may be the only thing that keeps Dr. Lam from kicking your drunk butt back to Macon."

Having sorted out his younger brother, Ray walked over to Val. He couldn't help grinning when he saw the bowtie Tom had made with the reins around the dashboard rail. He untied her and led the horse to the house. On the way, Tom kept trying to explain about Lanier and the drink he'd taken. Over to their right, men were busy building a pen of some sort.

At the big house, Bob Minish opened the car doors and let everyone out by the back door. His passengers delivered, he drove the car across a bridge to the carriage house. Two other men pulled up in a wagon with everyone's trunks and luggage. Ray grabbed his small bag from the pile. "I'll keep this with me for now," he said, tossing it by the steps.

Another colored woman—Tom later learned she was Pledger's wife, Ida—helped Big Mama and Isaac get settled. The two of them would stay in the cabin behind the kitchen. Half that bungalow was a smokehouse, but the other end was a make-shift bedroom.

Wirtha insisted on having two metal cots put on the back porch for them, too, in case the heat made that more comfortable than the cabin. Big Mama would assist Delia with the cooking, and Isaac would do odd jobs around the house while they were here.

Once Dr. Lam changed into more comfortable clothes, he and Minish spent the next hour showing Tom and Ray around the farm. Jack soon got acquainted with two other dogs. He romped with them, but only as long as they all stayed close to Ray.

Outside the long, two-story milking barn up behind the house, Bob Minish took Dr. Lam into a small office in the front corner to look over the herd's production records. Tom spotted Pledger's twin boys in the hallway of the big barn. They were helping other men wash down the concrete floor after the morning's milking. "Howdy," said Tom. "Do y'all remember me?"

"Yassir. Shore do," said one of the brothers. Since they were identical, Tom didn't know if it was Jody or Josh who answered him. "You dat new doctor. I's Jody. Dis here's Josh."

"How do folks tell y'all apart?" asked Tom. "You sure do favor."

"Dat's easy," said Jody. "I'm da black one." The brothers both grinned but kept working. They'd pulled this little joke before. Josh reached in his back pocket, took out a homemade slingshot and showed it to Tom. "I'm the one good wid dis flip," he said. "I can take down a squirrel at fifty yards!"

Tom laughed. "I bet you can."

"This is the biggest milking parlor I've ever seen," said Ray, as he walked up behind them and looked down the long corridor. Light poured through what must be fifty windows on both sides. Above him, on the barn's second story, unseen men tossed hay about, causing bits of chaff to drop through the cracks above their heads.

"Yassir," said Jody. "We milks ninety-six cows at a time, twice a day, ever' day." He pointed toward two rows of iron stanchions that lined both sides of the barn.

The blend of barn smells — manure, hay, milk, disinfectant and a dozen others — created an aromatic richness that Tom found oddly comforting. Apparently, Jack didn't. He sniffed the concrete floor and walked outside to sit and look in from there.

"I don't blame you, boy," said Ray, following him. "I'll come with you." Together, they walked over to the little creek between the house and barn.

"I'll catch up," Tom hollered after them.

He turned back to Jody and Josh. "So, your mother works for the Hardmans, too?" Both boys nodded. "Jus' about ever' body over on Bean Creek either works here or da Helen sawmill," said Jody. "Deys gonna keeps dat sawmill runnin' 'til ever' tree in the mountains is cut, I reckon. But me and Josh likes farm work better'n sawmill work."

"It's a long way over here from Bean Creek," Tom pointed out.

"It ain't a far piece," said Jody. "Ya see, deys a little road up over dat hill dar behind da barn. Hit ain't more'n two miles dat way. Sometimes we walk it three times a day."

Tom glanced through the door of the little office. It looked like Dr. Hardman and his farm manager were going to be reviewing those records for quite a while, so he decided to leave the two of them to their paperwork and join Ray and Jack over at the creek.

They heard Big Mama laughing in the kitchen across the way, but the big house, where everyone else was staying, seemed oddly silent. "Things sure did get quiet up at the house," said Tom.

"Yep," said Ray. "I reckon everybody decided to take a nap."

"Well, y'all have had a long trip," said Tom. "You look pretty tired yourself."

Ray yawned. "I've had my eye on one of those rocking chairs over on the porch ever since we got here. Want to try one out, little brother? I mean, if it won't interfere with your drinking."

Tom rolled his eyes, but they walked around the house to the big front porch and sat in two rockers. Jack lay down between them. After a while, Tom said, "Ray, I'm glad you came up. Seems like we haven't talked in a long time."

Ray rocked but didn't say anything. A minute later, he asked Tom a question. "Little brother, do you have an extra room at your place? If you do, I'd like to board with you while we're here."

"There is a spare room there, but it only has one little cot in it. You're welcome to use it, of course, but the accommodations down here are a lot better."

Ray took a deep breath and let it out slowly. "That cot will feel like paradise compared to what I got used to in France. The problem with me staying here is that I don't think Aunt Emma will let Jack in the house."

Ray looked at the dog, and paused, before adding, "There's another reason, too, Tom. You see, I have nightmares. Not every night, but I'm afraid I'll scare the children if I wake up hollering. But I can sleep down in the kitchen or with Big Mama and Isaac, or even camp out someplace, if it's a problem for you."

"Don't you even think that, Ray," Tom insisted. "You and Jack can stay with me for as long as you like. Only thing is, I need to start home pretty soon. I have to make sure no one needs me. People leave a note on my door when I'm not home if they do."

Inside the house, children's feet scampered down a stairway. Lamartine Jr. ran onto the porch first — his sisters chasing him. One of the front doors slammed as they raced down the steps laughing. Upstairs, the baby cried. Alma shushed it.

A few minutes later, Wirtha came through the door, closing it softly behind her. "So much for my nap," she said, laughing. "I've forgotten what it's like to have children around."

Both her sons stood the instant she came out. Tom pulled another rocking chair close to theirs. "Sit with us, Mother," he said. "We want to ask you something. Would you mind if Ray stayed with me while y'all are up here?"

Wirtha didn't seem surprised at the question. "I thought you might," she said, addressing Ray. "You're afraid you'll frighten the children, aren't you?"

Ray kept looking at Jack but nodded. His mother reached over to put her hand on his knee. "Actually, that might be a good idea," she said, looking at Tom. "I'm sure Emma won't mind at all."

"Thanks, Mother," said Tom. "I knew you'd understand. But I'm going to have to head back to my office before long. Would you make my apologies to Aunt Emma and Dr. Lam?"

"Certainly, son. You do what you have to while we're up here. We didn't come to be in your way."

"You could never be in my way, Mother." A gentle fondness smoothed his face. "You or Ray either one—we're family."

When Wirtha rolled her lower lip between her teeth, Tom knew she was thinking about something. "Son, do you like it up here?" she asked. "Was it a mistake for you to move this far from home?"

Tom leaned back and looked out across the Valley. "No, Mother, it wasn't a mistake," he said honestly. "I think these two valleys are beautiful. This whole county is a fine place to live. Most people have been friendly and, well, it's the strangest thing, but I felt at home here the first night. It's like this is where I'm supposed to be—for now, at least."

His mother seemed pleased with his answer. "This place does seem to suit you. Have you found a church yet?"

Tom laughed. "I'm sorry, Mother. I *have* been to church every Sunday, only not the Baptist one, at least not yet. I've been meaning to go there, but the Methodist folks held a dinner and all-day singing, sort of in my honor, when I first got here, and I've kinda' felt beholden to them for that."

Wirtha looked over at the cornfield across the road, then up at Yonah Mountain. "Well, as long as you're going to church somewhere." She clearly wasn't thrilled about her son spending so much time outside his own denomination. Tom decided it might be best not to tell her he'd been planning to attend a Methodist campmeeting later today.

Anyway, going to campmeeting was out of the question for tonight, and probably for the rest of the week. He hated to miss seeing Lenore, but family came first. His father taught him that.

After Tom and Ray walked back from the kitchen, where they said goodbye to Big Mama and Uncle Isaac, Ray picked up his bag from the porch. He tossed it into the buggy and motioned for Jack to jump in.

About a half-mile from the Methodist church, they met Lanier heading back to Loudsville. Tom stopped Val, introduced Ray, and explained how his family had surprised him by coming in on the train unannounced.

"Nice to meet, ya," Lanier said to Ray. "Any brother of our new doctor is a friend of mine." He weaved in the saddle some. Tom hoped Ray didn't notice. Looking at Tom, Lanier asked, "You not coming over to campmeetin' tonight? I expect they's gonna be some hellacious preaching."

"I won't be able to, tonight," said Tom. "I'll try to come one other evening, though, if I can."

"Suit yourself," said Lanier. "Oh, by the way, I ran into Alton Boggs up the road. He said he's had enough of campmeetin' for this year. He ain't going back 'til Monday mornin' to get his mama. Just figured you'd like to know that. Later, boys!" Lanier dug his heels into Custer's side and started singing again as the horse trotted away.

"He your drinking buddy?" asked Ray, grinning.

Tom chuckled. "He's the one. I hope you'll forgive him for tempting me with liquor."

"Why should I, little brother?"

"Well, the biggest reason is because that man is going to be my father-in-law one day."

CHAPTER ELEVEN

Home Again

August 11, 1919

F or Lenore, the rest of campmeeting dragged by. Her encounter with Alton at the spring had left her confused. She still hadn't told anyone about it, not even her mother or her friend, Jenny. She'd explained away her muddy dress by truthfully saying she'd tripped on a root and spilled the water.

When Preacher Yarbrough asked her to sing a solo on Saturday, she begged off, feigning a sore throat — another excuse with at least some truth to it. From her choir seat, she scanned the crowd every night, looking for the new doctor, but he never came.

When she casually remarked on that at Sunday dinner, her daddy said, "Oh, yeah. I ran into him Wednesday when I went back home. His family came up all at once. I imagine he's busy with them. I met his brother, but I can't call his name — it may have been Roy. He seemed right moody."

Lenore still hoped Tom would show up for the last service that Sunday night, but he didn't. Neither did Alton, thank the Lord.

Monday morning, they loaded up the surrey. It was a tight fit, but, somehow, Lanier got all their stuff in. They said their goodbyes and headed home. Lenore was usually reluctant to leave their old tent, but for the first time, she was eager to go home.

Lanier wanted to ride back through Helen. They were driving past the Morse Brothers Lumber Company just as the giant steam-whistle announced the twenty-minute dinner break. The two massive band saws went quiet and men poured out of buildings carrying tin dinner pails, which they sat on piles of lumber. Those neat stacks of recently milled boards stretched a half-mile in either direction. The smell of sawdust and freshly cut wood reached even farther.

Lanier stared up at one of the new, two-story buildings on the right as they rode past it.

"What are you looking at?" asked Hannah.

"One of the boys down at the store told me that's the new Jenny Barn," said Lanier. "I just wondered what one looked like, that's all."

A young woman leaned out the window of the building Lanier was looking toward. She waved to a group of workers getting ready to eat. Several of the men waved back — one even whistled. Lanier laughed when Hannah bumped him hard with her shoulder.

"What's a Jenny Barn, Daddy?" asked Lenore.

"Never you mind," said her mother, looking straight ahead. "Let's go Lanier."

The town of Helen was a noisy, busy place, and Lenore was glad when they put it behind them. Passing by the Hardman farm, they waved to the three children playing badminton in the yard. "Looks like the Hardmans are up," said Hannah.

"Yeah. I hear they're gonna stay several weeks this time," said Lanier. "They have a new baby, you know — a little girl. What about that? The old man's gotta be toppin' 60. It's a little soon to be traveling with a new baby, but I reckon it's cooler here than down in Jackson County. I bet it's hot as hell down there in the summer."

"Lanier! Watch your language," said Hannah. "Your daughter's sitting right here."

"Lenore ain't a young'un n'more," Lanier reminded Hannah. "She's bound to hear worse."

"Maybe so," said Hannah, "But she ought not to hear it from her daddy."

At home, Lanier was quiet and efficient as he unloaded the surrey and put everything away. Lenore gave Custer a good rubdown and turned him into the pasture so he and Ole Burl could get reacquainted.

At the barn, she peeked inside the stable at May's calf. "Goodness gracious, girl, you've grown this week. In a few more days, we'll put the muzzle on you and see how you like grass. In fact, I'm gonna give you a little sweet-feed right now and see how you like that." The calf walked to the door and stuck its tongue through a crack to lick Lenore's fingers with its rough tongue.

Lenore unlatched the feed-room door and stepped inside. She scooped up a bit of feed from the bag and walked back to the stable. Using her shoulder to turn the latch, she nudged the door open and dropped a handful of feed into the trough. The calf backed into the corner and stared.

Overhead, a bit of hay dust dropped from between the cracks. Lenore looked up. "Sly? Daisy? Why don't you come down and see me? Did Pledger remember to give you any milk while I was gone?" The cats didn't respond. "I guess it is nap time," she said, looking up at the ceiling. "I'll see you two this evening."

Lenore and her mother spent a productive afternoon in the garden picking anything that had ripened since the last time Pledger was here. Lanier took the wagon to the store to pick up more Mason jars. The first ones had all sealed except for one, and both women were pleased with this new way of putting up food.

"What all do you want me to bring back besides those glass jars?" asked Lanier.

"That's all we need," said Hannah.

"I'll be back directly, then," Lanier assured her.

"See you do," Hannah hollered after him. "Don't get into any long-winded political discussions."

"I won't. All anybody wants to jaw about anymore is whether or not they're gonna let women have the vote. Lord help us if they do!"

Hannah tossed a squash at her husband. Lanier grabbed it and put it on the seat beside him. "You got to stop throwin' produce at me, woman. People are gonna start talking."

After her daddy drove out of earshot, Lenore said, "It's gonna happen you know, Mama. We'll be able to vote come next election, just like men. Are you gonna vote, Mama? 'Cause I am."

"Let's cross that bridge when we get to it. I may be too old to vote by the time that passes. And, of course, it may not happen at all. A lot of folks are against it you know, including quite a few women — some say it goes against the teachings of the Bible."

Hannah turned back to the corn. When she'd pulled all the ripe ears, she helped Lenore with the green beans. Pledger had left enough mature ones at the end of one row for them to have a mess of white "shelly" beans for supper. Those were Lanier's favorite.

When they'd picked about half of them, Lenore asked her mother another question. "Mama, why do you think Tom didn't come to campmeeting? We invited him."

"Your daddy said his family came up this week. I imagine he's busy with them, plus his doctorin'."

"Still," said Lenore. "It looks like he could have come for one service anyway."

"Maybe he's bashful. What do you care? You haven't gone sweet on him, have you?" Hannah peered at her daughter.

Lenore thought about her answer before giving it. "Maybe I have. Would Daddy be mad if I was? He's so all-fired set on me marrying Alton Boggs. But I can tell you this, Mother — I'm through with that man."

Her mother looked up, but didn't say anything. When she reached the end of the row, she walked over to help Lenore with hers. "Your daddy only wants what's best for you. You know that. But I'll speak to him about Alton tonight if you want me to." Then she asked a question Lenore wasn't expecting. "Would you like for us to invite Dr. Garrison to supper one night?"

Lenore glanced at her mother, surprised. "Yes, Mama. I would — if you think Daddy won't mind. I don't want to upset him."

"He'll be fine. I promise." Hannah stood beside the basket and looked again at her daughter. "Have you and Alton had a fallin' out?"

Lenore emptied her apron into the basket. "No, not really. It was nothing to speak of. But I'd be grateful if you got Daddy to stop encouraging him."

Lanier still wasn't back when they finished in the garden, so they lugged the three baskets to the porch themselves. About six, Lenore headed to the barn to milk. Peeking through the stable door, she asked the calf, "Did you try any of the sweet-feed I gave you this afternoon?" When she saw it had, she decided to give it a little more.

She unlatched the feed-room door and pulled it open. The door felt heavy. When she swung it back on its hinges, it slammed against the wall with a bang. Lenore gasped when she saw what made the door feel so heavy. Someone had nailed a calf hide to the back-side planks. It hadn't been there when she'd opened the door this afternoon.

Her first thought was that Pledger had found June's calf dead somewhere. Saving the hide would make sense; it would bring a quarter at the store. The white spot on the front leg left no doubt that the hide belonged to June's calf. That's why she'd named it Snowflake.

When Lenore moved her fingers across the soft brown hair, an image of the rage she'd seen in Alton's eyes at the spring flashed through her mind. She stepped away and put her hand to her mouth. Alton said he'd been nearby that day. Could he be that mean? She remembered the sound she'd heard in the loft this afternoon and shuddered.

For a minute, Lenore panicked. Then she felt Lana's presence, her guardian. She calmly took the hide down from the door and rolled it up as tightly as she could. Inside the feed room, she grabbed a burlap sack and picked up a shovel. On the side of the barn, away from the house, she dug a hole in the soft dirt next to the building. She dug it as deep as she could and then made herself dig it deeper. She threw the sack in and covered it with dirt and manure.

From the little shed off the end of the barn, she struggled to pull out a piece of the rusty tin her daddy kept stacked there. She laid it over the spot she'd buried the hide, found two rocks and put them on top of it. Then she shoveled more dirt to cover the tin.

Her daddy must never know about this. There would be big trouble in the Valley if he found out and decided to get even with Alton.

Lenore was quiet at supper. Hannah noticed and asked, "Is something wrong, honey?"

"No. I guess I'm just tuckered out from campmeeting and all. I think I'll go to bed early tonight if that's all right with you."

"We're all tired," said her mother. "We'll get a good night's rest and get back to putting up beans in the morning."

An hour later, lying next to her husband, Hannah leaned on her elbow. "Lanier, you need to tell Alton Boggs Lenore's not interested in him. Why are you so dead set on them getting together, anyhow?"

Lanier rolled over to face his wife. "I reckon you're right, but here's the thing, Hannah; if she marries Alton, she'll stay in the Valley and live out her life here. It'll mean another generation tied to this land." He touched his wife's face. "Maybe I got no call to feel this way, but if she marries that doctor, I fear we'll lose her. He'll move off to Macon or someplace else he can make more money, and she'll go with him. We won't know our grandbabies—not in the natural way."

Hannah laid her head on Lanier's shoulder. "What will be, will be. But I've seen the way the two of them look at each other, and I'm pretty sure that's what's gonna be."

As an afterthought, she added, "Lenore wants to have him over to eat supper before long. You gonna be all right with that?"

Lanier sighed. "Aw, Hannah, if she falls for him, I won't stand in the way. But I *do* wish she'd consider Alton."

Hannah smiled at her husband. "She has, Lanier. Now she's considering this other feller."

CHAPTER TWELVE

The Broken Churn

August 15, 1919

T om pushed back from the table when he finished his first meal at the Conley home. It had been a fine one, but he was too nervous to eat much.

The young doctor had been pleasantly surprised when, last Tuesday afternoon, Lenore's daddy walked up in his yard unexpectedly. He assumed the man had come as a patient, but instead of medical advice, Lanier invited Tom over.

"My wife says we'd be tickled if you'd eat supper with us this Friday," Lanier had told him. "That is, if you don't already have other arrangements made."

Tom thought Lanier looked hopeful that other plans might indeed be in the works, but when he shook his head no, Lanier nodded and continued. "It won't be nothin' fancy," he said, "but Hannah's a good cook. So's Lenore, but I reckon you already know that."

Tom accepted the invitation, even though he, in fact, *had* planned to eat with the Hardmans that night. His mother and Aunt Emma would just have to understand.

As Lanier was about to leave, he turned to Tom. "Not that you would, but when you come over Friday, there's no need in tellin' on me about that snakebite medicine we drank over at the depot."

Just the thought of that burning whiskey made Tom touch his throat. "Don't worry. I won't bring it up if you don't." He decided not to tell Lanier how much trouble he'd gotten in over it himself.

When Lanier saw Tom's brother, Ray, walking down by the barn with Jack, he waved at him. "I forgot your brother's staying with you," he said to Tom. "He's welcome, too."

"Thanks," said Tom. "I'll invite him."

Later, when he did, Ray agreed to think about it. But, about 5 o'clock the next morning, he was standing by Tom's bed holding a railroad timetable. "Little brother," he said. "Would you give me a ride to the Nacoochee Station? The train leaves at 7:23, so we'll have to hurry."

"Why?" asked Tom, rubbing his eyes. "Are you going home?"

"No. I need to see an old Army buddy. He lives in Bogart over near Athens. He's a friend of Jack's, too."

It was still dark when they drove by the Conley house, but Lanier was already out and about, standing by his mailbox. His dog, Cornbread, was with him. Ray was in a hurry, but Tom stopped the buggy anyway. Lanier's hound barked some, but Jack didn't take it personally. Once the two dogs sniffed each other, the German shepherd yawned and lay down on the floor of the buggy.

Cornbread plopped himself by the mailbox, but kept his serious face pointed toward Jack. "He's a good hound," said Lanier, looking at his dog. He put a letter in the box and raised the metal flag on the side. "But I don't fool with him like I ought to." Lanier looked at Jack. "That's a right good-looking dog you got there," he said to Ray. "Kinda' different, though."

Ray just nodded. Since he didn't say anything, Tom did. "You're up early, Mr. Conley."

"Always am — just waitin' for daylight. Gotta' go, boys. See y'all later." Lanier and Cornbread walked away.

"Lenore's probably not up yet," said Ray, noticing Tom looking at the house. "You ought not to be calling on a girl before daylight, anyhow. Women like to be called on later in the day, and with a little advanced warning to boot."

"What do you know about women?" Tom asked.

"More'n you might think," said Ray, grinning. "Anyway, you're gonna see her tonight at supper."

"I know," said Tom clucking to Val. "Let's go."

At the depot, Ray bought a regular ticket but gave the conductor a nickel to let him ride in the baggage car with Jack.

The brothers said goodbye on the dock. "When will you be back?" Tom asked.

"Not sure. Will you make my apologies to Mother? And tell Big Mama I'm going to see Smallwood. She'll understand."

When the train pulled away, Tom drove Val the short distance to the Hardman house and parked the buggy. Jody and Josh were driving the last of the cows from the pasture across the road to the milking barn.

Standing by the kitchen, Tom smelled biscuits, sausage, and frying bacon. Ray was in such a hurry to leave they hadn't taken time to eat, and now he felt hungry. Tom walked up the steps and looked inside through the open door. Big Mama and Delia Cochran, the Hardman's cook, stood with their backs to him, cooking on the big wood stove. Uncle Isaac sat at the end of a table, eating a plate of eggs and sausages smothered in sawmill gravy. It was warm outside, but the kitchen must have been twenty degrees hotter.

"Howdy," said Tom, startling everyone. "What's a man gotta do to get something to eat around here?"

Big Mama grinned and motioned for him to come on in. "What you doin' down dis way so early? Did you smell Big Mama's biscuits all da way up to yore place? Sit down wif' Isaac, and I'll fix you a plate."

Delia looked concerned. "You sure he won't rather eat up dar wif' his mama and 'nem in da big dinin' room?"

Big Mama giggled. "Delia, has you met Tom? Dis here's my favorite chile. He always did love sneakin' off to da kitchen and eatin' wid me and Isaac ever since he was a young 'un. Ain't dat right, Tom?"

"It is," said Tom, as he walked to the table and sat down. "Food always tastes better right off the stove."

Isaac grabbed a tin plate from the cupboard, handed it to his wife and pulled up another chair. Big Mama filled the plate with eggs and bacon and sausage, spooned gravy over the eggs and put two hot biscuits on the side. Then she poured him a steaming cup of coffee. "Mr. Ray not wif' you?"

Tom blew on the coffee. "He caught the train to Gainesville a few minutes ago. He's going to visit a friend over near Athens. I believe he said his name was Smallwood."

Big Mama rubbed her chin and changed the subject. "You *do* know me and Miss Wirtha is comin' up to your place tomorrow, don't you?"

Tom shook his head no. "Well, we is. Mr. Minish gonna bring us in dat big green car. Can you see Big Mama ridin' in a Cadillac? Well, I sho nuf will be tomorrow! We goan make shore yore house is clean from top to bottom." Big Mama leaned close. "So 'iffin you got anything to hide up dar, like a jug of whiskey, you best get it gone. Break your mama's heart she find somepin' like dat in yore house."

"Big Mama, it's too hot in here for me to try to convince you again that I don't drink. That was a one-time thing, and an accident, to boot."

"Humpf," she said, going back to her cooking. Isaac grinned at him.

After he finished eating, Tom followed the three of them up the well-worn path to the big house. Each one, including Tom, carried a tray of covered dishes. On the way, Ida spoke almost apologetically to Big Mama. "Miss Emma say she gonna build a covered walkway from da kitchen all da way up to the Big House 'fore long."

Big Mama looked behind her. "Shore be nice if she do. Lot less dirt get tracked in dat way." At the house, the back porch had a side-room with its own outside entrance. Another door inside opened to the main dining area.

Alma, taking a break from the baby, held the entry door open, and they went inside to put the trays on the counter. Alma dished scrambled eggs on a tin plate and sat by herself at a small table near the end of the porch.

When Delia was satisfied the dining room table was properly set, she went to the oversized entry that opened to the foyer and rang a silver bell to announce breakfast. All of a sudden, Tom had an idea. Putting his finger against his lips, he stepped back inside the serving room and hid in the corner.

Dr. Hardman came into the dining room first and went to the far end of the table. He took his seat in front of three bay windows that reached from ceiling to floor. His well-dressed children followed; the two girls sat to his left across from their brother, his back to the fireplace.

Wirtha and Aunt Emma entered next, laughing. After Emma sat down opposite her husband, Wirtha took a seat by their son, Lamartine Jr. Once everyone was settled, Dr. Hardman announced, "You may serve now."

Tom swept through the door holding a covered dish over his head. "Yes, sir," he said, setting the platter on the table and uncovering it with great fanfare. "I've been cooking all morning, and I think you'll love what I've done with these rare turtle eggs and possum sausages."

All three children giggled, and the two girls clapped, but their father wasn't amused. Tom decided it was best if Delia took over the serving.

"What are you doing here?" asked Wirtha, laughing. "Is Ray with you?"

When Tom explained that Ray had left on the train this morning, his mother looked disappointed. "Did he say who he's going to see? Is it a someone named Smallwood?"

"That's right. I didn't ask any questions, but he said it's one of his Army buddies."

The baby cried in one of the upstairs bedrooms. Aunt Emma cocked her head to listen. "Alma," she said loudly, "will you please check on little Emma?"

Alma, come in from the porch, walked down the hall and ran up the stairs. The baby soon became quiet.

"Ray's never talked much about his time in the Army," said Wirtha to no one in particular. "But he *has* brought up this Smallwood fellow a few times. Maybe visiting him will do Ray good."

"I hope so," said Tom. "Those dreams he has are pretty bad. He didn't sleep much either of the last two nights."

Tom remembered the question he'd stopped by to ask. "Dr. Hardman, I appreciate your invitation to supper Friday, but would it be all right if we made it some other time? You see, I have another offer, and this one involves a young lady I'd hate to disappoint."

"A girl, you say?" asked Dr. Lam as he reached for another strip of bacon. "What's her name?"

"Lenore Conley."

"Ah, yes—Lanier and Hannah's child. I believe she had a mild case of poliomyelitis when she was little. Dr. Dyer didn't know what to call it at the time, of course. It wouldn't have made much difference if he had. She's a sweet girl—pretty, too. Why don't you bring her with you?"

Tom's mother listened to the exchange with interest.

"Well, sir," said Tom. "It's really her parents who invited me. I know they have everything planned and all. Maybe I can bring her another time."

"Suit yourself," said Dr. Lam. "You're the doctor. Sit and eat with us."

"No, thanks. I have to be going," said Tom, standing. "I have a woman coming to have her carbuncle lanced at ten."

"Tom!" said his mother. "People are eating." Pushing her chair back, she placed her napkin on the table. "Please excuse me, but if you don't mind, I'll see my son to his buggy."

Tom said his goodbyes, and he and his mother stepped into the hallway. This was the first time he'd seen any part of the house other than the dining room. He couldn't help looking up. The foyer felt massive—at least forty feet long with a fourteen-foot ceiling and crown molding a foot wide. Elaborate trim covered every door frame. A magnificent set of stairs led to the upper floor bedrooms and mysterious places beyond.

The tops and sides of the mahogany double-front doors were surrounded by red, etched cardinal glass. His mother saw him looking at this splendid piece of work and couldn't help admiring it herself. Tom would have looked around longer, but she took his arm and pulled him through the large back doors and into the yard. "Tell me about this girl, son. Dr. Lam mentioned she has some sort of physical defect. What is it?"

Tom hugged her. "It's nothing, Mother—barely a little limp. Besides you, she's the most beautiful woman I've ever seen."

Wirtha smiled. "Well, I can see from that look you've already made up your mind about her, so there's no need for me to say much. But you've only been up here a few weeks, Tom. I can't help being concerned. Is that really enough time to get serious about a girl?"

"I know, Mother. I promise I won't rush things. But I had *the feeling* the first time I saw her. When you meet her, Mother…well, you'll be meeting your future daughter-in-law. She doesn't know it yet, but I do."

"You say her name is Lenore? That's quite lovely. But son, in matters of the heart, it's best to take things slowly." Wirtha took his hands. "Still," she said with a sigh, "I want to tell you something, Tom. It's something I've never told you before. I *knew* I would marry your father the first time I saw him, too."

His mother squeezed his hands. "I can't explain it, but it felt like I already knew him before I ever met him." She kissed her son's hand and went back inside the house.

❧

Tom had never known a Friday to take so long to arrive. At least Thursday was kind enough to offer a diversion. Early that morning, Bob Minish drove the Hardmans' big, green Cadillac into his yard. Wirtha sat beside him with Big Mama and Uncle Isaac both grinning in the back seat.

After looking around, the two women went into a cleaning frenzy. Big Mama did most of the heavy work, but she and Tom's mother scrubbed his house and office until the rooms and furniture fairly gleamed. Isaac expanded Tom's now-crowded chicken pen and made repairs to the pasture fence before Mr. Minish picked everybody up at sundown.

Friday finally arrived. Tom didn't have any patients, so he spent the morning sawing up a tree branch that had fallen by the barn. It would make good firewood this winter.

About four, he washed up at the dry sink, dressed in his Sunday best and killed time reading last week's *Cleveland Courier*. He still left home a half hour earlier than he needed to. To idle away a few more minutes, he stopped inside the covered bridge to count the rafters — there were twenty-three on each side. Even with that, he arrived at the Conley house fifteen minutes early.

"Come on up, son," Lanier called from the porch when he saw Tom by the mailbox. "Supper's not ready yet, but we can sit a spell."

Lanier was more interested in his pipe than conversation, so Tom was relieved when Hannah hollered for them to come inside. It was a fine meal, but Tom was too focused on Lenore to pay much attention to food.

After supper, Lanier insisted Tom come out to the porch with him while Lenore and her mother washed the dishes. Hannah protested that she could use his help more than Lenore's, but Lanier didn't take the hint. "Cleaning up is woman's work," he said. "Come outside with me, Doctor."

Tom hated being away from Lenore even for the few minutes it would take her and Hannah to clean up. Still, he followed her daddy out the door. Lenore winked at him when he turned to go, and that made his face turn red. On the porch, Lanier took a seat on the top step and motioned for Tom to sit in one of the rocking chairs.

Lanier lit his pipe. "Watch out for those crocks there," he said, indicating a row of green churns lined along the edge of the porch. Each one had a cloth cover tied around its top with string. Tom imagined they were filled with green beans and corn, pickling. From the smell, he guessed at least one held sauerkraut in the early stages of fermentation.

"I'll take 'em to the cellar tomorrow," said Lanier. "We've had such a good garden we're about outta' churns to pickle in. They're out down at the store, too. Hannah's been after me to get some more, but I have to go way below Cleveland for 'em. That's why I been putting it off."

Smoke curled around Lanier's face. Inside the house, Tom heard Lenore and her mother stacking dishes. Neither man said anything else until Lenore and her mother came outside. As soon as the two women stepped on the porch, Tom jumped up. Looking at Lenore, he took a big step backwards. When he did, his leg bumped one of the crocks, knocking it over. The churn rolled off the porch and broke against a rock in the flower bed. Green beans and kernels of yellow corn splattered everywhere.

A big portion of the salty brine splashed on Lanier's overalls. "Damn, son," he said, brushing off the liquid. "Did you have some kind a fit there? Ever' time I see you, you're spillin' somethin' or other."

Hannah hurried down the steps. "Hush, Lanier. You know it's bad luck to make fun of an accident. Lenore, bring me a dishpan, and let's see if we can save some of this."

Red-faced, Tom raced down the steps behind her. "Here, let me help," he said, bumping into Hannah as he tried to scoop up a handful of beans. He stood there holding them as salty water dripped through his fingers.

When Lenore brought the dishpan out, he dropped the beans into it. "Move back," Hannah said, bumping him with her hip. "Let me and Lenore handle this. You have a seat on the porch."

Tom was too mortified to move. Why was he so clumsy around this girl?

Lanier picked a few more corn kernels off his overalls and flicked them into the yard. "Well, at least it isn't butterbeans this time." Then Lanier started laughing. So did Hannah, although she tried to hide it—at first anyway. Finally, her shoulders shook so hard she had to straighten up to keep from choking.

"I'm sorry, Dr. Garrison," she said putting her hand on his shoulder. "But the look on your face when that churn fell...well, let's just say I won't ever forget it."

Lanier and Hannah's laughter was so contagious, even Tom had to grin. After Hannah and Lenore salvaged what they could, Lenore turned to Tom. "You have to admit that was pretty funny," she said, smiling. "But I'm sorry they laughed at you."

"You laughed, too. I saw you," Tom accused with a grin.

Lenore put her hand to her face. "Maybe a little, but not as much as they did."

Tom looked at the broken churn. "I'll buy you a new one," he said to Lanier. "You said you needed more anyway. Tell me where this pottery shop is, and I'll get them for you first thing tomorrow."

Hannah glanced at Lenore. "That place is right hard to find," she said. "It's way down below Cleveland. But, if you *really* want to go for us, why don't you take Lenore along to show you the way? Would you have time, honey?"

Lenore looked at her mother before answering. When Hannah winked, she said, "Actually, I'd love to. That is, if it's all right with you, Daddy."

Lanier sat back down on the top step and rubbed the stubble on his face. "Why, Sugar Babe, she's never been..." A hard look from Hannah cut her husband off in mid-sentence. Lanier looked trapped. "Well, I don't know," he said, looking at Hannah. "A man and a girl going off on a churn-buying trip might cause talk. But we do need some new ware. And I reckon *somebody* ought to go along to make sure he don't break everything 'fore he gets back with it."

He tapped his pipe against the post. "It would save me a trip. There's a bee tree on the other side of the creek I been wantin' to find. This *would* give me a chance to look for it." Lanier breathed out more smoke. "You can take my wagon and pick up a dozen or so jugs for the store, too. They'll appreciate that, if you feel like foolin' with it. I'll put some straw in the wagon bed before you leave tomorrow."

"I'll be here first thing in the morning," said Tom.

Lanier flicked one last bean from his overalls. "Somehow, I don't doubt that one bit, son."

CHAPTER THIRTEEN

A Vase or a Pitcher

August 16, 1919

About nine-thirty the next morning, Tom rode Val up to the Conley house. He'd meant to be there earlier, but two patients showed up, even though his sign read "Closed on Saturdays." People around here didn't pay much attention to signs, he'd noticed.

Beside the house, Ole Burl stood hitched to Lanier's wagon and the bed lined a foot deep in straw, as promised. "Mornin'," Lanier said without looking up as he walked around the wagon eyeballing everything. When he was satisfied all looked in order, he came over to Val.

"I got a mighty fine day planned, thanks to you, son," he said. "I'm gonna sit by the creek and wait for a honey bee to come to water. I heard 'em swarm down there when I was plantin' corn this spring, and I've noticed 'em waterin' since. Once a bee comes to water, a man can follow him back to the tree. I think this honey will be sourwood, from all the blooms we had."

Lanier grabbed Val's bridle while Tom dismounted. "I appreciate you goin' down there for me," he said. "Otherwise, Hannah wouldn't approve of me chasing bees while she's short of picklin' churns."

"It's the least I can do after what happened last night," said Tom. "Is Lenore still coming along with me?"

"Yep," Lanier said, as he handed Tom five, one-dollar bills. "Now listen — get us three churns in the five-gallon size, and two or three four-gallon ones. They'll want some syrup jugs to sell at the store, so pick up a few of those, too." Lanier took out a stubby pencil and a scrap of paper from his overall's pocket. "Here, let me write this down for you."

He put the paper against the side of the wagon and began marking on it, squinting hard as he wrote. When he finished, he folded the list and handed it to Tom. "I didn't write it down there, but if they have any chicken drinkers, bring back one or two of those, too. If you push him, Cheever'll let you have 'em for ten-cents apiece. His brother, L.Q., will want fifteen-cents, but don't pay that. Use the rest of this money to get some pitchers and what-not for the store. You only need to pay us back for that churn you broke."

Tom didn't reach for Lanier's money because his focus was on the man's daughter. While Lanier had been giving Tom his instructions, Lenore had walked onto the porch. She was wearing a blue dress and matching bonnet.

"Here," said Lanier. "Take this money. Son, did you hear anything I said?"

"I did," said Tom, not taking his eyes off Lenore. "I'll take care of it." Tom folded the bills into his shirt pocket — not noticing he'd dropped one in the process — and walked to Lenore. He accompanied her to the wagon and helped her into the seat. When Tom had climbed up himself, Lanier handed him the dollar bill he'd dropped.

Hannah hollered from the porch, "Y'all be careful now. And have a good time."

"We will, Mama," said Lenore, waving. "Bye now." Tom slapped the reins, and Ole Burl pulled him and what Tom thought was the prettiest girl in Georgia toward Cleveland.

When they passed the Hardman farm, Tom considered inviting his mother to come along, but decided against it. The wagon ride would be too rough for her, and besides, this way, he had Lenore all to himself. Maybe they'd stop on the way back. He could introduce Lenore then.

Halfway to Cleveland, the rock cliffs near the top of Yonah Mountain came into view on their left. Tom kept Ole Burl moving, but he looked up at the mountain while he drove. "Frank Sosebee told me Yonah had some high cliffs on this side," he said to Lenore, "but I had no idea they were so huge."

"They are grand, aren't they?" said Lenore, looking up, too. "You should see them up close."

"You've been up there?"

"Yes. Quite a few times, actually. Daddy carried me up there on his shoulders when I was a little girl. That's one of the first things I remember us doing together. Mama came, too, and we had a picnic on top of Yonah." Tom thought Lenore seemed as proud of Yonah as Frank had been when he told Tom about the mountain.

"Did Frank tell you about the legend of Nacoochee and Sautee?" she asked.

"You mean the two valleys?"

"Well, about how they got their names, anyway."

"No. He didn't say anything about that, but I'd love to hear it." The truth was, he loved hearing Lenore talk about anything at all.

"Well, like I said, it is a legend. But a lot of people believe it really happened. Of course, Daddy calls the whole thing hogwash."

Tom chuckled. "He would."

Lenore smiled and continued her story. "You see, the Cherokee Indians hated the Chickasaw tribe. The Chickasaws hated them, too. But one day, the Cherokees agreed to let a few of their old enemies cross their land. The Chickasaws camped in the Valley, and that evening, some of the Cherokee went over to visit and trade. One of them was the beautiful princess, Nacoochee. Her daddy was Wahoo, the Chief. They say Nacoochee means Evening Star, but who knows, really?"

Tom gazed at the cliffs while Lenore talked. The reins lay limp in his hands. As they plodded along, Lenore continued on with her story. "A handsome Chickasaw brave named Sautee saw Nacoochee and instantly fell in love with her. Later that night, they ran up on Yonah Mountain and hid in a cave. Since he was a chief's son, and she was Wahoo's daughter, Nacoochee and Sautee thought if they got married, it might make the two tribes quit fighting each other. But Chief Wahoo got so mad, he had his braves throw Sautee off those cliffs up there. They made poor little Nacoochee watch. She was so upset she ran over to the side and jumped after him. After that, Wahoo felt so bad about what he'd done that he had them buried together in the Indian Mound, which was a great honor. Then he ordered those valleys to be named Nacoochee and Sautee. Forever."

"Wow, what a great tale," said Tom. "Do you believe it really happened?"

Lenore thought for a minute. "I'd like to. The story's been around a long time, and it's quite beautiful." Lenore stared into the distance. "Maybe," she said, "for the lucky ones anyway, there really is a love worth dying for."

"Perhaps," said Tom, smiling. "But it sounds a lot like *Romeo and Juliet* to me." Then he turned serious. "But I do believe one part of that story. I think it's possible for two people to fall in love the first time they see each other. That happened to my mother and father."

Lenore didn't answer. Instead, she went back to talking about the Indian Mound. "Dr. Hardman let some Yankees dig in the mound about four years ago. They found where people had been buried, but they didn't find any couples together. Of course, they only excavated half of it. Dr. Hardman got sick of the mess and sent those people back to New York before they finished."

"What all did they find?"

"Daddy said they found all kinds of things. Bowls, pipes, stuff like that. But they took everything with them. It's a shame, because all those things belong here in the Valley."

Lenore looked back at the cliffs until they disappeared behind them. "I never get tired of looking at those," she said, taking her bonnet off to see better.

"How far is it to Cleveland?" Tom asked when she turned around again.

"Another mile or two. The pottery shop is four miles south of there, down by Mossy Creek. So, we have a-ways to go yet."

Tom took out his gold pocket watch and looked at it. They were making good time, darn it.

When Tom turned Ole Burl into the yard of the Meaders family pottery shop, Lenore looked at the operation with interest. The whole place was designed for work and function with no consideration given to frills.

Among the old buildings leaning haphazardly around the yard was a low, brick structure with a three-foot opening in front. Pine poles and makeshift rafters held sheets of rusty tin over the top.

From its wide, brick chimney on the back, Lenore assumed this was the kiln.

She had used pitchers, bowls, and of course, churns, from this and other shops all her life. But, despite the fact that she was supposed to be Tom's guide down here, this was the first time she'd seen the source of those household items. Her mother wrote down directions to the shop last night. She'd memorized them this morning before Tom got to her house. But they'd found the place just fine, and she reckoned what he didn't know wouldn't hurt him.

A man about thirty, wearing a crumpled fedora, led a mule in a circle around a wooden cylinder filled with gray clay. A pole reached from the mule's harness to a larger post planted in the center of the mud mill.

"Are you Mr. Meaders?" asked Tom as he approached the operation.

"I'm one of 'em," the man said puffing on a homemade pipe. "But you can't hardly throw a stick around here without hitting a Meaders." He smelled of tobacco and roasted peanuts.

"I'm Cheever," the man said, dropping his hand from the mule's bridle. When he did, the animal stopped in its tracks. As Cheever walked over, he reached in his pocket and took out a handful of peanuts. He cracked one open and offered it to Tom. "That's L.Q. loadin' the wagon," he said. "And that man sittin' over there strokin' his beard is our pa, John." Cheever looked at the mule. "That's Lou, but I reckon you ain't here to meet an animal. What can I get up for you?"

"I'm Tom Garrison, and this is Lenore Conley," he said, shaking hands with Cheever and nodding to everybody else.

The older man with the long beard lifted his walking stick and waved it in Tom's direction. L.Q. was busy loading a wagon of his own, and when he'd stacked the last churn in place, he climbed into the seat. Looking at Tom, he said, "Nice to meet ya. Sorry to rush off, but I gotta finish out this load at my brothers, Wiley and Cleater's, shop and get on over to Blairsville." Waving, he drove the wagon out of the yard and onto the main road.

After watching him go, Tom turned back to Cheever. "We need to buy a few churns and things to take back to the Valley." He assumed, like everyone else in this county, the man would know which valley he meant.

"We got plenty," said Cheever, pointing to a table at the end of the longest building. Wide sawmill-cut boards stretched across two sawhorses holding at least fifty pieces of freshly-fired pottery. "I took those yonder out of the kil' this morning, so we got a right nice selection. Pick out what you need. They're five-cents a gallon — ten-cents for the smaller stuff. You need churns for pickling?"

"Yes," said Tom. "Churning, too, I guess."

Cheever nodded and took more peanuts out of his pocket. "Come on up here and let me educate you 'bout pottre', young feller." Looking at Lenore he added, "Missy, you can go inside the shop there if you want to. You'd be cooler. My wife's in there balling up clay."

The sun was hot, so Lenore decided to step inside. A woman, clearly in the family way, was pounding a ball of clay against the top of a thick table. She sliced the ball in half by pushing it down hard on a thin wire that stretched between a couple of short posts nailed to the sides of the table. Once the ball was sliced into quarters, she slapped the clay back together, rolled it around a bit and repeated the process. The woman was too absorbed in work to notice her visitor.

"Hello," said Lenore, knocking on the doorframe. "I'm Lenore Conley." When her eyes adjusted to the dark, she saw two boys in the shop, too.

"Oh, howdy," said the woman. She put down the clay and wiped her hands on her apron. "I'm Arie Meaders, Cheever's wife."

Lenore smiled when the oldest boy ran behind his mother and grinned at her from there, holding the sides of Arie's dress. "That there's John Rufus," said Arie. "He's right bashful. That's little Lanier on the floor down there getting as dirty as he can."

Patting her bulging belly, she said, "In here, we have Reggie or Margie, one or the other, but we won't know which one it is for a few days yet."

Lenore looked at the younger boy who she guessed to be about 18 months old. He sat straddle-legged on the floor, pounding his own ball of clay, in a serious imitation of his mother. She bent over in front of him, pulling the sides of her dress together to keep the bottom away from the dirt floor. "My father's name is Lanier, too," she said to the youngster, "just like yours." The boy didn't seem impressed with the information. He ignored Lenore to focus on his clay. This was the most serious-looking child Lenore had ever seen.

Arie laughed. "Be careful of that pretty dress, honey. A pottre' shop is a mess, and before long, so is anybody who comes in one. Is Lanier Conley your daddy?"

"Yes, he is. Do you know him?"

"When I see him. He bought some whiskey jugs from us last year."

When Lenore frowned, Arie added quickly, "Actually, now I think about it, seems to me he got those jugs for syrup, not whiskey."

Lenore liked this woman. "I'm fascinated by what you're doing," she said. "But it looks like you're mad at that clay."

Arie picked up the ball again. "Honey, I *stay* mad at this old clay. I'm airing some out for Cheever. You're welcome to watch, but I need to get back to work." She talked while she pounded and slapped. "See, ya divide the clay over and over. That's to work the air and grit out of it. Then you make it into a ball for the wheel."

Arie pointed to the pottery wheel in the corner below a muddy window. A makeshift seat covered in cloth sacks allowed the potter to lean, more than sit, when he worked the kick-wheel below with his leg.

"Give that-there old treadle a try," said Arie. "You have to kick that foot-bar down there to get it going, but it's right easy after that."

Lenore was tentative. "I might break something."

"Lord-a-mercy, girl, you can't hurt that wheel. Anything those Meaders boys battered around for thirty years can't *be* broke. Just kick it back and forth with your foot."

Lenore still hesitated. That was when Arie first noticed her special shoes. She put down the clay and turned around. "Law me, child. I didn't pay any attention to your leg. I'm sorry."

Lenore usually hated it when someone mentioned her leg, but for some reason, this lady's comments didn't bother her. "No. I think I *will* give it a try," she said, rolling up her sleeves. "Nothing ventured, nothing gained." She pushed the foot-pedal back and forth with her right leg, and the flat stone wheel began to turn.

"Wait a minute," said Arie. "If you're gonna go to that much trouble, you might as well put some clay on the wheel. You're gonna get dirty, though."

Arie centered one of the smaller balls of clay and showed Lenore how to cup her hands around it. "Use your thumbs to push down on the middle and start a hole." Arie splashed water from a clay container on the ball to make it slick. John Rufus tugged at his mother's dress and raised his arms. The pregnant woman lifted the boy with a grunt and held him against her hip.

Lenore thought she was making progress when the wet lump suddenly came apart in her hands. The wheel threw thick, clay-soaked water over her dress. John Rufus clapped in delight, but little Lanier never looked up.

"That's not bad for your first time," said Arie, handing Lenore a rag to wipe off her dress. "It takes a while to get the hang of it. I warned you you'd get dirty, didn't I?"

"You did," said Lenore, laughing. "It's my fault, and I normally wouldn't care, but I think he wants me to meet his mother this afternoon." She pointed with her thumb toward the sound of Tom's voice outside.

"Oh, my," said Arie. "Will you have a chance to change beforehand?"

"I'm afraid not. She's staying with the Hardmans, and their house is on the way home, so we'll stop there first."

"L.G. Hardman, the doctor?" asked Arie. "Whew me, we got to get you cleaned up, girl—best we can, anyhow."

Arie grabbed a cloth-covered pitcher from the back room. "This is our drinking water, and the cleanest cloth I got." She wet the rag, wrung it out and dabbed at the front of Lenore's dress. "This will get most of it out," she said. "But you're gonna have a wet spot, I'm afraid. Maybe it'll dry by the time y'all get back up there." Arie looked toward the door. "I take it that young man out there is your beau?"

"Can I tell you a secret?" Lenore asked, as Arie wiped at her dress. "I only met him a few days ago, but I really do believe he and I are going to get married. I know that sounds silly, but I dreamed about a man who looked just like him one night, and the next day, there he was, sitting in front of our house."

Outside, Lenore heard Tom call her name. "Lenore, I think we've got all we need. I'm ready to go whenever you are."

"I'll be right there," she hollered through the door. "I guess I better say goodbye, Mrs. Meaders. It's been nice meeting you and the boys. Thanks for letting me try my hand at the pottery wheel."

"Oh, you're welcome." Then, speaking in a confidential tone, Arie stopped her. "Wait a minute, honey." She went into the back again and came out with a small, gray vase with daisies etched on the sides. "I'd like you to have this. If you two do get married, this can be your first wedding gift. You don't have to tell anybody."

Lenore took the little piece of pottery from her. "Oh, it's lovely." She looked at it closely. "Did your husband make this?"

"No, I did, but you don't have to tell anybody that. And it's not beautiful. In fact, I couldn't decide if it was gonna be a vase or a pitcher, so I reckon it sorta' turned into both. See the little lip there? It looks funny to me."

"Well, I think it's gorgeous," said Lenore. "I'll keep flowers in it, and this lip will make it easier to pour water out. Do you make much pottery?"

"Oh, no," Arie said, shaking her head. "But sometimes I'll turn a little piece or two. Nobody knows 'bout it but Cheever. I like to decorate my pieces. That's why I put those daisies on there. Cheever thinks that's silly."

Lenore was moved. "This is the most beautiful thing I've ever seen," she said, hugging Arie. "I'll cherish it. But please let me pay you for it."

"Lord, no," said Arie. "I've not ever sold a piece in my life — probably never will, either." She turned back to the clay, laughing.

When Lenore stepped into the yard, it took a minute for her eyes to adjust. Once they did, she walked to the wagon where Tom and Cheever stood eating peanuts, dropping the hulls at their feet. The sun made the wet stain on the front of her blue dress stand out. "Did you men get your business taken care of?" she asked.

"Sure did," said Tom, pretending not to notice the wet places on her dress. "I got some pitchers, nine churns, six syrup jugs, three chicken drinkers and fifty-cents in change."

When it came to the stain on Lenore's dress, Cheever wasn't as discreet. "Lord-a-mercy, gal, did Arie try to drown you in there? Looks like you spilled half of Mossy Creek down the front of your dress."

Lenore laughed. "I just tried my hand at turning a piece of pottery," she said. "I'm not too good at it, though."

Cheever handed her a peanut. "Come back some time, and we'll teach ya how it's done," he offered. Arie came outside to wave goodbye. John Rufus was with her, but Lenore saw through the open door that Lanier was still pounding his ball of clay against the floor.

Tom noticed the vase Lenore held. "Did you buy that from Mrs. Meaders?" he asked. "What's it supposed to be, a vase or a pitcher? Looks like it could be either one."

"It can be," said Lenore, as Tom helped her onto the wagon seat. "That, plus the fact that she gave it to me, makes it special."

Lenore sat the vase on the seat between them while she tied her bonnet strings. Then she picked it up and held the prize in her lap as they headed north.

As they drove through Cleveland on the way home, Tom looked at the old courthouse built on a small hill in the middle of town. "I've never been here before today," he said, "but I'd swear I've seen another courthouse like that. I can't remember where, though."

"You probably have," said Lenore. "It's supposed to look like Independence Hall in Philadelphia. Only the war came along, and the county ran out of money before they could put the clock tower and all on top. My granddaddy helped build it."

As they rode around the red-brick building, Lenore told Tom all about it, including the fact that the bricks were made with slave labor. She waved at some old men sitting on benches by the open entrance. Tom didn't know any of them, but he waved, too.

"That's ironic," he said, as they passed the jail on the way out of town. "Only in America would a place made in the image of Independence Hall be built by the labor of slaves."

"I've always thought that, too," said Lenore as she turned in the seat to face him. "Tom, can I ask you a question? What do you think about women getting the right to vote? I think it will happen, don't you?"

"I hope so," said Tom. "My mother is a woman."

"Really?" said Lenore, looking at him sideways. "I'm glad to know we have that in common."

As he did so often, around her, Tom blushed again. "That didn't come out right," he said. "What I meant to say was my mother is one of the smartest people I know. Of course, she should vote. Either way, it's going to be decided soon. Are you going to vote if it does?"

"I certainly am."

"Good for you."

"A vote is a sacred thing," said Lenore. "You shouldn't keep sacred things from anybody. I hope Mama will vote if it becomes the law, but I'm not sure she will." Lenore looked at the vase in her hands. "Let's not talk politics. Daddy says if you talk politics or religion with your friends, before long, you won't have any friends."

"That's right," said Tom. "My daddy always said the problem with politics is that folks on both sides know so many things that aren't true." They both laughed.

About a mile from the Hardman house, Tom asked, "Would you mind if we stopped for a few minutes and had a quick visit? I'd like you to meet my mother. I'm sure you already know the Hardmans."

"Everybody knows the Hardmans," said Lenore. "But I don't know them well. We don't quite have the same social standing, you know. Still, I'd love to meet your mother, now that my dress is dry."

"Good. I want you to meet Big Mama and her husband, Isaac, too." Tom parked the wagon at the steps in front of the boxwood-lined entryway. He tied the mule to one of the metal rings anchored in a rock post and helped Lenore down. She carefully laid the vase Arie Meaders gave her in the back and pulled straw around the sides to protect it.

Wirtha and Emma were on the front porch, talking. "Mother, Aunt Emma," said Tom, as they walked up. "I have someone here I'd like you to meet."

The women turned in their rockers to look at him. "Hello, son," said his mother. "When did you start driving a wagon?"

"It belongs to someone else," said Tom. "I'm just borrowing it for the day to run an errand."

His mother and Aunt Emma leisurely moved hand-held fans in front of their faces. "We almost didn't hear you drive up, with all those cows bawling, waiting to be milked. Who's this with you?"

Tom walked Lenore up to the wide front steps that led to the porch. If the two women noticed Lenore's limp, their faces didn't show it. "This is Lenore Conley," he said. "She lives in the Sautee Valley, down below my place, in fact."

His mother and Emma kept their seats, but smiled at them. Wirtha extended her hand. "Nice to meet you, Lenore — won't you please join us?" Tom positioned two more of the rockers on the porch at right angles to the seated women. Once Lenore sat down, he did, too.

"Are y'all on an outing?" asked Emma.

"More of a business trip, really," Tom said. "We've been down to Mossy Creek to buy some churns and such. You see, I broke one of Mrs. Conley's — she's Lenore's mother — and I wanted to replace it."

Emma Hardman looked at the young woman. "I'm sure you don't remember this, Lenore, but you're one of the first people we met up here after we bought this farm. Dr. Dyer brought you down for my husband to examine your leg. I remember he said you'd been right sick sometime before."

Lenore was the one who blushed this time. She pulled her shoes close to the chair. Her leg was getting a lot of attention today. "No, ma'am, you're right. I don't remember that. I didn't realize I'd ever been here before today."

"Well, you have," said Emma. "In fact, you were lying on a cot in just about the same spot you're sitting now."

Tom noticed that Lenore seemed uneasy with all that talk about her leg. "Where are the children?" he asked Emma. "Lenore has been looking forward to meeting them. She loves children."

"I'm afraid you've come at a bad time to meet anyone but us," said his mother. "Mr. Minish took Lamartine Jr. and the girls over to Dukes Creek for a swim. The baby's taking a nap with Alma, and Dr. Lam is up at Nora Mill doing something or other. Big Mama and Uncle Isaac are here, though. They're building a new shelf down at the kitchen."

"We'll go see them before we leave," said Tom. "We can't stay but a minute anyway. I don't want Lenore's daddy out looking for us."

The four of them had only visited for a short while when Tom decided it was time to go. Lenore stood when he did, and Wirtha reached for her hand. "It's been wonderful meeting you, dear. I have a feeling we'll be seeing a lot of each other before I go home. I hope so, anyway."

"Me, too," said Lenore. "I enjoyed my time with you both." Then, remembering something, she added, "Oh, I want to show y'all the little vase Mrs. Meaders gave me."

Lenore made ready to fetch her treasure, but Tom stopped her. "Stay here, Lenore. I'll get it." He ran down the steps toward the wagon.

Lenore turned to Wirtha and touched her hand, which rested on the arm of the rocking chair. "Tom said you lost your oldest son in the war and your husband soon after. I can't imagine how hard that must be for you."

Wirtha lowered her head. "I did lose a son. But so did a lot of other mothers. I think the shock of Christopher's death killed my husband. But that doesn't make it any easier. Thank you for caring, honey."

"I didn't mean to upset you," said Lenore. "I just wanted to offer my sympathy. Tom speaks highly of his father, and his brother, too. Crick, I believe you called him?"

"That's right. When his other brother, Ray, was a baby, the closest he could come to saying Christopher was something that sounded like Crick. My husband and I thought it was cute. Somehow the name fit him better than his real one, so it stuck."

"My daddy calls me, 'Punkin,'" said Lenore. "I hope folks don't think that fits me better than my real name."

"I assure you it doesn't," Wirtha said, patting Lenore's hand.

Tom came back to the porch with the vase. He gave it to Lenore, who handed it to Wirtha. "Mrs. Meaders said this isn't very pretty," said Lenore. "But I think it is."

Wirtha looked at the vase in her hands. "It's almost like she couldn't decide what this little piece was supposed to be before she fired it. Still, it's lovely. I sense this is something you'll treasure one day."

"I already do."

Wirtha handed the vase back. Then she stood to hug Lenore. "I have a mighty good feeling about you, dear." She winked at her son over the girl's shoulder.

Tom winked back. "We've got to go now, Mother. I want to introduce Lenore to Big Mama and Isaac.

When they got to the kitchen, Big Mama came outside just as they started up the steps. "It's too hot in dis' here kitchen fer a purty woman like her," she said, shooing them back with her apron. "We'll come down dar' to say howdy."

Tom introduced Lenore and showed Big Mama the vase.

"Dat *shore* is special," she said, carefully handing it back. Turning toward the kitchen, she yelled, "Isaac, come out here and meet dis lady."

Her husband came down carrying a hammer. After they introduced him to Lenore, Big Mama pulled Tom back up the steps. "I got sompn' I wants to show you in da kitchen." When they were inside, Big Mama faced Tom. "Dis da girl you had your feelin' 'bout, ain't it? Your mama tol' me all 'bout dat. She got a face like an angel. She da one, ain't she? It's a shame 'bout that leg o' hers, though — pretty gal like that bein' crippled up. Jus' a shame!"

Big Mama peeked outside the door and shook her head. "I shore do wish your daddy could meet dat gal."

When Tom and Lenore got back to the Conley house, Lanier was in the yard, holding the ends of a feed-sack around his neck with both hands. Hannah was cutting his hair with scissors. Their clippings fell on the cloth draped over his shoulders.

"Hold still, Lanier," she scolded. "I'm almost finished."

"Well hurry up, Hannah. I'm tired of sittin' here. Let's go see what all they got back with."

Hannah made a few more snips, then pulled the cloth off Lanier's shoulders and shook it hard. They both came over to look at the pottery in the wagon. Hannah picked out three churns, and Lanier took those and two chicken drinkers up to the house. "Leave the rest in the wagon," he told Tom. "I'll take them down to the store tomorrow."

"I bought a pitcher and two drinkers for myself," said Tom. "Since I seem to be in the chicken business now, they'll come in handy." He looked at the other pieces of pottery in the wagon and then at Lanier. "Since I rode Val down here this morning, is it all right if I leave my pottery here until the next time I pass by in my buggy?"

"I figured you'd say that," said Lanier, turning to walk away. "I reckon I'll see you bright and early tomorrow morning then."

CHAPTER FOURTEEN

The Repast

September 8, 1919

O ver the next three weeks, Tom found plenty of excuses to drop by the Conley place. He'd been invited back for dinner twice and had gotten through both meals without spilling or breaking anything.

Lenore and Hannah visited him a few times, too. Once, while Tom was removing a fishhook from a boy's hand, and had two more patients waiting, Lenore started helping. "You don't have to do this, Lenore," he told her. "I can't afford a nurse."

"I'll leave, if I'm in the way," she said. "But I don't mind helping you, now that the garden's done."

Tom accepted her offer, and she'd been back every day since. Once, she even rode with him up to Batesville so he could treat a man who'd been kicked by a mule.

Tom hadn't heard from his brother, Ray, since he left for Bogart, but his mother had a letter from him last week. In it, Ray wrote that he planned to stay a while longer with his friend, Joe Smallwood. He wrote that he wasn't sure if he'd be back before his mother returned to Macon. "If I'm not," he wrote, "just leave without me. I'll come home later."

With her departure imminent, the Hardmans were having a farewell supper for Wirtha tonight, and Lenore had agreed to go with Tom to it. She'd never been inside the family's big house before and looked forward to seeing it firsthand.

Aunt Emma had said to come early, so Tom picked Lenore up at four. They pulled into the Hardmans' yard a half-hour later. Up at the barn, the afternoon milking was in full swing. Big Mama's husband, Isaac, was in the side-yard raking leaves from under one of the giant magnolias. The wrought-iron handle of the push mower Isaac had used earlier leaned against the porch steps.

"Howdy, Uncle Isaac," said Tom. "Where is everybody?"

"Dey in da house gettin' ready for supper. Nell is helpn' Delia wid da cookin'." He went back to his raking. Isaac was the only person Tom knew who used Big Mama's given name, and it always surprised Tom to hear her called Nell.

Tom and Lenore sat across from each other on the top porch step. It wasn't as hot as it had been, and the westerly breeze felt nice. The Indian Mound and its gazebo were framed perfectly between the two magnolia trees in the front yard. Beyond the mound, outlined against the sky, stood Yonah Mountain.

They didn't talk for a while — just listened to the sounds inside the house and the bawling cows. Tom stretched his arms out in front of his face and made a box with his thumbs and forefingers. He moved them back and forth and squinted like an artist viewing a scene. Suddenly, he bolted upright. "I see it, Lenore! I do! Look."

"See what?" she asked, shading her eyes and staring across the road.

"The sleeping bear — Frank told me the Indians called that mountain *Yonah* because it means *sleeping bear* in Cherokee. I haven't been able to see it until now, but it really does — see?"

Lenore looked at the mountain closely. "Where's the bear's head?"

"You can't see the head because it's tucked back against its shoulder just like a bear would sleep. The top of the mountain is its back — it's incredible!"

"When did you ever see a bear sleeping? I'm a little skeptical of your qualifications, Dr. Tom."

He loved that she occasionally called him Dr. Tom now.

"Isaac," said Lenore. "Do you see a sleeping bear when you look at Yonah Mountain? Because I don't."

Not looking up from his raking, Isaac said, "Yas'm. I seen dat bear first time I looked. Dem Indians was right 'bout dat." Isaac put down his rake and walked to the bottom of the porch steps. He looked up at Lenore. "You mind if I looks at yor shoes, Miss Lenore?"

Usually she would have tucked her feet under her dress if someone mentioned her shoes. But she didn't feel the need to do that with Isaac. Instead, she put her hands in her lap, turned toward him and extended her feet.

Isaac ran his finger around the soles of her shoes. He put his hand on the bottom of the left one and squeezed against the thick heel and outsole above it. "Dis' is good work," he said to Lenore. Then he raised his head and looked at her. "Dat leg bother you much?"

"Oh, I'm used to it. I used to be self-conscious about it when I was little, but not anymore. But I do hate these old ugly shoes." Lenore regretted her words as soon as she spoke them. "Actually, I don't know what I'd do without these shoes. Daddy goes to a lot of trouble to have two new pair made for me every year. Still, I do sometimes wonder what it would be like to wear shoes that aren't brown."

Isaac went back into the yard and picked up a few leaves he'd missed with his rake.

"Uncle Isaac is a cobbler," Tom said, feeling the need to explain the man's interest in Lenore's footwear. "He made the boots I have on. Isaac is always interested in unusual shoes."

Tom blushed again. "I didn't mean to say your shoes are unusual. I mean, they're quite common—not common in a bad way. Oh, Good Lord! Why do I get so tongue-tied around you?"

When Lenore grinned, Tom turned even redder. "You know," she said, "I don't believe I've ever seen a man blush as deeply as you do—or as often."

Thankfully, Tom's mother came out the door to his rescue. "What are you up to, son? You're red as a beet. Are you all right?"

"Yes, Mother, I'm fine. Here, have a seat." Tom stood and reached out both hands to help Lenore up. He arranged three rocking chairs so they faced each other.

When they were all seated, Wirtha asked, "Why is your face so red, son?"

Lenore laughed. "Tom's excited because he sees a bear in Yonah Mountain," she said.

When Tom explained the sleeping-bear theory to his mother, she looked at the mountain and shook her head. "I don't see it—not at all."

"Me either," said Lenore. "But Isaac does. Maybe only men can see it."

Wirtha reached over, touched Lenore's hand and winked.

Tom stopped focusing on the mountain and looked at the Indian Mound across the road. "That thing is something else," he said. "I just now noticed how its gazebo matches this house."

"That's right," said his mother. "Emma says the style is called Italianate. She and I took tea over there yesterday. It was quite nice." Wirtha looked at Lenore. "Have you ever been on the mound, dear?"

"No," said Lenore, "but I've always wanted to. It seems like a holy place to me. Did you know there were three or four other mounds in this valley until a few years ago?"

"Yes," said Wirtha. "Emma told me. She said most of them were plowed over not long after the first white people came. That's so sad." Wirtha suddenly had an idea. "Say, why don't you two have a picnic over there sometime?" She motioned in the direction of the mound. "Emma and Dr. Lam won't mind. They'll be going back to Commerce next week anyway."

"That's a fine idea, Mother," said Tom. "What do you think, Lenore? How about Saturday? I'll bring...well, I guess about all I can bring is a basket. I mean if you want to have a picnic, that is."

"That sounds good to me," said Lenore. "I've always wanted to see that mound up close — only I can't this Saturday. We're visiting Daddy's Aunt Joan and her husband, Kenneth, down in Cleveland that day. It's her birthday. But when we do go, I'll take care of the food *and* the basket. I *know* I can cook, but I'm not so sure about you."

The noise of a car rounding the bend up by the church interrupted Wirtha's amusement at Lenore's comment. "Whoever's in that car is driving way too fast," she said. "I hope they make the curve."

The driver obviously made it fine, because in a few seconds, a Model-T Ford stopped on the road in front of the house. Tom couldn't believe what he saw — it was the Dyers. He got up and ran over to the car. The top was down, so without opening the door, he reached in to give Miss India a hug, knocking her hat off in the process.

"What a surprise," he said, shaking her husband's hand. Tom looked back at the house and said loudly, "Mother, this is the doctor who sent the letter inviting me up here. This lady is his wife, Miss India."

His mother waved from her seat on the porch. "That's my mother, Wirtha Garrison," said Tom to the Dyers. I believe you know Lenore." Tom turned back to the porch. "Dr. Dyer is a legend around here, Mother."

The older man laughed. "A more modest man would argue about that," he said, waving at Wirtha. "But I reckon one can't fight the truth. India, you get out here, and I'll go park the car."

"You two are coming here?" Tom asked. "I had no idea, but I'm tickled to death if you are."

"We heard they spread a pretty good table over this way, and India has been wanting to try it," Dr. Dyer said before driving the car a little farther down the road and turning into the yard.

India Dyer put her arm in Tom's and walked with him up the wide path to the house. "Didn't David tell you that he and Dr. Hardman attended medical school together? They've been friends ever since."

"No, I didn't know that," said Tom.

"Well, we did," said Dr. Dyer, as he walked up and bowed toward Tom's mother. "He graduated when he was 19 and left me behind, but I was his broke sidekick down in Augusta for more than a year. I woulda' starved to death if it hadn't been for him, and he woulda' never got through chemistry class if it hadn't been for me."

India Dyer shook her head. "You said he was a whiz at chemistry. Are you changing your story now?

"Of course not," said her husband. "But the reason he was a whiz is because of all I taught him."

Tom chuckled. "You told me you'd never seen flatland before," he said.

"Well, I lied," said Dr. Dyer. "But remember, that was before I knew you all that well."

Just then, the doors behind him opened. "Well, speak of the devil," said Dr. Dyer, standing up as Dr. Hardman came out and held the door open for his wife. "Good to see you, David," said Dr. Lam. He hugged his long-time friend and pounded him on his back.

Emma walked around the porch, graciously offering her hand to each guest in turn. "Delia, would you please bring lemonade?"

She asked through the open door. "Does everyone have everything they need?"

When Emma felt sure her guests were all tended to, she asked Alma to bring the children out. Dr. Hardman beamed as his youngsters walked onto the porch and greeted every guest politely: Josephine and Sue with a curtsy and Lamartine Jr. with a smart handshake. Alma presented the baby by bending over to show her to each person. When the nanny stooped in front of Lenore, the baby reached out to her.

"Oh, may I please hold her?"

Alma glanced at Emma, who nodded. Lenore took the child and began rocking her. The other women exchanged approving glances.

When the children went back inside, Alma reached for the baby. "Oh, no. Please let me hold her a while longer," said Lenore. "She's precious."

Emma Hardman laughed. "She's usually fussy with anyone she doesn't know. You'll make a good mother one day."

"I hope so," said Lenore.

Dr. Lam slapped Dr. Dyer on his back again. "This is getting a little too girly for me, boys. Walk with me across the yard, and I'll show you my new play-pretty. Come on. Tom, I think you'll like this."

His new toy was a big, brown and black Jersey bull, named Manassas. The bull stood alone in a temporary pen across the road below the kitchen. It was built six feet high with thick two-by-ten oak boards. Behind him, in another enclosed area, were two smaller bulls, neither of which was as impressive as Manassas.

To see over the fence, the men stood on the bottom board. "Just look at him," said Dr. Lam. "Isn't he something? Once he gets accustomed to the place, we'll move him and those other two bulls up to the breeding pen above the barn."

Manassas moved his head up and down as he turned to face the three men who seemed about to invade his space. He pawed the ground with his foreleg, throwing dirt over his back. At the same time, he began a low, deep bellow that Tom imagined could just as easily have come from a lion. An iron nose ring made him even more imposing.

"Don't look like it would take much to piss that big boy off," said Dr. Dyer. He whistled, clearly impressed.

Tom thought this must be the fiercest-looking creature he'd ever seen. As Dr. Lam explained things like butterfat and the way something called casein coagulates into cheese, Tom studied the big animal. The hair around the bull's nose was off-white, but his head and face were black, like his underbelly and tail. Every other part of him, except his black hooves, was tan. Three-inch thick stubs of sawed-off horns jutted from both sides of his wide forehead.

"I always thought Jerseys were gentle," Tom said, when Dr. Lam finished explaining the history of the breed. "This fellow looks like he's aching to tear somebody in half."

Dr. Lam chuckled. "Jersey cows *are* the gentlest creatures you'd ever want to be around," he said. "But for some reason, the bulls are just the opposite. In fact, I'd say, pound for pound, there's nothing meaner on this planet than a Jersey bull, once he gets riled up, anyway."

"Why don't you just castrate him after he breeds a few cows?" asked Dr. Dyer jokingly. "It sure would quieten things down around here. And besides, bulls are just like people. Once the balls are gone, the brain comes back."

Dr. Lam laughed. "If I did that, he'd go from being a million-dollar bull like me, to a forty-dollar steer like you."

"Humpf," said Dr. Dyer, mumbling something under his breath. No one could hear what he said because of the bull started bellowing again while he spoke.

Dr. Lam explained how he'd just bought Manassas and those other two in the next pen from one of the top dairy farms in Wisconsin and had them shipped to the farm last week in a special railcar.

"I'd hate to tell you how much I paid for that big boy," he said, as if that were a secret. "But, I'll breed him to 100 cows and sell him at a profit in a year or two — you wait and see. It'll take a little time, but when his daughters go into production, they'll really boost my herd's productivity, not to mention butterfat."

"You always did know how to make money, Lam," said Dr. Dyer, as he climbed off the fence. "But this is about all the bull I can stand for now. When we gonna eat?"

The three men were almost back to the house when Delia rang the hand-held bell announcing dinner. A large dinner bell was mounted on a post in the yard, but the small one did the job this evening. Pledger's wife, Ida, had helped with the cooking, and because of the large group for supper, would assist Delia and Big Mama with serving the meal.

When everyone was seated, and after Dr. Hardman asked a long blessing, Ida and Big Mama brought out the platters of roast beef, chicken and pork they'd spent the afternoon cooking.

Dr. Lam sat in his usual place, with Dr. Dyer and India on his right. Tom and Lenore sat across from the Dyers. Josephine and Sue argued about which of them would sit by Lenore. Josephine, being the oldest, won the honor. Sue looked at Tom as if she thought he should give up his seat on the other side of Lenore, but he pretended not to notice.

"This is the best meal I've had since the last time we ate here," said Dr. Dyer, filling his plate. His wife looked at him hard but he didn't notice.

Most of the dinner conversation happened between the two older doctors. They reminisced about their days in medical school and about Dr. Hardman's work in the field of anesthetics. Eventually the talk turned to politics. "You plan on running for governor again, Lam?" asked Dr. Dyer. "You ought to. You'd make a fine one."

Dr. Lam beamed at the compliment. "Well, I don't know. I might. But it looks like women will get the vote, even though Georgia rejected that amendment last year. My friends in Washington say it's just a matter of time, though. Even Senator Hoke Smith thinks it'll happen. I'll have to re-think things if that passes. Because something like that will change the voting landscape pretty drastically."

"But don't you think most women will vote the same way their husbands do?" asked Dr. Dyer. "I'm sure India will, I mean, if she even votes at all."

India looked at Emma and rolled her eyes. The other women at the table glanced down at their plates and smiled.

"It's hard to say," said Dr. Hardman. "You'd think so, but what about the ones who aren't married? No, I'm afraid that if this thing happens, it'll change the country in ways we can't even imagine."

Dr. Dyer's head bobbed in agreement. "Well, Lam, you did some mighty fine work during your time in the legislature. A lot of people remember that."

"Why, thank you. I'm especially proud of helping get those dams built over at Tallulah Falls. They'll do the state good for a long time. Atlanta is already benefitting."

Beside Tom, Lenore folded her napkin and stood. "Excuse me, please. But if no one minds, I need a bit of fresh air." Tom stood too, but before Lenore got to the end of the table, someone knocked on the back door.

"Who in the world would come by unannounced at mealtime?" asked Dr. Hardman, visibly annoyed. "It must be some emergency on the farm."

"Big Mama stuck her head through the side-room door. "Miss Wirtha, you best get ready to be surprised — dat's Mr. Ray out dar." She went back into the little room and yelled out the side door, "Come on in this house, boy! Your mama and 'nem's eatin' right now. You git right on in dar and sit yosef' down."

They heard Ray open the door and say, "Sit, Jack. Stay here, boy." The big dog whined, but lay down on the porch.

"Ray, how are you doing?" asked Wirtha as she greeted him at the dining room door and kissed his cheek. "Are you coming to Macon with us?"

Before Ray answered, Big Mama burst from the side-room, again, wiping her hands on her apron and grinning. "Lawdy, Mr. Ray, ain't you a sight for sore eyes. I wuz afraid you wadn't goin' back home wif' us, but here you is!"

"Well, here I am," said Ray. "But Jack and I are gonna stay up here another week or two. We'll come back before long, but I'd like to spend some time with Tom first. We haven't had a chance to visit much."

Wirtha and Big Mama looked disappointed. Ray hugged them both, followed by Aunt Emma and the children. Then he shook hands with Dr. Lam and punched Tom on the shoulder. "Howdy, little brother. Good to see you're still ugly as ever."

"Back at you," said Tom, before introducing Ray to Dr. and Mrs. Dyer. Then he turned to Lenore. "Ray, this is Miss Lenore Conley. She's my..." Tom paused, trying to come up with a word to describe his connection to her.

"I'm his friend," said Lenore, taking Ray's hand. "It's nice to finally meet you."

Ray looked at Lenore and then at Tom. "She's all you said she is, little brother, and then some."

Tom had never seen it happen before, but this time, it was Lenore who blushed. "Have you boys been talking about me?" she asked.

Before either man answered, Aunt Emma said, "Delia, please bring another plate for Ray. Ray, darling, take the seat next to your mother." Just as everyone settled around the table again, Jack growled and ran off the porch, his claws scratching across the wood. He stopped at the edge of the rock wall, looked back toward the house and barked.

Down at the temporary bull pen, one of Ida's twins yelled, "HELP! Manassas has lit into Jody! Somebody come quick!"

Tom and Ray pushed back their chairs and dashed out of the dining room into the hall and through the back door. Everyone else followed. Jack raced ahead as the two brothers jumped off the low rock wall by the kitchen. Before they got to the pen, they saw through the boards that Manassas had Jody on the ground, pinned against the fence.

When he reached the rock wall, Dr. Dyer stopped and held up his hands. "You women take the children back to the house. We don't need a crowd over there scaring him worse."

Nodding their agreement, Emma, Wirtha and India started shooing the children in the other direction. "Ah," said Lamartine Jr, "I want to help, too!"

"There's nothing you can do, son," said his mother. "Let's go to the porch. You can see everything from there."

Each of the women and children returned except Lenore and Ida Moss. Ida had flown off the back porch screaming her son's name the instant she heard his cries. She reached the pen the same time Ray and Tom did. Lenore didn't run well, but she kept up a quick pace, walking toward them.

Before any of them got there, Josh had jumped in to help his brother. He was pounding the bull's head with his fists, yelling as loud as he could, trying to keep the bull away from Jody. Josh reached for the nose ring over and over, but Manassas kept slinging his head. The bull bellowed so loud it hurt Tom's ears. When the two in the next pen joined in, the noise became deafening.

Ray hit the fence running hard. Putting his hand on the top board, he pushed himself off, landing in the pen on both feet. Tom was about to follow, but Ray waved him off without turning around. "No! Go stand by the gate, Tom. I'll get his attention while you drag that feller out."

When the bull turned to face this new intruder, Josh pulled his unconscious brother closer to the gate. Manassas looked at Ray and snorted. Streams of drool dangling from his chin dragged across the manure-covered ground.

"If he comes toward you, grab hold of that nose ring," said Dr. Hardman, looking through the wooden boards. "Once you have that, you can control him. Be careful, Ray. Don't make any quick moves."

Tom knew Ray's dog understood a few words and phrases, but apparently "don't make any quick moves" weren't on the list, because Jack leaped at the fence. The big dog managed to get his front legs across the top board and kept scraping with his back ones until he'd propelled himself into the pen with Ray. He crouched beside him and alternated between growling and barking at the bull.

The animal moved backward, snorting and slinging globs of slobber with every step. Tom pushed the gate open and slipped through the opening to inch along the fence until he reached Josh and his unconscious brother. After they each took one of Jody's arms and pulled him through the gate, Dr. Hardman helped Dr. Dyer unbutton the boy's shirt.

"Ray," said Tom, who was still standing at the gate. "Back up towards me. Don't make a run for it, just back up, real easy-like."

"Come on, Jack," Ray whispered. He reached down to touch the snarling dog's back. "Easy boy, let's get out of here."

Manassas stood his ground but seemed calmer, at least compared to the agitated state he'd been in just minutes earlier. He'd stopped bellowing, too. The German shepherd backed up with Ray. When the man ran through the opening, so did the dog, although Jack stopped long enough to give the bull one parting bark. Tom pulled the gate shut, wrapped the chain around the post and locked it.

Just then, he noticed Lenore on the other side of the pen. She was staring at Manassas through the middle boards. Tom was about to suggest she move back when something lying just inside the fence caught his eye. It was Josh's slingshot. He reached between the bottom boards, grabbed it and slipped it inside his shirt before joining the other doctors. Lenore followed him.

"How bad is he?" Tom asked Dr. Dyer, who was listening to the wounded boy's chest.

"Not as bad as you'd expect. That soft dirt in there saved him. He's pretty banged up, but he's going to live."

Ida hugged her other son. "I tried to hep him, Mama," said Josh, crying into his mother's neck. "I tried hard. But dat bull is strong, and I never could get holt of dat ring in his nose."

"You did help him," said Dr. Hardman. "In fact, you distracted Manassas long enough to keep him from killing your brother. But how in blue blazes did this happen? You boys know better than to go in there."

Josh rubbed his face. "We fed dem bulls in the troughs just like we always do. Atter dat, Jody wanted to sit on da fence and 'mire Manassas. That's when dat rabbit's foot he totes fell out o' his pocket. When he climbed down in dar to get it, ol' Manassas lit out atter him." He turned to his mother, put his head on her shoulder and sobbed. "I aimed to help him, Mama, I really did."

When Jody started to come around, he tried to take a deep breath, but the effort made him cough. "Lordy, it hurts bad to breathe. Is Josh aw right?"

"He's fine," said Dr. Dyer. "Lay still. You're not coughing up blood, and that's good. You got a few busted ribs, but you're gonna be fine — that bull sure crawled your frame, though — he liked to killed you."

When Jody attempted to sit up, something fell out of his hand. It was his lucky rabbit's foot. "I gots my rabbit's foot back didn't I?" he said, looking at it. "I remember goin' atter it, but not what happen atter dat."

"After that, you hit a hornet's nest with a short stick," said Dr. Dyer. "That's what happened. But that rabbit's foot must work — what are the odds of three doctors sittin' a few yards away when you decide to wrestle a bull?"

Dr. Dyer looked up at his old friend. "We need to keep him flat for a while. Lam, you got anything we can carry him on?"

Dr. Hardman motioned two farm hands over. "Y'all run up to the barn and bring back one of those wide planks Bob picked up at the sawmill yesterday."

When Jody raised his head to watch them go, the effort made him moan. "Just stay flat," said Dr. Dyer. "Don't move around so much."

"Yassir," said Jody. "I'd agree wid keepin' me flat even if dere weren't no doctor here to say so. Dat bull's crazy as a Bessie bug."

The two hired hands ran back with the board and laid it in the grass beside Jody. "Help me out, Tom," said Dr. Dyer. Once they slid Jody onto the large board, Dr. Hardman motioned for the men to lift it. Before they could, Josh stepped to the front end. "Dat's my brother," he said, countering Dr. Hardman's instructions. "I'll help tote him."

Josh and a big fellow named Hill walked sideways carrying Jody toward the back porch. His mother, Ida, trudged beside them, saying, "Thank you, Jesus, thank you, Jesus," over and over.

Behind them, Tom noticed Lenore petting Jack, who licked at her fingers. "I see you've introduced Jack to Lenore," he said to Ray.

"Yeah, but I've never seen him hit it off like that with anybody else."

Tom watched Lenore and the dog for a few seconds. Then he put his arm on his brother's shoulder. "Ray, that's a brave thing you did, jumping in with that bull as mad as he was. You probably saved Jody's life."

"Hell, you were coming in, too if I hadn't stopped you, little brother. Lucky for you, I needed somebody to work the gate. There wasn't any need for both of us to get gored. Ol' Manassas ain't got much of his horns left, but there's still enough to do the job, I reckon."

Tom grinned at his brother. "Ray, would you mind walking Lenore back to the house? I'll run ahead and see if I can help."

When he got there, the older doctors had Jody lying on the grass by the rock wall. Isaac was coming out of the kitchen with a pan of water and some washrags. Jody let his mother and brother undress him down to his underwear. He'd been bruised about everywhere, and was still bleeding from a couple of cuts, but was in good spirits.

"Dat bull goan know not to chase ol' Jody Moss next he see him comin,' ain't he, Doctor?"

"Hush, Jody," said his mother. "Jus' be quiet and let da doctors look at you."

"Yeah, that-there bull was shaking in his boots when I got over there," said Dr. Dyer. "I reckon you made that bull run, all right." He looked around to see if anyone got the joke but him. If they did, no one let on. "Too bad Frank's not here," he mumbled.

Dr. Hardman took over the examination, feeling the boy's chest and arms. "I don't see anything too bad, other than three or four displaced ribs. His wrist is sprained, but it's not broken. I have some bandages upstairs, but there's not much more we can do but bind him up good and tight. Emma, have Alma fetch the bandages from my chiffarobe. They're in the bottom drawer. Bring my stethoscope, too."

Tom started to point out that he'd been taught it was best not to bind broken ribs, but decided not to go against the more experienced doctors.

After Dr. Hardman listened to Jody's chest, he stepped back to let Tom apply bandages. He patted Ida on her arm. "Your son needs rest, Ida. Why don't we let him sleep on one of those cots up on the porch tonight? I'll give him some laudanum. It's bitter as gall, but it'll make him sleep like a baby."

"No, sir," said Ida. "I 'preciates all you've done for my boy, but I gotta get him home so I can take care of 'im. I'll run to da house and get Pledger. He can bring our wagon 'round for him."

"A wagon ride will be too hard on him," said Dr. Hardman. "He could puncture a lung. No, you can't do that, at least not tonight. Tom, are you sure you pulled those bandages tight enough?"

Ida stepped between the two men before Tom could answer. "My boy's coming home wif' me, sir. Even if I has to tote him."

Emma Hardman touched her husband's arm. "Lamartine, don't get stubborn on this. She's a mama who wants her baby at home. Why don't you let Mr. Minish take him up to Bean Creek in the car?"

Dr. Hardman looked at the two other doctors. "What do y'all think?"

"You got him bandaged up pretty good," said Dr. Dyer. "I don't believe the ride would hurt him, as long as they drive slow."

"What on earth do you know about driving slow?" asked Mrs. Dyer.

"I'm the best automobile driver you ever rode with!"

Tom embraced his mother's shoulders. "I agree about taking him home. Nothing makes a man heal faster than being tended to by his mama."

Dr. Hardman pointed toward his farm manager, who'd come running from the house above the depot where he lived. "Bob, bring the car around and spread a blanket over the back seat. I want you to run him up to their place. Take the long way around. It's not as rough."

Ida hovered like a nervous hen while the three doctors helped Jody to his feet. After Minish drove the car as close to the wall as he could, Tom and Josh helped Jody to the car and laid him on a blanket covering the back seat.

When Emma Hardman opened the passenger door for Ida, the woman looked confused. "I ain't never rode in no car before. Maybe I oughta' walk home like I always do."

"No," said Emma. "Get in and ride with your son. It's fine."

Ida climbed cautiously into the seat. Emma closed the door behind her. Josh got in the back, crouching on the floorboard at his brother's feet. Minish turned the car around and headed toward Bean Creek.

The sun's last rays cast long shadows from the Cadillac as it rolled slowly up the road in front of the house. Out by the pens, one of the smaller bulls bellowed. When it stopped, the Valley was peaceful again.

"We've had quite an evening," said India Dyer. "David, we best be getting home now and let these folks get some rest."

Dr. Dyer shook his head. "No, I'm not ready yet—I barely finished my supper. Delia and Big Mama were about to bring out a blackberry cobbler before all hell broke loose. I plan to get me a bate of that before I go. I just had Miss Percole's headlights fixed, so we're good after dark."

Dr. Hardman laughed at his old friend. "David, I remember how much cobbler it takes for you to get a bate of it," he said. "I don't think Delia made that much. It looks like we're going to be here a while, so I'll call up to the mill and tell them to keep the power on. They'll shut the house lights off at 9 o'clock if I don't."

Tom let everyone go ahead of him and, to his delight, Lenore stayed back, too. "You're going to be late getting home," he said to her.

"Don't worry. I told Mama we might be. She'll take care of Daddy if he gets worried." As they moved toward the steps, Tom reached for her hand. He didn't think about it; the thing just happened.

Everyone went inside except Ray and Jack. When Dr. Dyer, who'd held the back door open for everyone, saw Ray sit down on the steps, he asked, "You not coming in, Ray? I know you didn't get to eat before."

Ray felt in his shirt pocket for his tobacco tin. "I think I'll sit out here with Jack and watch the sun go down."

"That's some dog," Dr. Dyer said, walking down the steps to sit beside him. "He was willing to die for you over there."

"I know."

Dr. Dyer patted Jack's head. "I think you must be part bulldog, big boy, the way you went after ol' Manassas. That's right, you're a bull dog, aren't you, big feller?" Jack ignored the doctor and laid his head on Ray's lap.

In the dining room, Dr. Hardman picked up the receiver of a telephone box mounted by the bay window. He turned the crank, held the receiver to his ear and spoke into the mouthpiece. "B.J.? Keep the electricity coming until ten. Yeah, that's right. No, it didn't hurt him too badly. Bob took them and Ida home in the car. Appreciate it. Thanks."

While he talked to the man at the mill, Delia served the rest of them coffee. Tom went into the side-room where Big Mama was dishing cobbler into bowls and setting them on a large tray. "Can I help?" he asked.

"Naw, I'll do it," said Big Mama. "But dat man better not ring no little bell nor holler, 'You can serve now.' Else he gonna have some blackberry juice ta clean off his shirt."

While everyone was eating, Lenore excused herself and took her own dessert outside for Ray. She needn't have bothered, though, because Big Mama had already brought him a big bowlful before she'd served anyone else.

CHAPTER FIFTEEN

War

September 9, 1919

T he next morning sun's first rays were just peeking over Lynch
   Mountain when Tom and Ray, with Jack on the floorboard,
turned onto Bean Creek Road. It was early, but Tom wanted to
check on Jody before they saw their mother and everyone off on the
train. Dr. Dyer told him last night that Pledger and Ida's house was
the one on the left across from the colored folks' Baptist church.

When they pulled up in front of the small, wood-frame home,
Pledger was in the garden gathering what looked like the last of
this year's tomatoes.

"Hello, Pledger," said Tom. "How's your son this morning?"

Pledger put down his basket and walked over to stand beside
the buggy. "He still sleepin'. He woke up 'bout four, and we give
him some more o' dat medicine Dr. Hardman sent. Ida ain't left his
side. It'd kill her ta lose another youngn'." Pledger looked up at
Ray. "Is you da man dat jumped in da pen wid' dat bull?"

When Ray nodded, Pledger extended his hand. "I's much
obliged to ya. Ain't many woulda' done it." Pledger shook his hand
a long time, his eyes never leaving Ray's face. "I reckon dat ain't da
first bull you faced down," he said before he let Ray's hand go.

Tom got out of the buggy. "Do you mind if I look in on Jody? I
won't wake him, but I want to make sure he's not running a fever."

Pledger nodded.

"Have you and your wife lost a child?" Tom asked, as they walked up on the small porch.

"Yassir, we did — our oldest boy, Howell. He got kilt in France two years back. Army man said he got blowed up wid two other colored boys taking shells outta' some field over dar. Dat was dar job — dat and digging trenches. Da man say we otta' be proud of 'em."

"I'm sorry. No one told me."

"Naw, sir. I 'spec not."

"Do you and Ida have any other children?"

"We got three girls. Dey all married. Jody and Josh is da babies."

In the bedroom at the back of the small, shotgun-style house, Ida Moss sat in a straight-back chair. She stood when Tom and her husband came in. Tom saw a little silver-framed picture of a young man in uniform on the nightstand by the bed. Ida noticed and looked at the picture herself. Then she turned her attention back to the son in her bed.

"How's he doing?" Tom whispered.

"Aw right, I recken," said Ida. "If prayin' works, he gonna be fine."

Tom felt the boy's forehead. "No fever. That's good. Let's let him sleep. When he wakes up, unwrap those bandages. Binding broken ribs tight is the way they did it in the old days, but we now know it's best to just wrap them loosely, or not at all."

Back on the porch, Tom asked Pledger, "How's Josh this morning? He seemed pretty shaken up last night."

"He fine. He got one o' his cousins ta hep' out wid' da milkin' 'til Jody's able to go back. I don't think dat'll be mor'n a day o' two."

As Tom climbed into the buggy, Pledger asked, "How much I owe you?"

"You don't owe me anything. And Dr. Dyer said you don't owe him anything either. You come get me if Jody starts feeling hot. Make sure he takes his medicine."

"Yassir. I's much obliged ta you. I'll slip a pullet in dat chicken pen next time I pass, jus' to make sure we square."

"Actually, I'd rather you take one out," said Tom, laughing.

Tom and Ray got to Nacoochee Station fifteen minutes before the train was scheduled to depart. The Hardmans were all there to see his mother off—even Bob Minish, who'd driven over with their baggage.

"Did you check on Jody this morning?" Dr. Hardman asked when they drove up.

"We did, sir," said Tom. "He doesn't have a fever. I think he'll be fine in a few days."

"Good. I don't know what got into those two."

Everyone hugged everybody else as the train from Helen came around the bend. Ray said he'd come home soon, and Tom promised to get back to Macon as soon as he could.

Jack walked up on the loading dock like he expected to get in the baggage car, but came back when he saw Ray wasn't following him. "We're not going home yet, boy," said Ray, rubbing his ears. "We will before long, though—I promise."

"You better," said Big Mama. "I's still mad at you fer not comin' 'long now."

Both boys hugged their mother. "I love you boys," she said. "You two are all I have now, so take care of yourselves. I'll write you both every week, and you better write back. That means you, too, Ray." She gave him an extra hug before she climbed into the car with the other passengers.

Big Mama and Isaac boarded last. The couple walked to the back and sat down in the back row.

A week later, after helping Preston White birth her new baby, Tom and Ray, with the big German shepherd on the buggy seat between them, rolled down Lynch Mountain Road. Tom pulled the mare up at the end of the flat bridge across Sautee Creek. Before he could set the brake, Jack jumped out and sprinted down the strip of wagon-wide grass that divided the corn from the water. In spite of the warm afternoon, steam rose from Val's back.

"Why are we stopping?" asked Ray.

"I always stop here when I'm over this way," said Tom. "I like this spot—it's the most peaceful place I know. Just look around."

The big creek poured through the Valley here. Thirsty birch trees grew along its banks and leaned toward the stream's middle to form a leafy canopy. The brothers got out and backed against the buggy's wheels watching Jack race across the grass. For no reason but the sheer joy of it, he splashed headlong into the stream, barking in appreciation of the thrill. Climbing back on the bank, he shook himself, filling the air with shimmering droplets of backlit wet.

Jack froze for a second, and then sprang toward a rabbit that bounced into the corn. He barked his annoyance at the cottontail's reluctance to play, but was unwilling to dash through dense stalks for a mere bunny.

A warm breeze dropped dozens upon dozens of yellow-tinged leaves into the water near the bridge—nature's notice that fall wasn't far away. "Jade to ginger," said Ray watching the leaves float by. Tom smiled. He knew what his brother meant. *The change from jade to ginger* is how their mother described late summer's slow transformation into autumn.

Tom hoped to persuade his brother to stay longer. Ray still seemed distant, and most every night, Tom heard him toss and mumble until Jack roused him from some dream. Tom thought a few more days in the mountains would be good for him—both of them, really. In spite of the nightmares, Tom believed Ray was beginning to win his battle against the war demons. He wasn't the happy-go-lucky brother he'd once been. That man was gone, and like Crick, he wasn't coming back.

"It won't be long 'til fall," Tom said. "Lenore tells me you've never seen anything like how the leaves paint these mountains. I'm looking forward to seeing it myself."

Ray looked at the cigarette he'd just rolled as if he was surprised to find it in his hand. He tossed it, unlit, into the water. Other than the occasional cigar, whose aroma reminded him of his father, Tom didn't approve of smoking. But nearly every soldier came back with a tobacco habit of some sort. The Bull Durham sign down at the store still hung with the company's wartime slogan: "When Our Boys Light Up, The Huns Light Out."

"Fall is nice in middle Georgia, too," said Ray. "Anyway, I've got to get back and start some kind of schooling or get a job, one or the other; can't keep playing sad soldier forever. But I might tolerate another week, if it don't take too much time from your doctoring—or your courtin'. What do you think, Jack?"

When he heard his name, the dog cocked his head and barked. "He agrees," said Ray. "I reckon we can stay a while more, but then, I got to be getting home."

They sat down on the bridge and swung their feet above the water like boys. As the stream flowed beneath them, they talked about home, the loss of their father and, of course, Crick. "I think the news about Crick killed daddy," said Tom. "He was healthy until that happened — never sick a day in his life that I remember."

"Well, he always got a pretty bad headache when Mother wanted him to go to one of those tea parties," said Ray. Both men laughed. Ray quickly turned serious again. "I hate that damn war for taking Crick," he said. "That's the worst part of it."

Ray tapped tobacco from a Prince Albert can into another rolling paper. With the subject broached, Tom did what younger brothers have done for centuries. He asked his older brother about the war. "What was it like over there, Ray?"

Tom immediately wished he could take the question back because Ray's smile vanished like he'd been slapped. The look he gave Tom made him feel like a child who'd asked an adult an inappropriate question. Flipping the still unlit cigarette into the stream, Ray glowered at his younger brother.

"You don't have the right to ask me that." Still staring at Tom, he spoke again, louder. "You may be a doctor and used to asking people private things, but you've got no right to ask me that. I don't want to talk about the damn war! Ain't it enough I have to dream about it without you wantin' me to talk about it, too?"

Tom wanted to crawl under the bridge, but he could only wither beneath his brother's glare. He didn't know what to say, but he fumbled for words anyway. "I'm sorry, Ray. I didn't mean to upset you. I didn't. But, with you and Crick going — going in my place, really, I can't help wondering what I missed. That's all." But the damage was done. The water flowing below them was the only sound. After staring at it for a while, Ray started talking again.

"What is it you want to know, Tom?" His hands trembled. "You want to know how when you put a blade in a man's belly he ain't dead unless you smell blood and shit both?" Ray ran his hands across his face. "You just smell one or the other, you gotta' stick him again. You weren't raised to know things like that! I'm trying like hell to forget I know it — and a million other things."

When Ray stood to pace back and forth behind him, Tom kept his eyes on the creek. Jack bounded back to the bridge, and the man and dog moved in lockstep. After a while, Ray sat down again. Jack laid his head on Ray's legs; brown eyes fixed on his master's face.

"I'm sorry, Tom," said Ray, stifling a sob. "I didn't mean to go off like that. I'm not mad at you. Hell, you're my brother. But I don't want to think about that damn mess. All I want to do is forget it...but I can't."

Tom touched his brother's arm. "I just wanted to know what you and Crick kept me from, Ray. That's all. I swear I'll never bring it up again."

Ray closed his eyes. "At least you have a reason to ask, little brother. Everybody else wants me to tell 'em how glorious it all was. But it wasn't glorious. It was hell. Only, men don't freeze in hell."

Ray's shoulders slumped, but his face softened some. "That time we met up on leave, Crick and I made a pact to keep you out of it. I don't know how we'd have done it, but we swore to, even if it took bribing the draft board."

Ray locked his fingers behind his head and made his elbows wave in front of his eyes. "I'm just trying so hard to not remember. The Army doctors said it takes time." Jack inched a little farther across his lap. Ray scratched the dog's ears. "I reckon Jack here is the only good thing to come out of that mess — for me, anyway."

Rising on his forelegs, Jack licked Ray's face. When the dog lay down again, Ray didn't say anything for a long time.

Tom was about to suggest they head home when Ray started talking. He didn't *want* to talk about the war, but suddenly, for some reason, he couldn't keep from it.

"I remember the smell more 'n anything," he said, staring at the rocks beneath the water. For a few seconds, Tom wasn't sure what smell his brother meant, but he didn't dare ask. The wind in the trees and the stream beneath the bridge were the only sounds until Ray spoke again. "New boys were put off by it the most. It always took 'em a day or two to quit puking."

The tone of Ray's voice kept Tom from looking at his brother. "Buckets full of shit, dead horses, and the cordite; God, I hate the smell of cordite! There were so many smells over there, Tom — all of 'em awful. If I could just forget one thing, it would be the Gawd-awful damn smell of it."

It still surprised Tom to hear his brother swear. And the truth was, he hated it. Ray seldom used profanity before he joined the Army — nobody in the Garrison family did, at least not in public. Once, their father overheard Crick say "damn" when, as a teenager, he'd missed a shot at a can the elder Garrison had put on a fence post for him to shoot. The next Sunday, at church, he made his son confess that sin in front of the whole congregation.

But civility of speech is war's first fatality. Tom knew Ray wanted to quit doing it, but right now, cursing came to him as naturally as breathing.

It seemed to Tom that his brother was in a daze. Ray stared at the water below them but kept talking. "They say eight million horses died over there. I don't doubt it; smelled like more than that."

Most of the loose tobacco Ray tapped over the cigarette paper spilled into the water, but after a few more tries, he managed to roll another. This time he lit it. "Rats were everywhere," he said, tossing the match onto the creek bank. "The bastards were as big as house cats. They'd walk across your face when you tried to sleep. Out in no man's land, if we couldn't get to the dead quick enough, they'd start eating 'em; eyes first, then the liver."

Tom winced, but Ray kept talking. "You may not believe this, Tom, but someway or other, those rats knew when either side was about to start shelling. A minute or two before it started, you couldn't see a rat anywhere. Those damn things knew! It was like the devil told 'em. I don't reckon a mortar shell ever killed a rat."

Ray stubbed his cigarette out beside his leg. "Now and then, the gas got a few rats, but that's about the only thing that did. Fritz would shoot it over in artillery shells when the wind was in their favor. 'Course we gassed them, too. That's about the only thing rats couldn't get away from. It floated down in their holes, you see. Gas is a bad way to go—even for a rat. At least we had masks."

Ray covered his face with his hands and moved them up and down. "When the damn flu hit that spring, as many men died from it as anything else. 'Course that didn't hurt the rats none."

Ray kept his hands over his face. "The trenches were trash heaps, and wet. They put planks at the bottom, but they were covered with mud, and so slick. Seems like we were always wet— and cold. A man wasn't made to live like that, but you know, Tom, you sorta' get used to that part."

He moved his hand to rest on Jack's head. "I reckon I was about done for when God sent me this feller. He sent him to remind me there was still something in the world besides killin'. You can call me crazy, Tom, but I believe in angels. They can take any form they want, you know."

His hand moved across the dog's back. "Jack here is my angel. Big Mama knew it as soon as she saw him—Mother, too, I think. It's why they let him come inside the house. I didn't even ask 'em. I'd 'a slept with him in the barn if they hadn't. When the nightmares come, Jack licks my face. It's the greatest comfort I've ever known."

Ray looked down at the dog. "This feller saved my life. It wasn't the other way around like folks think. Only, you was just a just little feller then, weren't you, boy?"

The dog's tail wagged just enough to sprinkle bits of grit into the water. Ray continued, "The day I found Jack, I'd already given up on ever making it home. We'd been at the front a week, and we'd heard it was gonna be a while before they rotated us back this time. The fightin' got pretty bad, and I reckon I had what they call shell shock. For some reason, I wasn't scared anymore. That shows how daft I was. I wanted to get dying over with and find some peace. Saying it here makes it sound crazier than it was. But that's how I felt."

Ray rolled another cigarette. "Fightin' over a damn ditch didn't make sense anymore. We didn't need their ditches; we had plenty of 'em—people killing each other over damn ditches; I got sick of it."

Jack whined and Ray stroked his head. "I told Joe Smallwood, the only other Georgia boy left in our outfit, that when they ordered us over the top again, it'd be my last time."

Ray took a deep breath. "Smallwood looked like I'd hit on something; something we should'a come up with sooner. Next time they ordered us over, we went, like we were supposed to. But this time, we didn't shoot; we just ran. I wanted them to kill me, Tom. I thought Smallwood wanted the same thing, because he stayed right beside me."

Tom kept looking down at the water as his brother talked. "I screamed at the Germans to shoot me: daring 'em; cussing 'em. 'Course they couldn't hear me—hell, I couldn't hear me! Bullets plopped in the mud around us, but none of 'em hit me or Smallwood. One boy on our left got tore in half, but we couldn't get hit—no matter how hard we tried. It got to be funny. Can you imagine laughing at a time like that? I did, though."

Ray flicked the cigarette upstream as far as he could. Both men watched it float by under their feet. "Our boys took that ditch without me or Smallwood helping much. We jumped into it—fell really — and he started pounding my back with his bloody hand, telling me to stay down. He'd got his hand cut up some on barbed wire while we were running."

Tom couldn't tell if the sound Ray made was a laugh or a sob, but either way he kept talking. "I thought I was a genius, Tom; I'd figured out how to stay alive; just *try* to die. The ones lying out there dead or screaming were the fools."

Crows flew over Tom and Ray's heads and landed in a tree farther up Sautee Creek. One stayed in the tree as a sentry when the others dropped to the corn. They cawed excitedly for several seconds, but Ray didn't notice.

"About then," he said, rolling another cigarette, "I saw something under the coat of one of the dead Germans. I thought the damn rats had started in on him, so I raised my rifle butt. I motioned for Smallwood to lift the flap. When he did, it wasn't a rat under there, Tom — it was two puppies. They weren't moving much, but they were alive. They must have been from one of the dogs the Germans kept on the line to carry messages and lay down communication wires — things like that. But there they were."

Ray looked down at Jack. "The gal pup, his sister, I guess, was too near froze to save. She died a few minutes later. Me and Smallwood bawled like babies. We cleaned this fellow up and got some canned pork in him. I kept him warm by holding him under my field jacket. About an hour before daylight, a captain came around the corner and saw Jack's head sticking out. He wasn't our captain, but I'd seen him before."

Ray took a drag from the cigarette he'd just lit. "At first, that captain grinned and reached down like he meant to pet him. But then he went back to being an officer and asked, 'Where the hell did you get a dog, Private? Knock it in the head and throw it outta here.' He walked on around the next corner — the trenches were laid out in sort of a zig-zag way — but we knew he'd be coming back."

It took a minute, but Ray composed himself. "I couldn't kill that pup, Tom. I wasn't *about* to. But here's the thing," he said, wiping his face with his hands. "The part I never told the Army doctors: You see, I decided I'd kill the captain instead of the dog. The little pup hadn't hurt nobody. He was dirty, but he couldn't help that."

When Ray spoke again, his voice cracked. "Smallwood watched me take out my knife. He knew what I was fixin' to do, and he didn't try to stop me. When we heard the captain coming back, I had my blade ready. But right before he stepped around the corner,

Smallwood handed me the dead pup. He put Jack in his coat pocket and pulled the flap over him."

Ray cuddled Jack's head. "When the captain walked back around and asked if I'd done what he ordered, I handed him the dead pup. He flung her over the sandbags and kept walking. I heard her hit on the barbed wire. It all happened so fast, he didn't notice it was a different dog."

Upstream, one of the crows, who'd been eating corn in the field, traded places with the lookout. Ray put his hands on his knees and rocked back and forth. "Look here, Tom. I *meant* to kill that son-of-a-bitch. I *would* have, too, if it weren't for Smallwood. In God's eyes, it's the same as if I did. The Bible says, 'As a man thinks in his heart, so is he.' I held a dog's life higher than a person's — maybe I still do. I don't know anymore. But I reckon that's about as bad a sin as a man can commit."

Tom looked at his brother for the first time since he'd started talking. "But you didn't kill him, Ray" he said. "You wouldn't have done that. I know you. You're a good man."

Ray pulled Jack further up on his lap with one hand and fumbled at his pocket for the makings of another cigarette with the other. "Here's the thing, Tom," he said, licking the paper. "You *don't* know me anymore. Hell, I don't know me anymore. I *would* have killed him, too, and not thought twice about it. What was one more dead man over there? Hell, I was trying to die myself."

He took one drag and tossed the cigarette into the water. Before it drifted beneath them, he'd reached for the Prince Albert can again. "Anyhow, a sniper killed that captain a couple of hours later, so it didn't make much difference, even to him."

Val looked at the two men. She snorted, shook her head and went back to grazing beside the road. Ray rolled his cigarette and continued. "Since I'd gone nuts, I thought Smallwood had, too. But he hadn't. It took me a long time to figure that out, but he wasn't running with me 'cause he wanted to die. He was trying to save me, Tom. He did, too, I reckon. How do you repay somebody for something like that?"

"I don't reckon you can," said Tom. He was struggling for something more to say when Ray started talking again.

"After that, me and Smallwood took turns hiding Jack. We put him in ammo boxes, behind sandbags — one time we even hid him under a dead man's hat. Jack never made any noise. He slept through artillery fire you'd think would wake the dead. We decided he must be deaf, but of course, he's not."

Upstream from the bridge, the crow's sentry cawed a signal, and the rest flew out of the corn and into the trees. They made a lot of noise doing it, but soon became quiet again.

"I know if the fightin' had kept up more than a day or two after we found him, Jack couldn't a lived," said Ray. "Damned lice would have killed him, if nothing else."

When Ray stood to pace again, Jack stayed beside him. "About 5 o'clock the next morning, a few big shots signed the paperwork to end the war. Armistice they called it. It would have been over by six, but some asshole noticed it was the eleventh day of November—the eleventh day of the eleventh month—probably when they signed the damned thing. So, they decided it would look good in the history books if the war stopped on the eleventh hour, too. They agreed to that, Tom! So, you see, it wasn't just me; even the generals were crazy."

Tom started to say something, but Ray kept talking. "By daylight, the *whole world* knew it was over. We heard church bells ringing. People were already celebrating, but we kept on fightin' because some damn fool decided we ought to stay at it 'til 11 o'clock. The war was *over*! It was like they figured up how many little white crosses they had left and needed more bodies to make the count come out right."

Ray pressed the heels of his hands into his eyes. "About sunup, both sides started some of the heaviest shelling I heard during the whole war—found out later, they wanted to use up the ammo before eleven so they wouldn't have to haul it off. In one place, the Germans stood up and waved our boys back, thinking they hadn't got word. They had, but we killed 'em anyway."

Ray rubbed the black hair on the back of his head over and over, but kept talking. "Three hundred men got killed taking a village so some damned general could get a bath. If the son-of-a-bitch had waited an hour, those boys could have walked right in—and he knew it. I reckon he wanted to smell good for the ceremonies. You see, he'd gone crazy, too."

He leaned back, like he was looking up at something, only his eyes were closed. "At *exactly* 11 o'clock, the war stopped. It took a minute or two, but I swear, Tom, it was like God snapped his fingers."

Ray kept his eyes closed, but for the first time since he began talking, he smiled. "That's when I first heard Jack bark. He barked that little puppy sound they make. I reckon he'd got so used to noise that quiet scared him. Smallwood whispered, 'That pup is taking credit for winning the war, Garrison. He's barking as loud as ol' Black Jack Pershing will be by tonight. You ought to call him Jack.'"

He scratched the dog's ears. "That's how it happened, wasn't it, boy? That's how ol' Jack got his name. Yes, it was."

Jack looked up, but kept his head on Ray's legs. "When it sunk in that the war was over, men on both sides started cheering. They threw their caps up and yelled like some game had finished. After a while, we walked over and shook hands with 'em. I saw a German machine-gunner take off his hat and bow like a play had just ended. Men who'd been trying hard to kill each other an hour before were passing around pictures of their girlfriends — all because a handful of bigwigs wrote their names on a paper."

Ray caressed Jack's back, unaware he was even doing it. "You may not believe this, Tom, but some of our men exchanged presents with the Germans, like it was Christmas or something — damnedest thing you ever saw."

Ray moved his hand from the dog to the tobacco tin. "When I let the pup put his head out so he could see, one of the Heinies spotted him. In a heavy German accent, he said, '*Shep pard. Ger man shep pard. You know breed?*' I shook my head and tried to tell him I was used to Blueticks and beagles, but he didn't understand. That man petted Jack and said, '*Fine dog. Smart. Hope he lives for you.*' Then he handed me a token for a pint of German beer. I don't know why I kept it, but I did. Here, you want to see it?"

Ray fumbled in his pocket and handed Tom the token, stamped with the words *Gut Fur Liter Bier* with a one-half symbol in the middle. "I kept it as a good luck charm, since he gave it to me on the last day of the war and all."

Tom looked at the coin. "Well, if you ever go back to Germany, you can buy yourself some beer." He immediately thought that must be the dumbest thing he could have said.

Ray looked at the token when Tom handed it back. Then he tossed it hard into the creek. "Damn think just reminds me of the war now."

After that, Ray told Tom how he and Smallwood hid Jack for the next few days and how they sneaked him onto the transport ship home. The big boat had plenty of hiding places, so they kept him out of sight at first, in case some other officer objected, but none did. With the war over, discipline was down a notch.

By the time they docked in New York, everybody on board knew about Jack—he was more or less their mascot. While everyone else lost weight on the rough Atlantic crossing, Jack gained three pounds.

The dog raised his head and panted as if he also had fond memories of the trip home. Ray rolled another cigarette and put the nearly empty Prince Albert tin back in his pocket. After a single puff, he dropped the cigarette into the creek. "I got to quit these damn things," he said.

Tom felt as tired as Ray looked. After a few minutes, he swung his legs back on the bridge and stood, extending his hand. Ray took it and pulled himself up. Tom wanted to hug his brother, but instead, he only looked at him.

In the trees upstream, the crows suddenly seemed in a hurry to be someplace else. They flew overhead again, and this time Ray noticed. Looking up, he asked, "Tom, did you know a group of crows is called a murder instead of a flock?"

"No, I didn't know that."

"Well, they are." Ray rubbed the back of his neck. "Some cultures believe crows are the souls of murdered men. You always see lots of them on battlefields after the fighting stops. I know that for a fact. Did you ever see a crow's court, little brother?"

Tom shook his head. "No, but I've heard of them. Big Mama used to talk about that sometimes. I thought it was just an old wives' tale."

"It's not," said Ray. "I saw one once, with Crick. It's funny how some of the strangest things that happen in this world are things only a few people get to see. Me and Crick were hunting, over in Baldwin County, and we saw a bunch of crows in a flat place on the ground. They were makin' a lot of noise, which is why we noticed 'em. Then they made a circle, and one of the crows walked in with its head sort of bowed."

Ray looked around like he half expected to see more crows here. "That ol' crow cawed for a while, but he was the only one that made a sound. Then he made a break for it, and the rest of those crows went wild. They flew after the one that took off and pecked him to death before he'd gone fifty yards. It was eerie."

Just then, Jack spotted the rabbit he'd chased earlier and dashed after it, barking. Closing in on the unwary cottontail, he was in midstride, when a gunshot shattered the quiet. The explosion vibrated the bridge. Both men recoiled.

Jack yelped, and crumpled into a heap, shaking violently. The rabbit bounded into the corn.

Shouting Jack's name, Ray jumped off the bridge and raced toward him, dropping to his knees by the dog's side. Blood poured from Jack's chest and left foreleg, and the dog thrashed in a darkening circle of matted grass. When Ray tried to cradle him, the pain-crazed animal snarled and locked his fangs on Ray's right hand, ripping away skin to expose white knuckle cartilage. Ray didn't flinch — he didn't feel it.

In the split-second before Tom sprinted after Ray, he saw a puff of smoke beside a tree across the stream. He briefly thought about running toward it, but decided to help his brother and the dog instead. In a second, he went from a stupefied brother to a doctor in charge. Ripping off his shirt, he ordered Ray to do the same. Pulling his brother's arm away, he wrapped the cloth around his bloody hand and tied the sleeves together in a knot.

Ray jerked away. "What the hell are you doing? Help Jack! Somebody's shot him for God's sake! Help him, not me!"

Kneeling behind the hurting dog, Tom wrapped Ray's shirt around Jack's jaws, forcing them shut, but keeping his nostrils clear. He used the rest of the material to press down on Jack's wound and tie it as tight as he could around him. Sliding his arms underneath Jack's shoulders, he lifted the struggling dog, nodding for Ray to help. Moving sideways in an awkward half-run, they carried Jack to the buggy. Val shied from the blood, but held her ground.

Ray climbed in, and Tom handed the bleeding dog to his brother. He jumped up beside him and showed Ray how to keep pressure on the wound. The man's blood mingled with the dog's as Tom pressed Val into a run.

He turned the buggy hard at the end of Lynch Mountain Road and urged Val faster. They galloped toward home at a dangerous pace. The dog was quiet now, but not Ray. "Oh, God," he wailed! "Who'd shoot Jack? He never hurt anybody. Don't die, Jack. I can't make it without him!"

When the buggy sped past the Conley place, Lenore and her mother saw the two shirtless men, with the dog across Ray's lap. "Something must have happened to Jack, Mama," said Lenore, putting the pails from the evening's milking on the porch. "Will you strain the milk, Mama?" she asked. "I'm going to ride up there and see if I can help."

"Of course," said her mother. "You just be careful."

"I will Mama. I'll be back when I can." Lenore ran to the barn, bridled Custer and bolted bareback after them.

As they pounded through the covered bridge, Ray's pleas became chant-like: "Our Father who art in Heaven...Our Father who art in Heaven." He repeated the words like they were the only part of the prayer that mattered—like he'd chanted them many times before.

Pulling a snorting Val up in the yard, Tom leaped out, opened the side-room door and ran back for Jack. Inside, he laid the whimpering dog on the table and ordered Ray to hold him down. As a physician, Tom worried about Ray's hand, but as his brother, he knew it was useless to bring it up until he'd done all he could for Jack. He grabbed a bottle of ether from the case, doused a medical rag with it and held it over the dog's nose until he lay still.

"How bad is it?" asked Ray, looking down at Jack.

Tom had to push his brother out of the way to get to the dog. "I'm not sure," he said, examining the animal. "I don't know what size bullet it was, but it's bigger than a .22. He's lost a lot of blood. Then again, his chest doesn't look too bad—just muscle, I think. If he'd been hit in the lungs, he'd already be dead."

Tom looked at the shattered leg bone and touched his brother's arm. "Ray, I can't save his leg."

"Just save him. I'll carry him everywhere, if I have to."

Ray didn't realize Lenore was in the room until she put her arm around his waist and rested her head against his shoulder. "How can I help?" she asked. Calm came into the room with Lenore. Even Jack's breathing seemed steadier. Her effect was dramatic.

Ray looked at his brother. "Thank you, Tom. You're going to save Jack. I know it."

Tom didn't pay him any attention. "Keep this rag by his nose," he instructed Lenore, "and try not to breathe any yourself." He handed her a washrag. "Here—hold this cloth over your face. I've never given ether to a dog before, so I don't know how much it takes. Too much might kill him."

Once he'd let Jack breathe as much ether as he dared, Tom found the main artery and tied it off as best he could—he'd deal with the smaller ones later. This wasn't that different from working on a person, he thought to himself.

He whipped soap and water together to make lather and used a straight razor to shave the dog's shoulder. With a scalpel, he cut through the tissue and tendons and removed Jack's leg. After cleaning everything with peroxide, he stitched the muscle together first, then the skin. The chest didn't need sutures.

After he finished, Tom took a deep breath. "You can take the ether rag away now," he told Lenore. "When I lift him, wrap this gauze around his chest to hold that bandage in place."

When that was done, he and Lenore laid Jack back on the table. "That's all we can do for now," he said. "At least for Jack."

Tom dropped the severed leg into a bag with the ether rag and motioned for Lenore to take it outside. He lifted his brother's hand and unwound the bloody shirt he'd wrapped around it earlier. "Ray, let me look at you now."

Ray looked at his hand as if this was the first time he'd noticed his injury. He held it out for Tom to examine. "It is beginning to throb a little," he said.

Despite deep gashes, the tendons were intact, and Tom didn't think there had been any permanent damage, although there would be scars. Tom grabbed more gauze and a bottle. "I'll clean it with peroxide, but this is going to need stitches, big brother. I'll numb it up the best I can, but you'd get a medal for this if you were still in the Army."

Ray looked at his hand. "Jack didn't mean to bite me, you know. He didn't mean to. He was just hurting so bad, he didn't know what he was doing. Don't blame him for this—either of you."

Lenore rubbed Ray's arm. "Who would do this?" he asked her. "Who could hurt my Jack?" Then he turned to stare at Tom. "When I find out who did this, I'm going kill the son-of-a-bitch! Tom, did you see anybody else back at the bridge?"

Tom shook his head. "It was likely just some boys out hunting," he said, not really believing that himself. "Jack was moving pretty fast when it happened. He may have looked like a deer from across the creek. You have to consider that it may have been an accident, Ray."

The look his brother gave Tom unnerved him. The calmness that had entered the room with Lenore was gone. "You already told me there ain't been any deer around here for twenty-five years," Ray said, "This is no accident, and you know it. Somebody did this on purpose. When I find out who—he's dead." Ray stroked Jack's side. "Looks like I'm bound to kill somebody over this dog yet."

By the time Tom stitched and re-bandaged his brother's hand, Jack was moving again. When his eyes opened, the dog looked across his bandage toward Ray, who'd never left the table, even while Tom stitched his hand. Ray put his forehead next to the dog's own and whispered. "I'm sorry, buddy. Tom couldn't save your leg, boy. But, I'm gonna take care of you, and you're gonna keep taking care of me. Just like always."

The dog lay still. "We're a fine pair, aren't we, boy?" said Ray, bending over him. "I cut my hand on some barbed wire back at the creek. That's all—just some damned old barbed wire."

Ray stayed with Jack while Tom and Lenore put an extra blanket on the dog's pallet beside the little cot in Ray's bedroom. When they came back, Tom suggested, "Let's move him while he's still groggy, Ray."

Tom reached for the dog, but Ray stopped him. "I'll do it," he said. He put his bandaged hand underneath Jack and gently lifted him. He carried his friend to the bedroom and laid him on the makeshift bed beside his cot.

When they'd made the dog as comfortable as they could, Tom put his hand on his brother's back. "You need to rest, Ray. So does Jack. I don't know if he's going to make it or not, but I've seen dogs get over worse—men, too."

"So have I," said Ray. "And I've seen 'em die from less."

Tom wanted to offer his brother something in the way of hope, but as a doctor, he had to be realistic. "Jack's young and healthy, Ray, but infection could set in, and he's lost a lot of blood. We'll have to wait to know. I'll change his bandage in the morning— yours, too." Ray sank to the floor and propped himself against the cot. He pulled his own pillow down to his lap and moved Jack's head a little until it rested on it.

Lenore stayed until dusk, sitting on the porch with Tom, listening to Ray rock back and forth, whispering that single, sing-song line: *Our Father who art in Heaven...Our Father who art in Heaven...Our Father who art in Heaven...*

CHAPTER SIXTEEN

A Dance in the Valley

September 18, 1919

Jack recovered from the leg amputation sooner than Ray's hand healed. They kept the dog in the bedroom for a while, but three days after the surgery, Ray took him outside. After that, they walked together every day — on the porch at first, then in the yard. Ray gradually increased the distance until, two weeks after the shooting, they walked all the way to the covered bridge and back — a mile altogether. The dog still hadn't mastered stairs, so Ray carried him on and off the porch.

Dr. Dyer drove over the following Sunday to check on him. He picked up Frank Sosebee at his house over by Lynch Mountain. Frank brought Jack a bone with a good bit of ham still on it, and a few biscuits.

Dr. Dyer examined the dog with Ray while Frank and Tom played chess on the porch. Frank still hadn't beaten Tom yet, but he was getting closer every time they played — at least he thought so.

"Jack will be fine," Dr. Dyer announced, after looking him over. "He may walk slower than he used to, but in a few days, he'll run better than he walks. Why, back when I was a boy, there were so many dogs missing a limb, I thought they all came with three legs and a spare."

He made Ray write down a liniment recipe for Jack. "Put four eggs in a pint of vinegar," he said, as Ray wrote. "Use the shells and all. Let that stand until the vinegar eats the eggs all up, then stir in a pint of turpentine." He assured Ray the mixture would make Jack's shoulder feel better, and Ray agreed to try it.

Because of the shooting, Tom and Lenore had postponed their picnic on the mound until now. Tom hoped to leave by eleven, but patients kept showing up all morning despite his official-looking, "The Doctor is Out" sign posted on the door. Lenore would understand — patients came first. In fact, she'd just rolled her pretty eyes when he told her he'd be there before noon, anyway.

When Tom pulled up to the Conley house at half-past two, Hannah was in the garden. Lanier's hound dog, Cornbread, walked out to greet him. He didn't bother barking at Tom anymore. An acorn fell from the tree he'd parked the buggy under and bounced off the top to roll along the ground. Another one fell on the tin roof of the house, making a noise loud enough to startle Val.

Hannah laughed when Tom put his hand over his head. "That's a sure sign fall's comin'," she said. "How are Ray and Jack?"

"Pretty good, thanks," said Tom, scratching Cornbread's ears. "Jack still has trouble climbing steps, but I'm amazed at how fast he's bouncing back." Tom tied Val and walked across the yard. "Where's Lanier today?"

Hannah put the last few ears of this year's sweet corn into the basket on her arm. "I think you mean, 'where's Lenore?' but since you asked about my husband instead of my daughter, I'll tell you. Lanier is helping Alton Boggs pull fodder. I don't pull fodder myself — makes me swimmy-headed."

She was teasing Tom by not mentioning her daughter. Finally, feeling sorry for him, she said, "Lenore's in the house putting y'all's picnic basket together. She figured you'd be late, so she didn't start on it 'til a while ago."

The sound of Alton's name irritated Tom. He hoped Hannah didn't notice. He took the basket and walked with her to the porch. On the way, he whispered, "Mrs. Conley, may I ask you a question? I can tell your husband sorta' wants, or at least wanted, Alton and Lenore to, well...I mean..."

Tom stood by the steps, but Hannah walked up them and sat in one of the porch rockers. She leaned forward and motioned for Tom to come close to the rail. "Let me tell you something," she said in a low voice. "You don't have a thing to worry about from Alton Boggs. Lanier may be interested in him, but Lenore isn't."

Before he could thank her, Lenore called from the kitchen. "Tom? Is that you out there? If it is, come give me a hand with this basket. I didn't mean to get it so heavy."

He raced up the steps and through the door. The basket *was* heavy. "Goodness gracious, Lenore. Do you think we can eat this much?"

"Oh," she said. "It's my tea cakes that make it weigh so much. They're not as light as Mama's."

Outside, Hannah looked at the sky. "I don't suppose you two would consider putting this picnic off a day or two, would you? It looks to me like it might rain."

Tom looked up, too. "Oh, it's just a few passing clouds," he said. "I don't think it'll do more than come up a drizzle. Even if it does, the gazebo has a roof."

"All right—suit yourself. I reckon you're both smart enough to keep dry. But I want you to take my old umbrella anyway. Stay here, I'll get it." Hannah ran into the house and came back with a black umbrella that she handed to Lenore. "Don't lose it, honey. It's the only one we have."

"I won't. Bye, Mama, we'll be back before dark."

"You better be. Else your daddy'll have a conniption. Don't hurry too much, though—I'll milk for you tonight."

Down the road, they passed the cornfield where Lanier, Alton, and a few other men, were stripping leaves from the brown stalks and tying them in bundles. Lanier waved. Alton glared and kept working.

As they drove alongside the Nacoochee Valley toward the Hardman farm, the clouds thickened a bit, but Tom didn't notice. Lenore did, but didn't say anything.

At the farm, they turned left on the little lane between Dr. Hardman's cornfield and the big pasture. The closer they got to the mound, the larger it loomed. Tom parked the buggy and helped Lenore down. When he picked up the basket, he grunted. "I still can't get over how heavy this is," he said.

When they reached the base, Lenore looked up at the grass-covered hill. "I've always wanted to come over here and see this mound up close," she said. "But this is the first time I've had the chance. Thank you for giving it to me."

"I'm glad I could," said Tom. "This old thing is a lot bigger than it looks from the road. It's higher, too, isn't it?"

"It sure is." Lenore was fascinated. She'd seen this knoll a thousand times, but never like this; never close up. Steps covered with thick planks led up the south side — the side closest to the river. There was even a little handrail, but Lenore seemed reluctant to use them.

"Is something wrong?" asked Tom, thinking the steps might be too much for her leg.

She put her hand to her chest. "No. It's just that this feels like a *holy* place — like the Indians are still here — like you can feel them dancing. This whole valley seems sacred from here."

"I feel it, too," said Tom. "Did they use this place for dancing?"

"I believe so. There's another mound east of here that people call the dancing ground, but I'm sure they danced on this one, too."

Tom looked up. "Frank told me the Indians kept a fire burning up there. Wouldn't *that* have been something to see?"

Lenore nodded. "Daddy says this is where the chief's house was. And since Dr. Hardman let those Yankees dig in it, we know they buried people here, too. It seems like we shouldn't go up there — like it might not be right."

"Well," said Tom. "If the Indians danced up there for hundreds of years, I don't see any harm in us having one little picnic, do you?"

Lenore still hesitated. "I guess not, as long as we treat it with respect."

Tom went up first, balancing the basket in front of him with his left hand. He reached back for Lenore with the other. The mound's top was surprisingly flat. And like the hill itself, the gazebo was larger than it seemed from the road. Four arched entryways faced all four directions with matching window-like openings between each one. At its apex, a decorated lightning rod pointed skyward like the tip of a spear. Everything except the wooden shingles was painted white. The meticulous detail of the woodwork fascinated Tom.

"How long has this been up here?" he asked, as he stood in the grass, running his fingers over one of the carved patterns on the side. "Did Dr. Hardman build it?"

"No, a man named Nichols put it up here shortly after the War Between the States. Daddy says, back when he was a boy, Mr. Nichols had a garden here on top."

They stepped through one of the openings and up onto the gazebo's wooden floor. There was a small table with four chairs in the middle. Bench seats lined the short walls below the window-like openings.

"Looks like there are plenty of places to sit," said Tom. He put the basket down on one of the seats along the wall. "This is astounding," he said, taking in the sight. "Aunt Emma said there'd be a breeze, but she didn't mention the view."

"I had no idea you could see so much," said Lenore. "You almost can see the whole valley. And look at Yonah Mountain and the river!"

Tom looked at the ancient hill to the south. Suddenly Lenore gasped. "Tom! I can see it!"

"See what?"

"I can see how the mountain looks like a bear from here! You and Isaac were right—the Indians, too."

Tom reached for her hand. The wide valley of Nacoochee stretched before them, its foreground dotted with cows. Below her, acres of corn trembled in the warm breeze that blew across the mound like the very breath of God.

"It's more beautiful than I imagined," she said. "No wonder the Indians danced up here." She pointed to the east. "Over there is the Sautee Valley. The Indians lived there, too, but this is the valley where they danced."

Tom moved to stand behind her and circle Lenore's waist with his arms. "You're right about this being a special place," he whispered. "And I'm right about you being the most beautiful woman I've ever seen."

Lenore pulled away playfully. "Oh, goodness gracious, Dr. Tom, I bet you say that to all the girls. I'm hungry. Don't you want to see what I fixed us to eat?"

Tom's cheeks flamed again. "Sure."

As if his red face reminded her of something, Lenore opened the basket and took out an even redder tablecloth. When she unfolded it, Tom saw it was wrapped around the little vase Arie Meaders had given her. She spread the cloth over the table and placed the vase in the middle. Then she took out a box camera.

"I promised Mama I'd take a picture from up here with Daddy's new camera. Let's do that first." She held the black camera at waist level and aimed it toward the river. Looking down at the viewfinder, she said, "This doesn't look as nice through the camera." She pushed the shutter lever down. "But, at least Mama can see how it all looks from here, even if it will be in black and white. Aren't you glad we can see in color, Tom? How else could I see how cute you look when your face turns red?" she teased him.

Tom just nodded and blushed again.

Lenore put the camera back in the basket and looked at the table. "Tom, on the way up, I saw some black-eyed Susans growing at the bottom of the mound. Why don't you run down and pick a few for a centerpiece? Anyway, Mama says a man's just in the way when a woman's setting a table."

When he came back with the flowers, Lenore had the table set elaborately. Slices of sugar-cured ham, field peas, corn on the cob and biscuits lay in a large china serving dish. Knives, forks and spoons rested in perfect order atop cloth napkins. Cups filled with water stood beside two plates on either side of the table.

"This looks wonderful," said Tom, handing her the flowers. "No wonder that basket was so heavy. Where did you get water?"

"There is a spigot over there. It must connect to the spring over at the house. I let it run for a while, so it's nice and cold." Lenore fiddled with the flowers in the vase. "Setting a formal table is one of the things they taught us girls at the Nacoochee Institute. Miss McAfee says it's never complete without flowers."

She looked over her handiwork and seemed pleased. "This is the first time I've had a chance to set a really nice table, except for practice. So, let's eat."

Tom thought this was the best meal he'd ever had. Overhead, the clouds lowered more, but inside the gazebo, neither of them paid attention. Instead, they talked. She told him about life in the Valley. He told her about growing up outside Macon and of some of his experiences in medical school.

"Did you always want to be a doctor?" she asked.

Tom folded his napkin carefully and laid it beside his plate. "It wasn't so much that I *wanted* to be one," he said. "It's just...when I turned six, on my birthday actually, I *knew* I was going to be one. It came to me as a feeling. It's hard to explain. Anyway, I've always liked helping people."

"I do, too — especially children."

For some reason, Tom felt a strong need to tell Lenore about this thing he called *the feeling*. The urge to do it was overwhelming, so he decided to break the ice. "Can I tell you something, Lenore? Something I've only told two other people?"

"Of course. I'd be honored if you shared a secret with me."

Tom took a deep breath. "Sometimes, I know things I shouldn't know."

Lenore tilted her head. "How do you mean?"

Tom leaned toward her and placed his elbows on the table. "To tell the truth, it's hard to explain. But I knew my brother had died over in France two days before the telegram came. There have been other things, too. I've known about them just as surely as if someone told me."

Lenore reached across the table and took his hand. "Maybe someone did. Maybe your guardian angel told you."

Tom looked over the pasture at the herd of cows moving as one toward the road. "Do you believe in angels, Lenore?"

Lenore didn't hesitate. "Yes," she said, "I do. And since you told me your secret, I'll tell you mine. I have a guardian angel. In fact, if you promise not to laugh, I'll tell you something even bigger."

"I won't laugh," said Tom. "You didn't laugh at me."

"Well," said Lenore looking down at the table. "I've *seen* my angel—several times, in fact. I even know her name. It's Lana."

Tom looked around the gazebo. "Is she here now?"

"I'm sure she is. But I can't see her. I haven't been able to do that since I was 5. The first time she appeared to me, I was 3 and burning up with fever. Suddenly, the most beautiful creature I'd ever seen was standing beside my mother. My eyes were closed, yet I could see everything. She didn't exactly *tell* me anything, because we could talk to each other without speaking. That's how I knew her name was Lana."

Tom was fascinated. "Lana is the name you mentioned that day your cow, June, had her calf, wasn't it? What did she say to you?"

Lenore gazed over the flat stretch of ground in front of them. Across the way, two men opened the gate so Dr. Hardman's cows could cross the road and walk single-file down the lane to the milking barn. Then she looked back at Tom. "Lana said for me not to be afraid—she said I wasn't going to die, which is what I thought was happening. She said even when I do, death isn't something I should fear. She said I was loved and to look around me. When I did, I could see the love she was talking about. Isn't that funny—that you can actually see love? It was like a liquid light pouring from the middles of Mama and Daddy and Granny and Paw-Paw Chambers, too. It all flowed toward me, and Lana was that same color."

Tom leaned back in his chair. "Lenore," he said, "I believe every word you just said. Am I the first person you've told about this?"

"No, but you and Mama are the only two who ever believed me—that is, if you really do. I tried to tell Jenny one time, but she said I was just hallucinating from the fever. The other children laughed at me, so after that, I kept Lana to myself—except for Mama, and now you." Lenore took a sip of water and put the cup back on the table. "When was the last time you had that feeling you get? What was it about?"

Tom got up and walked to the edge of the gazebo facing Yonah Mountain. Then he turned around. "Why did you ask me that?"

"No reason. I'm just curious. But you don't have to tell me if you don't want to. I know how personal something like that can be."

Tom sat again. "It's not that. It's...I'm afraid if I tell you, you'll think I'm...well, I don't know what you'll think about me, Lenore."

"I won't think you're crazy, if that's what you're worried about, no matter what you say. I promise."

Tom took a deep breath before he spoke. "All right, then. Here goes. The last time I had this thing I call *the feeling* was the first time I saw you—the day Dr. Dyer and Frank brought me over to the Valley. It was when you came out on the porch with your mother and daddy."

"I remember that very well," she said, looking into his face. "It was the day after I dreamed about you."

Tom was startled. "You dreamed about me? When?"

"It was before I ever saw you, Tom—the night before. I can't explain it, but it happened. I'll admit I *did* know a new doctor would be coming to the Valley, so that might explain part of it. But in my dream, you had on the exact same clothes. You were even sitting in Dr. Dyer's buggy. You looked the same in person as you did in my dream. You even waved the same way. That's why I stared at you so long—because I'd already seen you before I ever met you."

Once again, Tom didn't know what to say, so he just watched the cows. He didn't say anything until Lenore asked the question he knew she would.

"All right, I've told you about my dream. Now it's your turn. What did your special feeling tell you the last time it came to you? Did it have anything to do with me?"

Tom looked at her. "Yes, it did. But I don't think I should tell you what."

"Why not?"

"It might make you mad."

"But I promise I won't be mad, no matter what you say."

Tom pulled her hands to his face and held them there. "When I saw you for the first time, I knew you were going to be my wife. I knew it as surely as I've known anything in my life. Now don't you think I'm crazy?"

Lenore dropped her hands to her side. She didn't say anything, and for a few seconds, Tom thought she was about to laugh. Thankfully, she didn't.

"No, Tom. I don't think you're crazy, because, in my dream, you were my husband."

He didn't know what to say. He reached for this woman he suddenly needed to hold. "Did you just propose to me?" he asked before he kissed her.

A minute later, when she could breathe again, Lenore said, "I was about to ask you the same thing. Maybe we just proposed to each other at the same time. Would you mind kissing me again, Dr. Tom?"

He hugged her tighter. "The truth is, I've been thinking about proposing to you since the day we met," he said, granting her request for another kiss. "But I haven't even spoken to your father about it. That part isn't as much fun to daydream about. In fact, I'm not sure he approves of me — not as a son-in-law, anyway."

Lenore smiled at him. "Well, you might not be his *first* choice. But you're mine. You're Mama's, too, so he'll come around. And Daddy *does* like you. It's just too bad you don't have any bottomland."

"Then there's the matter of the ring," said Tom, not understanding her comment about bottomland. "I imagined I'd get down on one knee and present it to you. I've gone over it so many times in my mind. This isn't how I'd planned it at all."

"Well, I always imagined that if a man ever proposed to me, it would be after he'd said he loved me. I don't recall you ever saying that, Dr. Tom."

Tom pulled her to him. "You know I love you, Lenore. I love you so much I forgot to say it, that's all. I love you so much I feel it pouring out of me the way your angel showed you love can do. Saying it seems such a small thing compared to how I feel it."

"Say it anyway."

"I love you, Lenore."

"I love you, too, Tom."

As if she'd suddenly had an idea, Lenore reached over to the vase and took out one of the black-eyed Susans. "Pretend this is a ten-carat diamond ring."

Tom took the flower, dropped to one knee and looked up at her. "Miss Lenore Conley, would you please do me the honor of becoming my wife?" He plucked one of the yellow petals from the flower she'd handed him and wrapped it around her finger. She held it in place with her other hand.

"Yes, Tom Garrison, I would indeed, but there is a condition."

He looked perplexed. "What is it?"

"As much as I'd love to marry you right now, we have to wait at least a year. We can't even tell anyone we're engaged for a while. We'll know it, but for now, we have to keep it a secret."

"Why?"

"That's just how we do things up here. People will talk if we move too fast, and I'd never do anything to hurt my parents. And you *will* need to ask Daddy for my hand in marriage. He'll expect that."

"All right. But how long do we have to wait?"

Lenore looked across the Valley. "As far as I'm concerned, today is as perfect as one gets. Let's get married one year from now, September eighteenth of next year and make this day a part of our anniversary, too. What do you think?"

Tom rubbed his forehead hard. "But Lenore, we don't even know what day of the week this date will be next year. Won't that matter?"

"Not to me. We'll get married on whatever day this date falls on. Why should it matter?"

Tom sighed. "That's fine with me if that's what you want." Tom kissed her hand. "But, I can't believe you won't tell your mother you're betrothed. You tell her everything."

Lenore laughed. "All right. Let's say we both get to tell one person. But it has to be someone we trust to keep a secret. And, yes, Mama is the one I'll tell. Who will you choose?"

He considered her question before he answered. "Ray. I'll tell Ray. Maybe it will cheer him up."

Lenore smiled her agreement and laid her head against his arm. Tom put his hand on her back. "Didn't you say something about dancing a while ago? I've never felt more like dancing in my life than I do right now."

Lenore hesitated. "I've never danced before," she admitted, looking down at her shoes. "I don't know how."

"I'll show you," Tom reassured her. "Besides, *anyone* can dance up here." And so, on the giant mound where hundreds of ancients performed the ritual before she was ever born, Lenore danced for the first time in her life. Then, as if nature decided this occasion called for an accompaniment, it began to rain.

The rain wasn't heavy at first, but it didn't let up all afternoon. Neither of them was anxious to leave, but two hours later, when it turned into a downpour with no signs of letting up, Tom finally, reluctantly, made a dash to retrieve the umbrella from the buggy. Although he held it over Lenore's head as best he could, her dress was more wet than dry by the time she got inside. Tom was soaked.

"I don't think daddy's camera got wet enough to hurt it," she said, as Tom laid the picnic basket in the buggy and ran around to his side. "I wrapped it in the tablecloth and put the platter over it."

Looking across the seat at the man she was now totally in love with, she added, "I can't say the same for you, though. In fact, I believe you're the wettest man I've ever seen."

"Have you ever been kissed by a wet man before?" he asked, pulling her to him.

"Until today, I'd never been kissed by a dry one. Let's see how wet feels."

A half hour later, they slogged up the muddy road towards the Sautee Valley.

෴

At the Conley house, Tom walked Lenore to the door as fast as he could. He made another gallant, but mostly useless attempt to hold the umbrella over her head. Hannah opened the screen door and motioned him inside, but Tom stayed on the porch.

"I'm dripping wet, Mrs. Conley. I better not come in right now. I need to get Val in the dry, too."

"I told you it was going to rain," said Hannah, laughing. "Don't look to me like it's gonna fair off 'fore mornin'. You best run on home and get out of those wet clothes before you catch your death of something or other I can't pronounce."

Tom wasn't ready to leave. But Lenore came back to the door and touched a raindrop on the end of his nose. "You heard Mama. Now go on. I'll see you tomorrow."

He looked at Lenore for a second, then smiled and dashed through the rain toward the buggy. On the way, he jumped in the air and clicked his heels together — it wasn't hard at all this time.

Inside the house, Hannah looked at Lenore. "There's something different about you, daughter. Care to tell me what it is?"

"Is Daddy home?"

"No, he's not. He never came back from Alton's fodder-pulling party this morning. I suspect he went to the store and got caught in all this rain."

Lenore took both of her mother's hands in hers and looked at her. "Mama, if I tell you something, will you promise not to let Daddy or anyone else in on it — at least not right now?

"I'll keep the cat in the bag if that's what you want, honey."

"Mother, Tom and I are engaged. This is the best day of my life."

"Go change clothes, Honey. Then come back and tell me everything."

After Tom put Val in the barn, he gave the mare a quick rubdown. He tossed her some hay and checked to make sure she had water. Then he raced through the pouring rain to the house. Inside, Ray was at the kitchen table, writing a letter by lantern light. Jack lay in his customary place at Ray's feet. "Wet enough for you, little brother?" he asked without looking up.

"Is it raining?" asked Tom. "I didn't notice."

That made Ray look up. Tom pulled over a chair and sat down across from his brother, dripping water on the table and the letter Ray was composing. The rain started pounding the tin roof so hard it was difficult to hear, so Tom spoke loudly. "Ray, I've just had the best day of my life. I'm in love with Lenore, and I don't care who knows it. I only get to tell one person this, Ray, and I want it to be you. And Ray, you can't tell another soul — not even Mother. You promise?"

Ray nodded.

"Lenore and I are getting married! The wedding is one year from today, only she doesn't want anybody to know about it yet, on account of folks thinking we're moving too fast. And Ray, I want you to stand up for me at the wedding. Will you?"

Ray nodded again.

Tom couldn't quit talking. "Lenore laid out the most fantastic meal you've ever seen. She even put a little vase of black-eyed Susans on the table."

Jack got up, moved a few feet away and lay back down. Tom kept talking. "I didn't have a ring, Ray, so I used a petal from one of the black-eyed Susans we found to put on her finger instead."

Tom leaned back in his chair and clasped his hands behind his head. "Then we danced, Ray. We danced in the same place the Indians danced. Of course, we didn't dance like they did; ours was more of a waltz. But Ray, it was magical, absolutely magical."

The rain didn't let up until Sunday morning's daybreak. Tom lay in that netherworld between sleep and consciousness, not wanting to wake. Had the picnic with Lenore been a dream? Even after he was fully awake, he couldn't believe Lenore had agreed to marry him. He went over the picnic on the mound in his mind again and again. Once he convinced himself it really had happened, he lay still, remembering the taste of her.

As he lingered in bed with his thoughts, he sensed that something wasn't right. Neither of his two roosters had crowed this morning. Plus, he didn't hear the hens cackling and clucking as they scratched for any corn they'd missed yesterday.

He pulled his pants and boots on and went out the back door. Something didn't feel right. A few steps from the chicken pen, he rubbed his eyes, not believing what they were showing him. Inside, their lifeless brown feathers soaked from last night's rain, were twenty-three dead chickens, each one with its neck wrung.

Tom ran back to the house and into Ray's bedroom. "Ray, wake up," he said, shaking his brother's shoulder. Jack growled as he struggled to rise on his one front leg.

"Ray, come outside—and hurry!"

"Give me a minute, little brother. I'll be right there."

Tom waited on Ray at the porch steps, staring at the chicken pen. He paced back and forth, running his hands through his hair. When Ray came out with Jack, Tom pointed to the enclosure.

"Damn, little brother," Ray said. "Something killed all your chickens. Reckon it was a fox?"

"It wasn't a fox, Ray. A fox would have snatched one and headed for the woods. A human did this. I just can't imagine who, can you?"

"Or why," said Ray. "Who'd be that sorry?" He motioned for Jack to lie down, and the dog complied, staying on the porch while the brothers walked to the pen and looked through the chicken wire.

"I didn't get back 'til late last night," said Tom. "It was nearly dark when I put Val in the barn, and raining so hard I didn't even look up this way when I came to the house. How could this have happened with you and Jack here? I know he would have barked at all the commotion this must have caused."

Ray curled his fingers around the chicken wire and looked inside the pen. "It must have been when we walked down to the covered bridge yesterday. We got there right before the bottom fell out and got stuck. A one-legged fellow and his sister got stranded with us, and we got to talking. The rain never did let up, so they gave us a ride back up here. This must have happened then."

"Was the man's name Odell Stovall?"

"Yeah. Nice feller. His sister's husband got killed in the war. Turns out, me and him were in the same unit over in France. You know Odell?"

"I've met him."

"You don't think he did this, do you?"

"It would be pretty hard for a one-legged man to kill this many chickens."

Ray scratched his head. "Jack gets shot, and now your chickens are dead. I think somebody may not like us, little brother. You reckon it has anything to do with you courtin' Lenore?"

CHAPTER SEVENTEEN

Happy Holiday

November 13, 1919

Tom's reputation as a reliable doctor spread fast. By the time the first frost came in late October, people from as far away as Cleveland were regular patients. Even a few sawmill men preferred Tom to that doctor the lumber company kept on staff. If you counted June's calf, he'd already delivered four of the Valley's newest babies.

The chicken pen was full again. The afternoon following that mysterious slaughter, Pledger Moss had stopped by. He was carrying two dominecker hens and a red rooster by their legs as payment for Jody's treatment after the bull attack.

Tom showed him what had happened to his other chickens and asked, "Who do you think did this, Pledger?" The colored man went inside the pen, dropped the chickens he'd brought and picked up one of the dead roosters. "Can't say," he said, examining the lifeless bird. "A body'd have to be mean as a snake ta do dis."

Tom nodded in agreement. "I'd appreciate it you don't say anything about this. Let's give whoever did it a little rope and see if they hang themselves with it. Besides, I don't want word out that strange things are happening at the new doctor's place. No need to get the community upset."

Pledger helped Tom bury the dead chickens down by the barn. When they finished, he turned to Tom and said, "I appreciates all

you done for my boys da other day over at da Hardman place —
bof' of 'em."

"That's my job," said Tom, looking at the three new chickens in
the pen. "But, I only treated Jody. Anyway, there's no charge for
that. You're overpaying me by bringing three chickens. That's too
many."

Pledger shook his head. "Nawsir, the rooster's for the doctorin'
you done. Dem two pullets is for you not tellin' nobody 'bout dat
flip you found in da bull pen."

Tom grinned. "It looked to me like those two were in enough
trouble without me opening up another can of worms."

Pledger nodded. "Josh seen you get it," he said. "He thought
you wuz gonna tell on him. When Jody went in after his rabbit foot,
Josh shot ol' Manassas in his cod sack. Dat da reason he tore into
Jody like he done."

"I figured it was something like that," said Tom. "Here, hold on
a minute." He walked to the house and came back with the
slingshot. "You can decide if he gets this back or not," he told
Pledger, who put the homemade flip in his back pocket.

"Dey good boys, Dr. Garrison. But I reckon dey still boys. And
dat cod sack do make a mighty temptin' target for a young'un."

That afternoon, Tom bought five hens down at the store. There
were enough in the pen now that neither Lenore, nor anyone else
ever noticed anything had happened to the others.

Fall in the mountains was even more spectacular than Tom had
hoped. The leaves turned and twisted in more vibrant hues than he
could imagine before dropping to the ground like tiny ghosts.

Folks in the Valley were busy with quilting parties, corn
shuckings and cider presses. The smell of cane syrup cooking off at
Telford Nix's syrup mill came through Tom's windows for a dozen
days. He missed the aroma when it finally faded.

Thanksgiving was a fortnight away, and Tom had decided not
to go back to Macon for the holiday. Instead, he would stay in the
Valley. His decision was easier to make once he learned Ray
planned to stay with his friend in Bogart, and that his mother
wanted to spend the holiday in Valdosta. Tom couldn't imagine her
being anywhere but home that day, but she said she needed to
reconnect with friends back in her hometown.

"This is something I want to do for myself," was her only explanation. Tom decided not to argue with her. He guessed she probably didn't want to sit down to Thanksgiving dinner at the family table without her husband and all three sons—at least not yet.

The Hardmans spent Thanksgiving in Commerce, so Tom hoped he'd get an offer to have the meal at Lenore's house. He'd had several invites from various patients. The Dyers and even Frank Sosebee's family had invited him, too, but he was holding out for the one he hoped would come from the Conleys.

Lenore hinted it would happen, but so far it hadn't. She was sympathetic to Tom's concern but kept telling him to just be patient. "I'm working on it, darling. So is Mama," was all she'd say about it. On the Tuesday before the holiday, Lanier rode up on Custer as Tom finished removing a splinter from the eye of one of the sawmill men.

"Howdy, Lanier," Tom said, walking up to Custer and stroking his neck.

Lanier looked down at him without dismounting. "You sure you ain't a drinkin' man? 'Cause I'm always a little jubus of a man that won't drink with me. You and me'd get along better if ya did."

"I'm afraid I can't help you there," said Tom, grinning. "I reckon I wasn't cut out for strong drink."

"That's too bad," said Lanier, grinning back. "'Cause this would be a mighty good time for a snort."

Tom shook his head.

"Listen here," said Lanier. "It looks to me like I'm not gonna be welcome at home anymore if I don't invite you to supper Thursday. But before I do, I want to ask you a question."

"Certainly. Go ahead."

Lanier stared at Tom. "Is there something going on I need to know about, young feller? 'Cause the women in my house sure do act like there is."

Tom didn't know what to say so he just put out his hand. "Sir, I reckon I should have asked before now, but if you don't mind, I'd like to ask you for permission to court your daughter. I should have done it sooner. I'm sorry I haven't."

Lanier looked at Tom's hand but didn't take it right away. "I assure you my intentions are honorable," said Tom, not moving his hand away. When Lanier finally shook it, he gripped it harder than

Tom thought necessary. "If I didn't think that, son, I sure as hell wouldn't be askin' you to take Thanksgiving with us. As far as my permission, I reckon you did get around to it — finally."

Lanier headed Custer toward the road. "See you Thursday, Dr. Tom," he yelled back. "And, no, you don't have to bring nothin'. Lenore says you're not much of a cook anyhow."

That Thanksgiving at the Conley home was one he'd never forget. The food was good, but all he could recall about it later was Lenore's face.

It was the first big holiday of his life he hadn't spent around the family table at home in Clinton. Even while he'd been in medical school, he'd always made it back for the harvest feast Big Mama laid out every year.

Over the following weeks, Tom treated patients, visited Lenore's family as much as he felt proper and agonized over where to spend Christmas. He felt obligated to go home, and hoped to convince Lenore to come with him, but she refused. In fact, she wouldn't even discuss it anymore.

"As much as I'd like to go with you, Tom, I can't leave my parents at Christmas," she'd told him over and over. "Besides, Daddy would never approve of such a thing — he'd think it was scandalous."

So, five days before the big holiday, Tom left the Valley without her.

CHAPTER EIGHTEEN

Christmas

December 24, 1919

Well, Lenore thought to herself, at least it *smells* like Christmas. The aroma of ham baking in the woodstove, along with sweet potatoes and her mother's wheat biscuits, filled the house. It was a Conley family tradition to do all the cooking on the eve of the big day. They'd have a light dinner, a big meal for supper tonight, and eat leftovers on Christmas Day.

As it did every Christmas, the little manger scene her Granddaddy Chambers carved out of white pine fifty years ago, graced the kitchen table. But this was the first Christmastime Lenore could remember when she didn't feel festive—joyous even. The problem was, Tom wasn't here. He left for Macon last Friday and had now been gone five days. She stared at the coals in the fireplace and wondered if he missed her as much as she missed him.

"Hand me that dishrag, Honey," her mother said, walking to the stove. "I'm gonna open the oven door, and you can help me with the glaze. I think this ham is gonna be a good one."

Lenore was glad her daddy didn't keep hogs the way most people in the Valley did. Instead, he helped enough people out at hog-killing time every fall to earn a ham or two. Hannah bartered enough butter and eggs to get all the sausage and lard they needed without them having to put up with the awful smell of a pig pen.

She lathered the pork with the liquid her mother made from melted butter and some of the sourwood honey her daddy robbed from the bee tree last fall. "It sure does smell like it, Mama," she said. "Do you want me to start making the cornbread?"

"Yes, dear, if you don't mind. I'll put the lard in the pan and get it hot." Lenore's mother closed the heavy oven door and looked at her dejected daughter. "Honey, he's coming back in two days. I wish you wouldn't be so sad."

"I can't help it, Mama. I miss him."

"I know darlin', but you can't blame him for wanting to spend his last Christmas as a single man with his family. They weren't together at Thanksgiving, you remember. And he did invite you to come with him."

"I know. But Daddy would'a had a fit if I had. Besides, I couldn't leave home this time of year." Lenore looked at her mother. "I guess I just pictured this being the time when Tom and I tell Daddy about us being engaged, that's all. I know I'm being childish."

"No, you're not, baby; you're lovesick. Remember, it doesn't matter when you tell your daddy. You've already set the wedding date. That's not gonna change."

"I suppose so, Mama." Lenore gathered up the china plates they put out only twice a year — Thanksgiving and Christmas, and arranged them on the table. Some pieces had been used three times this year, though, counting the picnic she and Tom had on the Indian Mound. She'd been surprised back in September when her mother suggested she take two of the plates, her best platter and some silverware, on that excursion.

"Well," said Lenore, "when we *do* tell him, you better act surprised. I don't want to hurt Daddy's feelings about you knowing it first. Tom is going to tell his folks in Macon this week, so we'll have to let Daddy in on it pretty soon. Where is he this morning?"

"He went down to split the widow Boggs some firewood. Alton left her all by herself to go visit his brother. Can you believe that?"

"Let's not talk about Alton, Mother."

"I agree. Let's talk about your wedding." Before they could say much, they heard Lanier's boots clumping up the back steps. "Ay Gawd, it's cold out there," he said, coming through the door with an armload of firewood. He dumped it in the box by the stove, blew into his fists and took off his denim jacket. "A man can't even keep warm splittin' wood on a day like this." Lanier lifted the lid of a pot on the stove and peeked under it. Steam nearly burned his hand.

"Leave my arsh taters alone," said Hannah. "Sit down here and let me pour you a cup of coffee. How is Evelyn?"

"'Bout as cheerful as ever. I declare, that woman enjoys ill health moren' anybody I ever saw."

"She's got a lot on her," said Hannah. "I think we ought to invite her over for dinner tomorrow. I hate the thought of her spending the day all by herself. Alton sure don't think much of her — going off to Asheville at Christmas like he done."

Lanier reached for one of the cookies in the platter Hannah had just put on the table. "I don't think she'll come," he said, munching on the cookie. "I told you she's ailing."

"What's wrong with her?" asked Hannah.

"She didn't say, and I didn't ask. She looks like she's fell off some, though. I's afraid it might be one of them woman things, and I didn't want to get blessed out again." Lanier reached for another cookie. "She gets down in the mouth ever' Christmas, if you remember."

"Well, the least you can do is run a plate down to her tomorrow," said Hannah. "You can see how she feels then."

"All right, but I can already tell ya she ain't gonna come." He watched his daughter stir an egg into the cornmeal. "What's wrong, Punkin?" he asked her. "You look about as low as the widow Boggs does. Ain't you lookin' forward to caroling with the church choir tonight?"

"I'm fine, Daddy," said Lenore, pouring the batter into the pan.

Her mother stepped in front of her. "Leave her be," Hannah said to Lanier. "Make yourself useful and put some wood in the stove for me."

❧

They'd just finished supper when someone knocked on the front door. "Who in tarnation can that be?" asked Lanier, pushing his chair back. "It's too early for carolers."

He walked down the hall and opened the door. Tom Garrison stood on the porch holding two small boxes and one larger one, all wrapped in colorful paper and tied with ribbons.

"What are you doing here?" asked Lanier. "I didn't think you were gettin' back 'til Saturday."

"I changed my plans," said Tom. "We decided to celebrate Christmas early so I could come back up and see if anyone needed me. It was actually Mother's idea."

"Well, come on in the house, son. You're lettin' a draft in."

Lenore and Hannah came down the hall together. "Tom!" said Lenore, rushing to him. "What a surprise. Here, let me take those packages. I'll just put these over here under the tree with the rest."

"Don't get too excited. Your birthday is still a week away," he teased. "Those aren't all for you."

Hannah hugged Tom. "Merry Christmas," she said. "Let me take your coat. Lanier and I were about to clear the table. Have you eaten yet?"

"Yes, I ate over in Clarkesville with the Dyers. Mrs. Dyer insisted. I've been traveling since yesterday. I picked up Val at the livery stable and drove over here. I haven't even been home yet."

"Well, we're sure glad you came by," said Hannah. "Lanier, come to the kitchen and give me a hand."

"I'm fixin' to sit a spell with Tom," said Lanier, pulling up a chair. "You and Lenore do that while me and Tom get caught up."

"Lanier Conley! You come with me right this minute."

Lanier knew better than to argue with his wife once she addressed him by his first *and* last name, so he followed her down the hall. "Sorry, Tom," he said, as he walked away. "I reckon we'll have to catch up later."

As soon as her parents were out of sight, Lenore hugged Tom. "Thank you for coming home early — Lord, I missed you. I don't think I could have stood it another day!"

"Me, either, darling. I was in such a hurry to see you, I was almost rude to the Dyers."

"I can't imagine you being rude to anyone, especially them." She kissed him. "Merry Christmas, darling. I want to tell Daddy we're engaged today. We can't wait any longer. Mama's promised to act surprised when we do."

"But I haven't even asked him for your hand yet," said Tom, looking worried. "Don't you think I should do that first?"

Lenore backed away and smiled. "Daddy," she shouted. "Come back out here. I'll help Mama with the dishes while you and Tom visit."

Lanier walked down the hall mumbling, "I swear, I wish you women would make up your minds where you want me." He backed against the wall to let Lenore pass, came into the front room and flopped down on the sofa with a grunt. "Sit down, son, but throw some wood on the fire first. Why'd you decide to come back early? Nobody sick, I hope."

Tom put two sticks of wood in the fireplace and sat in the chair across from Lanier, the window at his back. The flames cracked and licked at their new fuel. "No one is sick that I know of," said Tom. He rubbed his hands together. "Sure is cold, isn't it? I thought I was going to freeze to death on the way over."

Lanier lit his pipe. Hannah only let him smoke in the house when it was too cold to go outside. Surely today would qualify.

Tom cleared his throat. "To tell you the truth, I moped around so much, I reckon Mother got tired of it. Also, it's hard to feel like celebrating much without Daddy and Crick being there."

Tom took a deep breath. He might as well get this over with. "Sir, why I came back was... well, the truth is...you see, the real reason I came back is to ask you for your daughter's hand in marriage."

Something in the fireplace hissed. Something else popped, and a glowing piece of wood landed on the hearth. Lanier glanced at it. Then he took his pipe out of his mouth and looked at it. He tapped it on the end table once and put the stem back between his teeth.

"You say you took dinner with the Dyers?"

"What?" Tom asked, surprised.

"The Dyers — you said you ate with them. How they doing?"

"Fine, I guess. Their daughter and son-in-law came up yesterday with the grandchildren. They're spending Christmas with them."

"Good," said Lanier. "It's good to have grandchildren around. Too bad theirs live so far off. If I ever have grandchildren, I hope they live right close by."

"The Dyers' grandchildren just live down in Atlanta," said Tom, wondering if Lanier had heard his original question. "That's only a few hours by train."

Lanier took out his pipe and studied it some more. "Mind if I tell you a story, son?" He didn't wait for Tom's answer before starting it. "A few years back...it don't seem like that long, but I reckon it has been, something happened I never got over."

Lanier motioned toward the rear of the house. "In that back room yonder, about sun-up one New Year's morning, Dr. Dyer handed me a baby girl. She was twenty minutes old. I always figured if I was somebody's pa, they'd be right ugly. But she was the prettiest thing I'd ever seen. And all she's done is get prettier."

Tom nodded his agreement. "You're right about that, sir. Lenore is beautiful." Lanier acted as if he didn't hear him. Instead, he pointed toward the mantle over the fireplace. "Look up yonder on the fireboard," said Lanier. "See that drawing of Lenore when she was a baby? Alton's brother, Charles, drew that back when he was just a boy — way back before he moved off."

"It's beautiful," said Tom looking at the little framed drawing of a grinning, curly-haired Lenore. "He was quite an artist."

Lanier nodded. "When I first held that young'un, it was the most powerful thing I've ever known. When she got to be three, we nearly lost her."

This time Tom nodded. He wasn't sure if he should speak, so he decided not to.

Lanier got up to put another stick of wood on the fire as if the ones Tom added a minute earlier somehow weren't doing the job. Then he sat back down. "I want to tell you something, son," he said, leaning forward. "The morning I held that girl for the first time, I bawled. I don't know why. It was the happiest I'd ever been, but I did, just like a baby."

Lanier looked out the window at the smoke coming from the Sosebee house over at the foot of Lynch Mountain a half-mile away. After a minute, he stood again and this time, Tom felt compelled to stand with him. The two men faced each other until Lanier put out his hand. "You wadden' my first choice, Tom, but I reckon you'll do."

Lanier laid his pipe upright in an ashtray and turned toward the hall. "Hannah! Come out here and meet your new son-in-law. And for Gawd's sake, don't you even *pretend* you're surprised by it."

A heavy frost lay the next morning, and Tom's breath came white as he rode Val through the covered bridge. It was 11 o'clock, and the morning had dawned cold, but clear. He'd tied a little sprig of holly to the top of Val's bridle, and it bobbed up and down in front of him as he rode along.

He rubbed the mare's neck. "It's Christmas, Val. And by tonight, Lenore will be wearing this." He felt in his coat pocket to make sure the ring box was still there. His mother had helped him pick it out earlier in the week at a Macon jewelry store. "I'm delighted for you, son," she'd said when he told her he planned to marry Lenore next September. "The two of you fit. I never thought my youngest would be the first to marry, but life is unpredictable."

Big Mama responded more heartily. "Lawd-a-mercy, chile! I knowed it was gonna happen. Why didn't you bring her wif' you? I want to hug her bad, but now she too far off."

When Tom rode up to Lenore's house, he decided it was too cold to leave Val outside, so he tied her in the hall of their barn before walking to the porch. Lenore met him at the door. "Merry Christmas," she said, hugging him. "Come in here before you freeze."

Inside, the fire blazed. Tom handed his coat to Lenore. "Wait a minute," he said. "Let me get something out of my pocket first. How was caroling last night?"

"Cold!" said Lenore, laughing. "But we had fun. "We made it to five houses. Olvia Lothridge seemed to appreciate our singing more than anybody. We sang six songs for her. It must be sad being alone at Christmas."

Tom walked to the fireplace and turned his back to it. "If your singing didn't cheer her up, she can't be cheered," he said to Lenore, who had followed him over. "Where are your parents?"

"Daddy went to take a plate to Mrs. Boggs. Mama's in the back getting ready. Why? Do you plan on kissing me again?"

He pulled her close. "I might. But I'd like to do something else first." Tom picked up the little box that held the engagement ring.

Lenore looked at it, then took a step backward.

"Don't you want to see it?" Tom asked.

"Not yet," said Lenore. "Come sit with me over here."

Together, they sat beside the fireplace in two chairs that faced each other. Tom scooted his chair close enough that their knees touched. He placed the wrapped box in her hands.

Lenore took the wrapping off and folded the paper. After she put it on the floor beside her chair, she opened the box. The diamond was small, but it sparkled as bright as her eyes in the firelight. She admired it for a minute, and Tom thought it was strange that she didn't put it on. Instead, she stood and handed it back to him.

"Don't you like it?" Tom asked, hoping she wasn't disappointed with his selection.

"It's beautiful," said Lenore. "But not as beautiful as that flower petal you gave me once."

Tom smiled at her. "I'm afraid black-eyed Susans are out of season now," he said. "You'll just have to make do with this ring."

"Put it on me, please, Dr. Tom." She held out her hand, and he slipped the ring onto her finger. Lenore admired it for a while, then sat down in his lap, put both her arms around his neck and kissed him for a long time.

After dinner, once Hannah and Lanier admired Lenore's new ring, they all retired to the front room to open presents. Tom gave Hannah a cameo brooch. His present to Lanier was a new pipe from the tobacco shop his father had admired so much in Macon. They gave Tom a new shirt that was from all three of them but, as Hannah pointed out repeatedly, hand-made by her daughter.

When there was only one box left to open, Tom handed it to Lenore. "This one is for you. It's from Uncle Isaac, but he had my mother wrap it."

Lenore removed the ribbon and took off the wrapping paper, folding it carefully before opening the box. When she looked inside, she pressed both hands to her chest. "Oh, my gracious," she said, reaching into the box.

"What is it, darling?" asked her mother.

"It's shoes, Mama. It's the prettiest pair of white shoes I've ever seen."

CHAPTER NINETEEN

A Leg To Stand On

April 12, 1920

L anier spoke to Ole Burl regularly as he trudged behind him in the soft dirt the plow turned up. "Haw, mule, gee...gee...haw back now." He stopped the mule in the shade at the end of the field, laid the plow on its side and looped the plow lines around the handle. Spring had come to the Valley.

Lanier loved the smell of freshly turned land and took in a deep breath of it through his nose. "Let's rest a spell, Burl. I see Lenore coming with my dinner." He reached under a bush and pulled out the metal foot tub he'd put there this morning. He drank from the clay jug filled with water he'd placed under the bucket to keep cool, or at least cooler than it would be in the sun.

He carried the bucket down to Sautee Creek a few yards away and dipped it in the stream. After slipping Ole Burl's bridle off to let it dangle around the mule's neck, he held the bucket up for him to drink. Ole Burl drank all it held, slurping the last bit at the bottom.

Lanier turned the tub upside down and sat on it while he watched his daughter come across the field toward him. Walking on freshly plowed dirt made Lenore's limp more pronounced than usual. Lanier's hound dog, Cornbread, plodded beside her.

"Howdy, Daddy," Lenore said from a few yards away. "Mama sent your dinner." The four-pound lard bucket Lenore carried held two warm sweet potatoes and a wedge of cornbread. There was also a quart of buttermilk in a Mason jar.

"Thank you, Punkin. Sit with me a spell." Lanier scratched the old dog's ears after it flopped down beside him.

Lenore rubbed Ole Burl's face. "All right, Daddy, but only for a minute. Mama wants us to get the rest of the beans planted before supper. Tom's coming over, you know."

Lanier drank some of the buttermilk and crumbled the cornbread into the rest. "I still don't think these new glass jars are safe," he said. "Did you bring me a spoon?"

"There's one under that napkin in the pail. And glass jars are perfectly safe, Daddy. You just have to be careful not to break them."

Lanier was about to tell her how he'd heard about a whole family dying from getting glass in their food, when they heard an automobile driving by. Dr. Dyer honked and waved as he flew past.

"He's going up to Tom's," said Lenore. "That pretend leg he got for Odell came yesterday, all the way from England. Dr. Dyer's going to take it to him in a little while."

"I bet it cost a pretty penny," said Lanier. "Surely Odell couldn't come up with enough money for somethin' like that."

"He didn't, Daddy. Tom's the one who got it all put together, but Dr. Hardman paid for it. They don't want Odell to know that, though. So don't tell on 'em."

"I won't." Lanier broke the skin of a sweet potato with his thumbs, turned it inside out and took a bite. "Odell's probably too dern stubborn to take it. That boy don't think much of your future husband you know."

Lenore shrugged. "That's why Tom asked Dr. Dyer to take the new leg over to Odell and help him learn to walk with it. Tom knows Odell wouldn't take it from him."

Her daddy rubbed the stubble on his chin. "Punkin, why don't you flag Dr. Dyer down on his way back and ride with him over there? You have a good way with gettin' men to do things they don't especially want to do."

Lenore looked toward their house where her mother was hoeing in the garden. Lanier eyes followed his daughter's gaze. "You tell your mama I'll finish plowing in time to help with the garden. And tell her I said gettin' a man's new leg to him is more important than plantin' beans."

As Lenore walked away, Lanier hollered after her. "Honey, see if there's enough poke salet growing up by the road for your mama to cook us a mess for supper."

When Dr. Dyer and Lenore drove up to Brenda Wiley's house, Odell was standing on the porch. He leaned on his crutch to hold himself upright and focused on his sister in the garden, where Brenda was trying to lay off rows with their mule.

"You got to get the plow point in the ground deeper," Odell yelled at her, "else the sweep can't spread out the dirt behind it."

Dr. Dyer turned off the car's engine and walked over to Brenda. Up close, he could see the woman was almost in tears.

"Afternoon, Dr. Dyer," she said, wiping her eyes on her apron.

"Howdy, Brenda. Are you where you can take a little break? I need you to help me with something over at the house, if you can."

Brenda tied the reins around the plow stock and let it fall on its side. She wiped her eyes a second time and nodded. "All right, but wait just a minute. I don't want Odell to see me crying; else he'll blame hisself for it."

"What's the matter, Brenda?"

"Oh, nothing. I reckon I'm not the only war-widow having a hard time. My husband, Michael, always did the plowing. I'm just not good at it, and Daddy's not stout enough to help anymore. Things are just a mess. Look how crooked these rows are, and not nearly deep enough — to suit Odell, anyway."

Dr. Dyer looked at the three rows she'd plowed under Odell's supervision. "Well, look at the bright side, Brenda. Crooked rows hold more corn than straight ones — beans, too."

Brenda wiped her face on her apron and smiled at him. "That's what Michael used to say. I don't mean to be rude, Dr. Dyer, but what are you and Lenore doing here? Is anything the matter?"

"No, I just have a little something for your brother. I need some womenfolk around to make sure he takes to it."

On the porch of Brenda's unpainted house, Lenore sat down beside Odell, who looked at her grumpily. "Are you mad at me about something or other, Odell?" she asked, "'cause it sure does seem like you are. Have I done something to affront you?"

Odell spat tobacco juice across the porch rail. "Damn right, you have, girl. And you know exactly what it is, too."

Lenore looked right at him and put her hands on her hips. "Are you talking about me getting engaged to Tom Garrison? 'Cause if you are, Odell, you're about to get on my bad side. He's a good man, and I love him."

Odell used his crutch to hobble over to a chair. "He's a dodger, Lenore. He didn't serve like he ought to have. That's all I need to know about him. If I had two good legs, I'd give him a run for his money, I tell you that much."

Lenore was glad when Dr. Dyer and Brenda came up the steps before she had time to respond to what she supposed was a compliment.

"Howdy, Odell," said Dr. Dyer. "You got a few minutes for me and Lenore?"

"Not many. Brenda and me got things to get done. I can't do like I used to, but I ain't helpless."

"I'll make it quick then." Dr. Dyer walked to the car and took out a package about three feet long. When he came back to the porch with it, Odell eyed it skeptically. "What ya' got there, Doc? Some new device to torment us cripples?"

"Hush, Odell," said Brenda. "Dr. Dyer has never tormented you or anybody else. Now behave yourself."

"What about when he put that white plaster over what's left of my leg last year?" Odell asked his sister. "That felt like torment to me." He looked up at Dr. Dyer and admitted, "But it did help with the itching—I'll give you that much."

"I thought it might," said Dr. Dyer as he opened the package. "Now, son, before I show you what's in here, I want you to promise me you'll keep an open mind about it."

"It's another wooden leg, ain't it?" asked Odell. "Damn it to hell, Doc, you know I can't make one of them things work. They're too dad-blame heavy. Anyhow, I don't take charity." Odell turned his head away and stared at the trees by the river.

"It's not charity, Odell. And anyway, you're only half right. It is an artificial leg, but it's not made from wood. It's made out of somethin' called aluminum. Here, feel how light this is."

The metal limb was a quality piece of workmanship with the exact contours of a human leg. It had a padded insert to cradle Odell's stump and an extension that fit up behind his hip for support.

"Look," said Dr. Dyer, "it even bends at the knee for when you sit down. This is nowhere near that ol' thing the Army gave you. It's top of the line, all the way from London, England. Go on, take it, son."

Odell looked at the contraption Dr. Dyer laid across his lap. He ran his hand over the polished metal that had star-shaped holes punched in it for ventilation. Copper rivets held the back together. It even had a wooden foot at the end.

"And that there foot is the same size as yours," Dr. Dyer pointed out. "So, you can put a shoe on it if you want to. That'll come in handy on Sundays."

Odell stared at the contraption. "Who paid for this, Doc?" he asked without looking up.

Dr. Dyer looked at the mule switching his tail at flies in the garden. "Aw, it's from one of those veterans' committees they got up in Gainesville a while back. It may be the same one who put that Confederate monument on the square down there."

"How'd they know about me?"

"You're famous, son, just like that York boy up in Tennessee. You have been ever since the newspapers all ran that letter from your commanding officer."

"I never read that crap."

"Well, everybody else did. They all know how you held off those Germans in that Argonne Forest, even after they shot your leg half off. Folks just want to help, Odell. You need to let 'em."

Odell raised the metallic leg and looked at the upper part, noticing its shape and contour. Then he looked at Dr. Dyer. "This here thing is why you put that plaster on me last fall, ain't it? It didn't have nothin' to do with killing a nerve to stop the itchin', did it?"

"Would I pull your leg about something like that, Odell?"

"I reckon I'm a damn fool," said Odell. Then he glanced at his sister and Lenore. "What are you two women gawking at? Come over here and help me up. Me and the doc gotta go in the house and try this thing on for size."

At the door, Odell spun around on his crutch and leaned against the opening. "Lenore, I ain't got much sense, but I got enough to know you wouldn't be here if that doctor you mean to marry wasn't behind this."

Before Dr. Dyer closed the door, Odell yelled through it. "Lenore, if it ain't too much trouble, would you mind tellin' him I'm obliged?"

CHAPTER TWENTY

Love and Marriage

September 18, 1920

T he morning dawned as bright and clear as Lenore had always dreamed her wedding day would be. This long-awaited date was the complete opposite of the rainy afternoon she and Tom spent on the Indian Mound a year ago—back when they chose today to get married.

Thankfully, September 18, 1920, fell on a Saturday, and Lenore was glad. A Saturday wedding wouldn't interfere with church and made it easier for most folks. The guest list had originally been small, but over the summer it grew every week. Most of Tom's patients told him they'd be there, as if they'd received engraved invitations, even though none were sent.

Most of Lenore's friends just naturally expected to attend, and every time someone mentioned it, all she could bring herself to say was, "Of course, you're invited. We're just not mailing out invitations."

Preacher Yarbrough had even brought up their wedding at campmeeting a few weeks ago. When Lenore finished her solo version of *The Old Rugged Cross*, he said, "Wonderful! Y'all know that little girl's gettin' married next month, don't you?" It wasn't exactly an invitation, but most of the congregation took it as one.

On her last night in the bedroom that had been hers since she was a baby, Lenore slept beside the box that held her wedding shoes—the ones Isaac sent her at Christmas. She hadn't meant to, but she fell asleep, and when she woke up, they were still right there.

Lenore was at her dresser brushing her hair when Hannah knocked on the door. "Honey, Jenny is here."

"Come on in, Mama. I know it's time to get ready."

Up at his house, Tom pinned a flower on his brother's lapel and stood back to admire his work. "You look good, Ray. Lenore may change her mind about which one of us she wants to marry when she sees you."

"I wouldn't be surprised, little brother. She's a pretty smart woman. Are you as nervous as I am?"

"Why would I be nervous? All I'm doing is getting married. You, on the other hand, have to get me to the church on time, not lose the ring in your pocket — at least I hope it's still there — and still look good enough to impress Odell's sister, Brenda."

"I'm not trying to impress anybody," said Ray, feeling in his pocket to make sure the ring was still there. "But if I was, she'd be a good one, wouldn't she?"

At the little Methodist church, Lanier drove the Conleys' surrey up the curved drive and stopped it by the front porch. He helped Lenore's maid of honor, Jenny Gee, and Hannah off the back seat before turning to Lenore.

His daughter was the most beautiful bride he'd ever seen. The dress she had on was a simple cream-colored one her mother made for her. Hannah had wanted it to be longer, but Lenore insisted she hem it high enough to show off her new shoes. Lord, how she loved those shoes.

"Are you ready, Punkin'?" Lanier asked, reaching out his hand. She handed him the black-eyed Susans she'd tied with a ribbon and arranged in that little vase she thought so much of.

Lanier had offered to find roses for her wedding bouquet, but Lenore insisted on black-eyed Susans. She'd even mentioned that the ones growing by the Indian Mound were especially pretty, so those were the ones he picked for her.

Lanier handed the vase to Hannah and extended both his arms toward Lenore. After she stepped down, she hugged him. "I love you, Daddy. You'll never know how much."

"You're the spittin' image of your mama, ya know," was all Lanier could think to say back. He didn't know it, but he couldn't have said anything that would have pleased his daughter more.

"You're the second most handsome man here," she said, as she kissed his cheek.

Lenore was smoothing her dress and getting ready to take the vase of flowers from her mother when Evelyn Boggs caught her arm. "Lenore, this may not be the time, but Alton wanted me to say he's sorry he couldn't be here. He had some business to attend to up in Batesville this week. Alton wanted me to give you this."

She opened the note Evelyn handed her. On the inside, it read, "I'm sorry I couldn't be there for you, but I'll see you soon."

Lenore thought the message was strange, but she hugged Evelyn anyway. "Thank you. I'm sorry he couldn't be here. But thank *you* for coming." She handed the note to her father who put it in his coat pocket.

About fifty people stood around the little church, which was filled to the brim inside. Her family and Tom's took up most of one side.

Over by a tree, Big Mama and Isaac stood with Pledger and a few other colored folks from Bean Creek. When Lenore saw Isaac, she pulled her dress up a few inches and stuck out her foot. She pointed to her white shoes and blew him a kiss. Isaac looked embarrassed.

From the porch, Lenore waved to everyone outside. When Fannie Stover began playing *Here Comes the Bride*, she took her daddy's arm and, together, they walked inside.

The ceremony was short and sweet. Tom turned red when Preacher Yarbrough pronounced them man and wife. He turned even redder when the crowd applauded Lenore's unexpected peck on his cheek.

On the porch, she tossed her bouquet in the air, about halfway between Jenny and Brenda. Brenda, being taller, made the catch, and Tom playfully elbowed Ray in the side.

Lenore hugged more folks than she could count, and Tom shook hands with every man there—some twice. When Odell Stovall hobbled up to hug Lenore, he whispered, "You and me are both standing tall today, aren't we, girl?"

She kissed his cheek. When Odell finally let go of Lenore's hand, he shook Tom's. "You got a fine woman there, Doctor. Take care of her."

"I plan to."

"Doc, there's one more thing."

"What's that?"

"I reckon Lenore got herself a good man, too." Ray slapped Odell's back. "Quit talking to my little brother. He's got a honeymoon to start on. Time's a wastin'."

Dr. Hardman walked over to the side of the church and waved his hand. When he did, Bob Minish started the Cadillac's motor and drove it down from above the cemetery where it was parked. The strings of tin cans Frank and his brothers had tied to the car's rear bumper made quite a racket. "Just Married" signs hung from both sides of the car.

"What's this?" asked Tom. "We were planning to drive the buggy over to Clarkesville and ride the railroad from there to the Falls."

"Nope," said Dr. Hardman. "Not after that train wreck they had last month. No sir, Bob's gonna run you two over there in my car. He'll pick you up next Saturday, too—my treat. That railroad's not safe. Bob's already loaded your things."

"That's very generous," said Tom. He shook Dr. Hardman's hand and looked him in the eye. "Sir, I never would have met Lenore if it wasn't for you and Aunt Emma." Tom looked at the crowd. "I wouldn't have met any of these people if it wasn't for you. How can I ever thank you?"

"That's easy. Now that women got the right to vote last month, just convince your new wife to cast her ballot in my direction when I run for governor."

"I'll do my best, sir, but I can't promise anything."

Dr. Hardman laughed and hugged Lenore. "Good Lord, if giving a car ride as a wedding present won't guarantee a man a vote, what's this world coming to?"

"I promise you this," said Lenore, kissing his cheek. "I will never vote against you, even if I can't vote for you."

"That's a resounding endorsement if I've ever heard one," he laughed.

Tom made his way over to Big Mama and Isaac. He hugged her and shook his old friend's hand. "Isaac, I want to thank you for those shoes you made Lenore. I think she's put them on every day since she got them. But today is the first time she's worn them outside the house. I thought about you when I watched her walk down the aisle a few minutes ago."

Big Mama rolled her eyes. "Shame on you! What you doin' thinkin' 'bout Isaac at a time like dat? You ain't been in dat snakebite medicine again, has you?"

Isaac stepped in front of his wife to address Tom. "Dem shoes is fer you readin' all dem books to me when you was a young'un— 'specially dat Lord Jim. Man, he was sompin', wadn't he?"

"He was, and you're welcome, Isaac. I enjoyed those times as much as you did."

He shook hands with Pledger next. Josh and Jody both extended their hands, too. "Give you a nickel if you can tell which one I am," said the one in front.

"Are you the black one?"

"Nope. I's da bull fighter. He's da one good with da slingshot."

Tom laughed and hugged his Aunt Emma, who was standing beside him. Dr. Dyer, clutching his hat in his hands and looking down at his feet, pulled him away. "Ah, son, this is a little awkward and a mite late maybe, but is there anything you need to know before you go? About the birds and the bees, I mean."

Tom rubbed his chin as if in deep deliberation. "Oh, you mean the Samuel Coleridge poem?

> *"All nature seems at work... The bees are stirring – birds are on the wing..."*

"He wrote that in 1825, I believe. Thank you for reminding me. I'll read it to Lenore tonight."

"You flatlanders are odd people," said Dr. Dyer. "Here I am trying to help." Turning thoughtful, he added, "Seriously, son, remember this: marriage is just a real good friendship that sorta' got out of hand on the front end. You don't forget that."

"I won't," said Tom as he embraced India. "It seems like I'm saying 'thank you' an awful lot today, but I owe you two a special one."

"You don't owe us anything," said India. "Although I do suppose it's your fault David bought that old car. But, I guess I can forgive you for that."

While everyone clustered around his new bride, Tom walked up to Val and his buggy parked in the shade behind the church. He stroked the mare's nose. "Goodbye, girl. I guess you won't have to take us to Clarkesville after all. You can just rest in the pasture this week. Ray will take care of you." He ran his hands through her forelock to straighten it and patted her jaw.

Back at the car, Tom took out his watch and checked the time. "We better get moving if we're going to get there before dark." No one paid him any attention. Everyone wanted to hug Lenore again, and he couldn't blame them.

When he saw his mother looking at him from a few feet away, Tom walked over and embraced her. "I'm glad you decided to stay until we come back next week. Now, don't you and Aunt Emma cook up any more plans for me while we're gone. Look how much trouble your last one got me into!"

"You don't look much like a man in trouble to me," said Wirtha, hugging him hard. "You look to me like a man in love."

"I am, Mother. I love you, too." With that, he pulled Lenore away from another group of well-wishers, waited for her to hug her parents one last time, and helped her into the Cadillac's big back seat. As soon as they were inside, grains of rice flew toward the car from every direction.

"Let's go, Bob," Tom shouted. "Get us out of here before they cover us up in this stuff!" The car pulled down the road with the tin cans banging behind them like a flock of crazy chickens. Tom and Lenore waved goodbye and headed to Tallulah Falls in fine style.

Inside the car, Tom snapped his fingers. "Darn it," he said. "I forgot my chess set."

"Don't worry, darling," said Lenore, leaning her head on his shoulder. "I promise you won't miss it."

CHAPTER TWENTY-ONE

The Honeymoon

September 24, 1920

The Cliff House was well-named. The hotel was perched on the rim of Tallulah Gorge almost directly across from the Tallulah Falls train depot. Its easy access, ground-level front porch stood in sharp contrast to the back one hanging high above the gorge. Stairs led from there down to a tall, thin structure with observation platforms and windows on the sides. Guests who were brave enough could take the steps down to the Tempesta Falls overlook.

"No way," said Tom when he saw Lenore looking at those steps on their first day.

"What's wrong with you menfolk?" she asked him. "Daddy won't go down there either."

"Well, I can't speak for *all* the other men, but for this one, those hundreds of steep steps have something to do with it. I bet it feels like several thousand on the way back up."

The town of Tallulah Falls had other hotels and boarding houses in the shadow of Hickory Nut Mountain, but Lenore had always thought the Cliff House was the grandest. Their first week as man and wife had been almost dreamlike. Since they'd been escorted to the hotel in the Hardmans' Cadillac last week, Tom and Lenore rode horses, shot billiards—a new experience for both—played lawn tennis, and—Tom's favorite—relaxed and read in the hammocks. At night, the hotel's band filled the air with music, so they danced—much more gracefully now than when they first danced on the Indian Mound last year.

It was now Friday morning; their final day lay ahead. As part of Dr. Hardman's wedding present, Bob Minish would come back tomorrow at noon and drive them home. By tomorrow night, they'd be back in the Valley, starting their new life. Tom had decided to wait until they got home to tell Lenore about the job he'd been offered at the St. Joseph Infirmary in Atlanta.

"So, what do you want to do today," he asked Lenore, peering at his wife over a coffee cup. "There can't be much more on your list, can there? And the stores can't have many souvenirs left."

Lenore waited for the waitress to finish clearing their table. Then she leaned forward to rest her chin on her hands. "I still have to get Mama something. And actually, Dr. Tom, there *is* one more thing I'd like to do before we leave. If you do this, I'll let you off the hook for not walking down to Tempesta Falls with me." She pointed out the window to the cliffs on the other side. "I'd like to take a picture of this hotel from over there. Won't that make a great keepsake?"

Tom looked at the rugged terrain and thought about her leg. "I don't know. I may not be up to that long a walk. How do we get over there, anyway? Is there a trail?"

Lenore leaned her face toward his. "Trail?" she teased. "Is my new husband afraid of a little walk in the woods?" Pretending to be serious, she said. "It *is* a little rough, Dr. Tom, but I think you can keep up. We just walk across the dam—at least it's good for something—then we'll be north of the old river bed. Daddy and I have gone before, lots of times."

Tom knew it was useless to argue. He took another look across the gorge. "Well, if you insist, let's go change clothes and get started."

An hour later—changing clothes proved time-consuming for the newlyweds—they strolled past the wicker rocking chairs in the lobby and through the front door. Lenore had put her blond hair in a bun and wore her favorite, bright yellow "everyday" dress her mother made for her. It wasn't long enough to cover her brown shoes, but that didn't bother her today. She thought Tom looked handsome in his blue jeans and khaki cotton shirt.

Lenore insisted on bringing the pottery pitcher or vase—she was still unsure which it was—Arie Meaders had given her. "Isn't that going be a lot of trouble to carry?" Tom asked, hoping she might leave it in the room. "You don't want to risk breaking it, do you?"

"I won't break it. I'm going to fill it with wildflowers and let that be the souvenir I take home for Mama. Black-eyed Susans from the far side of the gorge would be something she'd appreciate. I bet we can find a few. I'll carry the vase and you carry the camera."

Tom considered the feasibility of keeping wild flowers fresh on the trip home, but he didn't say anything. If Lenore wanted to take flowers to her mother, he'd carry them in his hat if he had to.

A few of the guests they'd gotten to know during the week waved as Tom and Lenore walked across the front porch. From one of the rockers, an Atlanta man named James, who was staying with his family for the entire month, spotted them. "You two ready for another go at badminton? Marlene and I practiced all day yesterday. I believe we might actually beat y'all today."

"We're ready," said Tom. "But it'll have to wait 'til this afternoon. We're walking over to the other side of the gorge this morning. Won't you and Marlene join us?"

The Atlanta man laughed. "Are you serious? Two newlyweds heading to the woods, and you want an old married couple tagging along? I hardly think so. Besides, it looks like a pretty far piece." The man looked across the ravine. "At least, you'll be easier to beat when you get back."

Tom eyed the empty hammocks in the side-yard. Lenore laughed, tugged his arm and waved goodbye to the Atlanta couple. As they walked across the dam, Tallulah Falls Lake, long and deep, sparkled to their left. The reflection of the town's tall train trestle twinkled on its surface. The deep gorge dropped off to their right.

When they got to the other side, they made their way through the hardwoods and scrubby pines above the remote north rim. They caught an occasional glimpse of Hickory Nut Mountain. Once, when Lenore stopped to pick a flower, Tom thought he saw someone slip into a patch of mountain laurel behind them. After staring for a while, he decided he was mistaken.

A few minutes later, he definitely heard someone flailing through the brush to their left. Tuning to look, he saw a man separating mountain laurel branches with both hands. Once he'd dislodged the binocular's strap, which had caught on a limb, he waved in their direction. Tom recognized him as someone they'd watched check into the hotel yesterday.

"Don't be alarmed, sir, and madam. I'm not stalking you. I've heard there is a pair of Peregrine falcons nesting in the cliffs above the gorge over on this side. They'll be leaving for their winter range soon, you know. I've spent all morning trying to spot them."

The stranger held a small notebook with a pencil attached. "I'm Warren Jones from Albany — the one in New York. I don't have the drawl for the one in Georgia. I'm doing a little bird watching. I've checked off a dozen so far, but those falcons keep evading me."

Tom laughed. "I'm Tom Garrison and this is my wife, Lenore. We walked over to see the sights from this side, too. I thought I saw someone behind us a while back. That must have been you."

"Probably was. But I wasn't following you on purpose. To tell the truth, I didn't realize there was anyone over here but me. I'll be out of your way in a moment. I think I'll look over that way," he said, pointing to his right.

After he ambled out of sight, Tom and Lenore continued their walk. At the place above the first of several waterfalls below the new dam, they finished filling Lenore's vase with black-eyed Susans, which were surprisingly plentiful.

Tom looked over the edge at the water below, holding on to a low hanging branch for support. "How did you pronounce the name of those falls down there?" he asked Lenore.

"Well, my French isn't very good," she said. "And I suppose most folks call it *La-door-ah* here in Georgia. But in French, it's *L'Eau d'Or*. That means, *Water of Gold.*

Tom came back from the big rock at the edge and took the vase of flowers from her. He set them and the camera at the base of a tree.

Lenore walked to the rock and looked down at the water herself, holding on to the same branch Tom had used. "Daddy says they named it that because when the sun hits it just so, it makes the water look like gold. I've never seen that — it always looks green to me — but I *have* tried. I guess I've just never been over here at the right time. Or maybe it's like that bear in Yonah Mountain. Maybe you have to look for a long, long time before you get to see it."

Tom nodded, reached for her hand, and held it. "The French word for those waterfalls is pretty close to your name, Lenore. Maybe you were named for them."

Lenore smiled. "I always thought that was a possibility. Daddy's French isn't very good — Mama's either for that matter.

And I *was* born nine months after Mama and Daddy's honeymoon. Maybe Lenore was as close as they could get to *L'Eau d'Or*."

Tom chuckled at the thought of his father-in-law trying to speak French. "Lenore is a French word, too," his new wife reminded him. "Mama says Lenore means *light*."

"Maybe that's why your name suits you so well," he said, kissing her hand. "You are definitely the light of my life." He looked thoughtful. "Edgar Allan Poe wrote a poem about a woman named Lenore, you know."

"I know," said Lenore. "Maybe Mama and Daddy got my name from that."

"I'm pretty sure your daddy never read much of Poe's work," said Tom, smiling at her. "But your mama may have."

Lenore looked into Tom's face. "You know," she said, "I've never asked Mama how I got my name. Remind me to do that when we get home."

"I will." Without warning, Tom began reciting a verse from *The Raven*. "*Ah, distinctly I remember, it was in the bleak December.*" After the first line, he stopped his oration and shook his head. "Oh, heck, I was going to impress you by reciting the whole thing, but I can't even recall the next line. It's something…something and then…'*For the rare and radiant maiden whom the angels name Lenore.*' That's the only part I care about anyway."

His wife smiled. "I've never liked that poem until now — until I heard you say it. I always thought it sounded sad. How is it that you know even that much of it?"

"One of my teachers made all her classes learn it. Back then, I never dreamed I'd be in love with '*the rare and radiant maiden whom the angels name Lenore.*' But here I am."

Tom took out his watch and checked the time. It was eleven-fifteen.

"Are you in a hurry to get back?" Lenore asked him.

"No, it's just a habit. I think of my father when I look at this watch — my grandfather, too. He carried this thing all through the War, you know. He even had it with him at Appomattox."

"May I see it?" she asked him. "I don't think I've ever really looked at it before."

Tom unhooked the chain's clasp and handed her the watch. While she studied it, he gathered pine needles and made a soft place for Lenore to sit. "Aren't you glad we came over?" he asked, as Lenore folded her dress and sat beside him.

"Oh, so this was your idea now was it, Dr. Tom?" She leaned her head against his shoulder. In a tangled mass of shrubbery below, the yellow eyes of a brown thrasher stared briefly before the bird fluttered away.

Tom idly put one of the pine needles in his mouth. "You amaze me, Lenore. Most women would rather stay at the hotel or shop in the village. But you, even with your..." Tom didn't finish the sentence.

"Even with my what?" asked Lenore, teasing him. "My dress? You're probably right. Most women would have worn britches today, but I guess I'm just an old-fashioned girl."

Tom's face turned crimson again. They both knew he meant Lenore's leg. But when she kissed him, they stopped thinking about it.

"I'm so happy, Tom. You make me happy." Lenore placed the watch on the pine needles. She stood to stare at the Cliff House. "It's so beautiful here," she said, gazing across the gorge, "and so vast."

The buildings were less than one hundred yards away, although they'd walked much farther than that to get here. In front of the hotel, the northbound train pulled soundlessly to the station. They could see the smoke and steam, but the wind blew its noise in the other direction, creating a dreamlike scene.

Again, Tom thought he heard something in the woods behind them, but after listening for a bit, decided it must be a squirrel. When he stood to put his arm around his wife's waist, his foot accidentally kicked a clump of pine needles over the watch where Lenore had laid it. He was too focused on her to notice.

"It is that," he said. "Vast and beautiful — just like you, Lenore." He pulled her to him. "But it's so incredibly different from those valleys you love. It's funny how your two favorite places are total opposites."

Lenore turned to him and looked in his eyes. "I'm a complicated woman," she said, smiling. She lifted her face for him to kiss her again. When she pulled back, she said, "But what I love most in this world isn't a place anymore, Dr. Tom — it's you."

Laughing at the smitten look on his face, she gave him a peck on the cheek, picked up the camera and handed it to him. "Are you ready to make my picture now, husband?"

"I'd be honored, darling," he said, picking up Lanier's camera. "Here, you should be holding your vase."

Tom held the camera at waist level and looked at her reflection through the viewfinder. She looked beautiful, he thought, standing there with that vase of black-eyed Susans. He pressed the shutter and turned the metal crank to advance the film. When he finished, the red circle on the camera's back showed a black 5, meaning there was only one image left. He watched Lenore pivot, arms outstretched, for one last look at the view before she walked to him.

She put both her hands behind Tom's neck, stood on tiptoe, and kissed him for a long time. "Now go over there where I was. It's my turn to take *your* picture. I want to remember right now forever. We'll get frames and put these two pictures side-by-side on our mantel. Don't get too close, darling — it's a long way down."

"There's only one more picture left," Tom reminded her, as he walked to the edge. "I should have bought more film. This is the last one, so make it good."

Lenore put the vase down and aimed the camera at her husband. Maybe it was just the viewfinder, but when she looked at him through it, something seemed different. For one thing, he wasn't smiling anymore. She looked up. "What's the matter, Tom? Don't you want your picture taken?"

Tom pulled a hand across his hair. "I don't know," he said, looking from side to side. "All of a sudden, I have a bad feeling. Let's get back to the hotel."

"All right, but smile first. We don't want our children thinking you weren't happy on our honeymoon."

Tom wasn't happy. That old sensation he called *the feeling* told him it was already too late to leave, but he forced himself to smile. It was an odd thought, but he decided he ought to look happy in what he knew would be the last picture anyone would ever take of him.

"I love you, Lenore."

"I love you, too," she said, pressing the shutter's lever. Suddenly, something rushed up beside her. A blur of gun metal flew past her right eye. The .45 caliber blast deafened her as Alton Boggs's powerful arm pinned her to his side. The camera fell hard, and from the corner of her eye, Lenore noticed that it knocked over her little pot of flowers.

In front of her, Tom dropped to one knee. When he clutched his thigh with both hands, blood oozed through his fingers from the flesh wound. Behind him, smoke poured from the train as it pulled out of Tallulah Falls, heading north across the giant trestle high above the town.

"Hush now," said Alton, covering Lenore's mouth with his hand. "Keep quiet, darling. This'll be over real quick. Then it'll just be you and me. I got everything took care of, darlin'. Be quiet now."

Lenore screamed into his hand. Alton ignored her and focused on Tom, who was struggling to stand. Tom looked at Alton and tried to move toward them.

"Hold on there, flatlander," said Alton, grinning. "You just stay put." Even with Lenore's squirming, Alton held the gun steady and pointed at Tom. "You didn't think you could get away with marryin' my woman did you, Doc? Are you that stupid? I thought doctors was supposed to be smart."

Struggling to stand, Tom looked at the crazed man. "Let Lenore go, Alton. I know you're going to kill me, but there's no reason to hurt her."

Alton laughed. "Hurt her? Why in Gawd's name would I hurt her? Naw, I aim to treat her real nice. After you jump into that there gorge, I'm gonna to take her up to my brother's place, outside Asheville. It's a fine spot to raise a family. She'll be happy there. We woulda' been happy over in the Valley if you hadn't showed up. But you ruined that."

Lenore kicked his leg and bit down on the hand shutting off her air. Alton flinched but kept his gun pointed. "Quit that, girl." He looked at Tom over the gun barrel. "I woulda' grabbed her sooner, but I's sure Lanier would put a stop to your stupid wedding. He never did, though — and you an outsider!"

Alton squeezed Lenore tighter. "Meant to get her 'fore you violated her," he snarled at Tom. "I reckon it's too late now, but she won't be the first widow-woman to take a new husband."

He motioned toward the Cliff House with the pistol. "There weren't never a chance to grab her over there. But I shore am glad you decided to bring her to this side of the ditch."

Alton waved the gun. "Now jump!"

Tom struggled to stand. "No," he said. "Alton, don't do this." He talked to the man but looked at his wife.

Lenore kept thrashing, but she did another thing, too. She nodded, and pointed with her eyes, indicating something above him. When Alton released his hand so she could take a breath, she gasped a single word.

"Lana!"

Alton covered her mouth again, but Tom understood. He looked at Lenore for what he knew would be the last time.

Alton took careful aim. "You quit looking at my woman!" Lenore struggled harder, but Alton held her in his grip. "Now, you son-of-a-bitch, I said jump!"

Tom took one last breath before charging toward Lenore and the crazed man holding her, but his wounded leg betrayed him. As he fell forward, another bullet tore into his chest. Across the gorge, the train disappeared into the woods above the lake.

When Lenore fainted, Alton lowered her to the ground.

Tom sensed the warm blood pooling around him on the rock, but he never felt the boot that shoved him over the edge.

Minutes later, water from Alton's canteen brought Lenore back to reality. Large hands cradled her head; gentle words found her ears. "Everything's fine, darlin'," said Alton, rocking her in his lap. "We're together now like we're meant to be."

Lenore felt something sweet against her lips. "Here," said the awful voice of Alton Boggs. "I brought you a stick of licorice. There's a whole box of it back at my camp. It's all for you, Lenore."

Struggling to stay conscious, she brushed the candy away and looked toward the place she'd last seen Tom.

"He jumped off, honey," said Alton, caressing her face. "He won't bother you no more." Alton pulled Lenore to her feet and turned her to face him. He put his hands on her shoulders. "You can be my wife now." Shyly, he asked, "Would you dance with me the way you did with him?"

Lenore watched, horrified, as he leaned toward her, his mouth slightly open. When the stubble of Alton's beard brushed her face, she bolted from his sweaty body and battled toward the gorge.

"TOM!" she shouted into the void. "TOM!!!!"

Alton was sure Lenore tried to stop when she reached the edge, but she must have slipped on the blood. Before she fell, the girl reached out like someone was there to catch her.

Alton thought that was the strangest thing.

During the split-second she faltered, Alton had grabbed at her dress. He almost had her, too—could have saved her if she'd reached for him and not out the other way—but instead, the sleeve of her yellow dress ripped in his hand as she went over the side.

Clutching the cloth that tore away, Alton crawled as close as he dared to the edge and looked down. The stream, so far below he couldn't hear it, continued its ancient trek to the sea. An unconcerned hawk caught a thermal and soared below him.

He watched the hawk for a while, then turned over and looked at the mess on his overalls. "Damn," he thought. "Why did that bastard of a doctor have to bleed so much?"

Alton sat up and reached for his canteen. He swigged the water and splashed more of it over his face. He used the rest to wash blood off his hands. What on earth had gotten into that girl? Now, she was gone, and it was that doctor's fault!

There'd been plenty of chances to get her earlier—he'd been stupid to wait. He'd been about to do it when that silly little bird watcher showed up. He had two or three other clear shots, but he wanted him closer to the gorge, so he wouldn't have to drag the body so far. He wasn't sure if Lenore would be willing to help with that or not.

Alton reckoned his papa was right about women not knowin' which man they're supposed to be in love with. But there was no use crying over spilt milk. He'd just have to find another wife— maybe that Jenny Gee girl—anyway, she was something to think about.

Alton picked up the camera and that ugly little vase Lenore brought with her. He nearly tossed them both over the side, but at the last minute, decided not to. He gathered the flowers lying around it and threw them over instead. Then he put the camera behind the bib of his overalls and wrapped the vase in the yellow sleeve of Lenore's dress. He picked up his gun from where he'd dropped it and started back toward his camp.

"What in heaven's name?" Warren Jones, the bird watcher, asked himself when he heard the gunshots. He wasn't a firearms expert, but he knew a pistol when he heard one—in this case, two. He hoped those nice people he'd met earlier were all right. Perhaps the man had been trying to impress her with his shooting skills.

Still, he really *should* check. He started in the direction the sound had come from when a flash of yellow caught his attention. It was a yellow warbler. He crept closer and looked at the bird through his binoculars. "Beautiful," he whispered, "just beautiful."

Other yellow birds soon joined the first one. He watched for a few minutes and then scribbled a notebook entry. After that, he headed toward the place where he'd met that young couple from the hotel. He was more likely to spot one of the falcons over there anyway.

No one was around when he got to the spot, so he headed in the direction they'd gone when he last heard them walking through the brush. Just as he was about to give up on finding them, he noticed something dark on one of the large rocks, by the ledge. "My God," he whispered, looking at the spot through his binoculars, even though it was only a few yards away. "That's blood."

He could see where something had made a dark smear across the rock. Two brass bullet casings on the ground reflected the sunlight. "Perhaps they weren't such a happy couple after all," he thought. He moved away as fast as the rough terrain would let him travel.

૨૦

Warren's shirt was soaked in sweat when he collapsed in one of the wicker chairs on the front porch of the Cliff House. "It's those newlyweds," he gasped, as a crowd gathered. "Something terrible has happened."

The desk clerk came out and insisted he come inside. "Sit here, sir. I'll get you some water."

"There was blood," Jones said between gulps. "And shots. But when I went back, no one was there. I think he shot her. I was just bird watching, you see."

"Where did this happen?" asked the hotel manager, Hammond Hamilton, who came out of his office.

Jones turned in his chair and pointed through the window at the other side of the gorge. "Right over there."

"Thelma," said the manager. "Send a boy to fetch Sheriff Grant. Since it happened on the Rabun County side, we better send for Sheriff Rickman, too." Looking at Jones, he said, "You best stay close. Both those sheriffs will want to talk to you."

Jones nodded and dabbed his forehead with a handkerchief.

Once Sheriff Luther Rickman got there, the bird watcher accompanied him and a deputy back to the place he'd found the blood. Jones was exhausted when they got there, but he pointed to the bloody rock before he slumped against a tree.

Rickman walked to the spot, knelt and looked around. He ran a finger through the blood and looked at it as if it held some vital clue. He wiped his hand on his britches and motioned for the deputy to pick up the shell casings. He looked around for more but didn't see any.

"Are those .45s?"

The deputy nodded.

Walking over to Jones, the sheriff looked down at him. "You see anybody over here other than them two?"

"No, sir. I don't believe many people come to this side. I was quite surprised to see anyone at all."

"You carry a gun?"

"No, sir. I've never shot a firearm in my life. That's preposterous! Surely you don't think I did this?"

The sheriff bent down and studied the little man. After a minute, he shook his head. "No, I reckon you didn't." He took the two casings from his deputy and put them in his pocket. Looking at the bloody rock, the sheriff said, "I think it's pretty clear what happened. This ain't the first time a new husband got buyer's remorse on the honeymoon. The little woman might not a' been as attentive as she should a been."

The deputy laughed. "I heard she was crippled in her leg. Maybe she didn't dance good enough to suit him."

"Folks have been killed for less, I reckon." The sheriff reached out to the bird watcher and pulled the exhausted man to his feet. "Let's go, Mr. Jones."

"Shouldn't we look around some first, Sheriff?" asked the deputy. "In case he's still here?"

Rickman shook his head. "Naw, he's long gone. She may wash up somewhere further down. Then again, she may not. We never found no sign of the last one that went off up here. What's that been, two years now?"

"That's about right," said the deputy. "They's enough pools and sinkholes down there to hide an elephant."

Sheriff Rickman nodded. "I'll get a description out on the husband. Didn't somebody say he was a doctor?"

Once he arrived at the hotel, Habersham County Sheriff John Grant didn't visit the crime scene on the north rim. It was a long walk, and not even in his county, so he took the other sheriff's word for what happened. "You sure that New Yorker didn't shoot 'em?" was his only question.

"Naw," said Sheriff Rickman, spitting tobacco juice through his fingers. "He ain't cut out for killin'. That feller couldn't hurt a piss ant without help."

Never learning he'd been ruled out as a suspect, Warren Jones quietly bought a ticket on the afternoon train and headed back to New York without bothering to settle his bill.

CHAPTER TWENTY-TWO

Alton Leaves

September 25, 1920

W ord spread fast that something awful had happened at Tallulah Gorge. The Dyers were sitting down to an early supper when Floyd Martin, the man who'd made Tom's mare fall when he first arrived, banged on their door to tell them Lenore and Tom were missing. No one knew much, but everybody said they'd gone for a walk on the far side this morning and never came back.

As Floyd turned to leave, he said, "There was lots of blood. They're saying Dr. Garrison shot her and threw her over the side because of her being crippled."

"That's a damn lie!" Dr. Dyer shouted. "Tom would have died before he'd let anybody hurt Lenore, let alone do it himself."

"I'm just telling you what folks are saying," said Floyd. "Sheriff Grant's taking a search party down tomorrow morning. I'm volunteering. He's got the law out on Tom."

Dr. Dyer grabbed his hat. "I have to get to Lanier and Hannah before they hear this from somebody else. I'm pretty sure Tom's mother is still with the Hardmans. I know his brother just got back from Bogart."

"Wait," said India. "I'll go with you. Those two women are going to need me."

They went to the Conleys first, breaking the news as gently as they could. They told them Tom and Lenore were missing, but didn't mention the blood, or that the sheriff considered Tom a suspect. That could wait.

"They could be anywhere," said Lanier. "They're probably just lost in the woods." He ran to the barn, saddled Custer and led him back to the porch. "I'm going over there," he said.

"Lanier, it's almost dark," said Dr. Dyer. "Why don't you wait 'til morning? There's nothing you can do tonight."

Lanier turned in the saddle and looked at his wife. "Pray, Hannah. I'll be back when I can." With that, he turned Custer and galloped down the road.

Dr. Dyer watched him go. When Lanier was out of sight, he said, "India, why don't you stay with Hannah while I drive down to the Hardmans and tell Miss Wirtha what's happened. Ray may be down there, too. I'm just not sure."

"No," said Hannah. "We'll go with you. Wirtha's going to need all the comfort she can get, poor thing."

Custer was completely spent when Lanier rode him into Clarkesville, so he rented a fresh mount at the livery stable. It was after midnight when he got to Tallulah Falls, but people were still on the porch, talking in low voices. Alton Boggs was the only one he recognized. "What are you doing here?" he asked him.

"I was in Batesville when I heard the news," Alton told him. "I've been up there visitin', you know. I want to help, Lanier. I'm going out with the search party in the mornin'."

"Me, too. Fill me in on what you know."

Alton told him about the blood and how both sheriffs were convinced Tom killed Lenore and ran off. Lanier took a step toward him when he mentioned blood. "Blood? Dr. Dyer didn't say anything about that. Where did they find blood?"

"Over on the north rim, close to the edge."

Lanier sat down in a rocker and put his head in his hands.

When someone told the hotel manager the missing girl's father was on the porch, he came out to offer Lanier the use of the couple's room for the rest of the night. "I'm sorry about this," he said. "I'd let you have another room, but we're full up. This way, you can at least have a roof over your head, not that I reckon you'll rest much."

Lanier was about to follow him to the room when he remembered his rented horse still tied to the porch rail. "Alton, would you see that horse gets put up and fed?"

Inside the room, Tom and Lenore's things were in neat order. Most of their clothes had been folded and placed in their trunk. That made sense — they were coming home tomorrow. Little gift bags filled with souvenirs lined the dresser. Lanier remembered how, even as a girl, Lenore always wanted to bring some little something back for the people who didn't get to go.

His daughter's wedding dress lay across the bed — its hem touched the pair of white shoes Isaac had made for her. Lanier slouched in the only chair the room had in it and spent what was left of the night staring out the window.

The next morning, Sheriff Grant's search party left at daylight. Grant wasn't happy when Lanier said he was going with them and ordered him to stay at the hotel.

"You ain't got enough men in Habersham County to keep me from going, Sheriff," Lanier told him. John Grant relented, but once they were in the gorge, he sent Lanier and Alton, along with two teenage boys, in the direction away from where he expected to find anything.

About mid-afternoon, after a long day, the sheriff fired his gun to signal they'd found something. Lanier ran ahead of Alton and the two boys over some of the roughest terrain in Georgia. When he was still several yards away, two men stepped in front of him, blocking his way. Lanier was too out of breath to resist much, but he could still yell. "Sheriff, you show me what you found! She's my daughter, damn it!" He didn't want to admit it to himself, but Lanier could see they'd fished one of Lenore's brown shoes from the water.

When the sheriff nodded toward the men in his way, they dropped their arms. "Let him come on over," said Sheriff Grant. "Somebody has to tell us if this is hers."

"Wait," said Alton as he walked up with the two boys. "Let me do this, Lanier. I can identify her shoe as well as you can."

"Get out'a my way, Alton."

Sheriff Grant looked at the shoe. "It don't look like a woman's, and it's too small for a man's. I can't understand how it was floatin'. Looks to me like it'd get water-logged and sink."

Lanier took Lenore's shoe from the sheriff and held it. When he sobbed, every man found a reason to look away. Lanier cleared his throat. "That's hers. It's floating because it has a two-inch cork for a sole. Her left leg is shorter than the other one." Lanier looked out over the river. "Where the hell *is* she?"

"Nobody told me she was crippled, said the sheriff. "I reckon the poor little thing never had a chance." He reached for the dripping shoe. "I'll need that shoe back, Mr. Conley. It's evidence."

Lanier waited a long time before he handed it back. Then he rubbed his hands over his face. "Is everybody over here crazy? Tom wouldn't hurt Lenore." He took a step toward the sheriff. "They were on their honeymoon, for God's sake!"

The sheriff shrugged and casually dropped a hand to the top of his sidearm. "Look, Mr. Conley, I know this is hard on you, but facts are facts. That's all I have to go on." John Grant wiped his forehead on his arm and looked around. "I don't know what else *to* think. Between that shoe and the blood Rickman found up yonder, I'd say it's pretty cut-and-dried. He ain't the first husband to get cold feet. Maybe they had a fight."

Alton Boggs put his hand on Lanier's shoulders. "I never liked that damn doctor, Lanier. You didn't neither, did you? I promise you this: if I ever do see that bastard again, I'll take care of him. You got my bond on that."

Lanier turned enough to make Alton's hand drop from his back. "Tom did not do this," he said to Sheriff Grant. "My wife's not gonna believe it either. Nobody who knows them will."

The sheriff lifted the dripping shoe and looked at it closely. Lanier noticed the shoestring was missing. "Look, Mr. Conley, I know this is hard, but why else would he take her over to that side of the gorge? Nobody goes over there unless they're up to no good." Sheriff Grant dropped the shoe into a bag and circled his finger in the air. "Wrap it up, boys. Let's go. It'll be dark before long."

Lanier moved toward the sheriff again. "Listen here. It would have been her idea to go over there, not Tom's. If I know him, he'd have tried to talk her out of it. I've been over there with her myself, for God's sake! I don't know what happened yesterday, but Tom did not kill my daughter, you hear me?"

Before the sheriff could respond, Alton said, "Well, I reckon it's plain enough he did, Lanier. Ain't that right, Sheriff? He had a .45 caliber pistol, too. He showed it to me one time, Lanier. It might take a while, but you'll come to see how it's the only way it coulda' happened."

Lanier stared at Alton a long time. He remembered the note Evelyn handed to Lenore at the wedding. It was still in his coat pocket, back at the house.

John Grant sighed. "Well, I reckon the best way to prove you wrong is to find him. I've already sent a bulletin out. I got the law down in Macon lookin', too. He'll likely show up back there. Women killers usually get to wantin' their mamas real bad. He'll turn up someplace."

Lanier clinched both his fists, but kept them by his side. "His mama is over in Nacoochee Valley," said Lanier. "And she'll be waitin' there 'til you find his body. If Lenore's dead, he is, too. I promise you that. You better keep looking, Sheriff. You hear me?"

Sheriff Grant put his arm across Lanier's back. "We'll do all we can. I'll bring some men back down tomorrow, but we better get going now. It's a hell of a climb out of here, and we want to get back on top while there's still light."

Tom's brother, Ray Garrison, was sitting on the porch of the Cliff House with his dog when Lanier and Alton walked up just after dark. A velour bag lay at the man's feet. Lanier shook his hand. Alton just nodded.

"I reckon you came to stay," said Lanier, indicating the bag.

"As long as it takes," said Ray. "I woulda' been here sooner, but Mother needed me. Plus, I had some thinkin' to do. Did y'all find anything?"

"Lenore's left shoe is all," said Lanier. "The sheriff kept it. I reckon that's proof enough she's down there. No sign of your brother, though — nothing."

Alton scraped some mud from the bottom of his boot onto the edge of the porch. Then he looked at Ray. "Sheriff thinks he's up and run off."

"Why would he do that?"

"Why you reckon?"

Jack growled without raising his head. Lanier stepped toward Ray. "Come with me, son. I've got a key to their room. Let's talk in there." He didn't invite Alton.

Inside the hotel, Ray looked at the tastefully decorated lobby and stopped. "Will they have a problem with Jack being in here?" he asked Lanier.

"Not if we don't ask 'em."

When they got to Tom and Lenore's room, Lanier slumped in the same chair he'd stayed in last night. Ray and Jack stood.

"Something ain't right here, Ray. I can smell it."

"Do they *really* think Tom would have done anything to hurt Lenore?"

"I reckon so, son. I told the sheriff it was horseshit."

"Alton Boggs seems eager enough to believe it."

"Yeah, I noticed that. You a drinking man?"

"Not normally," said Ray. "But Tom told me you are. I reckon I am tonight, too — only not here — not in this room."

"Come on then," said Lanier. He opened the door like he couldn't wait to get outside. "There's a man over at the train depot that usually has a pint to spare."

Ray and Lanier spent the night in two of the hotel's outside hammocks. Neither of them wanted to sleep in that room, although they did use it to wash up before breakfast. Ray changed clothes, but Lanier only had the overalls he'd worn over.

While they were sitting together about daylight on the back porch, the hotel manager pulled up a chair. Lanier introduced Ray to him as Tom's brother.

"I want you two to know that this hotel is at your disposal," he said. He looked at Jack. "The dog's, too." He handed Ray an extra room key. "Y'all can use their room for as long as you need it." Hammond Hamilton stood and cleared his throat. "However, there is the matter of the bill, of course. They never got a chance to settle up, you see."

When Lanier walked out the front door, to where Alton and the other members of the search party were gathering, Ray hung back.

"You coming?" Lanier asked him.

"Not yet. I want to look around on that side of the gorge first —
see what I can kick up."

"Suit yourself."

"Mr. Conley?"

"Yes?"

"Keep an eye on Boggs."

"I plan to."

The first daylight sparkled off Tallulah Lake as Ray and Jack
made their way across the dam. Once they were on the other side,
he slowed their pace. It would be a long walk for the dog over hard
ground.

Ray left his extra clothes in the hotel room but brought his bag
along. Instead of garments, it held a canteen of water and enough
biscuits to get them through the day. It also contained the German
luger he'd brought back from France. It was September and snakes
were still active.

It took most of the morning, but he finally found the spot the
hotel manager pointed out to him from the porch of the Cliff House.
Dried blood still clung to the rock by the edge. "Don't get too close,
Jack. It's a long way down from here." They turned around, and
Ray sat down with his back against a pine. Jack arranged himself
on the ground beside him. He sensed they were going to be here a
while.

Ray spent an hour gazing across the gorge with the wind
against his back, thinking mostly — smoking some. The flat rock
beside him had a little dip in it, and he poured water there for Jack
to lap up.

A crow lit in a scrub pine at the edge of the chasm. After cawing
once, it flew away.

As if he'd come to a conclusion, Ray took a deep breath and let
it out slowly. "That ol' crow's right, Jack. This was murder. Tom
and Lenore came over here for whatever reason, and somebody
killed them — right there on that rock. Whoever it was followed
them, and I think I know who."

Ray took out two biscuits from the bag, gave one to Jack and ate
the other himself. He poured more water for the dog, took a drink
from the canteen and wiped his mouth with the back of his arm.

When he put his hands back to push himself up, his fingers touched something cold. When he brushed back the pine needles, there lay Tom's gold watch and chain, the one that had belonged to their father and grandfather — the watch Ray refused to accept.

He opened it and polished the glass face on his shirt. "I'll be damned, Jack. Look what Tom left here. What do you make of this, boy?"

Jack sniffed it and lay back down. What was the watch doing here? Maybe Tom and Lenore were about to be robbed, and he'd found a way to hide it.

"I guess we'll never know, will we, Jack?" Ray pulled up the winding crown, turned it between his thumb and forefinger and held the watch to his ear. Satisfied it still worked; he set it to 2:45 — guessing at the time by the shadows — and put it in the bag.

"Let's go, boy. We got business to take care of."

About halfway back, Jack streaked off down a hill toward a stream. After running a few yards, he stopped and barked. Ray kept walking, but Jack didn't budge. He barked again.

"Jack, I said, let's go — come on, boy." When the dog took off down the laurel-covered hill, bobbing up and down on his one front leg, Ray had no choice but to follow. "Come here, boy! Don't get us lost."

When Ray caught up with him at the bottom of the slope, they were both panting. Jack stopped a few yards from a makeshift lean-to covered in canvas. Rocks circled a well-used fire-pit. "This is somebody's camp, Jack. "We need to leave it alone. Let's go, boy."

Ignoring him, the dog ran ahead, circled the fire-pit and went inside the lean-to. "Get out of there, Jack! You're gonna get us shot." Ray looked around. No one seemed to be here, so he walked down and peeked inside the tent. Jack glanced back, but kept trying to raise a blanket with his nose.

"What is it, Jack? Did somebody leave food under there?" There was a box of black licorice candy by the bedroll, but that wouldn't interest Jack.

Ray had to stoop to go inside and lift the blanket. When he did, there was a .45 caliber Model 1911 automatic pistol lying under it. Alongside that, wrapped in yellow cloth, was Lenore's flower vase — the one she'd carried at her wedding. Lanier's camera lay beside it. A pair of overalls, smeared in blood, was rolled up in the corner.

"Good Lord, Jack. What have you found?"

Ray picked up the pistol, checked to make sure it was loaded and dropped it in his bag with his luger. He put everything else back the way he found it.

He walked a few yards from the tent and found a secluded place to wait. "Lay down, Jack. We've got to be quiet for a while. After that, this is gonna be like taking another trench."

Two hours later, Jack grew tense when he heard someone coming. Ray put his arm around the dog. "Stay quiet, big fellow," he whispered. "Just a few minutes more, and I'll give you first crack at him."

When Alton—Ray could see his face now—was almost back to his tent, he whispered, "Sic him, Jack, now!" The big dog charged and lunged against Alton's chest, knocking him back, but not down. The man didn't fall until he'd grabbed Jack by his neck and tried to throw the snarling animal off him.

Jack tore into Alton's forearms. He stood on the man's chest with his jaws locked, his head shaking vigorously back and forth. Fangs ripped muscle until they hit bone.

With his free arm, Alton groped for a stick—anything. Just as his fingers closed around one, Ray's boot pinned his wrist to the ground. Alton looked up at the barrel of his own pistol.

"That'll, do, Jack," said Ray, touching the dog's neck. Jack backed away, snarling. Ray dropped to his knee and looked at Alton's face. "You ain't got much time left, mister. But I reckon you got enough to tell me what you did with my brother and his wife."

Alton's eyes followed Ray's when he looked at Jack. "Of course, if you don't feel like talking just now, I can let you and my dog play some more."

When Lanier came back from the second day's searching, he noticed the Hardmans' green Cadillac parked alongside the hotel. In the lobby, Dr. Hardman sat in one of the occasional chairs reading an *Atlanta Constitution* newspaper. As soon as he saw Lanier, he folded the paper under his arm and stood. "Mr. Conley, I am so sorry about what's happened. You look exhausted. What can I do?"

"Are you by yourself? Did Hannah come with you?"

"Yes — Wirtha and Emma, too. I wanted the ladies to stay home, at least until all this is resolved, but I couldn't restrain them past this morning. Your wife and mine are in your daughter's room along with Wirtha. They're gathering up Tom and Lenore's things." Dr. Hardman took a step backward and looked at Lanier. "I believe she brought you a change of clothes as well."

Lanier looked down at his overalls. "That's good. I'll go see my wife now if you don't mind."

At the room, Lanier knocked on the door. Inside he heard the women talking. When the door cracked opened a little, Hannah's face filled the void. Lanier was shocked at how much his wife had aged. What he didn't know was, she thought the same about him.

Hannah stepped into the hall, closing the door behind her. "You look half-dead, Lanier." She touched his face. "What you must have been through since you left me." She threw her arms around him and buried her face against his chest, sobbing. "Tell me Lenore is alive, Lanier. I can't keep living if you don't tell me that."

He pulled her close and hugged her so hard his sobs shook her body as much as they did his own. "I can't do that for you, Hannah. I wish to God I could, but I can't. Lenore's gone."

Lanier turned his face away and backed against the wall. His body slid down it, collapsing. Hannah sat on the floor beside him and leaned her face against his. It was only the second time she'd seen her husband cry.

Ray and Jack walked out of the woods and over to the edge of the gorge. The massive dam lay one hundred yards to their right. He looked at the German luger in his hand one last time, drew back his arm and flung the gun as far as he could into the abyss.

He watched it fall. "I never did get around to firing that thing," he said, sitting down beside Jack with a groan. "But I won't need it anymore. I shot a gun for the last time today."

Ray put his arm across the dog and pressed his face into Jack's neck. They stayed that way until the sun went down behind Hickory Nut Mountain, and there was barely enough light left to get back to the Cliff House before dark.

Two days later, Roscoe Nicholson, a man known locally as "Ranger Nick," dropped a sealed envelope on Sheriff Rickman's desk in Clayton, twelve miles north of the gorge. "A black-headed feller handed this to my wife at the store yesterday," said Nicholson. "He told her to get it to the Sheriff. She didn't know him, but here it is."

Scribbled on the note were the words, "The man who killed that couple is camped here." On the back, a pencil-drawn map showed a spot on a creek behind the gorge.

"What do you think, Roscoe? Should we check this out, or is somebody trying to pull my leg?"

"It's a nice mornin', Luther. I'm up for a ride if you are."

The map was accurate—the camp, easy to find. Once they got within 100 yards, the odor would have led them there, anyway.

"He ain't camped," said Rickman as they approached. "He's dead."

They pulled the man out of the lean-to by his legs and looked inside, holding their noses. The dead man's fingers were wrapped around a .45 caliber pistol.

"Can you tell if that gun's been fired?" asked Rickman.

"Well, from the side of his head, and that shell casing over there, I can tell you it's been fired at least once."

"Smartass."

Ranger Nick coaxed the gun out of the dead man's fingers. "Yep," he said, looking at the chamber. "Looks like they's two more bullets missing besides this one. Were those casings you found over by the gorge .45's, too?"

"Sure were."

"Then I reckon you got your man, Sheriff. Looks like some animal tore up his arms pretty good. I wonder how that happened."

"Probably after he shot hisself," said Rickman, knowing all that dried blood on the man's arms meant those wounds happened before the fellow died—dead men don't bleed. He'd have to think about that. Something wasn't right here.

"I reckon," said Ranger Nick, looking up at his friend. He decided to change the subject. "Look at these bloody overalls there, Luther."

"They don't prove nothin'. Maybe he skinned a coon."

When the ranger uncovered the camera and vase from beneath the yellow cloth, the sheriff changed his mind. "They said that couple had a pottery vase and a camera with them when they left the hotel, and she was wearin' a yellow dress. I reckon that does prove something."

"Who you reckon this feller is?" asked the ranger.

The sheriff looked down at the dead man. "I saw him over with the search party the other evenin'. I believe his name was Boggs something or other. I reckon this ol' boy must have got to feeling right bad about what he did up there." He decided not to worry about the dried blood on the man's arms after all.

Rickman looked around the camp. "I reckon me and John Grant owe that dead girl's daddy an apology. Hand me that box of candy, Roscoe. No need lettin' it go to waste."

CHAPTER TWENTY-THREE

Farewell

September 29, 1920

O nly a dozen people showed up at the Methodist Church for Alton's funeral. His brother, Charles, came down from Asheville, arriving just as the service started. He didn't bring his family. Two cousins and an uncle also scattered themselves around the pews.

In the front row, Alton's mother, Evelyn, dabbed her eyes while Preacher Yarbrough struggled to find a few kind words to say over her son. Charles sat rigidly beside his mother. Hannah held Evelyn's hand throughout the service.

The deacons refused to let a murderer—especially one who'd added suicide to his list of sins—be buried in the church cemetery. If they'd had their way, his funeral wouldn't be here either, but Hannah insisted.

"What about his poor mama?" she'd asked. "Don't tell me you don't have enough compassion in your hearts to let Evelyn Boggs give her son a Christian funeral. She's a good woman."

They relented, but she noticed none of them were there. Neither was Lanier.

Frank Sosebee was—along with his daddy and two brothers. If they hadn't come, there wouldn't have been enough pall bearers to load the coffin and haul the body to the grave they'd dug for Alton down below his mama's garden.

CHAPTER TWENTY-FOUR

Homage to an Angel

October 29, 1920

The little Methodist church Lenore attended all her life didn't have a bell. So, Dr. Hardman had Bob Minish pull the rope at nearby Crescent Hill Church nineteen times that morning — once for each year Lenore lived in the Valley. Its knells echoed over the hills. Buggies, wagons, and a few cars filled the space around the church. More of them lined the road in both directions.

A month had passed since Lenore and Tom disappeared. The number of men willing to search dwindled every day after the first one, and — within a week — even Sheriff Grant didn't come back.

When Lanier stormed the man's office, the sheriff stood his ground. "Look, Lanier. We've done all we can. We don't even know they're in that gorge. Maybe that feller just threw her shoe over. Either way, we're done lookin'."

Hannah insisted on holding a funeral, even without a body to bury. Lanier put her off for a month, but after that, there was no stopping her. When Preacher Yarbrough suggested they call it a memorial service instead of a funeral, she shook her head. "My daughter's going to have a proper funeral, and a grave to lay flowers, you hear?"

Hannah asked Wirtha to consider having a double service — one for Tom and Lenore together — but Wirtha declined her offer. "It's fine with me if the preacher talks about Tom some, but I'm not ready to have his funeral — not yet. Besides," she insisted, "Tom was raised Baptist."

Hannah reckoned Tom's mother still held hope they'd find Tom, maybe even alive. If that didn't happen within a year, she said, they'd hold a memorial for him back in Clinton. Hannah chose this day for Lenore's service because Wirtha planned to leave for Macon tomorrow morning.

Lenore's coffin was closed, of course, but Hannah sat beside it, alone, until right before the service started. Inside, she'd placed her daughter's wedding dress, along with a few of Lenore's other things. She'd almost put in that pottery vase, but decided against it at the last minute.

Local boys, including Frank Sosebee, finished digging the grave after sunup. When Preacher Yarbrough stood to start the service, Ray escorted Hannah back to the front pew and sat beside her. It seemed like everyone in both valleys — everybody except Lanier — turned out for the funeral. Despite Hannah's pleading, he'd left early this morning for Tallulah Falls to look some more. "I can do her more good over there than I can here," he insisted. His breath smelled of liquor, so she knew there was no need to argue with him, especially not today.

The church overflowed with people — they lined the back and both walls. Outside, Pledger Moss, his hat in one hand and a harmonica in the other, stood with his family beside a weeping Big Mama, her husband, Isaac, and a few other colored folks. Jack alternated between lying down and standing by the door, waiting for Ray to come back outside. Most people patted his head as they passed.

Preacher Yarbrough broke down twice while he spoke, and again when he led the congregation in a tearful rendition of *Amazing Grace*.

He said a few more halting words at the graveside, and they laid Lenore's empty coffin to rest surrounded by more flowers than anyone could remember seeing at a funeral in the Valley.

CHAPTER TWENTY-FIVE

One Dance More

September 18, 1921

E xactly one year after Lenore and Tom's wedding, Ray tossed
his losing poker hand on the dining room table in the Glen
House, a boarding facility a quarter-mile west of Williams' store.
"That's it for me, boys," he said to Joe Smallwood and Odell Stovall.
"I've lost two dollars tonight. It's bedtime for me and Jack."

As if he agreed, the dog hobbled to the door, looked back at Ray
and yawned.

"Hush," whispered Odell. "If Miss Lizzy and Miss Annie catch
us playing poker, there'll be hell to pay."

"Don't worry," said Ray. "I hear them both snoring upstairs.
We're fine."

In the year since Lenore and his brother disappeared, Ray had
made more than a few trips back to North Georgia. He'd given up
on finding anything of Tom's remains, but something—mostly
Odell's widowed sister, Brenda—kept pulling him back.

Brenda had caught his eye the first time he'd seen her up at the
covered bridge last year. It may have been a coincidence, but ever
since Ray met her, his nightmares had become less severe. Now
days, he rarely had them at all.

The job Ray had gotten as a fireman with the railroad brought
him to Atlanta fairly often. From there, it was easy enough to get
back to the Nacoochee Valley whenever he had a few days off.

Six months ago, Joe Smallwood met him up here with his new wife, Natalie, and their even newer Buick roadster — a wedding gift from her wealthy father. The couple fell in love with the Valley and this stately old Glen House, where two old-maid sisters rented out rooms.

When Ray finally accepted that his only other brother was gone, he went through Tom's belongings, selected a few mementoes to keep and distributed the rest of his property among the neighbors. He gave Frank Sosebee Tom's old chess set. Gus Miller soon rented Tom's house to someone else, so Ray, too, stayed here at the Glen when he came up.

Odell and Ray had become close over the past twelve months. As a gesture of that friendship, Ray gave Odell Val along with Tom's old buggy. He'd even modified the step and rigged up a rope handle to make it easier for Odell to pull himself into the seat. Once Ray introduced Joe and Odell, the three of them bonded the way war vets sometimes do.

"Let's have a smoke before we turn in," said Joe. "Natalie's asleep, so I'm not in a big hurry tonight." The other men laughed.

"I've quit myself," said Ray, "and Odell just chews, but I'll sit a spell with you."

On the porch, Odell stared into the yard. "Where the hell is Val and that buggy? I tied her right there where I always do. She ain't never wandered off before."

"That is strange," said Ray, looking around the yard. "Let's see if she went to the barn."

"Y'all go on," said Joe, yawning. "I'm gonna hit the hay. Crawling into bed with Natalie — even if she's asleep — is a lot more appealing than huntin' a horse with you two. See you boys tomorrow."

Ray grabbed his arm. "Oh, no you don't, Smallwood — you're coming, too. If we've got a horse thief on our hands, it may take all of us to nab him. Grab that lantern and come on."

"All right," said Smallwood, "but if she ain't at the barn, let's take my roadster to look for her. I ain't in the mood for a walk." He looked up at the sky. "The moon's so bright we nearly don't need a lantern."

"Bring it anyway," said Ray. Smallwood flipped his cigarette into the yard, grabbed the lantern and walked behind the house with them. The mare was nowhere around. "I bet she got loose and went home without you," Ray said to Odell. "You never do remember to set the brake."

"It's hard with only one leg," said Odell, hoping for a bit of sympathy.

He didn't receive any. "That ain't no excuse, and you know it," said Ray. "Let's drive down the road a piece toward your place. It's not hardly a mile. Come on, Jack."

"All right," said Odell, "but Brenda's already gone to bed, if you're aiming to see her tonight."

Ray laughed. "You never know. She might be up. Let's go find out."

The three men, along with the dog, climbed into the Buick. Joe drove with Jack sitting in the seat beside Ray. As they were about to turn down the road to Odell's place by the river, Jack barked at something up ahead. An automobile, its headlights pointing toward them, had pulled off the road and stopped just above the Hardman's house. In the moonlight, Ray saw the outlines of four people standing around it. "Looks like somebody might be having car trouble," he said. "Let's go see if we can help 'em."

Frank Sosebee and his friend, Arnold Self, sprinted after the hounds as soon as Sadie's bark changed from trailing to treed. They raced through low brush and jumped over fallen trees, their lanterns swinging wildly as they whooped and hollered in youthful delight.

Arnold's other dog, Track, joined Sadie, in tuneful resonance up behind the Methodist Church. When they caught up with the dogs, the out-of-breath boys held their lanterns up and saw the 'coon's eyes reflecting back.

"We got him," said Arnold. "It's an old boar 'coon. Looks like we're gonna have to do some choppin', though. Man, look at how bright that moon is."

Breathing hard, Frank sat on the trunk of another tree felled years earlier, probably for the same reason. "Let's rest a spell before we start. I'll take first turn with the axe."

Arnold plopped down beside him as the two dogs circled and yelped, looking up as if they were cursing nature for not giving them the ability to climb a tree, too. A movement in the churchyard to their left caught Frank's attention. He nudged Arnold, who stood to look closer.

Both boys were dumbstruck at what they saw. The dogs stopped barking.

Dr. Tom Garrison walked down the church steps, arm-in-arm with the luminous figure of Lenore in what appeared to be a white, translucent wedding dress.

"Is that who I think it is?" asked Arnold, rubbing his hands across his face. "It can't be."

"Hush! Stay still."

"But that's Dr. Garrison and Lenore. They say he killed her over at the gorge last year."

"He didn't kill nobody," said Frank. "I don't know what he's doing here, but I do know that much. He loved Lenore like the dickens. Now hush."

"But she's dead," Arnold protested. "They never found her body, but we went to the funeral! Most folks think they're both dead. You even got Dr. Garrison's old chess set."

"I know it, now hush!"

Frank took hold of an oak branch with both hands and squeezed so hard his knuckles turned white. Sadie and Track, as if unfastened from an invisible leash, bolted into the woods behind them, the raccoon forgotten.

"Good Lord, Frank! Look over there!" Arnold pointed at a horse and buggy in the little road that curved in front of the church. Neither of them had noticed it before.

"That's Dr. Garrison's old buggy," said Arnold. "And that mare is Val; the one his brother gave Odell. Do you think Odell's here, too?"

"Hush!"

Val pawed and moved her head up and down hard enough to make the harness rattle. The boys watched Tom assist Lenore into the buggy, then walk around and climb up beside her. He drove the nervous mare, under tight rein, onto the main road and turned west.

"Let's follow them," said Frank. "Grab that lantern."

"Are you crazy?" Arnold whispered. "You want to go *after* them? Even the dogs had enough sense to run home. Come on!"

"No! We have to find out what we really saw." Frank grabbed Arnold's arm. When Arnold pulled back, Frank let go and ran like a madman across the churchyard. Arnold—finding it more terrifying to be alone than to run toward God knows what—charged after him.

Sprinting hard, the boys hit the main road about 100 yards behind the buggy. They slowed their pace to keep from getting closer. Arnold grabbed his friend's shirt. "Stop, Frank. Look at me. It was Lenore who got in the buggy—and Dr. Garrison. But that can't be."

"Well, it was," said Frank. "Only that woman didn't limp the way Lenore did. It was like she floated." The boys gawked at the buggy as it rolled away. Up ahead they saw the lights of a car in the Hardmans' yard.

"I bet that's Dr. Dyer," said Frank, pointing toward the car. "They're supposed to eat supper with the Hardmans tonight. They'll have to pass that buggy. Let's wait here and see if they noticed anything."

Arnold nodded and swallowed hard.

It was late when Dr. Dyer and India drove out of the Hardmans' yard and headed the car toward Clarkesville. Before he'd put the automobile in gear, India nodded toward an area of fog that lay around the Indian Mound. "Look at that, David. See how the moon lights up that fog? Strange, isn't it?"

Dr. Dyer nodded and yawned. "It is, but I'm tired. All I can think about is bed."

"Well, you're the one who talked politics all night," she chided him.

Her husband stared at the mist across the road. It was amazing how the full moon made it look so surreal. It was late, at least for them. After supper—the Hardman's called their evening meal *dinner*—their political discussion lasted until long after dark. Dr. Dyer refused to get up from the table before his friend promised to at least contemplate running for governor again.

"This state needs you," he'd said. "You're the only honest politician I know. Think how much your being governor would mean to this area. You could do big things for us, Lam—big things!"

When Dr. Hardman agreed to at least consider running, Dr. Dyer was ready to leave, much to his wife's relief.

The lights were still on in the big house behind them. It was the only one in the Valley with electricity, but in a few minutes, it would soon go as dark as tonight's full moon would let it.

As Dr. Dyer pulled down on the throttle to move the car forward, his wife looked up the road. "What on earth is that, David?" A horse and buggy crossed in front of the car's headlights and turned down the lane that ran between the cornfield and pasture to the Indian Mound. "Who'd be going over there this time of night?" she asked. "Isn't that Val and your old buggy?"

Her husband stopped the car and looked where his wife pointed. "It sure is. I bet Ray's borrowed it to do a little sparking with Brenda."

"This late? I don't think so, David. Brenda's daddy wouldn't let her be out this late, not with a man, anyway."

"Well, she doesn't live with her daddy anymore. She lives with Odell. I know it's been a spell, India, but as I recall, daddies don't always know where their daughters are — brothers either."

"Wait a minute David." India's face was serious. "Didn't you see who was in that buggy? It wasn't Ray and Brenda."

"I wasn't paying attention," he admitted. "But who else would be driving it? Odell doesn't have a girlfriend."

"Well, if you didn't see it, I don't want to say who I thought it was. That can't be right anyway."

Dr. Dyer shrugged and pulled down the throttle again. They hadn't gone but a few yards, when lights bobbed in the road ahead. Two people held a lantern high and motioned for the car to stop.

"Are we being robbed?" asked India.

"Not sure. Just sit tight."

"Dr. Dyer!" said Frank Sosebee, holding the lantern up to his face to identify himself. Arnold Self was with him. "It's me and Arnold. Did you pass a buggy back there? Did y'all see who was in it?"

Before he could answer, India leaned across the seat. "Who did you see in that buggy, Frank? Tell me the truth."

Arnold pushed ahead of his friend and nodded vigorously. "It was Dr. Garrison and Lenore Conley!" he said, talking fast. "We saw 'em plain as day up at the church. We were 'coon huntin', and ol' Sadie treed a big 'un when we saw 'em get in the buggy and drive off. The dogs even ran, and Sadie's never left a treed coon in her life!"

Frank bobbed his head in vigorous agreement and blew out the lantern. Dr. Dyer killed the engine and stepped out of the car. The Valley was quiet, except for the shuffling of feet and the popping of the car's engine as it cooled down.

"We saw them come out of the Methodist church," said Frank, breathing hard. "Plain as anything. They got in that buggy and headed down the road. We followed 'em, but then we saw your car coming from the Hardman place. At least we were hoping like hell it was you."

"There's no need to swear, Frank," said Dr. Dyer, staring at the Indian Mound. "But, by God, look at that!"

The mound's gazebo fairly glowed in the moonlight and the fog around it. Val stopped by the end closest to the river. The well-dressed man got out of the buggy and walked to the other side. He helped the woman down, and together, the two moved toward the steps. It seemed like the woman pointed to something on the ground, and the man bent over to pick it up. He stayed in that stance for several seconds.

The four people on the road watched, enthralled, as the couple went up the mound's steps. At the top, they stepped inside the gazebo. They seemed to gaze across the Valley for a moment. Then, in the celestial light of an ominous moon that cast hard-edged shadows away from everything it touched, the couple on the mound danced.

The group on the road was so mesmerized by the couple dancing on the mound, they didn't pay any attention to the automobile that rolled to a stop behind them until Ray slammed its door getting out. Joe and Odell stayed inside.

"Dr. Dyer, is that you?" asked Ray, walking up to them. All four jumped and faced the intruders. "Good Lord, man," said Dr. Dyer, putting his right hand to his chest. "You nearly gave me a heart attack. What are y'all doing down here this time of night?"

While they were talking, a cloud passed in front of the moon, shielding the Valley from its light.

"We're looking for my buggy," said Odell from the car. "Val ran off with it. Then we saw y'all down here and thought you might need help."

"Your buggy is right down there," said Dr. Dyer, pointing behind him. "I ought to know it since it used to be mine. And Ray, you can believe this or not, but your brother, Tom, drove it there. We saw him — every one of us did."

Even in the darkness, the shock on Ray's face was clear. He leaned against the T-Model. "But that's not possible," he said, his voice trembling.

Jack ran a few yards up the road and barked in the direction of the mound.

"We saw them, too" said India. "Both of them. And Ray, I know it can't be, but they were dancing."

Dr. Dyer whispered, "The Indians claimed souls get to visit the one place on earth where they were happiest just before they leave for eternity. I never believed it myself, but maybe they were right."

Ray shielded his eyes and stared at the mound. "Blow out your lantern so you can see better," said Frank. As soon as he did, as if on cue, the moon returned to its fullness. They could see Val and the buggy again, standing in the fog, but no one was dancing on the mound anymore.

"They musta' gone down the other side," said Dr. Dyer. "They were there a minute ago, weren't they, India?"

His wife nodded.

Ray started toward the mound in a run. "I'll come with you," Smallwood yelled, getting out of the roadster. He raced after Ray who soon left the road, climbed the fence and cut diagonally across the pasture. Jack ran beside the fence as if he knew where Ray was heading.

"Get in that car," India said to Frank and Arnold, pointing toward Smallwood's vehicle. "Odell's already in there, and it's pointing in the right direction. I hope you can drive this thing, David. Let's get to the bottom of this."

"Now, Honey Pot, do you we think we really ought to butt in? I mean..."

"Get in the car, David."

With Frank, Arnold and Odell in the back seat, leaning forward as far as they could, Dr. Dyer hit the electric starter and the engine roared to life. "Damn," he said. "I gotta get me one of these!"

"Drive!" said his wife. When they got to the narrow lane that led to the mound, Dr. Dyer stopped the car and turned to his wife. "Lam and Emma aren't going to like all these goings-on over here so late," he said hopefully. "It might scare the young'uns."

"They're asleep — drive." When the Buick's headlights lit up the buggy, Val turned her head back toward them. Her eyes glowed in the light. Climbing a second fence, Ray and Smallwood arrived at the same time as the car. Ray was breathing hard when he walked up to them. "Let me have your lantern, Frank," he said. "Y'all stay here."

When they got to Val and the buggy, Ray stopped for a moment. He stretched out his hands for the reins, which had been tied in a bowtie knot around the buggy's dashboard rail. Ray ran up the side of the mound, not bothering with the steps.

"TOM!!" shouted Ray racing up to the gazebo. "TOM, ARE YOU HERE? ANSWER ME!!"

The Valley didn't answer, but the moon gave glimpses of Dr. Hardman's cows in the fog by the river. On the mound, inside the gazebo, something else caught Ray's eye.

A little pile of black-eyed Susans lay strewn across the table.

Later that night, Ray and the others gathered around Joe Smallwood's car and took a pledge of secrecy about everything they'd just seen. Ray and Joe hadn't seen the dancing couple, but those flowers and Tom's way of tying the reins to the dashboard rail convinced Ray his brother was there, or at least had been.

Everyone in the group kept that pact except one. About three weeks later, India Dyer had her husband drive them over to the Conley house. There, at the kitchen table, she told Hannah everything they'd all seen on the road and at the mound.

"You are the only person I'll ever tell this to," she said, as Dr. Dyer waited in the car. "But I thought you ought to know."

"I appreciate it," said Hannah, hugging her. "But, I saw Tom and Lenore that night, too — right here in this house. Lenore never spoke a word, but somehow, she let me know everything was all right. She did something else, too. I'll be right back."

Hannah went into her and Lanier's bedroom and came back with his camera, along with a little pack of pictures.

"I want to show you something, India. The night you saw them dancing on the mound — the same night they came here to me — Lenore looked at her little vase there on the mantel, but she put her hands on this camera and smiled. She looked so happy, India, so happy. Then she just faded away."

Hannah laid one of the pictures on the table. "That's why I sent the film off. It took me a year, but I finally did. Everything came back yesterday. This one here is what she wanted me to see. It's the picture Tom took of her at Tallulah Falls. Look at it, India. Lenore's holding the vase Arie Meaders gave her. Now look closer. It'll take you a minute, but once you see it, you can't see nothin' else.

"That's right. It's her angel, standing right there by her, holding her, really. I reckon that's the one she called Lana. Took my breath away, too first time I saw it.

"But that picture brought me peace."

EPILOGUE

When my interview with Hannah Conley was over, she leaned back in her chair. Her eyes fluttered before closing. She was clearly as tired as I was. It was a long way to Asheville, and I was aching to write down all she had said. Not wanting to wake her, I gently placed a stick of wood on the fire and looked at her one last time. I'd only taken a few steps when she called out.

"Wait a minute, Kelvin. They's another thing I need to say. I was gonna take it to my grave, but I reckon I've told so much now, I may as well tell it all — clear my conscience 'fore I cross over.

"After our daughter died, Lanier stayed liquored up more'n not. I got to where I quit pestering him 'bout it — weren't no use. He bought a Model-T Ford that summer and drove it all over the place — went to Tallulah Falls ever chance he got. I never understood that, 'cause he'd come to hate that place. And by then there weren't no hope of finding anything of Lenore or Tom. I never went with him, but the ones that did said he'd stare down into that gorge for hours.

"Lanier stayed mad at Sheriff Grant for not finding Lenore — thought he didn't look long enough. Last time he went was right at Christmas. He said something or other went wrong with his car, so he left it over there in a garage and hitched home. That night — well, it lasted two or three days — Tallulah Falls caught fire and burned. Even that big trestle that run up over the town went up. Some of 'em said a spark from the train caused it, but that's not so. It started in that garage where Lanier left his car.

"He told me he how he did it, sittin' there in that chair — drunk. I reckon he'd lost his mind, 'cause he planned ever' detail — even waited for a night when the wind was up. I hadn't decided if I was gonna put the law on him or not, but it turned out not to make no difference. A week later, Lanier passed out on the tracks below Helen and got run over by a night train the sawmill was running to Gainesville.

"That was in January of nineteen hundred and twenty-two. It seems like it happened yesterday, but I reckon that's how life is."

So now faith, hope, and love abide, these three,
but the greatest of these is love.

I Corinthians 13:13

ABOUT THE AUTHOR

Emory Jones' roots run deep in North Georgia's Appalachian Mountains. After a stint in the Air Force, he earned a journalism degree from the University of Georgia and joined Gold Kist, Inc. as publications manager. He has been Southeastern Editor for Farm

Journal Magazine and executive Vice President at an Atlanta based advertising agency. During his career, Emory interviewed farmers in all 50 states. His other books include: *Zipping Through Georgia on a Goat Powered Time Machine, Heart of a Co-Op — The Habersham EMC Story, and Distant Voices — The Story of the Nacoochee Valley Indian Mound.* He has written a play based on this book, *The Valley Where They Danced.* Emory and his wife, Judy, live on Yonah Mountain near Helen, Georgia.

Emory Jones
Photo by David Greear

ACKNOWLEDGMENTS

As I was writing this book, I tried hard to put myself in the middle of every scene and conversation and to recreate how my aunts and uncles, my grandparents or the other North Georgia folks I've known, all gone now, would have expressed themselves. I'm sure I didn't get it all right, but I tried to be close — preserving history is a sacred thing. So is preserving the vernacular of the Southern Appalachians.

So many people helped me with facts, expressions and terms that I can't possibly list them all. Still, I want to express a special thanks to folks like Judge Garrison Baker, and his wife, Susan; Ann and Mike Banke; Alan and Denise Boggs; Glenda Boling, Chris Brooks, Karen Casey, Billy Chism, David Cleghorn, Caroline Crittenden, Cara Joy De Celles, Duncan Dobie, Arnold Dyer, John Erbele, Horace Fitzpatrick, Luciano Georgescu, Mildred Greear, Dr. Scott Hancock, Betty Highsmith, Bill House, Nancy Kollock, Phil Hudgins, Mark Johnson, Linda Jordan, Jim Johnston, John Lunsford, Shirley McDonald, Cindy Mullinax, Dess and Jackie Oliver; George Prater, Jean Rice, Ivy Rutzky, Ellen Schlossberg, Buck Schneider, Walter and Marion Schade; Joe and Natalie Smallwood; Danny Tatum, Frances Young and Dr. and Mrs. Max White.

During the process, I phoned my aunt — the real Lenore — several hundred times to ask about things like the size of lard buckets or how to string leather britches. She always knew, bless her heart.

But the real reason this book exists is because of my wife, Judy. Like most Southern novels, this one was hashed out on the porch. Without her, this book would not exist — what a wife!

Judy will be mad if I don't mention our cat's role, too. Ole Sylvester's head lay on my left hand during almost every word I typed. Any zzzzzzzzzzzz or xxxxxxxxxxxxx or ....'s still in the book are his contributions to the process. (Also, any typos — darn cat!)